L. J. EPPS

JOURNEY TO TERRITORY M

EXTINCTION OF ALL CHILDREN SERIES BOOK TWO

To my Aunt Gayle, who was a go-getter and thrived at any job she held. Her example taught me to have fun and to go for what I want, like being a self-published author.

CHAPTER ONE

I GLANCE OUT of the rear window and see the gates of Territory L behind me. It's still so close my eyes sting. I can't believe no one is shooting at us. With Julian's help, we just strolled right through the guard's gate; they thought Julian was bringing back an empty truck. He does it all the time when he delivers supplies, so what would make them think today is any different.

It's hard to believe I was cooped up in a jail cell for thirty days because I went against the president's laws. The best thing about my time there was learning how to fight with Eric. I shudder thinking about President Esther and her values. She believes the poor should no longer have children because they can't take care of them. I once thought she killed all of the babies that were born and hidden, but I've since found out that some are illegally adopted.

Territory L is considered lower class, while Territory M is middle class and Territory U is upper class; but the labels are only there because she separated everyone and made up the division of classes. Just because the upper territories make more money than my territory doesn't make it right to send the babies there.

I still can't believe she planned to use me—her first female guard—as her personal mouthpiece, or I could be sent to the prison for lifers. I was able to escape that fate, for now; but what about the others who are still jailed for thirty days or sent to the prison for lifers? Will I be able to get them released or be able to get the walls torn down?

I take in a breath, glossing over everything that has happened. Territory L is my home—the only home I've known—but I need to do this to make things better for my family and all the people who live there. And I need to find my niece, Abigail, who was taken and may be dead or illegally adopted. I know that is my primary goal.

The back of the truck is dark. I am so deep in thought, I didn't notice that Eric moved away from me and is now up near the front, conversing with Julian, who keeps his gaze straight ahead, but nods as he listens to Eric talking behind him. I feel the bumps in the road as my body bounces up and down and I sway from side to side.

"Sorry," he says, turning from Julian to look at me. "I figured you needed some time to yourself. I was right because you didn't even notice me leave your side."

He crawls on his knees, back to where I am.

"You okay?" he asks, as he brushes a strand of hair from my eye.

"I'm fine now that we've made it into Territory M. I never thought that would happen."

"I feel the same and, so far, none of the guards or patrolmen have caught up to us, so we should take that as a good sign." He slides next to me. "Julian and I were listening on our radios and, so far, Rich hasn't reported us gone. I'm surprised but glad he hasn't."

"I'm surprised, too," I say. My chest aches knowing we could get caught and our speedy getaway will be for nothing. For some reason unbeknownst to me, Rich hates me. I think it's because his siblings died when the no children law started and I was the last one to survive. His dislike for me goes well beyond anything I've ever experienced.

I thought he would never stop coming for me but, for some

reason, he hasn't called this in. I thought, with him being the president's top guard, he wouldn't have hesitated to make light of what I've done. Was he injured so much when I fought with him he was unable to call it in? My hand trembles thinking about how I shot him back at the gates.

"I didn't know the radios would work over here," I say, trying to get my mind off Rich.

"Julian comes here frequently, and he says my radio has only a small range; but his is set up for longer distances, since he is allowed back and forth through the gates. Once we reach certain areas near the outskirts of the territory, mine won't work anymore but his still will."

"So where are we going now?" I ask, shifting my weight. The truck's floor is hard as a rock and uncomfortable. "Is it somewhere safe?"

"Julian knows a place where we can hide, in case this gets radioed in. No one should find us there—at least not for a while, and at least not until we figure out what our plan is."

He gives a half-smile that comforts me; but only for a moment, because my throat tenses when I hear a loud noise like a cannon going off.

"What was that?" Eric shouts up to the front.

"It's the construction workers. They get their day started early. They're redoing this entire stretch of road. No one lives in this area, so the noise levels don't bother anyone. They've already built a new college and a new library; now they're working on finishing up the improvements to our light rail. They should be done in a day or so. Territory U has a monorail but those are really expensive—our territory couldn't afford one."

It's nice they can afford such luxuries; we can't—Territory L has neither. It's still too dark for me to really be able to take in the sites of Territory M. I sit up more and I see the road we're on has a lot of large structures. I know they are buildings, but it's too dark to make out exactly what they're used for. I slouch back down, knowing that's not my main concern right now.

"What time is it?" I ask, after we have driven for what seems like hours.

"Four in the morning," Julian announces, looking down at the dashboard on the truck. "We're almost at our destination. When you first get through the gates into Territory M you'll notice a lot of unoccupied land. You couldn't see it from the back of the truck. You have to go about fifteen miles and then you reach some part of civilization. It takes about an hour…sometimes more if there's traffic…to get to where we need to go."

Eric clutches my hand and squeezes. The warmth is nice. I want to confide in him about the files I saw in President Esther's drawer, but I know this isn't the time or place to bring it up.

"This is it," Julian says.

The tires squeal as he pulls into a large driveway. He maneuvers along the driveway until we reach the back. I can't see what type of building it is because it's still dark.

"You two sit tight while I go check out the place. I need to make sure the building is still empty." I see him lean over and reach for something in the glove compartment. Then he hops down from the truck and slams the door.

"Everything will be okay." Eric touches my chin, turning my attention his way.

"I know," I say, even though I'm unsure. My chest is tight because I left my entire family behind, and I pray my efforts aren't in vain.

It seems as if several more minutes have gone by. My shoulders jump because the back door screeches open. "It's empty. We can go in now." Julian's eyes are wide. "Most of the entrances have been closed off. They've either been boarded up or blocked."

"Then how are we getting in?" I ask.

"There's a teacher's entrance on the east side of the building. That entrance wasn't blocked or boarded. There's only one single door there and it has an electronic locking device that's mounted directly to the door. It's the easiest way to get in, because it takes a code and I was able to hack the lock with some tools I had in the glove compartment. Once the door closes it locks itself, unless one of us uses the inside lever to push the door open—but once it closes again, it automatically locks from the outside. The workmen used that entrance to carry some of the furniture out. I noticed they only took what they needed, so a lot of the older worn-down tables and chairs are still in there."

Eric jumps down, and I jump down behind him in a huff. I'm still not used to the weight of my heavy black boots. I'm surprised I could run in them earlier when we were escaping L. I suppose my adrenaline was in overdrive and I didn't notice. We quickly follow Julian by a metal door into a dark building.

"What is this place?" I ask, once the door swishes behind us.

"It's Territory M's old college. They built a newer fancier one and now this one is empty."

"So, no one will look for us here?"

"No, they shouldn't." Julian shakes his head. "It's been unoccupied for months. We should be okay camping out here for a while, at least until we figure out our next move." The lights pop on as we walk in.

"The lights are connected to sensors, so they automatically come on when they detect movement. Once there is no movement they pop off, or you slap the button on the wall and turn them off," Julian walks ahead of us.

If they have automatic lights in the old college what must the new college have? Up ahead I see a long hallway and several doors leading into classrooms. It reminds me of the school I attended in Territory L, only bigger. The doors here look brand new—they don't have stains or discolorations or scratches like in my school. The walls look freshly painted—no chips or dirt marks like in my school either.

"We shouldn't have too many lights on. We wouldn't want anyone to get suspicious that someone's in here," Julian says. "If you notice a light doesn't go out automatically, then immediately turn it off once you reach your destination. I only had time to check the east and north sides of the building, since I had to hack the lock to get in here. I doubt if anyone is on the other side of the building."

"You doubt." I raise my eyebrow. "That doesn't sound reassuring."

He ignores my comment and grabs something from his pants pocket. It's black and has three red buttons on it.

"What's that?" I ask.

"It's an electronic key fob. There just a newer, fancier way to unlock and lock the doors of the truck. The upper territories have them, and of course all of President Esther's vehicles. You can also use it to start the engine, if you don't want to use a key." He dangles the key fob in his fingers.

When I used to ride on the school bus back in L, I never noticed if they used keys or that electronic key fob as Julian calls it. I'm sure, since it was only transporting the lower class, they just used a key. It's nice that they have fancy toys to play with—while we have none.

I ask another question, because I don't like being kept in the dark. "Are you going somewhere?"

"Do you two think you'll be okay by yourselves for a while? I need to take the truck back to the supply warehouse and get something else for us to ride in before daylight sets in." Julian shoves the key in his pocket, and then takes it back out like he's nervous.

"Won't you need some help?" Eric asks.

"No, I know the area. I'll be okay."

"If you're okay out there, then we're okay in here." Eric nods.

I remain quiet. My temples ache, and I don't know what to add to the conversation.

"You want to look around?" Eric asks, once the door bangs and Julian's gone.

"Maybe we should talk first," I say, softly.

"I would rather see if we can find some food first. You should eat. You look pale."

It seems like he's trying to avoid talking to me—or maybe he really is concerned about my well-being. I can't tell which, so I decide to let the conversation go until later.

"There has to be a cafeteria around here, somewhere," he continues. "Maybe something was left over."

I remain silent and follow him. We walk down the long hallway to a set of stairs. He's probably thinking what I'm thinking—the cafeteria is on the lower level. The lights click on in the stairwell as we enter and the light pops off in the hallway we just came from. I believe Julian's instructions are on point, so if the lights don't go out by themselves we will make sure to turn them off with the switch on the wall.

We exit the stairwell and continue down the long dark hallway, passing several large steel-like doors. The lights don't automatically pop on in this area. We keep walking until we see what looks to be a turnstile. It's silver and brings light to the dark area. Eric hops over it with ease. He reminds me of a horse hopping over an obstacle. I know I can't glide over it as smoothly, so I slide under it.

It's hard to see in the darkness, but I make out a long dark counter with glass above it. The glass above is used to cover the food while on display. It's where people used to stand in line and call out their orders or wait for their food to be placed on their trays. The counter is made of marble—it reminds me of the marble-top table in one of the conference rooms in President Esther's mansion. I remember sitting with her in the conference room as she grilled me on how my stay had been in the jails. This counter is even more beautiful to me because it's white with thin black streaks etched through it.

Over in the corner, there's one square window with blinds hanging from it. Daybreak has begun, which allows a small amount of light to seep through the closed blinds, making the glass above the counter glisten in the darkness, like frozen ice. Our school cafeteria wasn't this fancy. We had a wooden counter, and there was no glass above it to cover the food.

"Over here, Whisper."

I hear Eric calling my name, interrupting my thoughts. I follow his voice through a set of white hardwood double doors and find he's in the kitchen area. There is a large silver refrigerator, and I feel the cool breeze coming from it as Eric opens the doors. I'm surprised it's turned on, since the college is not in use.

"Did you find anything?" I ask.

"No, it's empty," he says. He sounds annoyed.

He shoves it closed with force, and I hear a bang. He moves over to an area with cabinets and starts searching through them. I start over to help; but before I can, I hear a noise. My heart pounds into my ears. It sounds like something is scuffling across the tile floors. I can't tell if it's animal or human. I lean down closer to the floor. I expect Eric to do the same but he doesn't. He reaches for the gun in his holster and pulls it out.

There are two rectangular-shaped illuminated signs up in the ceiling over the doors—one says EXIT and one says ENTRANCE. The light hangs over Eric, and I see his amber eyes glistening in the darkness. He looks like a mad man on a mission. Something about him is different—something that makes me uncomfortable. My shoulders tense.

"What are you doing?" I ask, like I don't already know.

"You heard that didn't you?"

"Yes, I did." I nod.

"Well, we need to protect ourselves."

"But our promise." I feel my jaw tense. "We refrain from violence unless we have to defend ourselves."

He grips his finger around the trigger. "I haven't forgotten. What do you think I'm doing?" he asks, as if I'm stupid for challenging his motives. "I'm defending us. We don't know what's out there."

We hear scuffling across the cold dark floor again. He points the gun in the direction of the noise. The scuffling now sounds like it's in the opposite direction. He swings the gun in that area. His breathing is heavy. The air is cold and smells stale.

This can't happen. We can't shoot into the darkness without knowing who we are aiming at. I say we even though my gun is still in my holster. I have already shot someone, once, this week. I don't want to do it again. *Not so soon…not now, maybe not ever again*, I think.

We need to know who we are protecting ourselves from. At least when I shot Rich, it was because he was coming after me. He was trying to stop me from leaving Territory L, and he would have killed me in order to do that. But we can't shoot an unarmed person.

I squint my eyes and focus. I notice the lights aren't automatic in the cafeteria or in the kitchen, so I need to find the light switch. The small amount of light coming from the illuminated signs can help me find the switch. I need to see what's scurrying around the room. There, near the entrance into the kitchen, I see a square light panel. I run to it and flip the switch. The lights click on and the dark kitchen is suddenly bright, while the rest of the cafeteria remains dark. I blink a couple of times to adjust to the light. Looking down, I see something brown and fluffy with a tail. Its small beady eyes peer up at me.

"Don't shoot," I scream. "It's only a squirrel. It can't harm us. It's probably searching for food like we are."

Eric puts the gun back in his holster and the fire in his eyes goes away.

"I'm sorry." His face drops. "I'm a little on edge."

I touch his shoulder. "It's okay. We both are."

The squirrel squeals and runs away. In its rush to leave the room crumbs are left behind. I bend down and pick up the crumbs. They are white and pasty.

"There's food around here, somewhere. We just have to find it," I say, standing up.

"I think I already have. I found a couple of cracker packages in this box way back on top of the pantry. But they expired three months ago," he says, turning to me.

"Expired food doesn't scare me."

"Me neither." He throws one of the packages my way. It crackles in midair.

We ate expired food all the time when things were sparse at home, so it doesn't bother me. The cafeteria next door is filled with chairs; but I'm exhausted, so I opt to slide down the hard wall and sit on the dusty tile floor. Eric does the same, sitting down across from me.

"Maybe I should turn off the lights," I say. I rip open the package and the wrapper rustles in my hands.

"Leave it on," Eric mumbles in between crunches. "If someone were here, they would have come for us by now."

I glance around. "I guess you're right."

I see a big silver walk-in freezer. The pantry is large and has wooden shelves. Everything here looks practically new. How can they say this is the old college when it looks newer than the schools we have in Territory L? Of course, we had no colleges in Territory L for higher education. The school we did have back in L had ripped drapes in the cafeteria. Some of the drapes were even torn down and never replaced. The windows I saw in the cafeteria here have blinds that look well kept-up.

The crackers crackle in my hands as I gnaw on them, reminding me of a beaver chewing on wood.

"You should eat all of yours. You'll need your strength," Eric says, after a few minutes go by. "I will save the rest of my package for Julian. I'm sure he's hungry, too."

"Now that you have a little food in you, are you going to tell me what else is going on?" I ask, skipping over the small talk.

"I don't know what you mean." He curls up the end of the wrapper to preserve what's left for Julian. It crinkles in his hands as he places it to the side. "I'm thirsty. You probably are, too. I'm going to get some water from the kitchen faucet. I don't see any cups around so I'll just use my hands." He glances over at the large silver sink near the back wall.

"Can we wait on the water?" I swipe my hands together to get rid of the cracker crumbs. "I really need to talk to you about something."

"Sure." He moves closer to me. His pants swish along the concrete floors. "What's bothering you?" He lifts my chin and my eyes bore into his.

"Can we really trust him?" That's not the first thought that comes to mind; but since it's bothering me, I blurt it out. I feel I need to sit with what I saw in Esther's chambers a little longer, before I reveal it to anyone else—and that includes Eric.

"Trust who?" His eyes stretch wide.

"Julian. Can we trust him?"

"Has he given us a reason not to?" His eyebrow rises. "Do you know something that I don't?"

It seems to me that we are going around in circles. He's answering my questions with a question, and I don't like it.

"It's just, how well do you really know him?"

"I told you, he was my roommate. We discussed a lot of private things during that time. He helped us escape, so why wouldn't I trust him?"

"That's just it, why would he jeopardize his freedom for us? I don't understand." I shift my weight on the floor. "He had a good thing, being able to come and go between the territories and visit his family. Why would he give that up?"

Julian brought supplies back and forth through the territories, so he was allowed in both territories when most people are not—even some of the guards who are the president's trusted companions.

"We've been through some things together." He shrugs. "He owes me a favor."

Before I ask about the favor, I hear footsteps slamming against the concrete floors.

"Why the bright lights?" Julian says, walking into the kitchen. "We're trying to keep a low profile here."

He's right. The lights are bright. Eric and I were engrossed in conversation and not paying attention to anyone—or anything—that may be approaching.

"I was only able to bring back one flashlight. I will try and get more next time I go out." Julian clicks the light off on the wall. "We will use it if we need light. I will keep it for now. I was also able to scrounge up some clothing. We can't walk around in guard uniforms without being noticed. We'll have to keep on our pants and boots; but I was able to get different tops, so we can take off these heavy guard jackets."

He has a large black duffle bag hooked around his shoulder, and it screeches as he unzips it. He hands me two black knit turtlenecks, a gray cotton hoodie, and what looks like girl's underwear. There's no bra, just panties and thin white socks. I see he has gray t-shirts and black hoodies for himself and Eric, and another bag which probably contains their underwear.

Although I am grateful for the change of clothing, I can't help but wonder where he got them from. Instead of waiting to see what else appears from the bag, I walk to the cafeteria so I can change clothing in private. Once my jacket is lifted from my shoulders, the air feels even cooler. It lands on the floor with a *thump*. I put the knit turtleneck on and it feels tight and warm against my skin. The light hoodie is a nice change from the heavy garb I am used to. The necklace that my mother gave me is cold on my skin. I leave it underneath the turtleneck, for now.

I plunk down in one of the chairs in the cafeteria and take in a breath. The chair is padded and soft to the touch—unlike the chairs in my school back in L that were wooden and creaky. I haven't had a moment to think about what happened back in Territory L, until now. My chest feels heavy. I have so much to do, but I don't know how to do it. How can I find my niece, Abigail, when I don't even know where to begin? What about my mother and father or my sister or brother that I left behind? What will happen to them?

Then there's Samuel—will he be in trouble? He was one of President Esther's guards. He let me get away. He was always good to me, always looking out for me. I sometimes wonder if he has feelings for me.

As my hand trembles, I sigh and close my eyes. My mind fills with darkness, just like the room, and my chest feels like it's sunken in. A tear dampens my eyelids, and I quickly swipe it away. I know there's no time for crying right now, but I can't help what I'm feeling.

I jump, feeling a warm hand touch the top of my shoulder.

Eric has come into the cafeteria where I am. "Whisper, you okay?"

"Yes," I say, wiping another tear from my cheek.

"Julian brought food with him. It's only white bread and one jar of peanut butter and one jar of jelly, but it's better than expired crackers."

I lie. "I'm good, for now. The crackers were enough." My stomach is growling, but I don't want to eat right now.

"Julian says we should try and get some sleep. We need to have clear heads. We will figure out our next move, once we all wake up." He leans down and grabs my jacket off the floor. "You can use this to lie on."

He balls up my jacket into a makeshift pillow and lays it in front of me on the cafeteria table. He sits across from me and does the same to his. I'm glad they left the table; it helps to have something to lie on.

"Julian will take first watch while we sleep, and then we will do the same for him. He said he will wake up one of us in about an hour…then it will be one of our turns to keep watch."

"It would be nice if we could start devising some sort of plan around eight o'clock," I say, even though I don't have a watch on and have no idea what time it is.

"Don't worry about that right now." His eyebrows slant together. "You need to rest for whatever comes next."

I nod okay as Eric closes his eyes to sleep. I stand. I go into the kitchen because the crackers did make me thirsty. The sink has two knobs and I turn the knob for the cold water. The water hisses and swishes out. I put my mouth under the faucet and guzzle some down. Once my thirst is quenched, I click the faucet off. I wipe my mouth with my hand and return to the table in the cafeteria. I plunk back down across from Eric. His body is so still that he never notices I left the table. I lay my head on my jacket and pretend to close my eyes. I know I won't be able to sleep now, and I don't want to. I would rather keep watch, like Julian.

CHAPTER TWO

I KNOW I shouldn't, but I decide to walk around the old college. I leave Eric sleeping in the cafeteria, and I'm not sure where Julian is. My legs won't stop trembling and my heart is racing. Every time I close my eyes, I see Rich's ruddy face. Not only do I see his face, I feel his long thin fingers and large hands plastered tightly around my neck and he is choking me.

I know everyone dreams from time to time, but now my dreams have turned into nightmares. Why don't I see President Esther in my dreams? Maybe because I feel she just wants to torture me and make me suffer, while Rich wants to see me dead.

I can't tell Eric about my nightmares, at least not right now. We have more important matters to deal with. We don't know what's to come. My brain is on overdrive. I can't pretend to be sleeping anymore for Eric's sake.

I enter the stairwell, walking up to the north side to the second floor. The automatic lights in the stairwell turn on, but I quickly find the switch on the wall and turn them back off. I bypassed the first floor because I saw a lot of it when we first arrived. Once again, I'm curious about my surroundings, so I'm eager to look around.

As I walk down the hall, I see many rectangular-shaped doors. I stop in front of a wooden door with a silver handle. There's a small rectangular glass panel to the left of the door. I go inside because it's different from the others. The glass panel has a bright white decal stuck to the window. It looks like a snowflake, and I wonder what it symbolizes.

The door creaks as I open it. I pat the gun in the holster on my right hip and the Taser on my left hip. I don't want to become dependent on them; but I feel more comfortable with them than without them and that terrifies me. I believe violence only begets more violence; yet I have to protect myself.

Inside the room are six glass windows with shades drawn for most of them. The one that has no shade glistens. Now that the sun has risen, it shines through so the automatic lights don't come on. The room smells like markers. I see several different colored markers sitting on the ledge in front of a whiteboard off to the right of the room. I'm used to whiteboards; we used them in L at the school I went to.

In the front of the room I see some sort of a screen. It has a small crack in the middle. It looks to be broken. My mother is a teacher back in L, and she told me some of the upper schools used an interactive display in the classroom. I suppose this is what she meant by that. I'm sure in the new college they have a brand new display to project their text and images on.

My mother also spoke of an e-reader. She explained that it was used to read books and magazines on and to display pictures. I keep looking around to see if they left one of those behind, but of course they didn't.

I do see a few books that were left here, and easels and paint. I recognize the easel from some of the old magazines that my mom had. This must have been some sort of art room. Art, I chuckle to myself. Why would someone study art? Maybe they can use it here or in Territory U. But Territory L wouldn't have use for it.

Art books are left on the beige-colored shelves. The hardcover art books are old and dusty. The pages are dingy yellow, instead of natural white. The side binders are damaged, faded, and worn.

That's probably why they left them behind, instead of taking them to the new college. I touch my fingers to the pages. The edges are wrinkled, like something wet spilled on them.

I continue to look around and notice two books unlike the others, laying on one of the cherry-colored square wooden desks. One says DIGITAL ART BOOK in red lettering on the black cover. The cover is shiny and feels smooth to the touch. It looks brand new. It looks to be more advanced than the other books on the shelves. I shift through the pages and see lessons and instructions. Digital art is foreign to me—actually any art is, since we had no classes in Territory L on this subject. It's nice that they were able to learn how to draw art the old way versus the new ways.

Next to it is a sketchbook. I move closer to the desk and trickle down. I can't help but notice the back of the chair along with the bottom is padded—like the chairs down in the cafeteria. It's soft against my back and nothing like the hard chairs we sat in…in my school back in L.

My fingers shiver as I smooth my hand over the sketchbook. It also looks new and is blue like the sky on a good day in Territory L—although we didn't have many of them.

I open the hardcover book and see the pages are heavy weighted—not thin like I'm used to. The paper is of high quality and expensive. The first page shows a drawing of a woman with a thin face and sunken cheekbones. She has blood red eyes and black bags under them. Her hair is silver and is braided up into a circle on top of her head. The way the braid surrounds her head reminds me of a snake. I am correct in my observation; at the end of the braid is a snake with beady eyes and a pinkish tongue hissing out of its mouth.

The woman has long red fingernails. I can only assume this drawing is of President Esther. The likeness is amazing and the drawing amuses me. I want to look at more. I glance down at the bottom of the page and there is a name in cursive writing: *Alexa*.

Alexa must be the owner of this sketchbook and the one who drew this amazing picture that could hang in a museum in Territory U. Better yet, it should be nailed to a tree in Territory L where all of the townspeople can come and throw darts at it. The picture looks like it was drawn with a colored pencil or maybe colored ink. It's hard to tell—but I'm leaning toward pencil. I think colored ink or even marker would smudge more and make thicker strokes.

The pages ruffle as I turn them to see what follows. The next few pages are blank, but I keep turning. I hope to see more. I reach a page with scribbles on it. *"Justice—freedom of speech—equality. That's what we need."*

My stomach clenches because I agree.

The next page has words and I want to read them; but before I can, I hear someone open the door. I slam the book closed. I stand as my hand automatically moves toward my right hip.

"Why did you leave the cafeteria?" Eric's face is hard and his tone is serious.

"I can take care of myself."

"I realize that, but I was worried." He moves closer to me. "When I awoke and you weren't there, my first thoughts were maybe they came for you." He strokes my cheek with his fingers.

I know he's speaking of Rich, the guards, and President Esther.

"I'm sorry. I didn't mean to make you worry." His fingers feel warm. "I couldn't sleep, and I wanted to look around. I feel like we're wasting time here. I want to go out and look for Abigail."

"What do you mean look for Abigail?" His tone drops and so does his fingers from my face. "Whisper, Abigail's probably gone by now. I don't mean to sound harsh; but even if we find the newbie camp you were talking about in the truck, she'll probably be dead before we get to her. I think we need to stick to the original plan and look for the one in charge of this territory to help us break down the walls."

"No. No. That can wait." My voice rises.

He looks at me like I've gone crazy. I haven't had a chance to tell him about the adoption files.

"She's not dead." I shake my head. "She's alive."

I walk toward the windowsill. I need to lean on it for support. I have to believe she is alive, but what if I'm wrong? I don't want to get my hopes up.

"You should move away from the window."

I know he's right. The window shades are all down except for on the middle window. Strange…there is no shade there, so I slide away from it.

"Don't do this to yourself." He looks at me with kind eyes, bringing my attention back to him.

"No, listen. With everything going on, I didn't have time to tell you. When I went back to President Esther's quarters to look for that map, I found something else instead. I-I found files." My voice quivers. "There were green files with adoption papers in them."

I see his amber eyes widen, but I continue on. "There were only a few files. They had the baby's last name on them and the families they were going to. Then I saw a file with baby Whisperer on it, but the name of the family Abigail was going to was left blank."

My speech is fast and my eyes are watering. "One of the guards was coming through the door, so I couldn't look at the file anymore. I had to try and get out of there."

My hands are shaking, like I'm in the room all over again, searching through the files.

He grabs my hands. "It's okay."

"No, if I just had more time, maybe I would have seen something that would lead me to where she is, what family she went to. Since there was no name, maybe she didn't get a chance to go to a family. Maybe they did kill her. I don't know," I say rambling. "That's why staying here is a waste of time. I need to get out there and look. That has to be my first priority, and then we can talk about getting the walls torn down."

"We're on the run. We can't just go out there all half–cocked when we don't even know where we're going." He squeezes my hands harder.

"But if we can just find the newbie camp. We should talk to Julian—he may know." My lungs hurt, and I take in a much-needed breath. "I know you told me before not to get my hopes up, but that was before you knew about the adoption files. Now that changes everything, and you can't tell me it doesn't."

He's quiet. I don't know what to make of his somber expression.

"We can talk to Julian, but I thought you didn't trust him," he finally says.

"I still don't, but it doesn't hurt to ask him about this."

"I don't think he will know anything, but we can ask."

"Why are you being so negative about this when it's a good thing?"

"The adoption papers do change things; but it won't matter, if she's already dead or gone to her new family. I'm sorry to be so blunt; but I think you should face facts, that way you won't be hurt."

"Let's just go talk to Julian," I say with a huff.

I turn and walk toward the door. I hear Eric's boots stomping on the hardwood floors behind me. I know he is cold, at times; but I need to remain positive, and his negative attitude isn't helping me.

I can't help but think of Samuel. If he were here, I'm sure he would tell me things would be okay and we will find her. That's what I need to hear right now.

CHAPTER THREE

"So you think your niece has been taken to this newbie camp." Julian pulls on his earlobe, like he doesn't believe what I'm saying can be true. He plops down in one of the padded cafeteria chairs.

"Yes, I do," I say, tugging on my turtleneck, because it's rubbing up against my chin.

The air feels cold in the dark cafeteria. We decided not to turn any lights on, since there are eight large square windows with blinds slightly ajar and the light from the outside world peers through them.

Earlier, Eric almost closed them but Julian said they were slanted enough so no one would be able to see in—and a little light shining in wasn't a bad thing.

"Have you heard of the newbie camp?" Eric asks. He sits on one of the cafeteria tables with one boot propped in the chair while the other leg dangles.

"Or the midpoint burial," I say, cutting in. I'm pacing back and forth and my boots are clomping as they scuff the tile floors.

"I haven't heard of those places, but that doesn't mean they don't exist. A lot of things are kept quiet around here. Only level six guards and the president would know about it." He tugs on his earlobe again. Maybe he does that when he's in deep thought. "The next time I go out to get us food, I will ask around."

"The next time you go out." I throw my hands up, in anger. "When will that be? This process is taking too long. We need to do something now."

"Whisper, calm down." Eric hops down from the table. "I told you we have to take our time and figure out a plan before we go running down the streets looking for Abigail."

"When will that be? So far, we've done nothing but lurk around this old college."

"I'm sorry that we aren't moving fast enough for you," Julian says, as if he doesn't like my attitude. "But we haven't even been here one full day yet." He holds up a finger, like I'm a child and I don't know what one means. "I'm the one who knows the way around the territory, so let me do what I need to do." His face is hard as he stands. "Like I said before, we should keep lying low for now; and when I go out to get more food, I'll ask around and see what I can find out."

"I agree," Eric says.

My throat tightens. Eric doesn't seem to have my back, so I continue ranting. "Who are the people you're planning on talking to?" I shrug. "And you never told us where you got the food and clothing from."

"I think it's best if I keep that to myself, for now," Julian says, as he fiddles with his fingers like he's all of a sudden nervous.

"Why?"

"Emma, leave it alone." Eric squeezes my elbow.

I know he's annoyed because he uses my real name.

"You two keep talking about we need this grand plan." I gesture my hands up to the ceiling to make my point. "Well, we're all together now, so can we start discussing what our first steps will be?"

"Fine," Julian says, plopping back down in the chair. "I was able to get a black pickup truck from some old friends of mine. They won't say anything."

He glances at me like he knows I have mixed feelings about his friend's involvement. "It's a little beat up, but it runs good and my friend says it's good for off-road travel. It has a bucket seat up front, so you can fold the middle seat down to form a center armrest. It seats up to six people, has an enclosed cab and an open cargo area with low sides, and a tailgate. I was fortunate that they were able to lend it to me."

"Why would we need something that big?" I ask. "Won't we be easier to spot?"

"I couldn't be picky. I had to take what they could give me." Julian snaps. "I was just happy to receive the help."

"Julian's right," Eric says.

"There's a wooded area about a half a mile down east from here that no one goes to," Julian starts speaking again. "I parked it there and walked back here. Since we're so far out from the wall, my radio doesn't work anymore. I thought it wouldn't cut out if we were near the outskirts, but I was wrong. But when I was closer to the supply warehouse, to drop off the supply truck, my radio was quiet—like they weren't even searching for us."

"And it was strange that Rich didn't radio this in when we first escaped Territory L," Eric says. "But we've been here for hours, so why hasn't he done it by now?"

"Or maybe he has and they're playing some kind of game," Julian says. "We can't be sure of anything. I think we should continue lying low."

He peers over at me again because he knows how impatient I am. "All three territories combined are shaped like the human brain, with Territory M and U taking up the top of the brain, and Territory L occupying the lower half because it's the largest. Territory L is about thirty-six square miles—"

"We already know that," I say with a huff.

"If you would let me finish…Territory M is a little smaller. It's around twenty-six square miles. I don't have a map of the territory, but I'll show you on my hand."

He sticks his right hand out so it's flat. He spreads out his hand so his fingers are far apart and I see that his fingers point to the left—which would be west. His palm faces in the direction of the ceiling and I see the inside of his palm is pink and has tons of lines like an old person. "The pinky finger is the gates coming from Territory L, the south side of the area. Underneath the pinky finger and all that surrounds it is the area beyond the gates. Most of the palm consists of the Territory where people work and live. The round curvature near the thumb is the outskirts of the Territory. They call that area the Hill. It's located on the north side."

"Why?" I raise an eyebrow.

"Because it's a hilly area that has executive buildings that only level-six guards, maybe some level-five guards, and President Esther are allowed to go to."

"That's probably where the newbie camp and midpoint burial are located." I swallow hard a few times, hoping my words are true.

"Maybe, but we can't be sure." He shrugs. "But I told you I will ask around. I do know that that's where the leader lives. The leader reports to President Esther, is supposedly in charge of the territory, and lives in a mansion on the Hill, above the executive buildings."

"Who is this person?" Eric asks.

"No one seems to know." Julian shrugs. "If they do know, they are not saying."

"Then how does the leader delegate?" I ask.

"With men called watchmen. They're like the guards of Territory L, only they wear dark brown instead of black clothing. They wear black boots and have no metal buttons to indicate what level they are at because they are all at the same level. There are about twenty-five of them to watch over the Hill and surrounding areas. The leader sends them down to crack the whip when bigger jobs need to be handled that the one thousand patrol-men can't handle; but that's rare, because this Territory practically runs itself."

That's the same thing Rich had said to President Esther the day I was hiding out near the kitchen of her mansion back in Territory L.

"Everyone knows the leader is just a mouthpiece for President Esther," Julian continues, breaking my thoughts. "Whatever she says goes; but since she rarely comes to this Territory, then the leader follows all of her orders—or is supposed to anyway."

"Yeah, I know they say she doesn't have time to come here because she needs to look over Territory L." I tilt my head. "Since we're so unruly, we can't do anything on our own." I roll my eyes.

"Yes, and she only goes to Territory U because that's where her rich friends—who are her class of people—and her other mansion are," Eric says.

"Then this should work in our favor." I scratch my forehead. "If this said leader and the newbie camp are all in the same area, we can talk to the leader about siding with us and we can find Abigail all at the same time."

"You make this all seem like it's going to be a walk in the park, Emma. It's not." Julian squints his eyes.

"That's not what I'm saying at all, but—"

Cutting me off, Julian says, "Once I feel it's time, we will make our move to the Hill. For now, I feel we should remain here and the next time I go out to get more food—"

"You keep saying that," I say, cutting him off this time. "Why do you always get to go?"

Eric glares at me, like I'm embarrassing him. "Because he knows the area."

"I'm going to scope out the surroundings again." Julian stands and heads for the door.

"What's going on with you?" Eric brushes a strand of hair behind my ear.

"I'm sorry." I shrug. "It's just this whole situation has got me on edge." My fists are tight, making my nails dig into my palms. "I left my entire family behind. I know we just got here, but I feel like I need to do something."

"It will be okay." He pulls me close and I lean into him with my whole body.

I feel the ripples in his chest beneath his thin t-shirt. His arms feel warm wrapped around me, and I welcome his embrace. He kisses my forehead and then my neck and his hot breath sends a tingle up my spine.

"I know what you need," he says, breaking away.

He walks away from me, and I wish he hadn't. The hug was nice and just what I needed. I have no idea where he's gone to, so I walk toward the window. The blinds are still slightly ajar. I lean against them to feel the warmth shine through. They crunch up next to my body. I feel underneath my turtleneck and touch my necklace. The coolness coming off the chain makes my hands prickle.

Hearing a screeching across the floor, I jump. I turn to find Eric pushing the tables away from each other.

"What are you doing?"

"I think maybe we need to train."

I scrunch my face up. "Eric."

"Look, we need to keep up our skills because we don't know what's to come."

"Fine," I say, and then let out a large sigh. Maybe this will help me to loosen up some. My shoulders feel tense and I haven't been able to calm down since we got here.

I take my stance. Eric stands across from me, with his arms up and fists tightly closed. I extend my right leg in a smooth but sudden motion, so I can hit Eric in his left hip.

"Remember to hit me before your leg is fully extended."

His voice breaks my concentration, so I put my leg back down.

"I already know that," I say. "We're not in training anymore. You don't have to keep coaching me."

"Oh, look who's suddenly cocky. Just because you fought off Rich doesn't mean you don't need more training. You can always learn more." He wipes his brow with the back of his hand.

"I know, I know," I say. "We never stop learning. Now stop talking. I need more action and less chitchat," I say, with a smile.

"Fine," he says, then laughs.

He takes his stance again. His arms are up, elbows and knees are bent. He's ready to block whatever I have coming for him.

I extend my right leg but make sure it's still bent a little as I go for his left leg. The first time I was going for his left hip; but now that he knows that, I switch up my strategy and go for his leg. His hands are blocking his hip area. I use all my power and hit his left leg with the ball of my right foot before he can block it. I feel the air swoosh across my face and instantly I feel my energy rise. Maybe this is just what I need to let off a little steam. He grunts and stumbles back a little.

"Nice move." He nods his head while trying to compose his stance. "Those boots really hurt," he says, rubbing his leg.

I'm now in my original position with both boots on the floor. The boots are heavier to kick with than the shoes we had in training; but I did it with Rich, so I'm getting used to it. I know he is trying to distract me with this impromptu workout, but it's not really working.

"Your kicks are even quicker now than in training." He licks his lips. "They're more powerful and damaging than a slower kick would be. Keep moving like that and I may need some water."

"Are you saying you're getting thirsty?"

"Maybe. But let's see what else you got."

He's still in coaching mode. I want to teach him a lesson. I kick with my left foot this time. When he goes to grab my foot so he can get my feet from underneath me, I quickly stomp it back down to the floor before he catches it. He's bent forward and not paying attention to my right hand. I use it to grab the back of his hoodie. I yank his hood toward me and stomp down on his left foot with my heel. I do the moves as fast as I can and it seems like it was done in one swift motion.

"What was that?" he asks, sounding like a child. "That move's against the rules. I never taught you that."

"No, but it worked, didn't it." I grin. "That was something I thought up. It caught you off guard, and that's all that counts. Sorry, if I hurt your foot." I wipe the beads of sweat from my forehead with my palm.

"I'm fine," he says, wiping his head with the bottom of his jacket. "But I need a shower. There should be one in the gymnasium. Why don't you come with me up to the gym? You take watch while I take a shower, then I will take watch for you. " Eric removes his hooded jacket.

"So, you're saying that I'm sweaty?"

"No, I'm not saying that. I am happy this short sparring session lightened your mood, at least a little. I know this situation is stressful."

"Thanks," I say, following him. It has also seemed to lighten his mood as well.

* * *

We walk up to the first floor. The gymnasium and the showers are near the south side of the building. The lights automatically click on as we venture down the hallway. There are black directional signs on the walls with words in silver pointing to where we need to go. Eric has his hoodie across his shoulder. We both have our guard jackets in hand. Eric says if we can't find towels anywhere, we can use our jackets to dry off. There is one big room to shower in, with one side for men and one side for women. There are two unisex bathrooms. One's on the left side of the room you shower in and the other bathroom is on the right. I take first watch while Eric takes his shower. Then, he will do the same for me.

It's gloomy and eerie here, like the jails down in President Esther's mansion. The air smells like mildew.

When we're all in the building, the east entrance locks automatically from the inside, and when Julian leaves out, he is able to get back in by disabling and enabling it at will. Since he's the one who hacked the electronic lock, maybe he knows what he's doing. He claims we don't have to worry about anyone else getting or being in the building. Eric should be fine if I run into the other room, to look around and to use the bathroom.

I lay my jacket on the white, hard ceramic sink. There's one long counter with individual bowls. I haven't looked in a mirror since we left Territory L. Every bathroom I've encountered either has the mirrors ripped from the walls or they're cracked, like a glass has splintered. Now that I finally see my reflection, I look older and I have circles under my eyes. I hadn't realized it until now, but my hair is disheveled.

I need to splash some water on my face, but I don't see any knobs to use the sink. The bathrooms down in the lower level near the cafeteria still had knobs to turn for hot and cold water—but this one has neither. There has to be some new way to work this. I wave my hands underneath the faucet and water gushes out. It's cold and wet to my fingertips. I suppose with this kind of sink you only receive cold water.

My guess is the small white dispenser mounted to the wall next to the sink would be soap. I place my hand underneath it and a small layer of white puffy soap plops in it, which smells light like perfume. I rub my hands together and let the soap sink in as the water makes it bubbly. I turn toward the wall and see a silver box.

I'm curious to what it is so I move closer to it. I wave my hands underneath and hot air blows out so I can dry my hands.

It's amazing how many automatic things they have here while we have none back home. The sinks in L are nothing like this. We have regular bars of soap on the sink for everyone to use; and our sinks don't come on automatically. We have a paper dispenser to dry our hands but most of the time the dispenser is found empty—unless it's the dispenser with the one towel that hangs down for everyone to use. I flinch at the thought.

"Emma."

Eric's voice breaks my concentration. I notice when he's angry with me he switches back to calling me Emma.

"You were supposed to be taking watch while I was in the shower." His eyes are stern and pierce right at me.

He wears his uniform pants but no t-shirt. The muscles in his chest glisten from the water. I have never seen him like this before—with no shirt on at all. My cheeks feel hot. I'm sure they're as red as a ladybug's body.

"There's no one else here," I say, trying to compose myself. "We're the only ones in the building."

"We can't be sure of anything. You know that." He clenches his teeth.

I shrug. "I'm sorry."

"Just go take your shower." He shakes his head. "I'll finish getting dressed while I take watch. I *can* do two things at once." He makes sure to emphasize *can*.

"Fine," I say, rolling my eyes and walking by him.

I see his foul mood has resurfaced. I thought this phase was over. He's still so hot and cold all the time—just like in Territory L. I don't know where his nasty attitude is coming from, but I don't like it. I realize I've been all over the place since we arrived here. And I haven't been the most pleasant person to deal with either, because of my accusations about Julian; but I have a reason—my family's lives are on the line. And I know I can do two things at once. Just because I ran into the bathroom for a moment doesn't mean that I can't.

* * *

The shower room is draped in a light tan color. The floors are tiled and tan colored like the tiled walls. It's very different from the dark black and brown colors back in L. There are multiple showers with glass doors on each one. The glass is frosted so you can't see through it. There's one shower head and a large silver knob underneath that reads H and C. If you turn it to the right you get cold water and if you turn it to the left you get hot. The water against my skin feels cool and refreshing.

I wish my shower could last longer, but I know Eric is waiting for me to finish. I don't want to piss him off any more than he already is. Now that I have toweled off with my jacket and I'm dry, it's a shame I have to put back on the same sweaty pants and knit turtleneck. Out of the two turtlenecks he brought me this one fits the best. The other one fits a little snugger so I prefer not to wear it. I wish Julian could have brought me some t-shirts. But I guess I should be happy to have gotten anything new at all.

There is a gray bench in the middle of the room. I sit down for a moment. The bench is hard and looks heavy like it is made of stone. I decide to take the thick strands of my wet hair and braid them into one. Back in L we weren't allowed to have gym classes because there wasn't money for such luxuries, so there was no need for a shower in our school. Even if we did have one, I'm certain our shower room would look nothing like this. It would probably have been in a dark color with only one shower stall.

I walk out of the locker room with my guard jacket tied around my waist to find Eric still standing there, waiting for me. He has his jacket in hand.

"I thought we could walk around some more and check the place out," he says.

I nod. "Sounds alright to me."

We walk to the gymnasium to look around. There are no windows, and the lights don't pop on automatically. I click one of the light switches on that's near the gym's entrance. Eric squints his eyes at me. I see a few deflated balls. I also see a dumbbell that looks rusted. It must be old equipment that was left behind. Eric remains quiet as we continue along the white walls into the next room.

There is no door to separate the two rooms, just a small entryway. The lights automatically click on this time as we enter. It's the room that swim class must have been held in because there is a large deep pool. I've heard of the indulgences that the schools in the upper territories have, but I never imagined I would see it. My hopes for such things have faded.

Since the gym room and pool room connect with the entrance we just came through, I didn't expect to see another way in, but I do. Off to the south side of the room I see a brown door. I'm gathering that's another way to enter the pool room.

I hear Eric's boots scuffling against the tiled floors as he turns around. I hear him say he's going back to see if there is a light dimmer.

I move closer to the pool. It's empty, just like I thought it would be. It's square-shaped and deep. There are railings on the side where I am and a couple of stairs to go down into the pool. I would guess it to be about twenty-five yards long and five to six feet deep, because I've read in magazines that that's the dimensions of a standard-size pool. I don't know how to swim; but if given the chance, I would like to learn.

I see something bright, like a stain against the concrete, on the opposite end of the pool. The room is silent and smells of decay. Once I reach the shallow end of the pool, I lean down to get a better look. The stain is circular and apple red. I assume it's dried blood, but I can't tell if it's animal or human. I wonder what could have happened here. I look over to the left and see something small and pink. I blink a few times. I must be imagining things. It looks like a blanket.

Once I reach the left side of the pool, I kneel down again and lean in. It looks like a baby's blanket. It's flat, square, and made of a knitted fabric. I jump down with a huff onto the bottom of the pool and pick up the pink blanket. I see red stains splattered all over the blanket. Underneath the blanket is a tiny white dress. It's bloodied, shredded, and the right sleeve has been sliced apart. My chest tightens and I call for Eric. I throw the blanket down and run to the side of the pool with the railings. I use them to lift myself up.

"Whisper, are you alright?" Eric runs from the gym room to where I am.

"I'm sorry," I say. My throat tingles. "I know we're supposed to keep a low profile, b-but…" I'm having trouble getting the words out. "There's a baby's blanket over there." I point. "There's a baby's dress underneath and it's bloody. Just go look over there."

The brown door I noticed earlier swings open. "W-what happened?" Julian runs into the room out of breath. "I c-could hear shouting from down the hall."

I feel nauseated. I assume someone harmed a baby here. Why would they do that? This can't be where President Esther brings the babies to kill them.

"Emma saw a bloody blanket and dress at the bottom of the pool," Eric says. He releases his jacket; it whacks and lands on the floor. His boots *thump* as he jumps down into the pool.

"Maybe you shouldn't touch it without gloves on," I say, seeing him reach for it.

"It's fine," Eric says. "There are no gloves around and no time to search for any."

He leans down and picks up the edge of the pink blanket with his thumb and index finger. He holds it up.

"The blood's dried up," Eric says, picking up the dress next. "I wonder how long it's been here."

"There's no way to tell," Julian says.

"This means someone was here," Eric says. "Maybe they left right before we got here."

"I thought you said no one was staying here." My eyebrow rises at Julian.

"As far as I know, there wasn't," Julian says. "No one's been here since the college closed." His eyes are wide. "I don't know why anyone would be in here, especially with a baby."

"Do you think they use this place to get rid of the babies?" I ask.

"No, that's not possible." Julian scowls. "They would never use a place like this. Our best bet for that would be up on the Hill."

"Well, someone's been here recently," Eric says, throwing the dress and blanket down in disgust. "Maybe we should leave."

"Maybe it's time we check out the Hill," I say.

"No." Julian's eyes narrow. "I told you we can't just go running around; we have to have a plan."

"How can we stay here? If someone's been here recently, how do we know they won't come back?" I ask.

"All the entrances are closed off, except the one I use to get in and out. And that door locks automatically when I leave. I even yank on it a few times just to make sure it's securely locked. Trust me." His eyes are sincere. "I know what I'm doing, and we don't have anywhere else we can go; so this has to be it, for now."

"Maybe there's another way out—a way we don't know about because we haven't found it," I say.

"We haven't seen anything, or heard anything, since we arrived; so no one's here now." Julian's voice is ruff.

He acts like I'm undermining his skills of protecting us. I don't want to argue about this, so I keep quiet. My throat constricts every time I glance over at the bottom of the pool.

"We should just make sure we stay in the areas we are familiar with, like we've been doing. If we need to come down here for showers, we should come together. We have to be careful, in case they come back." Eric swipes his hands together. "Do we all agree?"

"Yeah," Julian says.

"Yes," I say, nodding my head. But I'm hoping we aren't around long enough for that.

CHAPTER FOUR

WE'VE BEEN HERE for a week and I feel like my side is repeatedly being hit with a steel pipe. Julian comes and goes as he pleases, but I have to keep out of sight until he feels the time is right for us to make our next move. Every time I try to voice my opinion, Julian shuts me down and Eric agrees with him. My body trembles with anger, thinking about the time we're wasting while Abigail is being shipped off to a new family, like she's no better than supplies being shipped on a truck.

No more workouts with Eric to relieve stress. No more sitting in a dark drafty cafeteria, eating peanut butter and jelly sandwiches. I can't do this anymore.

It's morning—10:00 a.m.—and I'm at the back door of the college, the east entrance. Eric is still sleeping and I didn't see Julian, so I assume he is taking a shower.

I'm at the teacher's entrance, the way we first came in. I push open the latch to unlock the door. I know the door will automatically lock behind me and I won't be able to get back in. I don't care. If my plan works out I will be gone a while, and I may not even be able to come back. I will just have to meet back up with Eric later—after I've done what I feel I need to.

I will have to make my way on foot. It may take a while, but I can take the wooded area where no one will see me. If I can make it north to where the Hill is, maybe I can find the newbie camps.

I take my chain from beneath my turtleneck and place it on top of the knitted fabric. I want to touch it as I take this walk. My steps are quick and my boots scuffle against the dusty ground. I know it must be my imagination, but the air smells like daffodils and the sun shines so bright it blinds me. It's something I'm not used to.

Once I walk down to the wooded area, I feel more relaxed. There are birds squawking above and it reminds me of the area where I brought my sister, Taylor, food and clothing back in Territory L. She was pregnant, which is against the law; so she was hiding out from the patrolmen in our grandparent's old house. Once she had Abigail, she remained hidden there. I was her only link to civilization during that time.

The stiffness in my chest relaxes a little as my pace slows. I haven't stumbled upon the black truck that Julian says he left here. It doesn't matter; I don't have the key fob. But I would like to see what it looks like, since Julian claims—once it's time—it will be used in our escape plan.

My heart jumps because I hear tires screeching. I turn to find the black truck I've been hearing about turning into the wooded area. I don't keep tabs on Julian, so I had no idea he wasn't back at the college. He must have gone out before I did. I could turn my slow pace into a quick run, but he's seen me now so what good would it do.

The pickup truck squeals and stops right beside me. The truck has four doors, two rows of seats, and an open area in the back with low sides. We don't have many vehicles back in L but from magazines I've read that my mom had, I believe that's called a cargo bed. I also remember Julian saying it had a cargo bed when he was describing it.

"What are you doing?" he shouts, as he hops down from the truck. "Are you really taking off?"

He continues ranting. "You're going to blow everything by going out and searching around where someone can spot you." He rubs his hand through his hair. "You have no idea where you're going, but you feel it's best to ruin things for everyone."

"This isn't about us, it's about my niece." My teeth clench together. "I can't just sit around here doing nothing."

"I told you I would ask around, but you seem like you don't trust me."

His face is so close to mine that I feel the warmth of his breath.

"I don't know you well enough to trust you," I say. "Besides, how can I trust you when you sneak off without telling anyone?"

"I don't know you, and I don't owe you any explanations; but Eric is friends with both of us. If he trusts me, I think you should too. We should try to make this work," he says, scratching the back of his neck. "Look, I'm risking my life for Eric, so that extends to you and your family."

"And why is that?" My eyes squint. "Why would you stick your neck out for Eric?"

"We were roommates." He looks down and up, like he doesn't like the direction the conversation is going.

"I think there's more to it. He said you owed him a favor." I bite down on my lip.

"If you must know," he says, pausing and glancing around. "When I first became a guard after being kicked out of Territory M, I didn't have many friends. A lot of the guys didn't like me because they felt like I destroyed my Territory M privileges when they never even had a chance to go there." He blinks. "My roommate, Billy, didn't care for me too much—needless to say we didn't get along. We heard that one of the guys who drove the truck to carry the supplies over to the hospital suddenly had a heart attack and died, so they needed someone to take over the job."

I feel my eyes glaring as he talks.

"Billy really wanted it, but I got it. President Esther felt they needed someone fast who knew the area already—there was no time to train anyone on the surroundings of Territory M. Billy's dislike for me turned into hatred after that, and he started goofing off and not keeping up with his job responsibilities. So, he was kicked out of his room in the mansion. When the new guys came in, Eric was chosen to room with me. Billy had to move back home, which meant he was making less money since he wasn't a guard in the mansion."

A breeze blows and he looks over at the trees because the wind is howling in our ears.

"Anyway, one night I was alone in my room. Billy must have been still lurking around the mansion after training. He came in my room and put a gun to my head. I'm sure he was going to kill me. Eric walked in and saved my life."

He shrugs. "I told him I owed him a favor for what he did for me and if he ever needed any help to let me know. When he came to me with this, I said I would help out; but I didn't want to get in too deep. I feared my privileges of going back and forth may be taken away and I would not be able to see my child. If we get caught, I'm supposed to say that you two forced me to do this. You have some kind of leverage over me, so I had to help you."

"So you two came up with this plan and no one thought to tell me." My chest burns with anger.

"This was Eric's truth to tell, not mine." He glances around again.

"How did he save your life?" I ask, grabbing his arm to turn him back toward me. "What did he do?"

"I just told you." He frowns.

"No, you said he came into the room; but you didn't tell me what he did."

"He pulled his gun on Billy and—"

"Shot Billy in self-defense," I say, cutting him off because he's talking too slow. For some reason my hands shake.

"Not exactly," he says, with a low voice.

"What does that mean?"

"Look," he says, with annoyance in his voice. "I think you need to ask Eric about this."

"I'm asking you."

We hear a noise. Julian screams get down. I can squat down on my own, but before I do I feel the weight of his hand on my shoulder. He shoves me down to the filthy ground. There's a loud commotion of voices, like someone's having a party. There's a group of young people; they look around my age or a little older. I can't hear what they're saying, but they are walking back toward the old college.

"Maybe they're the ones who left that bloody blanket in the pool," I say. "We should follow them and see how they get in."

Julian doesn't answer back; he just nods, in agreement. We stay several feet behind them. I now see there are four of them. They are dressed in dark colors—blacks and browns—like we do in Territory L. All of them have on hoodies, so I can't see their faces. We stay low and follow them to the west side of the building. The wind is still gusting strong. I wish I had braided my hair this morning, so the strands wouldn't keep wafting in my eyes.

I squat down again and lean against the brown brick of the building. Julian is right next to me. I shiver a little. The air seems damper on this side of the building and smells like moldy cheese. The night we left Territory L, it felt like fall and now it feels like winter. The weather here seems no different than in Territory L. I can never tell what season it is.

I turn my attention back to the group of four. My eyes widen as I see them slide up a window. The window is small but they still manage to squeeze through it. I look at Julian and he looks back at me. I had no idea there was another way into the building, and I'm guessing he didn't either.

"They must be staying on the west side of the building," he says in a whisper.

"We need to go back and warn Eric." I swallow hard.

We make our way back to the east entrance. Julian is ahead of me.

"You said all of the entrances had been closed off or boarded or blocked."

"I said most of the entrances." He turns around and glowers at me. "I told you when we got here that I only had time to check the east and north sides of the buildings. But later on I went back and checked the other doors and everything was boarded and blocked like I said."

"If you would have checked all the entrances—like the windows—we wouldn't be having this problem right now," I say.

"Since you're so great at everything maybe you should have checked them yourself."

He's right I should have because I had my doubts about his abilities. But it's too late for that and I'd rather focus on his faults right now.

"I didn't think I had to, since you said we could trust you." I throw those words back in his face.

"We don't have time for this right now." He turns from me and continues toward the door.

He knows I'm right that's why he's changing the subject, and I know he's right—we need to get to Eric.

* * *

We find Eric down in the cafeteria.

"We saw them entering the west side of the college through an open window," Julian says.

"What were you two doing outside, anyway?" Eric asks. He leans back on one of the hard tables and plops his right foot in a chair. His eyes narrow my way. He seems to be talking to me more than Julian.

"That doesn't really matter right now," I say. "What are we going to do about the intruders?" My boots scuffle as I pace back and forth near the tables, trying not to look at him.

"We should just go and talk to them and find out who they are," Eric says. "Maybe they won't have a problem sharing the college with us. They're probably hiding out like we are."

"You think that's wise?" I ask. "What would they even be hiding from?" I stop pacing.

"I think I may know who they are." Julian's eyes lift. "I've often heard that the runaways use abandoned buildings to hide out."

I repeat his words. "*Runaways.*"

"Yes, they're young people who don't want to live in Territory M, because they don't want to follow the rules here. They run away and hide, so they can live the life they want to."

"Why wouldn't they want to live here?" I ask. "It's better than Territory L—at least that's what I thought. It just has to be." My voice quivers.

No one seems to be listening to me because Julian continues on.

"I'm sorry," he says. "I didn't know the runaways used this building to hide out or I would never have brought you here."

"It's not your fault," Eric says. "Are they dangerous?" His eyebrow rises.

"Some are and some aren't," Julian replies. "Maybe we should just leave. I can try and find us someplace else to go."

We hear a loud booming voice. "You aren't going anywhere."

Four dark figures walk toward us with hoodies on. They're the same figures we saw crawling through the open window on the west side of the building.

"Why are you here? This is our spot. We found it first." The tall skinny one is doing all of the talking. He takes off his hood and I now see that his skin is as dark as mahogany and he has short black hair and dark brown eyes.

"We didn't know anyone was staying here," Julian says.

I see the other three are standing back near the cafeteria doorway, watching the tall one speak. There are no lights on—besides the thin layer of light seeping through the blinds—so it's hard to make out their faces. Out of the corner of my eye, I see Eric has his hand on the gun in his holster, just like I have my hand on mine.

"Well, you do now." The tall one keeps talking. "So, you should leave." He steps closer, into Julian's face.

Eric moves closer behind Julian, my guess is if the guy lunges, he can help Julian out.

"We don't want any trouble." There's a growl in Eric's voice.

"Logan," the tall one says, yelling back to one of the others. "Check in the kitchen to see how much is still there. They've probably eaten everything we had left."

Logan's steps are quick, and I hear his shoes screech across the tile floors. Now that his shadow is closer, I see he is light-skin and freckles plaster his face. He marches by and a small breeze hits me in the face.

The others come closer and their dark shadows brighten. I see another guy who's short and husky with curly light brown hair. The last one is short and has skin the color of mahogany, like the tall one. I can't see his hair because he keeps his hood on.

"A lot of it's gone," Logan says, walking back in the cafeteria. "They've eaten it."

"That's a lie," I say. "There were only expired crackers when we got here, nothing else."

"And those expired crackers were part of our stash," Logan snaps back at me. "So, you did eat it." His blue eyes flash my way.

"We went out to get more supplies." The tall one is talking again. "To add to what little we had left." His face hardens.

"Look, man. Like I said before, we didn't know." Julian moves his head from side to side.

"Well, you know now." Logan steps forward. "And you guys need to get out." Logan's height matches Eric.

"Who's going to make us?" Eric's nostrils flair.

I can tell he's getting tired of the conversation, as am I, because it's getting us nowhere.

"We'll make you." The tall one thrust his shoulders forward. He slithers straight toward Eric like he's ready to throw a punch, but the little guy jumps in between the middle of them.

"Stop it—stop it now, the building is big enough for us all to stay here." I now know *he* is a *she* because the voice is soft and high-pitched. "Why don't we stay on opposite sides of the building?" She continues, "That way we don't have to cross each other's paths."

"How will we decide who takes which side?" I ask.

"Since we come and go from the west side, then we will stay on that side of the building. You and your friends will stay on the east side."

"What about the cafeteria?" the tall one says, with tight fists. "It's in the north corner of the building but closer to the east side than the west, so that would be left to them. If we follow your plan, then we can't come in here. We need to eat."

"We all need to eat," Julian says, hunching his shoulders.

"We don't need to use the cafeteria," she speaks again. "Most of the food we bring doesn't need to be refrigerated."

She seems to be the most reasonable one out of them all.

"But we do all need to use the locker rooms," she continues. "Which will be on our side of the school. I realize we all need to take showers."

"Why don't we share it," I say. "I'm sure we're civil enough to share a couple of showers. Besides, we're not going to be here that long anyway." My chest twinges. I pray that's true.

"You're that girl—that Emma girl we saw on the boxes. You gave that speech," Logan says.

"Yeah, it's her." Eric moves in front of me. "What's it to you?"

It's nice to see his protectiveness, but I don't need him to rescue me.

"Nothing." Logan shrugs. "I'm just saying—"

"Look, no one cares about the female." The tall ones voice is ruff. "But for now, we'll make peace like my sister wants." He glances over at the young woman. "But to make things fair, we'll use the showers in the morning and, if you need them, you will wait till the afternoon."

"How is that fair?" Eric asks, puffing his chest out.

"Because I say it is." His jaw hardens, as if he doesn't like being questioned.

"It's fine." I grab Eric's hand.

He brushes my hand aside. "Whatever," he says, shaking his head. He walks back toward one of the hard cafeteria tables. He leans on it in disgust.

"Why don't we disperse now and we won't have to see each other again," she says.

I consider her wiser than the others. I nod my head, in agreement. The runaways leave and Julian walks closer to me. We turn to Eric, who's still leaning on the table.

"I don't like this," he mumbles. "I don't like this at all."

"What's the big deal?" I ask.

"I don't want to share this school with them." Eric's jaw twitches. "We don't know them and I don't trust them."

"I agree with Eric," Julian says.

"As long as we watch our backs and stay away from them, I think we'll be fine. Besides, we don't have anywhere else to go right now. And we're not going to be here that long." I know I sound like a broken record—a phrase my mom said they used years ago—because I keep repeating myself, but I don't plan on being here long.

Eric and Julian talk among themselves and I walk toward the cafeteria windows. The sun seeps through and I stand there and sigh. My thoughts go to the one and only female in their group. I can't help but wonder if the blood in the swimming pool came from her baby. I don't know why it matters so much, but it haunts me. Then, I can't help thinking of Abigail.

CHAPTER FIVE

IT SEEMS LIKE months have passed instead of only a few days since we met up with the runaways. Since then, we steer clear of them. They stay on their side of the building and we stay on ours. We even manage not to run into them at the showers. Everyone sticks to their required schedules.

Eric and Julian are unusually quiet, and I don't know what to make of it. Since I'm going out of my mind, I decide to go exploring again. I don't dare venture outside after what happened last time, but I've been itching to go back to the art room. It's on our designated side of the building, so there shouldn't be any problems. I shouldn't bump into any of the runaways.

My hair is in one long braid; it's more manageable that way. I have on the same clothing as yesterday, since we don't have much to change in to here.

The door to the art room squeaks behind me as I close it. My head spins as I go back to where I left the sketchbook. I sit in one of the cushiony padded chairs and open the book. The pages ruffle as I turn them to get back to where I originally left off. My eyes blur, trying to find where I was. I don't know why this book unnerves me so, but my hands shake turning the pages.

Finally, I see writing.

What drives President Esther? What motivates her to do what she does? She claims she kills babies because she doesn't want them to grow up hungry or to be raped or to be treated poorly. Let their suffering stop, before they feel the pain. This is what she claims, but there has to be something more. Although I understand what she is saying, I still don't think that gives her the right to decide what we do with our bodies. It's our decision and our decision alone. I believe something else makes her do what she does. But will we ever know her real reasoning? She is the only president our world will ever see. What she says goes. So, at this point, does it really matter?

Her words send chills up my spine. I have never thought about it in that way before. She is right; there has to be something else that makes President Esther act the way she does. I can't help but wonder who this Alexa is and why she left her book behind. I keep turning through more blank pages, craving to read more. Near the end of the sketchbook, I see more words.

Day one: we are here hiding out. Hoping we won't be caught. I write this because I don't know how else to express myself and get out my thoughts.

Her words trail off, so I turn to the back of the book. There is a diagram drawn on the very last page, along with words. The numbers 2030 are circled. Next to it there is writing.

An internal war over farming land took place during that year in our small world—well, in the city of Craigluy. The elected officials took land away from some of the citizens that owned it, so the people fought for what was theirs and it tore everything apart.

She has written California on one side of the paper and Arizona on the other side of the paper. In between those words she has drawn a map of Craigluy that looks like the human brain; it reminds me of the picture I saw in President Esther's quarters and the description Julian laid out for us earlier.

Next to the brain picture she has written: near Blythe, along the Colorado River.

Craigluy…a small city of people who were too afraid to leave and start over in California or Arizona. They were stupid, so they ended up staying here. Since we became such a small group of people once the others left, the president started calling us a nation. I feel our stupidity is what makes us a nation.

I don't agree—some people did leave and go to those places; my mother told me so. Those that stayed, like my grandparents, weren't stupid; they just wanted to rebuild what we once had here in Craigluy. They wanted the chance to make it better. They had no idea that if they stayed walls would be built around Craigluy—walls that keep us from venturing to the surrounding states.

It's the president's doing; she wants us trapped here forever. She wants everyone to follow her rules no matter what race or ethnicity you are. No creed should be followed. Her word is gospel. Religion has no place here. The president says how much money you make is what's important and what class you belong to, not any religious affiliation. It's been that way since my mother was born in 2045. Now that it's the year 2098, I'm hoping to get things to change…my thoughts are interrupted because the door bangs. I jump to my feet and reach for my gun. It's not Eric this time; it's the female who was the wisest one in the cafeteria.

"You don't have to go there," she says. "You don't have to do that—go for your gun, I mean." She holds up both her hands.

She must have noticed my hand near my holster.

"I'm Alexa," she says, moving closer to me.

I know that name from the sketchbook.

"This is where I come to write my thoughts. I left my book here." Her chestnut brown eyes slant toward the sketchbook.

"Sorry," I say, while glancing down. I notice I'm still holding onto the book in my left hand, tightly, like it's mine and I'm afraid to part with it. "I thought this was left from when the college closed," I continue. "I didn't realize it was yours."

I didn't notice before because her hood was on, but now I see she looks a lot like her brother, except she is small-framed and not as tall. She is around my height; our eyes align in the same plane.

"It's fine," she says. "I know I'm not supposed to be on this side of the building. I wanted to retrieve my book." She still has on her sweatshirt. It's black to match her jeans.

"No problem," I say, handing her book over.

"I'll get out of here now." She turns to leave.

"Alexa, could you wait a minute?"

Now that her hoodie is not over her head, I see that her hair is in long black braids and they swing as she turns back toward me. "Sure," she says, shrugging.

"I wanted to say thank you for being the most reasonable one in the cafeteria. If it wasn't for you, I don't know if we would have all made it out of there in one piece. By the way, I'm Emma."

I feel the need to extend my hand to her. She extends hers as well and we shake.

"I already knew who you were when we saw you in the caf-eteria, even before Logan mentioned it. Everyone here knows who you are. How could they not?" She releases the handshake.

I glance down and back up, not knowing how to respond. I know everyone seems to look at me as some kind of role model, but all I want to do is save my niece—my family.

"If I hadn't spoken up, I'm sure you would have," Alexa continues.

"Probably," I say. But my chest tightens; I'm honestly not sure what I would have done. "I didn't mean to invade your privacy, but I read some of the words in your sketchbook."

She frowns, making her high cheeks droop. "It's just some gib-berish I wrote down."

"I think it's more than that. You have a different perspective on President Esther—one I've never thought of before. And that picture you drew eerily depicts her perfectly."

"Thank you," she says. Her frown turns into a small smile. "I guess I just like to know what makes people tick. Why they act the way they do. I was always curious about the history of Craigluy. It was never taught to us in school; however, my mother explained it to me when I was seven years old…how we ended up this way."

"My mother explained the war to me as well," I say, "and how it was an internal war. And the elected officials of Craigluy wanted to take farming land away from some of the citizens that owned it. The people fought for what was theirs and it tore everything apart."

"Some of my grandparent's closest friends died during that war." She shrugs. "And some of my great aunts and great uncles got out of here and ended up in California, while some other relatives scattered and ended up in Arizona. I wish my grandparents would have left, too; but instead, they stayed and now we're stuck here."

"My grandparents decided to stay here, too," I say. "They chose to stay here to rebuild. They had no idea years later Craigluy would get torn apart and divided by an evil woman. If the walls are torn down, I would stay here and make it nice again, like it used to be—everyone could become one unit."

"Not me." She frowns. "If the walls come down, I would try and make it to California. I hate it here—and I'm not just speaking of Territory M; I'm talking about Craigluy, in general."

"Is that why you are running away?" I ask. I'm not sure she will answer me.

"What do you mean?" The sketchbook shakes in her hands.

"Julian—he's one of the guys I'm here with—says they call you runaways because you hate the rules here. You hide out so you don't have to follow them."

"That's part of it." She glances away and back up.

"What's the other part?"

She walks over to the box-shaped windows. The shades are still down, except for the missing one. The light trickles through that window. She makes sure not to stand in front of it.

"This place isn't all it's cracked up to be," she says, then lets out a small sigh.

Her words remind me of the conversation I had with Julian when we were staring at the wall back in Territory L.

"I mean," she hesitates and turns back to me, "I know you think it's bad where you live, but here it's not much better. Sure the people here have more money; yet we still have to follow stupid rules and..." She stops talking.

"Some rules are good."

"And some aren't." She seems irritated. The book drops from her fingers and plops on the floor.

I reach down to pick it up at the same time she does. Now that I'm closer to her, I notice a large black bruise that surrounds her wrist. She notices my stare, quickly grabs the book, and stands back up.

"What happened?"

She shakes her head. "Nothing."

I know she doesn't want to discuss it. I ask anyway. "Did someone hurt you?"

"No, it's fine. I can take care of myself. Besides, my brother wouldn't let anyone touch me." Her voice softens. She deeply cares for her brother. It reminds me of my own brother—T.

"I have a brother, too," I say. "He's back in Territory L."

"You left him behind?"

My face drops. I shouldn't have mentioned T. I didn't want the conversation to shift from her to me.

"If you and your friends are hiding here, then I know your running from something. From that speech you made over the box, maybe. I'm sure you escaped Territory L and President Esther must be after you." Her eyes widen. "Since you just said your brother's back in L, then you must have left him behind. From the sad look on your face, I can tell you didn't want to. So, how could you?"

"It wasn't a choice I made lightly. Sometimes, you have to do things you don't want to for the right reasons and pray everything turns out okay."

"Were you and your brother close?" she asks.

She says *were* like he's dead now. I pray that's not the case.

"Yes, we were close—still are," I say, as my voice trembles. "What about you and your brother?" I ask, trying to shift the conversation back to her.

"Yes, we're very close. Like I said earlier, he would do anything for me. He would never let anyone harm me."

My eyes glance down at her wrist again.

"I know what you're thinking. He didn't do this. This is part of the reason we're on the run."

I don't think her brother hurt her. I wonder who did. I want to know what she means—why are they on the run now? Could the blood we found in the pool have something to do with her? I want to ask; but before I can, the door swings open and the one they call Logan walks in.

"Your brother's looking for you." His eyes are cold, dead-looking.

"How did you even know I was here?" Alexa asks, with a huff.

"I searched all the rooms and finally found you in here."

"Well, I'll be there in a minute."

"You should come now. You know Mason wouldn't like you being on this side of the building or talking to her."

"Fine then." She rolls her eyes. "Nice talking to you, Emma."

"Same to you." I throw my hand up.

She walks away and slams the door behind her. I fully expect Logan to follow. Instead, he turns to me.

Suddenly, the room feels cold, like there's a draft; but no windows are open.

"I should go, too," I say, trying to exit the room.

"You scared to be alone with me," he says, with a slight chuckle. His blue eyes glare right through me.

"No." I shrug. "It's just, I've been missing for a while. My friends are probably wondering where I've gone."

"I think they can handle you being gone for a little longer."

"Why would you want me to stay?" I ask. My knee wobbles. I don't know if I will like his answer.

"I think you should know that after all the things you said over the box, no one will hurt you."

"What does that mean?" My eyes stretch wide.

"I know you think President Esther will send men to look for you because you escaped Territory L; but even if she does, they won't harm you." He scratches one of the freckles on the side of his face.

I'm still confused. "What are you talking about?" My jaw tightens.

"She won't harm you; she wants you here. She needs you in this territory; she has plans for you."

His tone is serious, but I can't believe him and I don't want to talk to him anymore. I stomp toward the door.

"So, you don't believe me then?"

"Why should I?" I shout back. My cheeks feel hot. "I don't even know you. You're some runaway. Where would you even get any of this information from?"

"I wasn't always a runaway. Up until about a year ago I worked up at the Hill, so I heard things."

"What things?"

"If Emma Whisperer ever makes it into Territory M, no one should ever harm her." He blinks.

None of this makes any sense. A year ago, no one even knew I wanted to make it into Territory M to go to college—except for my family. I just escaped Territory L a few days ago, so why was my name mentioned up at the Hill a year ago? He said he worked there up until about a year ago...so who knows when he actually heard this information. How many years did he work there? Exactly when was my name mentioned? Was it a year ago or several years ago? My ears sting. I can't believe what he is saying.

"I don't believe you."

"I also heard," he continues, ignoring my last comment, "your parents were once offered a chance to go straight into Territory

U, but they had to do something for President Esther and they refused." He sucks his teeth.

"I still don't believe you." My fingers twitch. The conversation makes me nervous.

"Why would I lie?" His face hardens. His frustration makes him run his hand over his sandy head of hair. It's so short that his fingers touch his scalp.

"I don't know but you are and…" My voice drifts off because the door squawks open.

"Whisper, I've been looking for you." It's Eric. "You shouldn't leave without telling someone where you are going."

"Sorry, I was just coming back to find you."

He glances over at Logan and then back at me. "You sure about that?"

"Yes, I'm sure," I say, grabbing his hand so we can leave the room.

I feel Logan's glower on me as I exit with Eric but I don't care. His words make my body tense, and I don't want to hear anything else he has to say.

* * *

"This is starting to become a habit," Eric says. His hand is cupped over his chin and he's rubbing his face as if he's trying to figure me out. "Me finding you in that art room."

The glow from the sunlight oozing under the blinds hits the back of his neck, making a shadow along the wall. We're back in the cafeteria—our usual spot to converse—sitting at the tables.

"I like to go there to think. It's on our side of the building, so I don't see a problem with it." I bite the inside of my jaw.

"Well, since we aren't the only ones occupying the building anymore, I don't like you being there alone. It isn't safe." His eyes find mine.

"I'm fine," I say, even though I know where the conversation is going.

"Why were you talking with that guy…I think his name was…" he hesitates, "Logan. Why was he on our side of the building, anyway?"

"It's not a big deal." I shrug and throw up my hands. "I was looking at this sketchbook I found, and one of the runaways—Alexa—came in. We started talking. She seems nice and smart. That Logan guy came in and interrupted us. She left. I was about to, but he started talking to me. I was fine. It wasn't like he was going to hurt me or anything." I don't feel the need to tell him what we talked about because in my mind it was all nonsense. I can't believe anything he said.

"It just seems like you've been taking off by yourself a lot lately."

"Are you upset because I was outside with Julian?"

He remains silent, so I continue. "I just felt like we were sitting around wasting time. If I could find the Hill, then I could find Abigail before it's too late." I shift my hips in the chair. "But Julian saw me and stopped me from going."

Eric lets out a slow grunt but says nothing else.

"Now you're mad and you're not going to say anything else." I cross my arms defensively, and search his face for warmth, but there is none.

"I'm not mad, just disappointed that you wouldn't confide in me—that you would choose to leave me behind."

"I'm sorry I made you feel that way." I move from my chair to the top of the table, sitting next to him. I touch his cheek with the palm of my hand. His face feels warm. "I realize we're in this together and you have my back. It's just sometimes I get a little impatient—you know me."

"You have to stop running off and start telling me where you're going. If we're a team, then you need to tell me things."

His words make me angry, and my ears burn because I know

there are things he is keeping from me. I drop my hand from his face and stand.

"I would like to be a team as well; but how can we, when you just keep going along with whatever Julian wants. But I guess I know why."

His eyes dull. "What does that mean?" He stands, as if he's unhappy with what I just said.

"I asked him why he would risk his job and seeing his family to help us. He told me about the favor and how you saved his life when his roommate, Billy, was trying to kill him."

"He told you everything?"

"Not everything." I shrug. "He said it was your truth to tell, not his. But the part he did tell me, I wish you had."

"I didn't want you to be disappointed in me."

"Look, I already know you almost killed your father. So, how bad could it be?"

"This is different. I actually did kill someone. That's why—"

"In self-defense," I say, cutting him off.

"No, not in self-defense."

"Could you please tell me what happened? If you can't, then maybe whatever we are to each other should end now." I'm grasping at straws, so he will tell me the truth.

He lets out a large sigh, like the weight of the world is on his shoulders. He glances down at the floor and starts to speak. "How much do you already know?"

"Only that Billy had a gun on Julian."

"When I walked in, I saw the gun to Julian's head. Billy told me not to make a move or he would shoot Julian. So, I couldn't reach for my gun. I just stood there, trying to figure out what my next move would be. Then, he hit Julian over the head with the gun and knocked him out. He turned his attention to me. The next thing I knew, I lunged at him before he could shoot. We struggled and the gun went off. I wasn't hit and neither was he.

The bullet hit the ceiling and ricocheted into the wall. We tussled back and forth for a while until…" He pauses.

"Until what?" I ask. My jaw twitches.

"I knocked his gun out of his hands and kicked it across the floor." He shrugs. "Then, I pulled my gun out and held it toward his face. He smiled and laughed this wicked crazy laugh, like he knew I wasn't going to shoot him. I lost it, for a moment. The laugh reminded me of the last time I saw my father, when I left that house and vowed to never go back. Billy kept laughing and saying if I didn't shoot him, he would keep on trying until he killed Julian. I believed his words to be true. My hand shook. I pulled the trigger. But I only shot him in the shoulder. He stumbled closer, toward me, and I shot him again in the gut."

He lets out a large sigh. "It wasn't self-defense because I had the gun on him and he was unarmed. I could have let him go, but I knew he wouldn't stop coming for Julian. So, I shot him."

"What was all that stuff you said to me? You only maim, you don't kill. We only kill in self-defense?"

"I meant that. This happened before we had that conversation. I vowed, after that, to never let it happen again."

"Why weren't you thrown in jail for what you did?" I feel my anxiety rising. My throat is tight. "Did you cover it up?"

"There was no covering it up. When Julian came to, he saw Billy's lifeless body on the floor. I explained to him what happened and he thanked me for saving his life. Billy was crazy and, like I said before, he would have never stopped coming for Julian. We reported it to the other guards and President Esther was told. Since I had just joined the guards, I wasn't sure what she would do to me; but she said it was considered self-defense, and I did what I had to do."

"But that really wasn't self-defense." I shake my head in confusion. "He was unarmed."

His eyebrows slant together. "See. That's it right there."

"That's what?"

"That's the look in your eyes I never wanted to see. Like you are disappointed in me or you don't know who I am."

"There's no look in my eyes. I'm just surprised, that's all." I shrug. "After all, we don't know each other that well. We still don't know everything about each other. But I understand why you did what you did. I don't think any less of you." I turn away and walk toward the other side of the room. My heartbeats are unsteady. "I only wish you would have told me."

"I'm telling you now."

"Only because I had to pull it out of you, after Julian already told me most of it," I say, still not turning around to face him.

"Part of the reason was fear of the look you would give me; but the other part was because I didn't want you wishing Samuel was here instead of me."

I turn to him with wide eyes. "What are you talking about?"

"You know," he growls.

"No, I don't." My jaw tightens. "Where is this even coming from?"

"I saw the way Samuel used to look at you, and the way you looked back at him, sometimes. I'm not stupid." He wipes his hand across his mouth, as if he's getting really angry. "If you could have, you would have had him come with us."

"I feel bad for leaving anyone behind." My face feels flush. "I wanted T to come with us, but he refused."

"And you know I'm not talking about your brother. Do you or do you not wish Samuel could have come with us?"

He moves closer to me and his breath blows hot on my face.

"Why is this even an issue? He's not here."

"You're avoiding the question."

"I'm not. If you must know, it would have been nice to have him here. We may need his help. And yes, he's my friend. He was good to me, and I do miss him; but not in the way you're implying. He was good to me, so this whole conversation is pointless."

He opens his mouth to speak, but before he can, we both turn toward the door because we hear banging and shouting down the hallway. We both take off in the direction of the yelling. I'm running so fast my feet feel like fire, as if I'm trying to get off hot coals. I'm about ten steps in front of Eric.

We race up the stairwell. Our steps are loud as we run south down the dank hallways. The hall seems narrower as the screaming continues. We are almost to the gymnasium when we see what's causing the commotion. Mason has Julian pinned down in the hallway in front of the gymnasium. I see Logan, Alexa, and the other guy standing around screaming and watching.

"I found him in the showers. He's supposed to wait until afternoon, but he didn't," Mason yells, looking up at us. His arm is still holding Julian's neck down.

"Get off him," Eric roars.

"Fine. Fine," Mason says, letting go of Julian's neck. He stands and pulls down his black cotton shirt.

Julian shakily stands. "It's almost n-noon now." His breaths are jagged. "What's the big deal? It wasn't like I was in the showers. I was waiting outside them. We have the showers in the afternoon, remember?"

The nervousness in my gut tells me there's something more. "What's really going on here?" I say.

"I walked down here and I was waiting outside the door, but I heard talking. I heard Emma's name mentioned and I walked closer to the opening to hear more. They're hiding something and I want to know what it is."

"Look, I was speaking to Dwayne in private," Mason says. "You had no right to eavesdrop."

"That's right," Dwayne says. "It's none of your business." He squints his light brown eyes in my direction.

"What were you saying about Emma?" Eric asks.

"Yeah, what's going on?" Alexa stares at her brother.

Apparently she's in the dark like I am.

"If you must know…" Mason pauses and looks my way. "The president read a statement over the boxes that said if anyone sees Emma Whisperer they are to notify the authorities immediately and whoever brings her in will be compensated by getting into Territory U. But she is to be brought in unharmed. I saw the announcement on a box in a store when we were out searching for food. I just remembered and told Dwayne. "

"So, what is your game plan? Wait until we are asleep and kidnap Emma, so you can bring her in?" Eric's eyes harden.

"Why would we want to touch your precious Emma?" Dwayne's shoulders tense. He scratches his hand roughly through his scraggly, thin hair. "We are runaways. Why would we care about getting into Territory U, when we have no desire to go there? And why would we want to get caught by the patrolmen, when we are hiding out as well?"

"Then why are you keeping this such a secret?" I say. "I don't think you just remembered to tell Dwayne…I think you've been devising a plan ever since you saw me in the cafeteria. I think you were just going over the details and Julian overheard you."

"You're wrong." Mason's jaw hardens.

"Maybe you don't want to get into Territory U, but you were planning to offer me up for something else. Like I don't know…" I cock my head to the side. "Money? Maybe if you brought me in, they would look over the fact that you're runaways and let you go. That's the only explanation there could be…otherwise you would have told us about the reward earlier."

"You already know they're searching for you," Mason says. "Why is it our responsibility to tell you the price on your head, if you're brought in?"

He didn't really answer my question, but now I'm bothered by my earlier conversation with Logan.

"Did you know this?" I look at Logan. "You told me that if I ever came to Territory M that no one was to harm me because she wanted me here." I didn't believe his words earlier; I don't understand why my name was even spoken about a year ago…maybe several years ago or why someone would want to harm me back then, but I still want an answer.

"I told you that's what I heard. But I believe that was if you came here for schooling, not if you got here by escaping." He turns to me with kind eyes. "I have no idea why she would want you here or why she would or wouldn't harm you. And I had no idea that now that you are here there was a reward out for your capture. Apparently, Mason and Dwayne were keeping this a secret. I was kept in the dark, like Alexa was."

I'm not sure why, but my stomach settles down like a boat on a smooth river. I tend to believe him. But I look over at Eric and he rolls his eyes. That tells me he thinks differently.

"I had no idea about any of this, but my brother's not going to turn you in." Alexa stares at her brother. "If I get any whiff of that, I won't go along with it. I think if we just stick to the rules and stay on our designated sides, everything will be okay."

Julian and Eric exit the room. I follow.

"We can't stay here much longer," Eric says, as we walk down the hallway. "Now that we know this, we really can't trust them."

"I guess we should sleep with one eye open." I look at Julian. My boots stomp on the floors. "Can you find another place for us to stay?"

"I've already been working on it." He nods. "It should only be a few more days and we can get out of here."

"Good," I respond back. My hand is trembling and I have a bad feeling.

CHAPTER SIX

THIS TIME OF day only a little light dribbles in through the cafeteria blinds. I decide to pack the few clothes I have gathered while I've been here. It's not much, just a few white socks, a black turtleneck, a gray cotton hoodie, and the jacket I wore with my uniform. Julian was able to bring back more clothing for him and Eric—a few more t-shirts.

He claimed he couldn't find anything in my size, so he brought me a gray t-shirt that's too tight around the arms and a pair of blue jeans that are tight around the hips, and more underwear. I will pack them with the other things and just keep on my uniform pants and turtleneck, for now. He did bring back cleaning supplies. I was able to wash my clothes out, so at least they're clean. I also still wear the black boots that weigh me down.

Julian says he knows of a place we can go, but he needs another day or so to get it ready. I'm giving him one more day and then I'm leaving on my own. I can't wait on him forever. Eric can come if he wants, but I know what I need to do. My body shivers, dwelling on the journey ahead of me, and on all the people I left behind.

Eric and Julian have gone down to take their showers. I took mine hours ago.

I hear Alexa's voice. "You packing up to leave?"

My eyes widen.

"I know I shouldn't be down here, but I wanted to apologize for what happened the other day."

"You don't need to."

"No, I am really sorry."

"That's okay. I believe you." The zipper screeches as I undo the bag Julian brought to put all our clothes in. "What happened in the swimming pool?"

She looks down and back up, like the conversation is making her uncomfortable.

"I saw blood and a baby's blanket." I continue. "What happened?" I ask again.

"Can we come with you?" she asks.

She hasn't answered my question, but now my thoughts go elsewhere. I'm more curious as to why she wants to come with me and what she means by we.

"We?" I say, as my jaw tightens.

I hear Logan's voice. "I'm coming, too." He steps into the room with us and sucks his teeth as he talks. "Alexa and I discussed it after the fight Julian and Mason had. We need to get out of here with you guys."

"Why would you leave your brother?" My face scrunches up. "I don't understand."

"My brother and I have always been on the same page—that is, until today." Her face saddens.

"Why today?" I ask.

"This morning, I overheard him saying he wants to get rid of your two friends and turn you in. I can't go along with that. I was wrong about him—"

Cutting Alexa off, Logan says, "He doesn't want to get into Territory U; but it's just like you suggested earlier, he wants to bargain a price for your head."

"Even if that's true, why would you want to come with me and my friends? Why wouldn't you two just go off on your own?"

"I think we're better in numbers. I think we should stick together," Alexa says. "My brother said the last information they heard on the box while we were out getting supplies was that the president is saying you're here to cause trouble and start a war against the territories."

"Did she state the reason I was trying to start a war?" My heart pounds.

"No, she just said you and your friends were not to be trusted because you were trying to start a war and that's why she wants you captured," Logan says.

"There's a good reason why I'm doing what I'm doing and it's not that I'm trying to start a war." I blink, because it bothers me that people don't understand my reasoning. "I hope it doesn't come to that, but I believe people should be treated equally and there shouldn't be any discrimination among the different classes. In fact, there shouldn't even be classes; the rich and the poor should be able to live together in peace."

"I remember those words in your speech." Alexa's eyes brighten. "That's why we would like to help."

"She's right," Logan says. "That's why I left the Hill. And that's one of the reasons we are runaways. No one takes us seriously. They just think we're screw-ups. This is our chance for people to see us differently."

I take in a deep breath. "I don't know."

"So, you don't trust us?" Alexa looks at Logan and then back at me.

"I don't know." I shrug. "That doesn't matter right now because even if I did, it's not just my feelings to consider. I have two other people with me and I would have to talk this over with them."

Alexa's shoulders slouch. "We understand."

"But you need to hurry before the others find out what we're doing behind their backs." Logan scratches the back of his neck.

"Logan's right," Alexa says. "My brother won't be happy that we've betrayed him."

"You two stay here." The duffle bag bangs as it hits the floor. "I'll go find Eric and Julian and be right back."

I only walk about two steps before I hear what sounds like someone screaming and shouting over a bullhorn in the first-floor hallway. I hear glass shattering and it makes my whole body quiver.

"What was that?" Alexa shouts.

"Whatever it was, it don't sound good," I hear Logan say, behind me.

I track to the stairwell. I race up the stairs. Once I'm in the hallway, I run toward the shouting. I know I should run the opposite way, but the sounds are coming from the south side of the building. That's where Eric and Julian are. My first thought: the patrolmen must have found us. I will be turned in. My heart drops. I haven't found Abigail or helped my family or any of the people back in Territory L.

I'm halfway down the hallway, nearing the gymnasium. I hear Alexa's and Logan's shoes stomping behind me. We stop because Julian and Eric are running our way. They are making loud coughing noises.

"What's happening?" I shout. Before they answer me, I see white clouds of smoke coming under the gymnasium door.

"Go back!" Eric shouts. "It's t-tear gas," he says, in between coughs.

"I suggest you surrender now." I hear a loud voice booming through a bullhorn. "We already have two of you. I know there are more," the voice continues.

"Keep running," Julian says.

I hear something crash to the floor. I know it's another canister.

"Get down on the floor and try to hold your breath. Close your eyes and crawl as fast as you can," Eric says.

We crawl on the floor. The air smells like chemicals and gun powder. I've never experienced tear gas, but I've heard horrible stories of how it feels like being kicked in the chest by an elephant. It can burn your eyes and induce vomiting.

"I can't see," Alexa says.

"Don't close them all the way," Julian says. "Just squint."

"Here, let's get in here," Logan says.

We haven't been crawling that long. We end up in a semi-dark room that I haven't been to before; I only walked by it while going down the hallway. The lights don't automatically click on, which is a good thing. There is still some natural light left from outside that trickles in the room. Eric is still on his knees and turns to quietly close the door. It clicks as he pushes in the knob to lock it behind us. He turns and sits down on his butt.

"Are you two alright?" I ask, now that I'm not holding my breath anymore. "What happened?" I sit up on my knees.

"I finished my shower and put my clothes on. When I walked out into the locker rooms, Julian was standing there. He said he heard shouting coming from the gymnasium. We went to the gymnasium to check and heard Mason and Dwayne arguing with someone. When we cracked the door a little, we saw patrolmen… with gas masks…dressed in black, telling them to get down on their knees. When they refused and tried to run, the patrolmen threw a canister of tear gas. That's when we took off running, but we knew they heard the door creak behind us—"

"That's when we saw you guys running this way," Julian cuts in.

"How long can we h-hide out in here?" Alexa asks. Her voice is shaky. I know she's scared—not just for what's happening to us in this tiny room, but for what has happened to her brother.

"Not for long," Logan says. "They'll check every room, just like last time."

"What do you mean last time?" Eric's voice hardens.

"Every few months, the patrolmen check certain abandoned buildings for runaways. They almost found us before, when we were hiding out in the abandoned library. They checked every room, but we were able to get out of a door they didn't know about."

"Last time they didn't have tear gas though," Alexa says.

"Yeah, that's something new." Logan shakes his head. "Mason figured they wouldn't check here for a few months because they already ran through here a couple months back. I guess he was wrong."

"None of that matters now," I say. "What matters is how we're going to get out of here without getting caught. Where are we, anyway?" I notice a red leather sofa in one corner and a long table with four brown chairs in another corner.

The room is getting darker by the minute; and I left the duffle bag behind, with our extra clothes, and anything else we might need. I keep looking around and see a large white refrigerator is unplugged and pulled away from the wall.

This must have been a teacher's lounge or break room, because I see a framed sign hanging on the wall that says: T*eachers guide and inspire.*

I scrunch up my nose because the air smells stale, like no one has occupied this space in a long time.

"I don't think there's any way out." My chest throbs, for fear of getting caught. I get off my knees and slide down to the floor with the others. Logan is the only one standing. I continue, "But I know I'm not surrendering without a fight."

Eric's eyes narrow. "We could just give those two up." He glances over at Alexa and Logan. "After all, they're looking for the runaways—not us. If Alexa and Logan surrender, they'll take them away, and then we can stay here like nothing happened."

"And what makes you think we're just going to surrender without letting them know you three are in here? Once they find out Emma's here, they may let us go and take you in. She's worth more to the president than a few runaways," Logan says.

"Stop it," I say. "No one's turning anyone in. We will find another way. Just think and stop turning on each other."

Alexa remains quiet and so does Julian. The rest of the room falls silent. I hear only shallow breathing.

The room is suddenly dark now, like the sun has disappeared.

"I have a small flashlight." Logan reaches in his pocket. I hear rustling as he takes the flashlight out. He clicks it on and shines the light in each of our faces. He turns it on the room. Then he quickly snaps it back off.

"Where's the flashlight you had, Julian?" I ask.

"It had a short in it, so it didn't last long," Julian says. I hear him shift his weight on the floor. "I haven't had a chance to go out and find another one."

He should have told us that earlier. What if we needed it? I know that doesn't matter now—we have more pressing matters to deal with. I move over to some drawn shades. I kneel and peer behind them. From what I can tell, we appear to still be on the south side of the building; we aren't far from the gymnasium. The sun is still gone; a cloud sits in front of it. Down below, there are black cars with headlights flashing, so they must have this side of the building surrounded.

I stand. "We have to get out of here."

"I have an idea," Alexa says, standing as well. "Logan, flash the light this way." She points. He clicks the light back on.

She picks up one of the wooden chairs and carries it across the room. She quietly lowers it to the floor, so it doesn't bang. She puts one leg on top of the chair. She balances her weight and puts the next leg up. "Shine it here," she says. "I'm sure they have all the entrances and exits surrounded; but I think if we remove this panel in the ceiling, we can crawl in the ventilation shaft through the air ducts and to the west side of the building. If we make it there, we can get to the small supply room where the window we used to come and go is. They probably don't know about it."

"Aren't we too big to fit up there?" I ask.

"It's larger if we enter through the cover of the cold air duct." She hops back down from the chair. "The farther away from the supply fan we go, the smaller it gets, but we don't have far to go to reach the room with the window. The cold air ducts should be above us. We should get where we need to go before running into any filters, or anything else that may block our path. "

"How do you know all of that?" I ask.

"We've hidden in a few different places and I always try to find ways to escape if needed. I've been in the ducts before."

"In this building?" I ask.

"No, in others."

"Then how do you know it will hold all of us?"

"Because most of the schools in Territory M have air ducts that were built with larger shafts, so workmen could get to the fans if they need to work on them. They found it more efficient to get bodies inside the ducts to see and do the work properly."

"Where'd you get this information from? Forget I asked that," I add, knowing we don't have time for another long explanation right now. "I'm not sure that's going to work, but what other choice do we have," I say, even though my knees are wobbling.

She answers my question anyway with a shaky voice. "I have family who used to clean air ducts, so I know things…my f-father." She picks the chair up again and moves it over a few steps. She gently places it back down.

"It's worth a try. What do we have to lose," Logan says.

"How do we know she's not leading us into a trap?" Eric asks.

"I think it will be fine." I walk to Eric. "Do you have another plan?"

Logan flashes the light our way and I see Eric's amber eyes, burning bright in the darkness.

"Are we going to shoot our way out?" I ask, continuing on my rant. "We would never make it. I'm sure there are way more of them than there are of us."

"You're right." He blinks. "I suppose there is no other way out."

I hear the bullhorn in the hallway again. "I know I saw others," a deep voice shouts. "Start checking all of these rooms." The voices are coming closer.

"We need to hurry." My chest constricts.

"Let's get going," Julian says.

Alexa is standing on the chair again. "This chair isn't tall enough to bring me close enough to the panel," she says.

She hops down. Logan steps onto the chair. He takes in a breath, then shoves the panel to the side with a *clunk*. Dust falls down like leaves from a tree. Logan and Alexa start to cough.

Once they compose themselves, Logan reaches up into the air duct and uses both hands to pull himself up. He grunts. When he is up, he grips Alexa's wrists and helps pull her up. The voices outside the door get louder. My heart beats unsteadily in my chest.

"Hurry," Eric says.

I go next. Logan grabs my wrists and pulls me up, while Eric pushes me up by my boots. I land in the air duct with a *thump*. I cough from the dust secreting in my lungs. We help pull Eric up next and then Julian. Once we are all up, Julian replaces the panel so it will look untouched if anyone enters the room.

Alexa says she is good at tracking. Since she's done this before, she goes first. We follow. Logan is behind her. I'm behind him, with Eric and Julian in the rear. The air duct is dark and dank. I can't help but wonder what other creatures are hiding up here. The dust is so thick I feel like the air is choking me.

We head straight. Alexa says we are going south over the part of the building where the gymnasium and pool are—the exact spot where her brother and Dwayne were captured. My nose wrinkles because the smell up here leaves nothing to be desired. It smells like expired milk.

"West is this way," Alexa says. "Turn here. Make sure you guys stay a few paces away from each other. We wouldn't want to put too much weight on the ducts in certain areas. Also watch out for any sharp metal edges, and try to move quickly but quietly. Any noise up here tends to echo."

We listen to her instructions and keep following her. The more we follow, the more my knees get scraped. I'm sure they're only battered and bruised, but they feel like they're bleeding. I distribute my weight and slide on my knees instead of crawling. My braid, along my back, feels thick and heavy.

"Augh," I hear Julian scream. He's in the back, taking up the rear.

"What's wrong?" Logan asks from in front of me.

"Something's biting my leg. I think it's a rat."

"Hold on. I got it." Eric tries to turn around in the tiny space. I hear him grab his gun from his holster. He pulls the trigger and a loud bang fills the ceiling walls. It's so loud my shoulders shake. It's so dark up here, I can't see what's going on. I do hear the squeal of the rat. I hear scratching like its tiny feet are running away. I believe the bullet pierces the air duct. I'm just glad it didn't ricochet and hit one of us.

"Is everyone okay back there?" Alexa asks.

"I'll be fine," Julian says. "I think it just scratched me."

"I think we need to hurry," I say. "I'm sure the patrolmen heard that noise. They probably know we're up in the ducts now." I'm talking fast, so I stop and take in a breath.

"You're right," Eric says, continuing my thoughts. His voice comes from behind me. "They probably don't know where in the ducts exactly—since the sound echoes but they will probably stop searching the rooms and come toward the direction of the noise."

Alexa crawls faster. We follow but make sure to stay a few paces back from each other to keep our weight dispersed on the ducts. The air is thin up here. I feel faint. I try to take slow steady deep breaths and keep going. I've never been afraid of small spaces. I can't start panicking now.

"How much farther?" Eric asks.

Maybe he's finding he can't breathe, just like me.

"Logan, lift the panel up here and see what room we are over," Alexa says. "I'll move out of the way."

Logan slowly lifts the panel and it scrapes a little against the panel next to it.

"What do you see?" I ask.

He slides the panel on top of the panel next to it. He removes the flashlight from his pocket. "It looks like we're above one of the classrooms." He glides the light around. "I see a poster that was left on the wall. It says classroom rules in big letters. I don't see any patrolmen."

"I remember going in that room. That means we only have a few feet to go before we reach the supply room."

The panel scrapes again as Logan puts it back in its original position.

"How do you know there's not another room with that same poster?" Eric's voice echoes behind me.

"I don't think there is—and we don't have time to worry about that right now." Alexa turns and starts forging ahead. I hear her knees scraping as she moves faster. "Check again, this should be it." She stops.

The panel screeches as Logan lifts it. He moves it to the side close to where I am. He yanks out his flashlight and whips it around. "This looks like the room where we came in. I'll go down first. I see a few desks and chairs. I'll try and land on one of them." He hands me the flashlight.

"I don't remember any desks being in that room," Alexa says.

Logan ignores her comment. "I'm going down."

His legs dangle toward the floor as he holds on to the left and right sides of the duct. He jumps down with a wallop. He plops down so hard that the desk he lands on topples over. He bangs on the floor. The lights don't pop on.

"Logan you're making too much noise," I say in a whisper so he will hear me but the outside world won't. I shine the light in his face.

He rolls his eyes and ignores my comment—just like he ignored Alexa. The desk wobbles as he tries to stand it back up. Once the desk is upright he walks away from it.

"I need something sturdier," he says.

He retrieves a wooden table from across the room. He carries it over to underneath where we are. Then he turns and picks up a nearby wooden chair. He places it closer to the table. He places one foot on top of the chair. Then he places his other foot on the chair. He uses the chair as if they are steps so he can get on top of the table. Once he is on the table he balances his weight as he stands straight up.

"You go first, Alexa." He puts up his hands.

Alexa scoots herself out of the duct. Her legs dangle. Logan is able to grab on to her. He holds her by her waist. She hops down the rest of the way with a thud onto the table. Then she steps down on the chair and balances her weight so she can step down onto the floor. I'm next to go down. I hand the flashlight to Julian so he can shine it over the area. Logan helps me down in the same manner. I hop from the table to the chair. I quickly thump down from the chair to make way for the others. I feel a breeze as Eric jumps after me. He doesn't need much help from Logan. He lands on the chair I was just in.

Julian throws the flashlight down to Eric, and then takes his turn. Julian appears a little wobbly—maybe from the bite he sustained up in the ducts. He seems to need help so Logan reaches up his hands around Julian's waists to give him some support. Julian wallops down on the table. He's still wobbly as he turns and splats down in the chair everyone else took their turns in. Eric turns the flashlight on the room. I notice my once-black pants look gray from the dust. I swipe my hands across them and watch the specks fly.

"This isn't the right room." Alexa's eyes are big. "You said this was the room."

"I know, but we couldn't stay in the ducts forever. It was hard to breathe up there and I saw a desk nearby I could easily jump down on. I figured we were close enough that we could make it by walking now. The patrolmen should be finished searching this end and should be on the other end of the building."

"But what if they're not? What if they are still here?" Alexa's voice is high-pitched. "You know they heard the shot...or all the noise we made jumping down—they're probably headed this way."

"If not already outside the door," Julian adds. His voice is shaky.

"I agree with Logan. I'm sure they're on the other side of the building by now," I say, trying to sound positive. "Besides, we're down here now, so let's just make the best of it."

"I'll check the corridor," Eric says.

The door squeaks as he opens it to peek outside. "I don't see anyone. Let's move. Hurry," he yells.

The hallway lights pop on. I quickly search the wall for the button. I click them back off. We move as fast as we can. I hear shallow breathing from everyone's mouths. We make our way pass two classrooms. It's now dark as we reach the last room on the west side of the building—the room with the window. Logan swings the door open. Besides a metal garbage can and a few wooden stands with brown boxes on them, the room is empty. We all rush in and head for the small window.

"We can't go this way," Alexa says, reaching the window first. "They've broken the lock at the top, so it won't open anymore. It won't slide up." Her voice is panicky. "They probably figured we would try to escape this way. They're waiting for us. I see them hiding behind some trees."

She's right. Now that I've reached the window, I see the patrolmen standing there. The sky is still dim, but the sun has moved from behind the clouds so I see them, waiting. This way won't work, either.

"What are we going to do now?" Alexa asks.

"Everybody calm down. I'm sure we'll think of something," Eric says, looking at Julian.

My heart is beating in my ears. "I know a way. I will distract them, that way you can all get away. Mason has probably already offered me up in exchange for himself. Even if he didn't, once they know I'm here, I'll be more important to them than a few runaways. Logan said it earlier. He's right."

"There's no way I'm letting you do that." Eric grabs my hand. "We'll think of something else."

"No," I say, shaking my head. "I know what I'm doing." I remove my hand from his. "I'm not going to go with them, but I have a plan. They won't harm me—remember, the president wants me brought in unharmed. We can break the glass, then I will jump out and run. When they try and surround me, I'll keep running south of the woods, while you go east—"

"Whisper—"

"No, Eric, I'm doing this. You guys run to the truck. Once I lose them, I will meet you there."

"Are you sure?"

"Yes, I am."

"I know you're a fast runner, but what if you don't lose them?" Eric's eyes sadden.

"Don't worry, I will." I'm trying to reassure him and myself at the same time. My throat feels tight.

"Look, if we're going to do this, we need to do it now," Logan says.

"He's right," Julian chimes in.

"We can use this garbage can to break the glass."

The tiny metal garbage can swooshes as Logan grabs it in his hands. He throws it at the window. The breaking glass sounds like wind chimes blowing in the air. I run over before Eric stops me. I kick the rest of the shards away from the window with the ball of my foot and jump down with a bang. The patrolmen move near me. I hold up my hands, so they see I'm not reaching for my weapon.

"It's Emma Whisperer," a tall, curly haired patrolman says.

"When they broadcasted your name over the box, I didn't think it would be this easy to find you," a blond-hair patrolman with long toothpick legs, says. "In fact, I never thought you would give yourself up." His blue eyes flicker. "We were only looking for runaways, but I suppose we've found the ultimate prize."

"This should surely get us into Territory U." A short stocky patrolman, with a belly as large as a ball, chuckles.

Two more patrolmen walk up—now five stand before me.

"Well, I'm glad you're so pleased to see me. I can't say the same though." I'm trying to sound tough, even though my stomach twinges. "But what makes you think I'm giving myself up? I was hoping I would never see you or have to use this."

My hand trembles. I reach for my gun. I pull it out. I wave it at them. The metal is still cold and heavy to the touch. This reminds me of when I had to shoot Rich not too long ago because he was trying to stop me from escaping Territory L.

"Hey now," the short stocky one says. "You don't want to use that now, do you?" He holds up his hands. "We're trying to take you in peacefully."

"There's no need for that," another patrolman says.

I point the gun straight up in the air, making sure to aim over their heads. I fire three rapid shots. The ground seems to shake.

They glance around to make sure no one's hit. I put my gun back in my holster.

I take off running in the opposite direction. I run south as fast as I can. I hear them shouting. They've taken off behind me. I hear the soles of their boots, pounding the ground. The sound of heavy breathing fills the air. I just need time for Eric and the others to make it to the truck, without being noticed. Hopefully, if there are any other patrolmen out, they are still in the building or surrounding the opposite areas from where the truck is located.

I decide not to run in a straight path. Instead, I zigzag. My breaths feel uneven. I weave in and out between the dense trees. I'm hoping my unusual pattern will slow them down and make them out of breath. My ankle wobbles as my boot stumbles over a rock. I have to keep my stride or they will catch me. The tall one with the curly hair and the blond one seem to be faster than the others. I need to stay away from those two. Their long legs give them an advantage. The short one with the large belly can't seem to keep up. I shouldn't have a problem staying ahead of him. I know they can't shoot me or harm me to slow me down, so I could keep this up all day—even though I don't want to. I'm ready for this to be over, so I can go back and find the others.

I keep running in circles around the trees. It seems like only three are after me. Where are the other two? I hear footsteps all around me. Instead of chasing behind me, they have broken off into pairs to surround me. They don't seem to be tiring. They've come up with a new plan, so I have to as well. The weather here today is weird; the air reminds me of spring. We have so many cold spells that the trees are growing new leaves but the grass is still brown.

Far off in the distance I notice a stretch of land that's not kept up. I see a tree stump that's double my size in width—even with my arms stretched out it would still cover me. The stump is covered with dead grass, moss and wormy old wood. Some of the weeds surrounding it are taller than the stump. The stump rises up to my waist. Maybe it will hide me while I rest for a minute.

I pick up speed. I hear my breathing become heavier. My heart thumps in my ears. My boots clomp against the ground. I stop once I reach the stump to catch my breath. In school, we learned the number of rings you see on the stump once you cut down the tree is how old the tree is. I squat down. My breathing goes in and out. The moss covers the stump so I can't tell the age of the tree. Why is my mind racing? I need to hide myself better. I see a small ditch in the decayed section of the tree stump. It's big enough for me to fit in. I glide into it. I hope to blend in with the weeds, so they don't notice me.

"Where'd she go?" I hear a patrolman shout.

"I don't know. I don't see her anywhere."

"I can't believe she gave you guys the slip."

"Don't try to blame this all on us. You lost her, too."

"That's because I stood here watching you run after her like fools. I don't care if the prize is getting into Territory U. I'm not wasting my energy running after a little girl. If I had chased her I would have caught her."

"You say that now because you didn't try."

"Pipe down, you two."

I'm still crouched down. I can't see whose speaking, but I keep listening to everything they say.

"We might as well just forget about her now and go help the others find the runaways."

"Yeah, the runaways are probably gone, too."

"We better check and see."

"We'll go back…while you stay here. In case she magically reappears." I hear a chuckle.

I hear several footsteps clump away. But my feet are frozen there. I need to find my friends; but I know some have stayed behind and I don't want to encounter them again. My knees ache, so I change my position from squatting to sitting on the hard ground.

I haven't been here that long. It's getting dark, and I feel like it's time to seek out my friends. I need to double back and make my way east, toward the truck.

I stand up and my legs wobble beneath me. I take in a deep breath and start my stride in a northerly direction. I no longer hear or see patrolmen in the area. Even so, I duck here and there, behind trees, in case the ones that stayed behind are still out.

I'm closer to the college now. Everything is still quiet, until I hear a loud laugh to the left of me. I turn to find two patrolmen standing before me.

"See, I told you if we pretended to be gone, then waited around long enough, she would come out," the short stocky one says.

"Guess you were right," the blond one says.

"I'm not going with you." I start walking backward, but I keep my eyes on them.

"Now Emma, this is such an easy process. Let's not make it difficult." The short stocky one leans his head to the side.

"I said I'm not going with you." My hand is on my gun.

"Don't do it, Emma," the blond one says. "Don't even think about it. We have guns, too. Don't make us pull them out—"

"And use them," the short stocky one cuts him off.

"You're not going to use them. They want me unharmed!" I yell.

"I'm sick of this." I see a patrolman, with a neck as thick as a brick, walk toward me. His shoulders are four times the size of mine. He places his hand over the gun in his holster. It's the same voice I heard earlier that said he wasn't chasing after a little girl.

He scares me and I feel my legs tremble.

"You can't shoot her." The blond one glares at him.

"I don't take orders from you," He yells back at the other one.

"Those orders came down from the president. You can't kill her."

"I don't care who they came from." His right hand goes down near his holster. "No one tells me what to do."

He doesn't seem to care about my well-being. He won't listen to the president's orders. I know there's only one way I can stop him so I can get away. I need to do this while he's distracted and yelling at the others. My hand shakes. I yank my gun out. I aim for his right shoulder. I pull the trigger. I hear a loud *pop*. The muscles in my body jolt. I know I hit him because blood gushes out. He yells out in agony, and reaches for his arm with his left hand. I aimed for his shoulder but hit his arm.

The other two look shocked, like they don't know if they should help him or come after me. While they fumble around, I take that as my cue to get away. I bang my gun back in my holster. I turn and run as fast as I can in the opposite direction. I hear pounding behind me. I guess they decided to sprint after me. The two behind me were trying to follow orders so they won't shoot at me—but now that I've shot the other one maybe they've changed their minds.

I'm a few steps ahead when I hear rumbling, like an engine roaring. My stomach tightens. I turn to run away from the noise. It's probably just more patrolmen gunning for me. I have enough already running behind me. I pick up speed. I'm probably twenty steps ahead.

"Whisper, it's us—slow down." It's Eric's voice.

I slow down and catch my breath. My heartbeat slows down to a snail's pace. I turn to see the black pickup truck beside me. Julian is driving and Eric sits on the passenger's side. Alexa and Logan sit in the backseat.

"They're right behind me," I yell, in between jagged breaths.

"We know," Eric says. "Hurry and get in." He bobs his head to motion me toward the door.

I run toward them. Eric pops the door open for me. Eric slides the center armrest up to make a back for the middle seat. He moves over and sits in the middle. I glide in next to him, onto a cloth seat. The darkness of the interior matches the darkness of the exterior of the truck. Eric stretches his legs out. His left leg remains out front while his right leg is in front of the passenger's seat, next to mine.

I hear the patrolmen shouting behind us. Loud pops are heard as they shoot at the tires. The engine revs and Julian takes off. We're several feet ahead. They know they will not catch us on foot. I see them turn around and run back toward their vehicles.

"What was that?" I ask, hearing a screeching noise coming from the back of the truck.

"There's a shovel and some other supplies on the bed of the truck," Julian answers. "It probably just moved forward."

"We need to drive faster, before they catch up to us," I say, because my thoughts quickly move back to the men chasing us.

"That won't happen," Logan announces from the backseat.

"While some of them were in the old college and the others were chasing you, we decided to shoot out their tires...just like they were trying to do to us," Eric says. "They won't be able to get anywhere."

"All of them?" My face feels hot.

"Yes, all."

"They had at least four vehicles that I could see—that's a lot of ammunition."

"We only shot out one tire per vehicle. Just enough to stop them in their tracks. We can pick up more ammunition later. Only watchmen and patrolmen have guns here; so there are no public places to buy ammo, but Julian said he knows where he can get some without being noticed," Eric says.

"They'll probably call this in...if they haven't already." Julian grips the steering wheel.

"They'll probably set up roadblocks around the area and send for more patrolmen," Logan says, from the backseat. "I know a few backroads we can use. Being a runaway leads me to a lot of areas you guys wouldn't know of. We can make it there faster using the backroads…that way we should make it there before they have time to set up any kind of blocks or get extra manpower to surveil the area."

Alexa's a runaway, too; but she remains silent. Maybe she's focused on what happened to her brother. If it was my brother, those would be my thoughts right now.

"Give me the address to where you're thinking of going…I'm sure I'll know a backroad to get there." Logan sucks his teeth.

Julian nods, in agreement.

I stop listening to what they are saying. My thoughts drift to how I just shot another person. I shot Rich back in L and now I've shot a patrolman in M—I don't even know what his name is. My hand trembles, because I've shot two people. I know I had to so I could get away. I also know I had to because, given the chance, I know the patrolmen would have harmed or possibly killed me… but that still doesn't make my stomach feel any less nauseated.

"I'm sorry it took us so long to come for you." Eric places his hand on my knee, breaking the thoughts grinding over and over in my mind.

"No." I shake my head. "I was supposed to find you, but I was trying to wait until the patrolmen left. I had to be sure they were gone, but they never left."

We're speechless for a few minutes, and all I hear is the truck's engine roaring and the bumping of the tires over rocks. I'm not sure where Julian is taking us, but I hope Logan is right and he knows a back way to get there—otherwise, we will be caught and me shooting someone a second time will all be for nothing.

CHAPTER SEVEN

THE SKY IS dark and the moon looks fuller than it has in a long time. I'm not sure of the time because Julian says the clock on the dashboard is broken. We are driving through some wooded area that Logan knows about. I hear soft snoring coming from Alexa in the backseat. Logan has settled back in his seat as well, since he has finished belting out instructions in Julian's ear.

I realize Eric doesn't trust them, but we couldn't leave them behind. It wouldn't have been right to go without them—especially since Alexa's brother was taken into custody. I fear she depends on him more than she has let on.

I must have been more tired than I thought because my eyelids feel like lead. I lay my head on Eric's shoulder. I'm half asleep but hear Eric talking to Julian.

"Do you think this is wise?" Eric asks. "Maybe you shouldn't involve her."

"You think I want to—I don't, but I don't have any other choice," Julian says. "I don't have another place for us to go."

"Even so, I wish those two weren't with us."

"Me neither. I only told her I was bringing two others with me. Now I have to tell her I've added two more." Julian lets out a small sigh. "Even so, if it weren't for Logan we wouldn't know the quickest way to get here to beat the patrolmen…that's if they decide to come here."

"Don't give him so much credit. You used to live in this territory. I'm sure you could have found a fast way to get here, too," Eric says.

"Yeah, but I don't know all the backroads to get us here faster. And we wouldn't know the quickest way to the alley…and who knows what could be waiting for us in front of her house…so, this is the best way in. I guess we do owe him for that—maybe we should be grateful."

"How do you think she will take it?" Eric asks, ignoring Julian's kind words about Logan.

"I guess we are about to find out. If Logan's instructions are correct…we should be there soon. Fortunately, her back alley is gated off. Every street doesn't have that, but her neighbors wanted to feel a little more secure…so they blocked it. There's a keypad and a code to open it. The patrolmen would probably wait at the front of the house instead of the back because of the gate. Even if they do come to the back…by going this way, I think we will beat them."

Julian keeps saying the same things over and over and he's talking fast like he's nervous. I know he hopes we beat the patrolmen here. I feel the same. The truck sways back and forth. I adjust my weight to the right. I turn my head toward the window and lay my cheek back on the cloth seat. I want to see where I am but also appear to be asleep so I can continue hearing their conversation.

The truck stops moving forward. I hear Julian's door screech as he swings it open. I hear his feet thump as he hops out. I can't look over to see what he's doing now because I want Eric to think I'm still asleep—but I would guess Julian is putting in the code to unlock the gate.

I hear roaring, like the gate is swinging open. I open my eyes halfway and see the gate is metal and would reach well above my head if I were standing next to it. We're on a smooth road—it's the alley Julian kept talking about. I can't help noticing how clean and well-kept it is. There is no garbage strewed about or stray animals lurking around, like the kitten I saw get shot by guards back in L. Maybe if it was lighter out I would see some…but I seriously doubt it.

I hear Julian hop back in. We continue driving by a few garages. The garages look well-made, brick, not like the shed we had in the back of our home in L. The garages are big enough to fit two of my family's sheds in. Everything is neat and clean. The colors are bright. I see yellows and oranges.

There are fancy streetlamps hanging on black steel poles, to make the alley a little brighter. The streetlamps are also black, oval-shaped, and covered with glass casings. They seem like they should be in front of the house instead of in back. These lights remind me of the lights in the old college because they are motion activated. They click on when you drive in the area and click off when you leave. It's not continually dark like back home.

"Most people park in their garages…there are privacy bushes to the left and right sides of each garage. They're only allowed to be as high as ten feet and six to eight feet in width. They're artificial bushes. That's why they look so green. That way people can sit in the rear of the garages with the rear door open and have some privacy."

"Why would someone want to sit in the rear of their garages when they could just sit in the garage or in the backyard?" Eric asks.

"People have hobbies here. Some like to restore old vehicles and they don't want the mess in their backyards or in their garages. Some of the younger people like to play skate flight…you're on a skateboard with wheels that go about two feet off the ground in different directions. They open the front and rear garage doors and if their parents have the vehicles out of the way they go from the backyard all the way to the back alley. Other people have three vehicles and only have a two vehicle garage, so instead of clunking up the backyard with the extra vehicle they park it in the rear in the alley." He takes in a breath. "I'm going to leave the truck here. I need to go inside first and smooth things over…and find out if anyone has set up shop in front of her house." The engine stops humming as he turns the motor off.

"I'll keep watch here," Eric says.

I see we have stopped in front of a mauve-colored garage. The privacy bushes are quite large and beautiful.

The door swooshes as Julian swings it open. "Be right back." The door slams closed.

"Go ahead and say it," Eric whispers in my ear.

"Say what?" I look around and see he's leaned closer to me.

"I know you weren't sleeping and you heard everything we were saying." His jaw tightens. "I can tell by the look on your face you think this is a bad idea."

"If we're at Julian's ex-girlfriend's house, then yes, this is a bad idea. He told me all about Whitney when we first met, and I don't think we should throw our problems onto her. It's not right." I sit up straighter.

"Look, it's Julian's call. You heard what I said to him. He decided on this. We didn't."

"It's still unfair to her. Especially now that we have extra visitors." I'm trying to speak softly. I peek in the back and see Logan's awake but Alexa is still sleeping. "She has a child to think about." My hand tenses. This whole situation doesn't feel right. "Besides, we already know this is probably one of the first places the patrolmen will look. I'm sure they will search anyone who is close to Julian—his parents, his ex-girlfriend. I know Julian said he didn't see anyone around…yet." I shift my weight again. "But that doesn't mean they won't show up any minute."

Before Eric answers, the door rushes open and Julian jumps in.

He's quiet as he takes out a remote and presses a button. I

hear grinding as the rear garage door goes up. He uses the key fob and starts the truck engine back up. The motor revs and the truck sways as we drive into the garage. It's a two-car garage. The lights click on as soon as we enter. I see another vehicle to the left of us. It's light green and its headlights remind me of eyes on a bug—like a beetle. The bug car's headlights face the rear door while our headlights face the front. The garage is so large that I see an area for hanging tools. There are also rows of shelves with boxes on them and some lawn furniture.

"Okay you guys, everything's all set." Julian shuts off the motor. "Hurry, let's get to the house." His door hisses open at the same time I open mine.

I hop out. Eric slides over and gets out as well.

Logan swings open his door.

"Alexa, wake up," Logan says.

I hear a pat as he pushes her shoulder.

Logan's voice grows louder. "It's time to go."

"What's g-going on?" Her words are slurred as her brown eyes flutter open.

"We need to get inside before someone sees us."

"Fine—fine. I'm up." Her voice is still groggy. "Stop shoving me."

Logan jumps down with a smack and Alexa hops down behind him.

"The side door squeaks so she wants us to come to the front door."

"What was the point of going through the alley, if we will still be seen walking around to the front of the house?" I ask.

"There is a privacy fence surrounding the property, kind of like the privacy bushes along the garages. The leader or should I say the president allows the people here to put them in if they like—but they can only go as high as six feet. The top two inches is lattice-style which means there are holes there; so it doesn't really provide as much privacy as one would like, since someone could peer through those holes—also a rule from the government." Julian opens the side door to the garage and ushers us out. "You should slouch down as you walk or crawl on your knees if that's easier, so you won't be seen."

We follow Julian from the garage through the backyard. The motion lights attached to the back of the house click on.

"Sorry, I told Whitney to turn them off," Julian says. His voice is frayed because the wind is starting to howl.

If the motion lights didn't pick up our movement, they would surely pick up the winds. A gust of wind splashes strands of hair in my eye. I wipe it aside and look around. I now see what he's talking about. There is a long solid white fence—it looks like wood. I see the holes at the top he was talking about. The fence surrounds the side of the house along the driveway and leads all the way around to the front. The motion lights click on in the front as well—I suppose Whitney forgot to cut those off, too.

There is a large white gate that attaches to the fence. The gate has the lattice-style holes he was speaking of at the top, so no complete privacy there, either. It looks to me like the gate could open with a remote—I imagine it being a struggle to try and pull or push it, but I suppose it could be done. You could fit six of the trucks we are driving in, side by side, in the front yard and there would still be room left over.

We end up at a set of cement steps. There are three large steps that we walk up. It's still dark—but with the lights still clicking on and off, I now see the home is brick like mine was. But the porch is much larger than ours was and there are two chairs sitting in front of the bay window. We walk inside the oval-shaped front door and the house smells like vanilla.

Once we are standing in what I've seen in magazines is called a foyer, I hear the scuffling of shoes across the floors. I see a female, maybe a little older than me, walking down the hallway toward us.

She has on bright red slippers that look comfortable and plush. I assume this is Whitney—Julian's ex. She has on blue jeans and a red V-neck shirt that matches her slippers.

"Everyone, this is Whitney," Julian announces, as if we can't figure it out for ourselves. "Normally, she prefers you take your shoes off at the front door; but since this is an unusual circumstance and we m-might have to exit the premises in a hurry, you can leave them o-on." His voice shakes as if he's nervous.

"My parents are away for a few weeks on business, so you won't be able to stay here long. As a favor to Julian, I'll let you stay until they call and let me know they're on their way back." She bites down on her lip. I suppose she's not too happy with wanted strangers occupying her private space.

Whitney has beautiful high cheekbones and chestnut-colored skin. Part of her hair is blonde. I've never seen a dark-skin person with that color in their hair—at least there were none in Territory L.

If Julian's girlfriend is dark-skin, then that would make their baby biracial. When I was young, I always felt out of place because my father is light-skin while my mother is dark-skin. I wonder if their baby will grow up with the same feelings I had—or will his life be different since he lives in Territory M.

"The house has three floors. The top floor is where the bedrooms are. I would like it if no one went up there. The living room, dining room, kitchen, and den are on this floor. You can use the den if you like; you can watch the information box in there. You can also use the kitchen; there's food in the fridge but not much. I will have to go to the market once we figure everything out. The lower level is where you will be staying. It's the basement." She stops and takes in a deep breath, making her flat-shaped nose expand. "Follow me," she says, like the words were hard to come by.

I search my surroundings. The living room is quite

large—about twice the size of my living room at home. The walls are bright in color—I would say a bright sky blue—and not the darkness that I'm used to. I see a matching love seat and sofa that look soft like a baby's skin. It's bright red like Whitney's lipstick, one of the colors we are not allowed to wear in Territory L. There is a beautiful stone fireplace. Above the fireplace is a painting of a lion. I can only imagine how much that piece is worth.

As we make our way out of the living room, my boots float along the beige carpet like I am walking on a cloud. The carpet is not rough and kinked; I know it is expensive as well. We follow her down a long hallway, pass what I can only imagine is the dining room, and we stop at a set of stairs.

"Behind this wall is the dining room, around the corner to the right is the kitchen, and to the left is the den. I will show you those things later; right now, I want to take you down to where you will be staying." Her voice is strained.

The dark stairwell suddenly becomes light—like the upper floors—as we enter the area. My feet tramp along with everyone else's as we walk down ten tiled steps that curve until they reach the basement. All I hear is small breaths coming from everyone's mouths. Julian is right behind Whitney, then there's Eric, me, Alexa, and Logan. I fully expect us to stop, but she walks us pass what looks to be an exercise room and a playroom. I see exercise equipment and a pool table. The motion lights clicked on in those rooms as well. She explains that the pool table has an automatic ball return, and some other fancy features.

We keep stamping until we reach another room that houses a washer and dryer. We never had a washer or dryer where I lived. We used to wash our clothes by hand and hang them outdoors to dry. A washer and dryer in someone's house looks unusual to me.

Just by the room with the washer and dryer is another smaller room with a brown antique bookcase. There are three bookcases against the wall. She pushes the bookcase in the middle and it squeaks open. Whitney steps pass the open bookcase into a small room that reminds me of a closet. She takes three steps through the small room to a door that hides in the back of it. Then she swings open the back door that's hidden behind the bookcase.

"This is where you will stay," she says. "This is the panic room." She clicks on a switch that's mounted to the wall and the lights pop on.

"What's a panic room?" I hear Alexa asks.

I'm thinking the same thing, but she asks before anyone else can.

"A panic room is where rich people hide their valuables so no one will get to them," Logan blurts out.

"First of all, my family is not rich," Whitney says, sounding annoyed. "Secondly, that's not true."

She lets out a sigh.

I'm sure this is hard on her and she would rather not have us here.

"A panic room," she continues, interrupting my thoughts, "is where people or families hide if someone tries to break into their house, or if there is a natural disaster—like a storm. People hide here until the intruder leaves, or the storm passes, or they find another way out. Some of the homes here have panic rooms."

"That's right," Julian adds, cutting in. "Some people here like to take things that don't belong to them. So, they break into people's homes and steal things. You don't want to be around if that happens."

I'm not understanding—since we've arrived here I've seen privacy bushes, privacy fences, and a gate for the alley—now there's a panic room. I thought the middle class had money to take care of every little thing they needed, so why would they need to break into other's homes and steal from them? I don't ask my question because I can tell Whitney wants to show us the room. The way she's wringing her hands, I can tell our presence here makes her nervous.

"The home my family has doesn't have one," Alexa says.

"Neither does mine," Logan announces.

"That's why I said *some*." Whitney rolls her green eyes.

"Yeah, the richer ones," Logan mumbles under his breath.

"Could everyone just pipe down so Whitney can show us the room?" Eric glances around at us. "She was nice enough to let us stay here, so the least we can do is show her some respect."

Logan and Alexa glance at each other and quiet down.

Whitney continues. "There are no beds down here, so some of you can sleep on the sofa and some can sleep on the floor in sleeping bags. I will get the sleeping bags for you." She glances down, then back up. "You can use the bathroom that's around the corner in the playroom or the one on the first floor. You can also use the kitchen and den. When you are not using those rooms, you should remain in the panic room. You should especially stay in the panic room at bedtime. That's when the patrolmen are likely to come looking for you. They've already searched the house twice for you during daylight and I'm sure next time they come it will be during the night."

"Probably tonight," I mumble, knowing they just chased us from the old college.

I search the room and see a square tan sofa that reminds me of the colors of President Esther's living quarters back in Territory L. There is a white ceramic table in front of the sofa, and a screen on the wall that looks like several little information boxes plastered on it.

"That's the monitoring system," Whitney says, noticing my glare. "It's set up so you can see every room in the house. I turned off the monitoring units for the upstairs bedrooms and bathrooms. That's where the baby and I stay. I would like to keep some things private." Her eyes squint. "If anything happens and you need to see that area, you snap this button on the wall under that box and it quickly turns back on."

"Make yourselves at home. I will go and get the extra sleeping bags." She turns and exits through the hidden doorway that leads back into the tiny room in back of the bookcase. "By the way," she turns back around. "Make sure you don't touch the red button on the wall. That alerts the patrolmen that there is an intruder and they come right away." She turns around again and her slippers swish as she slides them across the floor to leave.

My mouth goes dry as I stare at the red button next to the screen. Everything's so different here—and not what I expected at all.

"Are you okay?" Eric asks. He squeezes my shoulder.

"I don't know." I glance down at the floor and let out a small sigh.

Julian leans near the doorway, waiting for Whitney to come back, while Alexa and Logan plop down on the plush sofa, making themselves at home. They both let out large grunts, like this has been a horrendous day—which it has. I walk to the opposite side of the room and lean my shoulder against the wall. Eric follows me. Now that I have the wall for support, I slide down it and sit on the hard floors. It's cold, but I don't care. I need to rest for a moment and let the weight of the last couple of days wash over me. I take in the air, which smells like cinnamon. I notice an air freshener plug into the outlet on the wall. Eric slides down next to me.

"Everything's going to be okay, you know." His tone is reassuring.

I glance around and notice two large gray floor lamps that occupy the ends of both corners of the room.

"You can't know that," I finally say. My chest pounds. "We just keep wasting time. The more time we spend in all these different places, the more time we lose not searching for Abigail. By now, she could be anywhere. And what about my parents and my sister and my brother—what's happening to them? I was supposed to help them and the people back in Territory L." I shrug. "So far, all I've done is hide out in an abandoned college and now in a panic room. Oh yeah…I've shot two people. I can't forget that. Maybe I shouldn't have come here." I slide my knees up to my chin. "Maybe I should have stayed in Territory L and accepted my punishment from President Esther."

A strangled cry comes from my throat. "Nothing's going the way it should. This is all wrong." My eyes well up. I don't want Eric to see, so I bury my face in the palm of my hands.

"Look, I know they're your family, and I care about them because you care about them. Besides that, I got pretty close to your brother and I don't want to see anything happen to him." I feel the warmth of his hand squeezing my shoulder again. "When I left with you, I also made a promise to help the people in our Territory and that's what I intend to do."

I look over at him and our eyes meet. He brushes my wet cheek with his finger.

"I know it may seem like we're wasting time, but we're not," he continues. "Everything happens for a reason. Julian told me that he has a plan; he just hasn't had time to share with us what that is because we had to leave the old college so unexpectedly. We're in this together—please remember that."

Before I answer him, I hear Whitney walking in the room, sighing. She throws three sleeping bags on the floor and they swish as they land.

"The women can take the sofa, so that leaves three bags for the men." Her eyes are wide. "Adam's going to be awake soon and he's going to need changing and feeding, so I will take you upstairs and show you the kitchen and den before that happens. Once the little guy gets going, he needs most of my attention."

CHAPTER EIGHT

THE KITCHEN IS enormous and bright orange. The lights are on motion sensors in here as well as most of the house. That is except for the panic room. The lights have silver cone-shaped covers surrounding them that hang down from the ceiling in various areas of the kitchen.

There is something in the middle of the room that Whitney calls an island. It's white and curved in a circular shape. The island has a sink in the middle of it. The faucet comes on automatically when a hand is waved underneath—reminding me of the faucets back in the old college. Further down the island is the stove along with an oven attached to it. The stove and sink are stainless steel.

At the end of the island there are four white swivel stools. The back of the chairs are curved to match the curvature in your back. The chair has one leg attached underneath in the middle that reminds me of a tall pole—it's stainless steel as well. The seat on the chair looks like leather but feels soft to the touch. How fancy that you can sit and eat at the same place your food is prepared.

My eyes blur over as she shows us everything.

There is a long glass countertop up against the wall. The glass looks bubbly around the edges and appears to have bubbles etched throughout the top. There is a square-shaped appliance sitting on top of it. Whitney calls it a see-through toaster. It's stainless steel, but the sides are glass—that way you can see the bread as it is being toasted. We didn't have toasters back in L—let alone one that was see through.

I turn my attention away from the counter because Whitney is showing them the refrigerator—it's also stainless steel. There's a box-shaped panel attached to the front with several buttons lit up in blue. Underneath the panel is a dispenser.

"If you hit this button, ice will drop down from the dispenser," Whitney says. "If you hit this button, you get water. If you hit this one, you get juice. You could also have fresh fruit drop down…like sliced apples or grapes."

It's beautiful, like something out of a magazine. If the houses here are this spacious and striking, what must the houses in Territory U look like?

The refrigerator swooshes open, and I shiver as the cold air hits me. Whitney says the bottom shelf will be for us—although it is empty right now. She also tells us not to touch the things on the upper shelves. The vegetables that her mother grew in her own garden are on there—they are not to be eaten. I didn't see a garden on the way in—but I wasn't exactly looking for one either.

I see baby bottles on the second shelf and jars of baby food. I blink, trying not to tear up because it reminds me of Abigail. Funny how they have real baby food here; but in L, we had to make our own because, of course, babies are not allowed.

She also shows us a bottom cabinet underneath the counter. It's filled with round metal cans of soups that she is willing to share with us. Since our visit was unexpected she hasn't had time to go shopping for extra food and she hasn't been given extra money for food either. She glares at Julian as the words come out of her mouth.

There are two large square-shaped windows in the kitchen with shades drawn. I peek out of one of them and see the back-yard. I know we just traipsed through it, but we were in a hurry and I couldn't really focus on how enormous it is. The motion lights are still on. The wind is still strong, making them click on and off—I suppose Whitney still hasn't turned the switch off to deactivate them.

Maybe I shouldn't be looking out of the windows, but I'm curious—like always—as to my surroundings. I doubt if her neighbors will be able to distinguish her frame from mine. If anyone is lurking out on the streets—like the patrolmen—the privacy fence should block any view of me. No one will notice me peering through a narrow opening between the window and a drawn shade.

I take in a breath. The grass is so green—I can tell it has been chemically treated. It has smooth lines that show it was just freshly mowed. I glance back over at the garage we just came through. It's almost as big as the main house. I know I've said this before but it's nothing like the little shed we had outback of our home in Territory L. It fits two cars while ours barely fit one. I suppose that's fine though since we had no car to put in our shed anyway.

I turn around to see the group is leaving me. I catch up to them and we move on to the den, which is a mixture of burgundy and green with soft green carpet. Funny, when we first arrived, Whitney said there was an information box for us to watch; but now she tells us not to touch it. All of a sudden, she remembers that it's broken and we shouldn't go in there. It sounds kind of strange to me, but I move on to explore the dining room with the rest.

The dining room is also bright blue. The table is cherry mahogany and seats at least ten people. I wonder why a family of three with a small baby would need such a large dining table. Maybe that's how people with more money live. Maybe they purchase bigger things than what they really need. I have to say it's nice to be here, and warmer, instead of in that dusty old college.

Once Whitney was done with Adam, she made something called tuna macaroni salad and brought it down to the panic room for us. It was quite good. And from the way I heard everyone else chomping and smacking their lips, I think we all enjoyed it. She called it leftovers, but to me it was just as good as if it was freshly made.

I'm ashamed to say, I don't really know how to cook. My mother never wanted me or my siblings in the kitchen. She always said that was her alone time, to reflect on her day. I believe she was embarrassed at the small amount of ingredients she had to cook with, and she didn't want us to see her struggle to make us a decent meal each day. We mostly had beans, with other things thrown in, when available.

Once the eating fest is over, we all decide it's time to get some much-needed rest. I lie at the opposite end of the sofa—down from Alexa and fall asleep.

* * *

I wake up and glance around. A small night-light is plugged into the outlet along the wall, giving the room a little brightness. I notice Alexa's not there. Then, I see her rustle back in with a disturbed look on her face.

"Everything okay?" I ask, as she plops back down.

"I'm fine." Her mouth scrunches up.

"You sure?"

She shrugs. "Why wouldn't I be?"

"Earlier, I went in the bathroom after you and saw something bloody wrapped in a paper towel in the garbage can."

She bites down on her lip. "If you must know, I have menorrhagia."

"Maybe you should see a doctor."

"How do you suggest I do that?" she asks with a snap to her voice.

"I know you're on the run but maybe you should turn yourself in." She glares at me so I continue. "They can get you a doctor. I'm just saying it can't be easy bleeding so heavily on the run. Do you even have—"

"Yes, I have some...or I did." She cuts me off and glances around to make sure no one has woken up and is listening to our conversation. "I did have some sanitary supplies, but when we escaped out of the old college I didn't have time to grab my bag... they were in there. So now I have to use what little I found in Whitney's bathroom. Towels will have to do for now. I don't need a doctor."

"Maybe you should ask Whitney if she has something you can use. That can't be too hygienic."

"Well it's not your body, so don't worry about it!" There's a growl to her words. "And if I did turn myself in—which I won't—I would never tell them where you guys are hiding. I'm not a snitch."

"Why are you bringing that up? I didn't say that you would."

She rolls her eyes at me.

"Sorry, I don't mean to pry," I add, trying to calm the conversation. "I just wanted to know if I could help is all."

She turns away from me. "I'm fine."

I let the subject go. I can tell it must be embarrassing for her, and she doesn't want to talk about it.

Alexa seems to fall right asleep, unless she's pretending so she doesn't have to converse with me; but I can't sleep.

Hearing a noise, I shudder. I shift on the soft tan sofa. I guess anything would be considered soft after sleeping on the floors and the chairs in the cafeteria. I glance around the panic room, before trying to go back to sleep again. Eric, Julian, and Logan haven't budged from their spots on the floors; they are still knocked out.

I hear something again. The noise I hear is the howling of a baby. The howling seems to only be bothering me—maybe because I was in and out of consciousness all night. I thought this was a soundproof room—but the cry is so high-pitched I can still faintly hear it.

Leaving the old college and arriving here happened so quickly, I haven't had time to dwell on my parent's secret. They were offered a chance to go straight to Territory U and they declined.

What did the president want them to do? Why would they decline? Why does my family seem to keep so many secrets? How do I even know Logan's words are true?

I can't lie here anymore, so I slowly rise and creep out of the door of the small space we now call home. I know Whitney says we should stay in the panic room at night, and Eric said we need to stay on the lower level at all times; but now that I'm awake, I need to move around.

I'm in the living room now. The lights don't automatically pop on. Maybe Whitney turned the motion sensors off. I try to adjust my eyes to the darkness; but before I can, I stub my toe on a vase propped on the floor. I wince in pain but try to hold in my yell. I still don't want to disturb anyone.

At that same moment, I hear light footsteps along the carpeted stairs, coming toward me. Whitney hits a switch on the wall and lights pop on.

"What are you doing up here?" Whitney asks. "I told you to stay in the panic room at night."

She has on a shiny pink bathrobe and fluffy blue slippers this time.

"I know," I say, shrugging. "I'm sorry. I heard the baby crying, and I couldn't sleep. Is he alright?"

"He's fine." She waves her hand. "He's just hungry. Sometimes, it seems like he just can't get enough food. Seems like I just fed him, but he always wants a midnight snack. I am on my way to the kitchen to get a bottle out of the refrigerator for him." She walks pass me. I take that as my cue to follow.

She stops in the hallway and opens a panel. She hits a switch.

"I usually turn off the motion sensors down here and upstairs at night. Sometimes, I walk around the house at night with Adam in my arms when he can't sleep and I don't want the lights constantly popping on and off. I also like to check on him from time to time during the night and if the lights were constantly going on and off in his room it would wake him. But when my mother is here she leaves them on constantly. She's lived here long enough to know where things are in the dark. But she just doesn't care what I want or about what Adam needs."

From her tone, I can tell she must not always agree or get along with her mother.

"Since we're awake now, I'll just turn the sensors back on."

I'm grateful for that. I stubbed my toe earlier. I'd hate to do that again.

She opens the refrigerator and a cold breeze splashes on my arm. She bends down and grabs a plastic baby bottle filled with milk. The refrigerator *thumps* as she closes it and walks away.

"Do you warm it up for him?" I ask.

"No, he likes it cool." Her eyes squint. "What would you know about babies?"

I know what she's getting at. Since there are none in Territory L, I guess I have no right to understand what they may want or even need.

She asks, "Would you like to see him?"

That was a question I wasn't expecting. "Really, could I? I thought you didn't want anyone to go up to the bedrooms."

"I'll allow it, this one time." She smiles. "Besides, no one will know. It will be our little secret."

The staircase that leads upstairs is spiral and the carpet is soft as butter. Every step I take makes my stomach do flip-flops because her home is so much nicer than mine...brighter, more hopeful—instead of dark. I get a whiff of the strong smell of baby powder.

We reach the top step, and I see four white doors. Two are on the left and two are on the right.

"That's my parent's room." She points to the left. "And that's the bathroom. My room is on the right, and Adam's room is next to mine."

We walk into the first room on the right where the strong smell of baby powder is coming from. The room is light blue with hardwood floors. The wall to the right of us is also painted blue. It's quite lovely. It has a tall brown tree with bright colored flowers surrounding it. There's a yellow sun at the top and gray and orange birds flying around. What a beautiful room for a young child to have. I only wish Abigail could have had something like this—instead she hid out in a dark house with boarded windows and no light. But that was before, now she's—well, I don't even know where she is, or if she's hurt.

"You okay?" Whitney asks, seeing the expression on my face. "You looked sad, all of a sudden."

"I'm fine," I say.

"Well, this is Adam." She walks over to the brown crib. The crib is unlike anything I've seen in magazines. It's circular instead of rectangular. It has two large round wheels attached to the front and two large round wheels in back. The wheels don't move, they are just for show, but it looks like a carriage. It looks to be made of wood, and the bottom has what Whitney calls a crib skirt—it reminds me of tiny curtains, surrounding it.

She leans down, picks him up, and places him on her hip. She tickles his chin and he giggles and smiles. He's the same complexion as she is, but his eyes are blue like Julian's. The thin amount of hair on his head is also brown like his fathers, and there are small creases on his forehead.

"Nice to meet you, Adam," I say, shaking his little hand.

His skin is soft like Abigail's. "How old is he?"

"He's ten months. He's crawling now." She smiles.

She carries him over to a gold sofa that's near the other wall in his bedroom and plops down. She waves her hand, so I will sit down next to her. The sofa is so soft, I melt down into it.

The baby's cheeks move in and out as he drinks from the bottle. My eyes tear. I look down at a gold blanket, laying over the edge of the sofa. I smooth out the wrinkles with my hand.

Except for the sounds of baby Adam sucking the nipple on the bottle, everything is quiet.

"Emma, you look like you want to ask me something." Whitney holds on tightly to the bottle. "Go ahead. I don't mind."

"Are you happy here?" I ask. "I mean, happy living in Territory M."

"Yes, I'm content. I may make it into Territory U, someday—but if that day never comes, then I've adjusted here so I'll be fine."

"But I thought if you didn't make it to Territory U, then Adam would be taken away from you."

"He will only be taken if I'm not holding up my end of the deal, which is to do my best in college and find a job. If I keep doing the best I can, and the president sees that I'm trying, I won't have to worry about him being taken away."

"But why should you have to live that way?" I shrug. "I mean, always in fear that your baby will be taken if you can't act accordingly."

"Did Julian tell you why we broke up?"

"No," I say. Julian and I aren't the best of friends, so I don't know all of his secrets.

"Julian was living here, in M, already because his father was a senior accountant. I was here as well because my father is a neurosurgeon. When I grew older, my mother didn't feel fulfilled staying at home anymore, so she went to college to become a nurse. Once she became a nurse, it almost put our family into another tax bracket. My parents almost made enough money to get into Territory U. So, my mother decided she would pick up extra shifts, sometimes, to help us get into the next tax bracket. My father didn't want to move. He told my mother no matter how many shifts she picked up so we could move ahead, he wasn't leaving. He liked working here. He liked the people and the area, so he wanted to stay. I can't say the same for my mother; she wanted to move ahead. At the time, they fought a lot."

I adjust my hip on the sofa and continue listening to her story. She takes the bottle from Adam's mouth and he whines, so she places it in his mouth again.

"I met Julian in school, and we started to date. Our school didn't have segregated classes, so we had a few together. He is an only child and so am I. We sort of clicked. Julian was kind of a bad boy, or he tried to be—he talked a good game—while I was considered the good girl. You know," she says, squinting her eyes, "I never got in any trouble, while Julian was always messing up and skipping classes. I was attracted to him—those blue eyes of his just drew me in. We continued to date after high school."

She looks around the room.

"Julian and his father fought continuously; his father thought he could do so much more with his life than be a patrolman. I found out I was pregnant; the protection we used didn't work, one time. So once that happened, his father blew a gasket and so did my parents."

She blinks a few times, like she's holding back tears.

"I wanted to get married. My parents and his parents thought it was for the best. Julian didn't want to marry me. He said he did love me but didn't want to be tied down. He would still go to patrolmen training and take care of me and the baby, but he didn't want to be married. I felt it was best if we broke up—he could still see his child and help raise him. I would never keep him from Adam; but we both just wanted different things, so the relationship wasn't going to work out."

"Weren't you hurt that he didn't want to marry you?"

"Of course I was." She places the bottle on the floor. She turns Adam toward her, places him on her shoulder, and pats his back. "At first, when he would visit Adam, I would go in the other room.

I didn't want to have anything to do with him. But then he got kicked out of Territory M, and I have to say I missed him stopping by to visit Adam—and, I guess, me."

The earlier tears still remain. "So when he became a guard that traveled back and forth between the gates to bring supplies, it ended up working for the both of us. He could come see Adam, and we became friends again."

"And you hoped you two would get back together?"

"How did you become so smart?" She stands and pats the baby's back again, until a small belch trickles out.

"I don't have to be smart." I shrug. "I see it all over your face. You still care for him."

"Yeah, I guess I do." She glances down, then back up. "Would you like to hold him?" She holds the baby out to me, trying to hand him over. I think she's trying to change the subject.

"I'm not sure that's a good idea." My chest feels hot.

"Why? He's not going to bite."

I don't know why she's so adamant about it. I think holding him will make me think of things that I don't want to.

"Did Julian tell you why I'm here?" I ask, never taking the baby.

"I know the patrolmen are looking for you because you're here illegally."

The baby scrunches his face up and starts to whine. She holds him close to her again and bounces him on her hip.

"You want the walls to be torn down, so everyone will be treated equally. And since you were the last child to be born and kept alive before the killings started happening, you feel like the whole burden of fixing everything is on you."

"You're right. I just want to make things right for everyone."

The baby has calmed down and is resting his head on her shoulder. "I know we just met, but I hope you know I will help you in any way I can."

"I do know that—and you're proving it by letting us stay here." I stand. "Do you know anything about the Hill?"

She shrugs. "Not much."

"Can you tell me what you do know?"

"No one talks much about it. It's all kept hush-hush. The Hill is on the north side of town. It consists of the mansion and the executive buildings that surround it. The watchmen guard the area and make sure only the invited are allowed in. The leader lives there."

"Do you know who that is?"

"No," she says, shaking her head. "I don't know—and it doesn't matter. No matter what they say, President Esther is still in charge of us. Her rules are what matters. The leader just watches over us for the president, since she doesn't have time to come here."

"Yeah, I know. She mainly divides her time between Territories L and U."

"I know you want to go there. I also know Julian is going to take you there. Yes," she pauses and kisses Adam on his forehead. The conversation must be boring him; he is falling asleep. "I know all of this because I had to ask him questions about you guys before I let you stay in my home. If someone's after you, I need to know—I can't let someone jeopardize me and my baby."

"That's understandable."

She walks over to the crib and lays him down on his back. His nose twinkles and he lays his head to the side to get more comfortable.

"He'll be asleep for a while. We can go in my room and talk." She nods toward the doorway, and I follow behind her.

We go one room over—the lights pop on and my mouth drops in amazement. As my feet connect with the hardwood floor, I see burgundy walls in this room.

Approaching the canopy bed draped in taupe, I notice the similarly colored dresser against the wall with its large mirror, reflecting the vanity on the other side of the room. Her slippers scuff up against the floor as she walks to the vanity. She sits down and stares at herself. I remove my eyes from her and glance at the table next to her because it has an information box on top of it.

"I don't think Julian should be the one to take you to the Hill."

"Why?"

"Julian will do anything for you all. He's a wonderful friend..." she hesitates.

"But?" I ask.

"But," she turns around to face me. "He's not very good in violent situations. He means well, but I don't think he does well under pressure. When he was a child, his dad was always on him. He would scream at him and tell him he would never amount to anything. I think that's why he's always trying to prove himself now. I think that's why he pretends to be a bad boy—when he's really not."

My thoughts go to what Julian told me about Eric saving his life. But to be fair, Billy had a gun to his head so it wasn't as if he could easily get out of the situation.

"I don't understand. If the people here have enough money to live comfortably, why can't they get along? Why would his father scream at him?" I ask.

"People with money still have problems. I think his father knew that and just wanted him to stop goofing around and make something of himself." She crosses her legs. "I know he's a guard so he should know what he's doing—but all I'm saying is he sometimes takes on more than he can handle. He doesn't know his way around up there, so I think you should find someone that does. Just to make sure everything goes safely."

My thoughts go to Logan. He used to work on the Hill, so he's my best hope. I just don't know if I trust him, or if he's willing to even go with us.

Whitney looks down at the gold watch on her wrist. "It's

almost three in the morning." The watch jiggles as she moves her arm around. "We should try and get some sleep. I have to drop Adam off at the babysitter's in the morning. Normally, I have classes on Saturday, but school has been out the last few days because a pipe burst on the first floor and it hasn't been fixed yet. I figure since I don't have class, I will go shopping at the market and pick up some groceries for you and your friends."

"How far is the market?" I'm still standing, because I never asked for permission to sit in her room.

"It's only a few blocks from here. It takes about ten minutes to get there."

"I want to go with you."

"Emma, do you seriously think that's a good idea?" Her eyes sharpen in my direction. "They're searching for you—you can't just walk around in the open. But I know you already know this."

"I'm waiting for Julian to give the word on when we can go up to the Hill. He said he was looking into some things. I'm hoping we won't have to put you out for too long. In the meantime, I can't stay cooped up here. I just want to get out of here and see what Territory M looks like in the daytime. So far, I've only seen it at night."

"I don't—"

"I will wear a disguise." I cut her off and shrug. "I can wear those glasses." I point to a pair of dark black-framed glasses on her dresser. The lenses are tinted, so it will help me stay disguised. "And put my hair up under a cap. No one will know it's me."

"You mean my sunglasses?" Whitney asks. "Have you ever worn sunglasses before?"

"No, we don't have them where I live, but I've seen pictures in old magazines. And I'm sure you have some kind of hat I can borrow."

She lets out a large sigh.

"You should get back down to the panic room, in case the

patrolmen stop by tonight." She stands and I know she wants the conversation to end. It's making her uncomfortable. "We can discuss this more in the morning. Besides, I'm sure you'll have to talk it over with Eric first. Isn't he your boyfriend?"

The word *boyfriend* makes my spine tingle. I've never had a boyfriend before. Although I do have feelings for Eric, and I know he has feelings for me, we haven't had time to discuss what our actual relationship is.

"He's not my boyfriend." I walk toward the door. "And he can't stop me if I want to go."

She gives me a weird grin as I leave the room, like she still thinks I'm lying about Eric being my boyfriend.

CHAPTER NINE

"I vote no," Logan says. He's sitting on the tan sofa in the panic room.

"I vote no, too," Julian says. He's standing, leaning on the arm of the sofa.

"My decision to go isn't up to you all, so I don't know why you're voting." My throat burns with anger. They can't make me stay if I want to go.

Everyone is up and staring at me. They all have on the same clothes they slept in last night. I have changed, so I can go out with Whitney.

"We're just offering suggestions, so you can think over your decision a little more. I think you're crazy to do this. But what do I know," Alexa says, sounding aggravated. "I mean, my brother was taken in and you don't see me running out trying to save him; I know what will happen if I try. I will be locked up, just like he is." Her tone is rough. She folds her arms and shifts her weight on the sofa next to Logan.

"I'm not trying to put myself, or you, in jeopardy. Besides, no one's going to recognize me. I know how to disguise myself and keep a low profile."

Alexa talks, while all other voices remain silent. "If you get caught, they'll ask about us. They know we were all hiding out at the old college together."

"If that happens," I say, shrugging. "I won't give you up. I know you haven't known me that long—but I wouldn't do that."

Alexa glares at me because those are almost the same words she said to me last night.

"Look, I'm sorry. I need to get out and look around. I can't stay cooped up here. Who knows how long it will be before we can go to the Hill." I glance at Julian.

"I told you I was working on that." His eyes squint together. "We woke up last night and the four of us discussed it. You were nowhere around. Since Logan used to work up there, he wants to go with us. He knows his way around and can be of help."

"I'm going, too," Alexa chimes in.

"Then when are we leaving?" I ask.

"We'll leave tomorrow evening." Logan looks at me. "The Territory leaders normally have a meeting on the first of every month. So the leader of Territory M takes some of the watchmen and they all travel to Territory U for a few days. They meet President Esther there, and they discuss matters involving the three territories."

I nod my head and continue listening.

"Monday marks the start of September, so Sunday evening will be the perfect time for us to go. The leader and the watchmen usually leave during the afternoon. They like to rest up in U the night before, to be ready for the morning meeting." Logan sucks his teeth. "If we leave tomorrow evening, when we get there… there will be less foot traffic up on the Hill. We can try to sneak in unnoticed."

"That sounds like a plan," I say.

My first priority is to look for the newbie camp, but they don't need to know that. The only ones here that know about the camp are Eric and Julian. The others don't know my secret, and I don't care to divulge it right now.

"Maybe I can look around and see what makes the head honcho vulnerable," I continue. "Even if I can't look around, I want my chance to speak. I can hide up there unnoticed until they come back and then get my point across about the walls coming down. But that will never happen if they take me into custody before I get to speak with them. I still need to go with Whitney," I add, to despondent faces.

I hear groans from everyone in the room.

"I hope you understand," I say. "Maybe while we're out getting food, we can pick up more clothing for us. We left the school so suddenly, we left all our extra clothes behind." I'm hoping this strategy will appeal to them, and they will side with me.

"If you're intent on doing this, then here is some money," Julian says. He stands from his slouched position. He walks toward me. He reaches in his pocket and takes out some bills and coins. The bills crinkle as he smooths them out to hand to me. "Bring back what you can." He lets out a sigh. "I don't have much money left. Since we went on the run, I never got a chance to go stand in line for my rations, and neither did Eric. And I can't get some from my parents. If I went to their house, I'm sure my mother would give me what I need, but my father wouldn't hesitate to turn me in."

He says rations, meaning his last paycheck. Once you received your paycheck, you would go to the local banker's office to cash it. In Territory L, there was one banker's office near the marketplace where the clothing stores and pawn shop was located. There was also a banker's office for the government workers who worked for President Esther at the city council building. Now, I need to know the inner workings of Territory M.

I glance over at Eric. He leans against the wall, with one leg bent up and the ball of his foot against the wall. He has a hard look on his face. I know he is not pleased with my decision, but he remains silent and still listens.

"It's going to be okay. I won't be gone long." I walk over and stand next to Eric, while Julian, Logan, and Alexa talk among themselves. "Aren't you going to say anything?"

"Whatever I have to say isn't going to change things." He shrugs. "So, why should I waste my breath? I know you have your mind made up, and there's nothing I can do or say that will matter." He glances down.

I turn his chin to face me. "I would at least like to know what you're thinking."

"I'm thinking, why do you have to be so pig headed and run off on your own? Julian just said we can go to the Hill tomorrow night. Why can't you wait to go out? That is what I'm thinking."

His eyes are glued to mine but not in a good way.

"If you must know, I think Whitney is hiding something. I can't explain it, but I have a feeling. I think if I spend some time with her, outside of the house and away from the baby, maybe I can get it out of her." I glance down then back up. "I think it's strange that she claims the information box in the den is broken. They have one in the den, one in her parent's room, and one in her room. She says the ones in her room and her parent's room are not to be touched. I think there's something she doesn't want us to see."

He remains silent.

"While I'm out, I hope to run by a supply store or whatever store they have here that sells boxes. They normally leave one on. Maybe I can find out what she's hiding."

"I found that strange, too." He leans in to me. "I asked Julian about it, and he said boxes break here all the time. He said Whitney can be trusted. I'm not sure what to think." He leans back. "How are you going to get there?"

"Whitney says she normally takes the light rail. They are

finished with the improvements on it now. Since her parents are out of town, she's going to use her parents' other vehicle—you know, the one we saw in the garage when we first arrived. Then we won't have to make the five mile hike down to the station."

"Two vehicles…must be nice."

"Yeah, I agree. She says today is rare. When her parents are here, her mother normally has the second vehicle…since they are gone, this is her chance to use it."

"That's a good thing, because they saw what we were riding in when they caught up with us at the old college. So it's good to let the truck lay low for a while, until the heat is off us."

I'm not sure the heat will ever be off us. The thought makes my insides crawl.

I hear Whitney's voice. "Let's go, Emma."

"Be careful," Eric says. He grabs my hand in his and his palm feels warm.

"I will." I release his hand.

* * *

The air smells clean and the sky looks aqua blue. I have the window rolled down in the car. We just dropped baby Adam at the sitter's house. I sat in the car while Whitney went in with him.

I stare at the houses on the streets. They are all beige brick. They all look big, beautiful, and the same. There are no humongous fields in between them, no woods, weeds, or dirt roads surrounding them. It reminds me of Whitney's street, except for the colors.

When we arrived at Whitney's it was nighttime, so I couldn't see much. I made sure to check the area surrounding Whitney's house when she pulled out of her driveway this morning.

Whitney's home is brick; the trim is red. There's a big square window in the front of her living room. The grass is smooth like it has been mowed several times over. You could double the house I lived in back in L and it still wouldn't be as big as her home.

While we're sitting in front of the babysitter's house, I see red and pink flowers aligning the driveway. Now that fall is arriving, they will be dying off—although the weather's so strange here, it could snow or be a heatwave tomorrow.

Whitney gave me a pair of black jeans and a black t-shirt to wear. They feel foreign against my skin. I've worn nothing but those uniform pants for weeks. I have to say the rubber-soled shoes she lent me feel weird. They're so light, not like the heavy boots I am used to. It feels strange but nice to have on new clothing. I believe now I will fit in with the others who live here. Whitney says I should blend in nicely.

Whitney is a little taller and skinnier than me, so the jeans are tighter than I like. The jeans are about ankle level, but I won't be wearing them long. Once I get back to her house, I will put on the looser clothes I had on before. That is unless I have a chance to buy something new with the money Julian gave me. My first priority is to buy food and then clothing with whatever is left. The t-shirt she gave me is just oversized enough that I am able to wear my holsters with my gun on one side and Taser on the other. The t-shirt nicely hides the duty belt that holds them. My necklace remains underneath.

We decide, since I was determined to come along, it is best to go to the market that's farther away. The people who work at the Mainstream Market near her house see her all the time and would wonder who the female with her is. She says there are several markets in the territory; but to be on the safe side, we're going where no one will know her.

I have to say, Eric wasn't happy when I told him what I was doing. I also know the others think I have a death wish. Maybe they're right, but I can't hide out in that house like I did at the old college. I need to know what's going on here. I've disguised myself enough, so I won't be recognized. I know how to be careful and to be aware of my surroundings.

Maybe Whitney knows something about what Logan said to me. It still bothers me that I was spoken about up on the Hill. I feel like if I get her alone, maybe she will divulge some secrets. I also wonder if she knows anything about the babies being adopted, but I'm afraid to ask her. If she doesn't know anything, it will just bring up a whole new subject that maybe she shouldn't know about.

I look around the car's interior and give an inner sigh at how beautiful it is. It's on the smaller side but the seats are cloth and cushiony.

"You like the car?" Whitney asks.

"Yeah."

"I thought so."

"How could you tell?"

"You're staring around like you're amazed."

"I am...a little."

"You were riding around in that truck that Julian borrowed. I know it's an older model."

"Yeah, and nothing like this." I look from left to right. "It didn't have all these fancy gadgets...and the clock on the dashboard didn't work. What's that for?" I point at a small square mirror in the middle of the dashboard.

"It's a backup camera. It helps see what's behind you when you're backing up. Hence the name." She lets out a small giggle. "If you like that, then check this out." She clicks a button on the dashboard near the bottom.

My body tingles because I feel heat underneath me.

"Heated seats." She grins. "You can also use that button to make the seats cold."

"That's a nice feature."

"Yes, it is. It's such a nice car. I try to enjoy it when I can.

When my mom's here, she won't let me drive it. She says I got myself pregnant and it's my responsibility to take care of my child and to go to college. Once I've done all that, then I can get a job and buy my own vehicle. Until that time, I have to make my own way around. Sometimes, she drops me and the baby off at the sitter's and then I take the light rail the rest of the way to college—but it depends on what mood she's in."

She rubs her left temple, like she's in deep thought.

"Funny, she always wanted something sporty like this, but now she's changed her mind. She now wants something bigger, fancier, and more expensive. I'm sure she will be getting rid of this one soon and buying something else. "

She's quiet for a minute.

"The screen that shows the backup camera also turns into a navigation system if you hit a certain button. If you don't know your way around the territory, it talks and guides you to where you need to go," she says, speaking again. "That's the radio system." She points downward, while her other hand is on the steering wheel. "There is also one channel that broadcasts the speeches President Esther gives…and gives us any important updates, if needed." She gives me a funny look, like she shouldn't have mentioned that.

"Can we turn it on? I would like to hear what's going on."

"No, my mom had that feature disconnected. She doesn't like any distractions while driving. She doesn't even want to be tempted—so she had it disassembled. It's better to be safe than sorry she always says."

For some reason, I tend not to believe her—just like I don't believe her about the information boxes. I shake that thought off and focus in on her driving. She grips the wheel of the car and whips the corners like it's nothing.

Watching her now makes me long for things I missed out on. Being here in an unfamiliar place reminds me that I don't know how to drive. I've never driven before because we don't have cars where I come from—at least not cars for the underlings to drive, as President Esther would say. I bite down hard on my tongue because I feel like I've missed out on so much.

I don't have any girlfriends. I've always felt out of place in school. I'm not sure if it's because I'm mixed, or something else; but I could never bring myself to get close to any of the other girls. Once Taylor became pregnant, my standoffishness became worse. I had to make sure no one found out about Taylor, so I didn't want to get close to anyone.

Looking at Whitney now makes my foot twitch. She's only a little older than me, but she seems to know so much more than I do. She drives, has been in love, and has a baby. She's in college and making a life for herself—making her way into Territory U.

I'm not saying I want to have a baby; but I've never been in love, and I only just recently had my first kiss. She's beautiful and probably has tons of friends.

I don't know why, all of a sudden, I am throwing a pity party for myself. I had my sister, Taylor; she was my best friend, and I confided in her about many things. But once again, I was jealous because she was considered pretty while I was only considered average.

"What's wrong?" Whitney asks.

I squirm under my seat belt. "Why do you think something's wrong?"

"Because you're staring at me and you have a weird look on your face."

The tires squeal as she turns the corner. She drives down streets with nice large brick homes and now we're on a street that has shops. I see a building with a bright yellow sign that says: CONVENTIONAL ICE CREAM SHOP. Next to that is another building with a white sign and blue lettering that reads: TRADITIONAL BAKERY. We didn't have those types of stores back in Territory L. I see thick trees with a mixture of brown and green leaves. The sidewalks are wide, instead of narrow.

"Did you hear me?" she asks.

"I've never seen anyone with blonde coloring in their hair. That's not allowed in Territory L."

"It's not all blonde." She sniffs. "Only part of it is. They're called streaks."

"Streaks," I repeat.

"Yes, only the women in Territory U are allowed to get all of their hair colored. The president believes the rich deserve to do what they want with their bodies…meaning their hair, nails, face lifts. My territory doesn't make enough money to be able to indulge in all those things. We are limited to what the president believes we deserve. We can have streaks here, if we want." Maybe she sees the confusion on my face, because she continues. "It's just something to make us look better, if we want."

"Did you ever feel awkward in your own skin?" I ask, since she's talking about what makes her look better.

"No. Why do you ask?"

"It's nothing." I look back out of the window.

"It's something or you wouldn't have asked."

I hear a bird squawking above. I stare out of the open window and see a black crow, circling the sky.

"You just seem like you have it all together, that's all." I shrug.

"I have it all together." She lets out a small giggle, again. "That's wild. I have a baby with someone who doesn't want to marry me, and now Julian and I are not even together. My baby's father is on the run and if he is caught and thrown into prison for life, my baby may never know his father."

She takes in a breath and continues. "My mother desperately wants into U; but like I said earlier, my father doesn't want to go. Even if he changes his mind and they are accepted, it doesn't mean I can go just because I live with them. It all depends on how well

I'm doing. I mean, I have to do as well as I can in college, so I can be put on the list to go to Territory U or my baby might be taken away. Since I'm of age now, my going doesn't depend on my parents anymore or how much money they may make," she says, rambling. "Mind you, I don't even want to go to Territory U."

The car hits a bump and my stomach flips. Not just from the unsteady road but also from what she just said.

"I thought you told me earlier that if you never made it to Territory U you could keep Adam as long as you were trying."

"I did say that, but it all depends on President Esther's mood that day. Some people have done their best and made it to U with their child, and others have done their best and have been held here and had their child taken. I'm just trying to remain positive about the whole thing."

The brakes screech as we stop at a red light. There are a few cars ahead of us. But for the most part, the streets look empty. I suppose most people are at work or at school during this time of day.

She turns her head to look at me. "To be perfectly honest, I only want to get into U because I may lose Adam. If it wasn't for that, I would prefer to stay here."

"I remember you saying you were content here."

"I am. Why would I want to go to a territory with uppity rich people who think they're better than everyone else? They treat people with less money with no respect, like they are gum under their shoes."

"Maybe all rich people aren't like that." Her face looks so withdrawn, so I'm trying to make her feel better. The engine roars as she steps back on the gas.

"I hear stories from my parents. My father goes all the time for business and training at the hospitals there. Like I told you earlier, he doesn't want to move there; he likes his work here. But I think it's more. He says all the people do there is talk about how much money they have and how they can make more. My mother, on the other hand, is just like them. She always wants more money."

Listening to her now, I would say her life isn't all that happy living in Territory M and she would be less happy moving to U.

"Do you know what happens to Adam if he is taken away?"

"They say the babies are killed. I prefer not to think about it." She blinks like her eyes are tearing and then she changes the subject. "Enough about me—now back to you. I think we kind of got off topic. You were talking about feeling awkward in your own skin. I take it someone made you feel that way. Am I right?"

The motor slows down to a soft hum as we sit at another red light. I see a couple of females jog across the street, trying to make the light. One has on a yellow pants suit and the other one has on a red one. They look around my mother's age. There is a large four-story building across the street—maybe they are walking to work. I turn back to her, to answer her question.

"When I was younger, around ten, my mother asked me to walk to the marketplace and buy some milk. When I got to the store, there was one container of milk left. I grabbed it and walked to the checkout counter." I turn toward the window, then back to Whitney.

"Well, a girl my age came up to the counter and she said she was looking for milk. The clerk said there was no more in the back, and there wouldn't be another shipment in until the morning." I take in a breath and continue. "When I placed the container on the counter to pay for it, he said I couldn't have it. He said he was giving it to the other girl because she was prettier. I figured it was because she was light-skin and I wasn't."

"He really said that?" Her eyebrow rises, like she doesn't believe me. "Who would say something like that?"

There was silence in the car, for a moment. The light shifts to green and then Whitney causes the motor to roar back into gear.

She continues with her questions. "Was he an older man?"

"What difference does it make?" I ask, not waiting for an answer. "Older or younger, he shouldn't have treated me like that," I say, with fury in my voice.

"No, I'm sorry." She shakes her head. "I didn't mean it like that. It's just sometimes older people say things without thinking first. They are set in their ways, and they blurt things out."

"Yes, he was old, like my grandfather—before he died, that is." I glance out the window. "But that's not a defense."

"I'm trying to make you feel better. I guess I'm not doing a very good job of it."

"No, it's fine." I look back at her. "It's just that there were more instances like that one—I never talk about them. I've never shared that with anyone before, except for my sister, Taylor. I always felt different, until I met Eric; he treats me like skin color makes no difference."

"I'm sorry that happened to you. I think you're beautiful. I think every skin color is beautiful. They're all the same. If people say things about me, I just ignore it. I don't let it bother me." She shrugs. "I'm glad you felt you could share your story with me." She slowly blinks, with resolve. "I will make you an honorary girlfriend now. I don't have many."

I smile, knowing I shouldn't judge people. I was wrong about her having a lot of friends; maybe I'm wrong about her hiding something as well. I will just ask her about the information boxes and see what she says.

"I don't think the things that happened to you can all be blamed on skin color," she says. "You shouldn't think like that."

"I'll try not to." I chew the inside of my cheek.

"We're here," Whitney announces, as the car races into the parking lot of a large market.

The sign out front says: COMMON MARKET. The lot is not smooth and the spaces aren't defined. It looks like they started to repave the lot but never finished.

We have gone about twenty miles and have driven for a little over thirty minutes. I am happy to vacate the vehicle. My feet stomp as my shoes hit the ground. I take a look around. A block down from the market is a gas station. I only saw a few gas stations back in Territory L. The ones near my house were closed because we didn't need them. There were others closer to downtown, near the president's mansion, which her henchmen used to gas up their vehicles.

The station is blue and silver and the signage above is all in white. I see four pumps standing asymmetrically. Across the street from the market is a clothing store. The sign says: ORDINARY CLOTHING SPOT. Maybe once we leave the market we can go there to buy new clothing. Although I don't know how much we can get with the little money Julian gave me.

This part of Territory M seems more isolated than where Whitney lives. Whitney says Common Market is smaller than Mainstream Market. Mainstream Market is located in the middle of town and they have more upscale items to choose from—maybe like that fancy cheese I had at the so-called party President Esther threw for me. Common Market is near the outskirts of the territory and carries only the essentials; but that's all we really need.

Whitney belts out instructions. "Make sure you keep your sunglasses on and your cap lowered. Try not to speak."

Although I already know how to stay incognito, I listen to what she is telling me.

"Don't worry about using the money Julian gave you. You, and the rest of your group, will probably need it later for other things." Whitney takes in a breath, like she's nervous. "I'll use my money card for the things we need." She glances around.

"What's a money card?" I ask, while shutting the car door.

"We receive our paychecks in the form of a money card. Our paycheck is downloaded directly to our money card and we use that card to make purchases. Those in college trying to better themselves also receive a money card. The government places money on our cards to help us out while we are in school because they know we are trying to better ourselves and make it to Territory U."

"So, the money Julian gave me won't work here?"

I lower my head because I hear voices. I look out of the corner of my eye across the way and see a male and female around my parent's age coming from the clothing store. They both have on light colored clothes, which I'm not used to seeing. Pinks and yellows aren't worn back in Territory L. They walk a few steps to a lot next to the store and get into a gray vehicle. It's small and rugged and reminds me of the square boxy-shaped military vehicles I've seen in old magazines—of course, it looks more up-to-date. The outside shines with a glossy finish and I'm sure the interior features are similar to Whitney's mother's car.

"No, it still works here," Whitney says. I glance back at her. Her taupe leather flats scrape the ground as she walks over to my side of the vehicle.

"I can go to the local bank office and have them release some of the money from my card if I want to pay with coins or bills. But for larger items, like an information box, or food, or clothing items that amount to more than fifty dollars, they like us to use our cards. The purpose of the cards," she continues, seeing the confused expression on my face, "is so the government can keep track of our spending. We don't have tons of money like the people in Territory U, so the government tries to control our spending. If they feel we're spending too much in any given month, they cut off our cards and we can't spend any more until the next month. President Esther says she's doing it for our own good; some of us aren't good with money and we would overspend and end up poor and have to be shipped to Territory L. No offense." She glances down, then back up.

"Then why not use the cards for everything?" I ask, glossing over her 'no offense' comment. I'm not offended by her comment. I know I'm poor. I lean on the side of the car. "Why even bother to go to the bank and take money from your cards?" I'm ready for her to answer my question.

"Some of the gas stations don't have the special machines that are needed, and some of the stores don't either. The money cards are holographic and they are coded with your fingerprint. The special card machines cost thousands of dollars and some of the smaller businesses can't afford them just yet. Some of the smaller businesses are still saving up for their machines." She taps her fingers on the top of the side mirror of the car. "I hear President Esther has given them a deadline and if they don't have their machines by then, their stores will be shut down. Once the changeover happens, there will be no need for bills or coins anymore. Everyone who lives here will have a money card."

I feel a cold rush go down my spine. This money card thing bothers me. I understand President Esther wanting to help people so they don't overspend, end up losing everything, and have to go to live in Territory L; but something still doesn't seem right. I didn't think she cared anything about the people in L, so why would she care if people ended up there?

I bite down on my lip. I don't think the government should be able to see everything we spend our money on. I also don't think they should be able to cut our cards off if they feel we've spent too much. People should be able to decide what to do with their money on their own.

"Why is it so quiet here?" I ask. "It's kind of eerie."

I hear the loud motor of a blue vehicle pull up next to us. The car's front and back remind me of camel humps. There are humps over each headlight and a higher hump where the trunk and hood are. It has four doors, and the roof has a window on top of it. I adjust my cap. I pull it down even further on my forehead. A man, who looks to be in his upper thirties, exits out of the car. He stares at us for a moment, then slams his door and goes into the store without speaking.

"People also seemed more polite in Territory L," I say. I know I haven't encountered that many people here but something just feels off. I adjust my weight on the car and fold my arms.

"It's the end of August. Normally, the end of the month is when people start getting their cards cut off because they've over-spent. Around this time of the month, people aren't in the best moods. People start looting and stealing to get what they need. So, although there's no curfew—like Julian tells me Territory L has—it's best to stay off the streets during this time. Most people go to work, to the market, or wherever they need to go, and then hurry home so they won't be robbed." She pulls down the blue button-down shirt that she's wearing.

Her words cause me to pat the gun on my right hip. No one else sees it because of the oversized t-shirt, but I feel protected knowing it's there.

"You'll find more patrolmen out this time of the month as well, since they know people get a little crazed. I guess we should get inside. You are a wanted fugitive." She smiles.

She's right. We've been standing out in the parking lot of the market talking, like no one is searching for me. Thinking about extra patrolmen being out and about makes my skin crawl.

There is a squealing noise as the front door automatically opens so we can enter the store. My mouth drops. Whitney said this is the smaller market, but from what I see just standing in the doorway, it's much bigger than the one at home. We only have one market in Territory L, and it's located in the marketplace in the middle of town. It's about half the size of this market. You could fit our market, Mr. Thompson's pawn shop, and one of the clothing stores back home in it—if they were merged. I'm sure Mainstream Market—the one we passed up to come here—is almost three times as big as this one.

My shoes slam against the concrete floor as I follow Whitney inside. The fluorescent lights are bright. There are a few registers off to the side, and I see two clerks ringing up customers. They have on white shirts and dark pants. I notice near the front is a stand and a sign above it that says: INFORMATION AREA. Whitney grabs a cart from the carousel that's off to the side of the store. The cart is rectangular, black with a silver handle. The handle has buttons on it and wheels that glide along the floor.

"I wrote out a small list." She takes out a piece of paper from her blue jeans pocket. It crunches in her hands. "This should hold everything. We don't need much," she says, pushing a button on the handle. "The cart pushes itself. You walk behind it to control the direction you want it to go. If it veers off too much in one direction, you hit a button to get it back in line. You also hit a button for it to go backward."

I feel my eyes stretch open. I've never seen anything like it before. Back in L we had baskets we pushed ourselves and sometimes we didn't have that. Sometimes, if the store was full with shoppers, there weren't enough baskets to go around so you would have to carry what you could and come back another day for the rest.

I see aisles and aisles of rations. Back home, there are about ten aisles filled with food and supplies. But here, I see around thirty. We walk pass the breakfast section and I see boxes of cereal and cereal bars. I see different flavors of oatmeal, instead of the one original flavor we have back home. There's apple & cinnamon and strawberry & cream. I sniff and a whiff of strawberries enters my nose. There's another one called maple brown sugar, and I smell the maple through the box. Whitney stops and picks up something called oatmeal raisin bars. That's a specialty we don't have back home. Oatmeal that's crammed into a bar, I didn't even know such a thing existed.

We continue our strides to the next aisle where Whitney picks up several cans of soup. I feel my mouth twist as I look at the beans—it reminds me of the tons of beans we endured at home. Whitney grabs white crackers and wheat crackers. She drops bottles of orange juice and grape juice in the cart. The bottles clash as they hit the side of the cart. She says those are Adam's favorite juices. We could only afford one type of juice on our trips to the market, not two. I also see apple juice and cranberry juice. We didn't have those back home.

As we round the corner, we arrive at the snack aisle. The store is mostly empty, except for the man who came in before us and an older woman with gray hair who's pushing a squeaky cart. She has on a pretty bright floral dress and carries a shiny square pink purse. I push up my sunglasses as my eyes glaze over. I see items we never had at home—different kinds of cookies and snack cakes. There's an aisle filled with nothing but chips. There are barbecue chips, ranch chips, and something called kale chips.

"What do chips taste like?" I ask.

"They're good. Do you want me to buy a bag for you and your friends?"

"No." I shake my head. "You're buying enough for us already. I don't want you to buy anything extra. The money on your card is for you and your son—you shouldn't spend it all on us."

"I keep track of it. I know how much I spend and how much I save."

"If the government assigns the money cards to each individual," my eyebrow rises as I continue, "and they monitor what you're spending, then they know where you're spending the money. If they see you're at this out-of-the-way market, they will probably figure you were helping Julian out and—"

"I know what you're getting at," she says, cutting me off. "Don't worry, the tracking system here is slow. When I purchase an item, it doesn't go in the government's system immediately; it takes a few days. By the time they see what I've spent—and where—you and the rest of your group should be gone. If they question why I came here, I will just say I visited friends in the area and stopped here on my way back."

"That's good to hear." My chest rises and falls with my words. I just don't want her getting in trouble for helping us, but she doesn't seem worried.

We move over to the bread aisle. I run my fingers over the plastic exterior of a bumpy bread called rye. I feel the bumpiness of the grains, sticking out. Next, I come upon wheat bread. It looks just like the white bread we have at home, except it's darker in color—brown—and there are some white grains that glaze the top of it. The wheat and rye bread both smell like flour dough to me.

I move down the aisle and I smell different cheeses; the loaves next to the wheat are cheese breads. I touch the plastic packaging and feel the cheese protruding over the bread. It smells wonderful, like cheese and garlic. I could stand here all day taking in the aromas.

"We're almost done," Whitney says, as I follow her to the last aisle in the store.

"Whitney, do you know what aisle the sanitary products are in?"

"If you mean for Alexa," she turns toward me. "I already know…I have extra at home and I gave her what she needed."

"How did you find out?" I'm curious if Alexa went to her.

"I was gathering the garbage together from each room this morning so I could take it out to the dump. It's my responsibility once or twice a week depending on how much garbage we have. I noticed the bloody towel. I went to Alexa first, then I was going to come to you…but she said it was hers. I gave her supplies from my stash. She stuffed it in the pockets of her jeans, and she put some in her sweatshirt pockets. I have more I can give her—if she needs it, before you guys leave."

I'm glad to hear Alexa is all taken care of.

"We better get moving." Whitney turns from me.

My breaths get caught in my throat; we are at the baby food aisle. I see small glass jars of mixed carrots, green beans, peaches, and peas. My fingers tingle as I touch the jars. It's not homemade like what my mother had to make for Abigail. I'm looking at real jars of baby food. I saw baby food back at Whitney's…but touching the jars now makes it more real. I rapidly blink as my eyes water, thinking of baby Abigail. I still don't know where she is or if she's alive. The sunglasses begin to fog up.

"I'm almost done here," Whitney announces. I hear the clanging of bottles as she puts them in the basket. "Why don't you go to the back of the store where the refrigerated items are. Just pick up a container of whole milk and then we're done."

I'm not sure how she could tell my eyes are watering under these sunglasses, but I think she knows I'm not used to seeing baby food. Maybe she feels I can't handle looking at the jars and it saddens me because there are no babies in our territory. Or maybe she doesn't know anything and I'm projecting my own insecurities on her.

My mind is scrambling all over the place. Maybe I'm trying to forget about the jars I just looked at, but I think back to something she said earlier.

"Whitney, you said you took the garbage out to the dump. I didn't see a dump when we arrived."

"The dump is a few miles down from my house—so I suppose I don't really take it to the dump…but I put the garbage out back in a secure bag and a drone picks it up and takes it down to the dump two days a week. The government gives each house a monthly schedule so we know what days to put our garbage out."

"Drone?" My eyebrow rises.

"Yes, a drone," she says, like I should already know what that is. "They use drones in Territory M and Territory U for certain things. The ones in Territory U are more advanced." She looks from side to side because the gray-haired woman with the squeaky cart passes by us. "Anyway, they look like small toy helicopters... but someone commands them from a distant location."

My face scrunches up so she continues.

"It's like a remote controlled robotic vehicle that's able to pick up the garbage and transport it to the dump so we don't have to. The garbage can't weigh more than fifty pounds or the drone won't be able to lift it." She turns from me and continues grabbing jars of baby food.

I let her words sink in while I walk to the back of the store. In Territory L, we had to walk our garbage down to the actual dumpster—which was a mile from our home. The air is cool as I open the refrigerator door, making me shiver. I see whole milk and something called two-percent milk. I'm not sure what that is. I grab the whole milk because that's what Whitney asked for. The door slams shut. If I turn to the right I can go to where Whitney is, but I hear voices coming from the left. The voice sends a prickle up my spine; it sounds just like President Esther. I grip the cold plastic milk container tightly in my fingertips and forge ahead to the left.

There is some sort of doorway that leads to a stockroom. I walk in just enough to see an information box sitting on a stand. Light flickers from the box. No one watches the box but the sound blares.

My whole body shudders. I see President Esther standing at the podium. I haven't seen her in over a week. Her silver hair is still scary, and her eyes are still a piercing bold blue. Her mouth still tics up like a witch from a fairy tale. She's giving some sort of speech. Two of her guards stand by her side. From where I am, it looks like Jason, the tall guard who trained my brother, and Mike, the gray-eyed guard who tried to take me into custody when I went back to the mansion in L to look for the maps. The last time

I saw Jason his face was purple and badly bruised from his fight with Eric when we were escaping L—now he looks fine.

I wonder why she's on the box now. Back home, she only broadcasts her speeches on Monday nights at eight o'clock, when everyone had to be home—or at least stop wherever they were—and go to a box and listen. That is unless she had something important to say that couldn't wait until Monday; then loud sirens were heard and, once again, we were to stop and listen to what she had to say.

I wonder if it's the same here. I wonder if she gives them a special speech on a different night. I know she broadcasts to all three territories at the same time when needed—like she did during the party that was thrown in my honor. I also learned from Whitney in the car ride over that they have a special radio station here to broadcast the speeches on, but she changed the subject before I could ask her any questions about it.

I tilt my head in closer through the doorway to hear what she is saying. Her lipstick is ruby red and her mouth moves slowly. Her tone is still as crackly as I remember as I listen to her voice go in and out.

"Ever since Emma Whisperer fled Territory L with two of my disloyal guards, things have gotten out of hand here. I have stood at this podium every night and put out a warning that Emma should be brought in unharmed. The ingrates here have proceeded to tear apart this territory, so now that warning has changed."

The picture changes from President Esther's sickling pale face to pictures of Territory L. I see burned down houses and trees up in flames. I see people protesting in the streets with signs. I see those very same people being handcuffed and thrown to the ground by patrolmen. I blink a couple of times because I swear the camera now shows the pawn shop owned by Cassandra's grandfather—Mr. Thompson—up in flames.

"If anyone sees Emma in Territory M, I suggest you turn her

in to the patrolmen as quickly as you can or you will be brought up on charges along with her." I hear President Esther's voice continue. "The people here thought by burning, looting, and ripping down the territory I would change my mind and let her roam freely within Territory M; well, those people were wrong. Emma wants to start a war, to tear down the very walls that help us remember our place, the very walls that help us keep order. Now that my blood boils even more because of the cruel disobedience I have been shown, I have changed my warning. Emma can now be brought in harmed, just not dead. Once again, in case you didn't hear me the first time—Emma Whisperer," her voice gets louder as she uses my whole name, "can be brought in harmed. If you need to shoot her, stab her, tie her up—you can do just that. But she must not be dead."

Every bone in my body seems to go limp from the words she just said. I tremble. Her words terrify me. I now hear Rich's voice in my head. Vivid pictures go through my mind of his finger going down my cheek when he had me trapped in my cell.

Another flash comes of him grabbing my ankle and me falling to my knees when he brought me up to my new living quarters.

The last flash is when I shot him in the leg when we were trying to escape Territory L. I rub my head, trying to remove the thoughts of him; but I can't because I hear his voice. I glance back at the information box. It shows the townspeople rioting in the streets. There is no sign of Rich.

"Have you seen this female?" Rich's voice is louder now, like he's screaming in my ear.

I turn to my left over to where the information desk is and my legs buckle beneath me. I see him. Rich is here. I'm not dreaming or losing my mind. Rich is really here. My feet go numb. I want to run, but I can't move. Why can't I move?

"T-that's Emma," I hear the clerk stutter. "T-the girl the p-president is looking for."

"That's right, old man. Have you seen her?!" Rich shouts. He clicks his tongue like he's disgusted with the situation.

"N-no. No, I haven't seen her. No one matching her description has been in here," I hear the clerk say.

During their conversation, the clerk keeps flicking an index finger at beads of sweat running from his bald head, pass his horn-rimmed glasses, and into his widely stretched eyes.

My chest moves in and out, rapidly. I take in a deep breath to control it. I slowly take steps back until I'm safely hidden behind one of the aisles. The milk container is still gripped tightly between my fingers. My hand shakes. I place the container lightly on the floor. My shoulder jumps because someone touches it. I turn around to find Whitney standing there with a plastic bag in her hand.

"We need to go," she whispers. "Two guards are here asking questions."

"I heard them." My throat constricts.

"When you didn't come back, I got a container of milk, got in line, and paid for everything. I was coming to look for you, but then I spotted them at the information desk. If we bend down, stay low, and hide behind the aisles until we reach the front door, I don't think they will notice us," Whitney says.

"What if they do notice us? I think bending down makes us look suspicious." I shake my head. "You already paid for your items. We should just walk to the door and leave. They're busy conversing. Besides, as far as they know, we're just two shoppers minding our own business." I'm trying to show strength even though my knees are shaking.

My heart is beating in my ears. Maybe my disguise would have been good enough for a patrolman from this territory; but I've had so many encounters with Rich, he will probably recognize me right off.

I shot him in the leg. How is he even walking? Maybe the

bullet just grazed him. But I thought I saw blood coming from his leg. My mind is racing.

We slowly walk toward the door. I hear my shallow breaths as well as my shoes hitting the floor. We walk pass several aisles. We reach the front. Before the door automatically opens, I hear Rich's voice and my heart drops to my knees.

"Excuse me, miss." I hear his voice again.

My feet are frozen, like they are in blocks of cement. I'm not sure if he's talking to me or Whitney; but I know I can't turn around or he will recognize me—even with the sunglasses, he will probably still make me out.

Maybe this is my punishment for leaving the panic room. Everyone said I shouldn't go out; but I'm so bullheaded, I wouldn't listen. I thought I knew best. But in my defense, all I wanted was to get out and see if I could hear anyone mentioning the newbie camps. I wanted to get closer to Whitney and find out what she is hiding. I couldn't do that hiding in a panic room.

All and all, I did find out that the people are rioting in Territory L because of me. And President Esther now wants me brought in, harmed or unharmed. I'm sure Whitney knows these things and she's hiding them—that's why she claims her information boxes are broken. But why would she hide that info? Why would she hide anything?

None of that will matter if we are both taken into custody. I will be shipped back to the prison in Territory L, and Whitney will be punished for helping me. I'm deep in thought when I hear Whitney's shoes squeak as she turns around to walk toward Rich.

"Y-yes, sir." Her voice trembles.

Maybe she feels if his attention is on her, he won't look at me. Does Rich know who she is?

"You dropped this earlier when you were at the register," I hear him say. "It's some kind of list. It fell on the floor."

"Thank you," Whitney says.

I hear the paper crinkle in her hand as she takes the shopping list from him.

"Have a good day," Rich says.

"Thank you," Whitney says again.

How can he be so polite to her? It's like he's a different person. If he realized I was standing there, he would have pounded me into the ground.

Whitney doesn't wait for the door to open automatically. She pushes the door. It shrieks open, and I follow behind her. All I hear are our shoes scuffling the ground as we make our way to the car. The plastic bag rattles as she throws it in the backseat. Then, she puts the car in gear. The engine growls as we take off down the street. We are both silent for a while, like we don't know what to say to each other—or maybe we are both just trying to catch our breaths from what just happened.

I finally ask, "Do you know who that was back there?"

"He's President Esther's right-hand man. He's the guard she uses for her most important tasks." She takes in a breath and continues. "He comes to Territory M all the time to conduct business for her. Everyone knows who he is. But I had no idea he would be here, searching. I thought she would let her grunts do a menial task like that and leave him to handle more important things." Her eyes widen as she looks at me, then back at the road. "If he's looking for you, then you must be special."

I'm nothing special, just the most hated, I think. Especially in Rich's eyes.

"Does he know your Julian's ex-girlfriend?" I twirl my one long braid of hair around my finger. The conversation makes me nervous. "What if he recognized you?"

"I knew he would recognize you, that's why I turned around and spoke up first, so you wouldn't have to. He knows Julian has an ex-girlfriend, and he knows my name. But I don't think he knows what I look like. When the patrolmen came to search the house a few times to see if you were there, they were always patrol-men from my territory—Rich was never with them. I've never met him before; so unless he's somehow seen a picture of me, he wouldn't know what I look like. Even so," She turns the corner. "I think that's enough shopping for today. We will have to pick up clothes another time."

"I agree." My hand jerks. I glance out the rearview mirror to make sure we aren't being followed.

CHAPTER TEN

"This is why we didn't want you to go!" Julian screams at the top of his lungs.

We are all sitting in the panic room. I have already changed back into my black pants. The jeans were much too tight. I did keep on the oversized black t-shirt she gave me—it's more comfortable than the turtleneck. I also keep the rubber-soled shoes, since they are easier for me to move in. Whitney and I are sitting on the sofa next to Logan and Alexa. Julian stands in front of us, while Eric observes everything from the corner. Eric's glare on me is intense as he leans on the wall. I can tell he's not happy with what happened.

"What if you were caught?" he continues.

I know Julian's concern is more for Whitney than for me. Maybe he still has feelings for her, or maybe it's because she's the mother of his child. Whatever the reason, his face is as red as a fireball as he paces back and forth. He takes five even steps to the right, then turns and takes the same number of steps to the left.

Eric finally speaks. "Do you think he recognized you?" His eyes squint.

I move my head from side to side. "I don't think so. I just can't believe Rich was standing—walking even. I shot him in the leg. Maybe I only grazed him. I guess none of it matters now. He's here. But he only saw the back of my head. Whitney had the most interaction with him. She was the one he spoke to."

"I don't think he knew who I was. He's never seen me before." Whitney adjusts on the sofa.

"If Rich had recognized us, do you think we would be sitting here right now?" I say, with toughness in my voice. I want everyone to calm down, so I can discuss what I saw on the information box. "I think if he knew who I was, he would have taken me in on the spot. I'm surprised he's even here." I scratch the top of my head. "I expected to see patrolmen from this territory, not guards from ours. Even if patrolmen or guards from Territory L did come here, I wasn't expecting Rich—not after I shot him in the leg."

"Maybe he recognized you and he followed you here, so he could take us all in," Logan says.

"No one followed us," I say. "We were careful."

Logan rolls his eyes like he doesn't believe me. "If he catches us with you, we will be lumped in and taken in with you."

"You didn't care about that when you got in the truck and came here with us."

"She's right," Alexa says. "We all escaped the old college together because we had no place else to go. And it was nice of Emma and her friends to let us tag along with them. Who knows where we would be if they didn't. We could be doomed, like my brother." Her face saddens.

"Yeah, I know," Logan says, sucking his teeth. "Sorry, it's just this whole situation is starting to get to me. I ran away with my friends because we didn't like what was going on here." He stops talking and glances at Alexa. "But now, since we're with you..." he stops and stares back at me. "We are getting in deeper and deeper."

"If you don't want to take us to the Hill anymore—"

"No, I will still take you to the Hill," Logan says, cutting me off. "It's just hiding out with you is taking us to a whole different level. Runaways get a few months in jail...depending on the circumstance, sometimes a little more. But being with you might mean prison time—or death."

"If that's what you're worried about, then why would you still want to help me—or should I say us?" I look around at Eric and Julian.

"Because you want to talk to the leader to see if the walls can be torn down, and we believe in that cause," Alexa says.

"What she said." Logan nods his head. "Maybe, since you're the last eighteen-year-old that was allowed to live in your territory, they will listen to you."

"There had to be some reason that you weren't killed." Alexa bites her lip.

"Like I told you earlier, I heard them say if you made it to this territory they weren't supposed to harm you," Logan says.

"Yes, but you never told me who said that. You never finished your story. You also never told me what favor the president wanted from my parents, so they could go directly to Territory U," I say. I'm wondering what Eric is thinking because I never had time to speak to him about what Logan told me.

"That's because Eric walked in and interrupted us." Logan looks at Eric. "I have no idea what the favor was for the president. I do know that the watchmen were the ones I heard talking about you. And if they said that then, maybe you would be able to get through to the leader, because for some reason they don't want you harmed."

"That's all changed now." I glance around the room and stand. "When Whitney and I were out at the market, I was able to see an information box. It was on in a storeroom."

Whitney has a look of shock on her face.

"I saw horrible things going on back in Territory L." I sit back down. The weight of the conversation is making me sick. "People were looting and rioting, and I saw businesses burned down. Mr. Thompson's pawn shop was one of them."

I blink, thinking about Cassandra and her family. Cassandra was imprisoned and put in the jail cell next to mine because she was pregnant and her parents turned her in. Her grandfather, Mr. Thompson, owns the now burned down pawn shop.

"The President was making a speech and she said that she no longer cares if I'm brought in harmed—she just wants me brought in." My throat constricts. "She still doesn't want me killed though." I adjust on the sofa, turning to Whitney. "I know your boxes aren't broken…and I know you telling me the boxes upstairs shouldn't be touched was just an excuse. Why did you lie?"

Whitney clears her throat. "I'm sorry I lied. I knew what was going on back in Territory L. President Esther gave that speech the day before you got here. It's on a constant loop; they just keep replaying the footage over and over again. I didn't want Emma to know how bad things had gotten since she left home. Julian said she's a good person. If what he said was true, I knew she would feel bad about what's happening there and feel it is her fault. I felt like it would take her away from what she's trying to do here, and I didn't want that."

Her eyes are soft, and she talks like I'm not sitting right next to her. "I want you to carry out what you're doing here." She turns to me. "And not feel like you need to go back there so the rioting will stop."

"Can we see the footage?" Eric asks.

"Sure," Whitney says, standing. She walks pass the monitors on the screen. She goes to a portrait of a white boat floating on a blue sea that, frankly until now, I hadn't really noticed. She removes the picture from the wall. A square silver information box appears on the wall behind it. It pops as it turns on.

"The speeches are on channel three," she says, then pushes a button on the side of the box. "We also have a remote that you change channels with." The channels whiz in and out.

"You have other channels?" I pull on my ponytail. I've never seen other channels before. I'm nervous as to what they show. We only have one channel back home and it only shows the President's speeches.

"Yes." She nods. "We have seven channels here. Channel three is for the president's announcements. They broadcast old shows from back in my grandparent's day on four of the channels and the other three channels are streaming channels that come from the surrounding states where the other people fled to after the war— before the walls were built and we weren't allowed to leave. Those three stations stream new shows. There are dramas and some comedies. Streaming takes the video from live sources and broadcasts it over our boxes."

The box swooshes again as she continues. "We don't have a special speech night like I heard Territory L has or a siren that blares for us to stop and listen. When she wants to speak with us, our boxes just automatically turn to channel three. If our boxes are off, they automatically switch on and we are supposed to listen."

"What if you're out and not near a box?" Eric taps his fingers along his chin. "If there are no sirens and you don't even know she's speaking—what happens if you miss it?"

"It's not a big deal because they replay messages over and over, sometimes. Just like I said, the message about Emma is on a constant loop."

Whitney holds her stomach. Maybe she's worried about our well-being, because the message said to harm me. Maybe that's why she was intent on me not going with her.

"My parents tell me Territory U's information boxes have over one hundred channels. It's very grand there." Whitney continues, "They not only broadcast old shows, but they stream live shows from the surrounding states like here…and they have on-demand shows. That's where you can go on your boxes and watch a pre-recorded video twenty-four hours a day—and as many times as you like. I'm sure their setup to listen to President Esther is much like ours. They don't have a siren to make them stop and watch the speeches. But I'm sure they have a constant loop, so they won't miss anything either." She glances down, then back over at me. "Once again, I'm sorry." Her face saddens and she walks away from the box.

"Don't be. It's okay." I stand. She thinks it's grand there, while I think it's grand here. I walk over to the corner where Eric is.

The room is noiseless as we watch the constant loop Whitney was talking about. I've already seen part of President Esther's speech and the rioting going on there. The rest of the room is eerily hushed as they stare at the screen. Once the loop is done and starts to replay, I close my eyes for a moment, to pretend I'm somewhere else.

"You alright?"

"I'm not sure." I shrug. "Maybe Whitney's right. If I had known when the fighting first started, I would have been so upset I would have gone running back to help my family and all the others."

"And now?" His eyebrow rises. He takes my hand and gently squeezes. The warmth feels nice.

"Now, I'm so close to going to the Hill and talking to the leader here. I don't want to lose out on that chance. If I go back now, will the people really stop the rioting because I say so? Maybe they'll riot even more because she will take me into custody. I'm happy the people there finally found their strength, and they're not sitting down and taking President Esther's nonsense anymore." I squeeze Eric's hand this time. "But is looting and burning a way to show that? What about peaceful protest?"

"There's been peaceful protest before and that never seemed to work."

"Well, this isn't working either. It's making everything worse. How can they burn down the place where they have to live? If they ruin the territory, where will they go? I don't understand."

"I don't either." Eric removes his hand from mine and squeezes my chin. "But I guess they are doing what they feel is right and that's all any of us can do."

I know he means well, but I still don't feel any better. I feel nauseous. Maybe I should go home and try and help my family; but I also need to help Abigail who, I pray, is still here. So much time has been wasted; she could be anywhere by now. My main focus has to be on getting the leader to tell me where she is. And then, my next move can be negotiating the walls down.

Before I reply or finish my thoughts, I hear a loud buzzing that makes me jump. Whitney says it's the doorbell.

We look at the monitor that shows the front door. There are two patrolmen standing on the porch. My fingers go numb.

"They're p-probably here to s-search again." She flips on the switch for the bedroom monitors. "J-just in case they go up there, you'll be able to w-watch."

She reminds us not to leave the room, as if we didn't already know that. She slams the door behind her. We watch the fourteen monitors on the wall.

We watch Whitney open the front door. We hear and see them through the monitors. "May I help you?"

"We need to come in and search," a tall patrolman with dark hair says.

Another patrolman with beady blue eyes and light hair stands next to him.

"They've already searched here several times," Whitney replies.

"We realize that, but there are two guards here from Territory L and they would like to be involved in the search this time."

"Yes," Rich says, moving in front of the patrolmen. "Now that my partner and I have come here to search the territory, we are researching all the places the patrolmen have already gone. Do you have a problem with that?"

"N-no," her voice trembles. "It's fine. Come in."

Four men step into the foyer—Rich, along with Rob, the shorter huskier guard who also helped train my brother, and two patrolmen from here. Rob must have been at the market with Rich earlier. I was so nervous, I didn't even notice him.

"I saw you a little while ago at Common Market. I didn't know you were Whitney Flowers," Rich says. "Where is the young lady who was with you?"

My fingers—once numb—now tingle, knowing he's talking about me.

"That was just a friend who lives on the other side of the territory. I dropped her off before coming home."

I'm surprised at how fast Whitney thinks on her feet. By the hardened look on Rich's face, I don't think he believes her.

"Are your parent's home?" Rich asks. "I see the house is registered in their names."

"No, like I told the patrolmen when they searched the last time, my parents are in Territory U on business. Only my son, Adam, and I are here. He's at the babysitter's house, right now."

"So, Julian Harris hasn't come by to see his son?" Rich asks, more like an interrogator.

"No." She shakes her head. "I heard he's on the run. He wouldn't jeopardize me, or the baby, by stopping by."

I look at Julian and his eyes are big, like he feels bad because he has done just that.

"Fine then, we'll look around now," Rich says, then clicks his tongue.

I noticed him doing that at the market when he seemed annoyed.

"You will first show us the upstairs rooms," Rich continues, breaking my thoughts.

"Okay," Whitney says.

My knee shakes, watching them walk to the upper floor on the monitors. I know it's only on screen, but seeing Rich's copper red hair makes my skin crawl. We watch the monitors as they go in and check the adult bedroom and Whitney's room. We see as they go in Adam's room. Rich's green eyes go wide as he looks around the room. I have no idea what he's thinking. My brain races with all kinds of thoughts. Maybe he thinks babies shouldn't be alive in Territory M and that's why his facial expression dulls.

The door clunks behind them and echoes over the monitors as they leave Adam's bedroom. They go through the living room and the dining room and check the den. Rich and the others are unnervingly silent as they search all of the downstairs rooms. Rich overturns chairs and tables, as if he thinks I was stupid enough to leave something lying around.

They go in the kitchen and check the refrigerator and cupboards. Knowing Rich's mind, he's probably looking to see what kind of foods are there. Maybe there is something there that younger people my age would eat—then he could tell if we've been there or not. Maybe he's deciding if it looks like there is more food there than a normal three-person home with a baby would eat—that way he would decide that the extra food was for me or my friends.

"We'll check the basement next," he says, in a ruff, irritated voice. He's probably upset that he's not finding any evidence of us being here.

Whitney nods and leads them down the steps to the basement. Their boots trudge against the tile. The closer they get, the more my eye twitches. My heart stops knowing Rich is right outside the door. He's so close I would swear I hear breaths coming from his mouth—but I know that's just my imagination.

"You okay?" Eric asks, in a whisper. He strokes the top of my hand. Maybe he can feel the tension coming from my body.

"He's so close..." my voice fails me as I take a breath, in and out. "But I know there's no way he will find us in here," I say, reassuring myself before he can.

"That's right. He won't." He strokes my hand again.

I glance around the room and I feel the tension dripping off everyone else as well.

"The room back here has a pool table and my father's exercise equipment," Whitney says, "and a small bathroom." Her eyes quickly move from side to side.

Rich and Rob, along with the patrolmen, look around the room and check the bathroom. Whitney takes them to the next room with the washer and dryer. Then, she walks into the room with the bookcases. I watch the screen as Rich and Rob stand in front of the bookcase that hides the secret door.

"We don't see anything, so I guess we're done here," says the patrolman with dark hair.

Rich's teeth clench. "I'll decide when we're done here."

"Sorry," says the other patrolman with lighter hair. "He didn't mean to overstep." He glares at his partner.

Rich gives the room one last once-over. He stares at the bookcases for a minute, and I bite down on my lip so hard I taste blood.

"I want you two to stay here." He looks at the patrolmen. "Whitney, I will need you to show us out back to the garage. Rob, you come with me." He signals.

I can't see what's happening now. None of the monitors lead out to or show the garage. I'm just happy Julian moved the truck away from the garage—in the back alley. After the patrolmen almost spotted us at the market, Eric decided it would be best to take the truck out of the garage, in case someone came searching.

They parked it two houses down, behind a garage. The owners are in their eighties and never leave out the backway, according to Whitney. It won't be parked there for long—and with the privacy bushes in the way, the patrolmen won't be able to see it.

I can't help but wonder why Rich told the patrolmen to wait in the basement, right by where the panic room is. Does he know something? After about ten minutes, I see them making their way down the basement steps—stamping all the way.

"No one's here," Rich says, with disgust in his voice.

Apparently, he didn't go searching down the back alley.

He turns to glower at Whitney. "If Julian and his friends show up here and you don't report it, you know what will happen to you for hiding wanted ones—don't you?"

She nods. "Yes, I do."

"Rob, recite the laws again for her," he says, ignoring her answer.

"If anyone willingly hides or helps a wanted person, they can be thrown in jail for a minimum of thirty days, or more. If said person lives with their parents, their parents can be taken into custody as well. If this person—or persons—has babies they are trying to bring into Territory U, their application for Territory U will be revoked and their babies will be taken."

My jaw flexes. I never knew all of the things Whitney is putting in jeopardy to help us. I mean, I know the laws; but I never dwelled on what could happen to Whitney. Her whole life could be ruined because of our presence here. As soon as Rich and the others exit, we need to leave and go far away from here—before we jeopardize her freedom any further.

The front door bangs closed and I can finally breathe again. Whitney opens the bookcase and I watch as she crawls through it and opens the door to the panic room. Her face is flushed and little beads of perspiration lay on her forehead. I can only imagine what she was feeling while Rich interrogated her.

Julian stands. "We need to leave, now." His words are the very ones echoing in my head. His face frowns and his fists clench.

"I'm fine." Whitney holds out her hands. "I can handle myself." Her eyes squint and I see the lines in her forehead.

"That was too close. You could have been caught." His chest

rises then falls. "I don't know what I would have done if you were taken away and jailed because of me."

"Julian, it's fine."

The way they talk and look at each other, you would think they were still together. I feel like they think they are in the room by themselves and have forgotten we are all watching. I want to speak my peace but don't know if I should butt in.

"The next time they come around, we should be gone. I suggest we leave in the morning," Eric says, before I can.

"Sounds like a plan to me," Alexa chimes in.

"But if we leave too soon, the watchmen and the leader will still be up at the Hill." Logan's brows pull in. "They won't leave until tomorrow night, so they will be in Territory U by Monday morning."

"It's fine," Whitney says. "Stay here tonight and most of tomorrow, then leave tomorrow evening to go to the Hill. I doubt the men will be back before then to check the house."

"What if they do come back?" I ask.

"Then you'll be safe in the panic room, just like you were today." Whitney voice is strong and the sweat no longer aligns her forehead.

I like her spunk, but I still feel bad for putting her in danger.

"I'll have Mrs. Hutchings watch Adam, to make sure he's not in any danger. I'll tell her I'm not feeling well and would appreciate if she could watch him overnight," Whitney says before she exits the room with Julian behind her.

Alexa and Logan engage in conversation, while Eric grabs my hand to pull me over to the corner. I see worry lines under his eyes.

"Why didn't you tell me what Logan said?" He shifts his weight.

I play dumb for a minute, although I fully know what he's talking about. "You mean about me not being harmed?"

"No, you know I already knew about that when you blurted it out at the school. I'm talking about the other thing."

"Logan mentioned that before the patrolmen searched the house. Why are you just bringing it up now?"

"I've had other things on my mind." He sounds annoyed. "Answer the question."

"I needed to let it all sink in first." I rub the side of my cheek. "I couldn't believe my parents were keeping another secret from me. What favor could the president possibly want from them? Everything happened so fast. I haven't even had much time to dwell on it myself." I bite my lip.

"More importantly, I didn't understand why the watchmen or anyone in Territory M would have spoken about me over a year ago—or say I shouldn't be harmed if I come here. I wasn't sure if any of it was true, so I thought it best not to discuss it until I knew it was. Besides, there were so many other things going on, I figured that could wait."

"Do you trust me?" His glare is hard. "I realize we're still getting to know things about each other." He takes in a breath. "But I thought somewhere during the time we've been friends that you had learned to trust me."

"Of course I trust you. We've been through a lot together." I move closer. I rub the top of his forehead with my fingers. "You taught me how to stand up for myself."

"No, you already knew how to stand up for yourself." He moves his face and my fingers fall.

"Well, you taught me how to fight, how to defend myself, and I appreciate you taking the time to do that."

"No problem." He strokes my chin. "I enjoyed it."

The moment sends a shiver up my spine. Now, I feel like we're Whitney and Julian when they spoke to each other like no one else was in the room. All the things we have been through makes me feel close to him, and thinking of all the things we have yet to endure makes me feel even closer to him. I want to lean in and kiss him, but I know Logan and Alexa are still in the room—so I don't.

Our gazes hold for a moment. He leans in to my face as if he doesn't care that we aren't alone. I lean in as well, but my shoulders jump because the room goes dark.

"What happened to the lights?" I hear Logan shout. "The monitors are out, too," I hear him say.

The door squeals open. It's too dark to see. I'm guessing it's Julian and Whitney.

"The upstairs is out, too," Julian says. "The whole house is out."

"The power must have gone out," Whitney says.

"Or someone cut it," I hear Eric say.

"Where's Alexa?" I say, because I only heard four voices in the room.

"I'm here," she says. I hear a door thump behind her. "I went around the corner to the bathroom. What the heck happened?"

"We don't know," Eric says, roughly. "Whitney, do you have any flashlights? I had one at the old college; but in all the commotion, I must have dropped it somewhere."

"There should be a few in the table. If you can find it in the dark."

"I'll get them." I hear Julian's shoes squeak across the floor—closer to the table. The latch squawks as he opens the drawer. I hear him fumbling around—there's a *thump* and a *thud*. He takes out the flashlights.

I make out three small lights as they click on so he can make sure the batteries are working.

"The flashlights are half the size of my fists...but I think it'll be enough light for us to make our way around," Julian says. He conveniently finds the guys in the room and throws one to Eric and hands one to Logan.

I hear Alexa's voice. "So the females don't get one." Her voice is stern and she echoes the very words I wanted to say.

"Sorry, there's only three and I just figured—"

"You just figured the males can handle the situation better, so we don't need one," Alexa says.

"We don't have time for bickering," Logan says. "If you want to hold the flashlight that bad, then take mine."

"Just forget it," she says, with a snap to her voice.

"We should take a look around to see if this was done intentionally." The light pops as Eric presses the on button. I hear Eric's footsteps forging ahead, so I follow. "They've already searched the house and didn't find anyone. If someone did cut the power, then that means they know we're down here and they will be coming in here to get us."

"If that's the case wouldn't it be better to stay in here?" Whitney asks. "This place was built so no one could enter it."

"I agree with Whitney," Alexa says. "I think we should just stay in here."

"I don't trust it," Eric says. "I feel like there's some way they will be able to get in here—and then we'll be sitting ducks."

"He's right," Logan says. "I rather we find them, then the other way around."

"Let's go," Eric says.

"I really think we're safer here," Alexa says again, but everyone ignores her.

We all follow behind Eric. The door rustles open as he pushes it. We walk through the small crawlspace. There's another squeak as he pushes the back of the bookcase. Once the bookcase is open, we huddle together. The basement is so dark, it's hard to see where we're going. Eric flashes the light around and we see the steps.

We make our way to the kitchen, then to the den and the dining room. No one's there. Eric's flashlight circles the living room and we search all of the upstairs bedrooms. No one is there.

"This is crazy," I hear Julian say. "No one's in here. Maybe the power did go out on its own."

My heart races as I think crazy thoughts. What if Rich is somewhere hiding and leaps out as soon as he spots me? I can't stand to hear his voice in my ear or have his hot breath on my neck again. My hand trembles reaching for the gun on my hip.

We now all stand in the living room. Everything is still dark, except for the three flashlights, circling the room like stars in the sky. Alexa has on a white t-shirt under her unzipped hooded jacket. I make out her shadow easily from everyone else's as she moves toward me.

"I heard something outside," she says.

"Coming from which direction," Logan asks, pointing his flashlight in the direction of her voice.

"From the front entrance," she says.

"I'll check it out." Eric's shoulder brushes against mine as he makes his way to the front bay window.

I follow him. We crouch down in front of the window. The blinds clack as we move them a little to peek through. I see that the rest of the neighborhood still has lights; we are the only house in the dark. I also make out, through the lattice-style holes in the top of the gate, two large trucks parked in the driveway with lights dimmed. We see several dark figures, sitting in the trucks.

"I can't make out anyone, but I know one of them is Rich," I say. "Why are they just sitting there?"

"Maybe they are waiting a few minutes to make their move." Eric switches knees and crouches on the other one. "We need to make it out back to the truck before they come in here to get us." Eric takes in a breath.

"How do you suppose we do that?" Julian asks.

Eric stands without answering. He scans his flashlight around. I hear his footsteps as he walks over to the other dark figures in the room. I stay behind him.

"I saw a side door when we arrived. We could leave out that way," Logan says, "and just crawl to the garage, since the holes in the top of the gate won't completely hide us."

"I think the patrolmen will hear us if we leave out that way. The door is very loud. It squeaks." I hear Whitney's strained voice somewhere in the darkness, reminding me of Julian's words when we first arrived.

"Whitney, is there another way out of here besides that one?" Eric turns his flashlight toward the area her voice came from.

"There's a window in the kitchen that I think we could fit through. The den also has a back door, but we haven't used that door in years. The lock is broken and my parents never had the time to call someone to fix it."

I hear Logan's voice. "So, we can spend time we don't have trying to get a broken door open or we can see if we can squeeze through a small window. I say we take our chances with the squeaky side door."

"I think the window's our best bet," I say. "It doesn't squeak and it's closer to the garage where we need to be, in a hurry." My throat constricts. "We're wasting time. They'll be busting the door down any minute."

Whitney says, "Since the fence surrounds the backyard, if we crawl on the ground to the garage they won't see us. But we should stay to the left and out of the view of the driveway because we already know the top of the gate won't hide us. If the power is out in the house, I'm sure it's out in the garage; but there's a bypass. We can open the rear door manually."

He shines his flashlight on Whitney's face. "Won't they hear the front door rolling up?" Julian asks.

"We can crawl to the side door of the garage. If we go in that way, no one will hear us. Once we're inside, I'll jerk on the cord and unlatch the rear door. It won't matter if they hear it going up because we will be long gone down the alley before they get to us."

"How do we know they aren't in the back alley waiting for us?" Alexa asks.

"Rich checked the garage and there was no truck there," Whitney says.

"That makes me think that since they didn't find a truck they feel some of us left in the truck…but obviously they know some of us are still here—otherwise why would they still be sitting outside. They probably want to stampede the house from the front and catch the ones who stayed behind," I say.

I hear Logan's voice. "That's all speculation."

"I agree with Emma. That's probably why they are sitting outside…and will be in here any minute," Julian adds.

"I think Whitney's plan could work," Eric says. "But we should go now."

I nod, in agreement.

"Why don't you guys go ahead? I'll stay behind and distract them," Alexa says. "That way, I'll buy you some time to get away. While you're crawling through the window to the backyard, I'll go out front and make a run for it. Maybe some of them will chase me; and when they find me, I won't mention you all were ever here." Her speech is fast, like she's nervous. "I'll tell them I'm friends with Whitney. Since I'm on the government's list as a runaway, I'll say she was nice enough to hide me in her panic room."

"What will you say when they ask you why you decided to leave while they are sitting in the driveway?" I ask. "Which clearly means you knew you would be caught."

"I'll tell them I decided it was unfair for Whitney to keep hiding me and I kind of wanted to get taken in because I have nowhere else to go." She blinks. Either the flashlight is blinding her or the conversation is making her weepy.

"You would do that for us?" I ask. "You barely know us."

"Well, it's not all for you." She glances down and back up. "My brother was taken. If I'm taken too, then maybe I'll get locked up in the same facility they took him to. He's always been there for me and now I need to do the same for him."

Her words are touching. The thought reminds me of how I left my brother behind. Suddenly, my stomach feels queasy.

"That's nice and all," Logan says, "but there's no need for you to do that. If we leave now, I'm sure we can all get away."

I wonder if there is more to their relationship than just friendship. I know this is not the time to ask or to dwell on the subject.

"He's right," Eric says. "Let's go."

The carpet bends as we walk across it, making our way into the kitchen.

The three flashlights shine throughout the kitchen.

"Whitney where did you put the bag we got from the market?" I ask.

"It's in the cabinet under the sink. Why?"

"Shine your light over here," I say to Eric.

The light hovers over the cabinet. I rush to it. I tear the cabinet open and snatch out a bag.

"I'm going to grab a few bottles of water from the fridge. Maybe someone could get those oatmeal raisin bars you bought earlier."

"I'll get them; they're in the upper cabinet." Whitney snatches another bag from underneath the sink. Then she rushes over to get the bars from one of the cabinets.

The guys are still bobbing their lights all around the kitchen so we can see.

The cold air from the refrigerator splashes in my face. The bag crinkles in my hands and my fingers tremble as I throw in five bottles of water. I don't see any more and I don't have time to look.

"Good thinking," Logan says. "We may need that for later."

"Hurry," Whitney says. I hear the window screech as she opens it. She says there's a trick to unbolting the latch. "Since the power is out we don't have to worry about the motion lights in the back-yard being set off."

Eric goes first. He hands me the flashlight. I hear him grunt as he squeezes through. His shirt scrapes against the top of the frame. Once he reaches the ground, I hand him the flashlight and the plastic bag. He lightly places both on the grass.

I place one knee on the ledge. I twist my body until I lean one leg out of the window, then the other. He holds out his hands and grabs onto my waist. I plop down on the ground. I take a breath. He lets me go.

Whitney hands me her bag. Then I watch as she goes next. Once she's down on the ground, I hand her the bag back. Alexa and Logan plop down next. Julian goes last.

Whitney crawls in front of everyone. She takes the lead since she's familiar with the area. The plastic bag around her wrist swipes across the ground. We stay to the left like she suggests and crawl along the grass. The grass is freshly cut and low to the ground but smells like chemicals—pesticides probably.

I place one knee in front of the other and forge ahead. I make sure to stay clear of the area that the gate won't hide. The bag surrounding my wrist scrapes the ground as well. I'm not sure what time it is, but the sun is down and a half-moon sits in the sky. It is growing dim here. I'm sure in a few hours it will be completely dark.

My knees feel like lead as they drag against the hard ground. The only thing I see in front of me is the sole of Eric's boots. He's a few strides ahead of me. Alexa is almost next to me. I hear small breaths coming from her mouth. I hear grunts from Logan behind me. I know Julian is behind them. I can't hear any noises coming from him.

I'm used to running, not crawling and the dirt grinding into the palms of my hands feels gritty. Being so close to the grass makes me want to sneeze. I hold it in, knowing I can't make any sounds. As I crawl, I swear I feel a small bug creep across my hand.

"The side door's not locked," I hear Whitney say.

Eric's still ahead of me. I see his head move up and down in response to what she just said. We crawl a few more steps until we reach the garage. Whitney reaches for the knob without standing up, turns, and opens it. There is a small squeal but not so loud that the patrolmen or guards will hear. We keep crawling into the garage and the ground now feels cold and solid. Once everyone is inside, Julian closes the door. We stand. Julian, Logan, and Eric shine their flashlights across the garage.

"Logan, you should drive since you know your way around the off roads," Julian says.

Logan nods. He snaps off his flashlight and puts it in his pants pocket.

"Here are the keys." Julian throws them at Logan and they clink in his hands.

"I think it would be faster if I ran down and got the truck. It would take longer if we all went—"

"And I think it would cause too much commotion if the neighbors heard all of our footsteps stampeding down the alley," I say, cutting Logan off.

"Julian, shine your flashlight on the ceiling. I'll use the emergency bypass and disconnect the doors." Whitney rushes to the middle of the garage.

Julian's flashlight shines in her direction. There is a cream box plastered on the ceiling with a chain that hangs down. A red cord hangs from a bracket on the chain. She jerks on the cord and I hear a small snap. Julian still has the light shining her way.

"It should be unlocked now." She takes in a breath. "We can open the rear door."

Eric and Julian walk toward the door to help her. They use both their hands and lift the door. I hear grinding as the door goes up on a metal track. Once the door is halfway up, Logan glides under it and takes off down the alley. The grinding continues until the door is all the way up.

It seems like only a few seconds have gone by when I hear the motor of the truck blaring our way. Logan stops the truck in front of the garage. It's decided, since Alexa is the smallest, she will sit up front in the middle, that seat is smaller because it's the one that converts into an armrest. Eric hops in the front passenger's seat, next to her. I take the spot behind Eric, while Whitney slides in the middle next to me. Julian sits next to her, behind Logan.

Logan shifts gears and moves the truck forward.

"Maybe I should put the garage door back down," Whitney says, once we're out of the garage.

"We need to get going," I say. "The door will just have to stay up."

"She's right." Eric nods his head from up front.

I blink a few times, once again noticing how clean the alley is.

Once we're clear of the alley, I breathe a little easier. I'm sure everyone else feels the same. I glance behind me. Seeing that no one is following us makes my heartbeat slow down to a normal rate.

We continue driving for a while. To the left of me, I still see many houses and garages. As we make our way down the road, I see storefronts and businesses on my right. Logan says since we had to leave earlier than expected, we need to keep out of sight until tomorrow evening. Just until we are sure some of the watchmen have left with the leader to go to Territory U.

If I'm taken in to custody now and imprisoned back in Territory L, none of my plans will take place. I try not to think about the uneasiness in my stomach. I settle back in my seat and try to take in my surroundings.

Alexa turns around and looks at me. "You alright?"

"I should be asking you that." I look up at her. "You were will-ing to sacrifice yourself for us back there."

"It was nothing." She shrugs and adjusts her weight.

She's talking right by Eric's ear, so I know he hears us; but he turns toward the window like he's not listening.

"No, it was something. You didn't have to do that. I will always be grateful," I say, with a smile. "Thank you."

She smiles back. "You're welcome." She turns back around and looks ahead.

I notice Whitney is twisting her hands in a nervous kind of way. "You okay, Whitney?"

"My watch must have fallen off when we were crawling in the grass." She twists her right hand around her left wrist. "It's not important...it's just..."

Her words drift off as she glances down.

I know this is more about Adam than some watch that got left behind.

"I'm sorry," I say. "About everything."

She looks over at me but says nothing.

"I know this isn't how you wanted things to go. You were nice enough to hide us and now you had to escape with us." I take in a breath. This can't be easy for her and I'm sorry for what we put her through. "I know it was hard leaving Adam behind."

"She's right," Alexa says, turning around again. This time she turns to the left to face Julian and Whitney. "We should be thank-ing you. It's hard to lose a child."

"I didn't lose a child," Whitney barks. "I'm going to see him again, once this mess is over." She blinks away tears.

"I'm sorry. I didn't mean it that way." Alexa snaps her head forward.

"You will see him again," I say, trying to help the conversation. "At least you know he's safe at the babysitter's house right now."

My mind races. What if the patrolmen go pick up Adam

because she helped us and left with us? What if they take him away and kill him because of us?

"Yeah, but for how long?" She shrugs. "All I wanted to do was help you guys, not get caught helping you and be forced to leave with you." A tear graces her cheek. "But I know if I had stayed in that house, they would have taken me into custody because they knew I hid you all. Maybe this way, if I can talk to the leader of this territory, they will see how much my son means to me and that I don't have a prior record of wrongdoing. Maybe they won't bring charges against me or maybe they will lessen my sentence."

She's talking fast, like she's trying to convince herself what she is saying will come true. A minute ago she said she was going to see Adam when this mess was over, and now I think she realizes she may never see him again. She's babbling on and on, trying to see if there is a way out of this for her.

Julian is silent, but I know he hears our conversation. I watch as he takes Whitney's hand and slowly rubs the top of it. Whitney turns toward her window, and I turn toward mine. We don't know what else to say.

I don't know how else to comfort her, so hopefully Julian can.

CHAPTER ELEVEN

THE ROAD WE travel on has turned from smooth to bumpy. We have been driving for what seems like forty minutes, and it's dark out now. I still have no idea where Logan is taking us. Logan says the area we are going to is mainly deserted—meaning there are no stores up this way.

I did see a few markets, clothing stores, and gas stations during our drive here—probably about twenty minutes from here. But this area has none at all. It's a good thing we brought a few water bottles and oatmeal bars with us. We will need them when we get hungry.

Alexa has fallen asleep again like she did on the way to Whitney's house. Maybe long car rides do that to her. I see her head is leaning toward Eric's shoulder. The way my heart beats through my ears, I'm too nervous to sleep.

Whitney glares out of her window, probably wondering what will happen to Adam if she doesn't return. She can't be certain. I don't know if they will give him to her parents when they return from Territory U, or if they will hold him in custody for an illegal adoption, or if they will kill him for her disobedience.

"This is where we will stop and hide out. I will park here until morning, and then we'll move to a spot that I know," Logan says.

We stop in a wooded, out of the way area. There are enormous trees around that hide us from anyone's view. Good thing the truck is good off-road, as Julian says.

"I used to come here sometimes during my lunch breaks from work to think and such. It's quiet and no one's around here," Logan says, slouching down more in the front seat.

"I suggest we get some sleep while one person stays awake as the lookout," Julian says.

"I'll take first watch," Eric says. I see him sit up straighter in his seat, like he's gearing up for a long night. "I'll stay outside in the flatbed. I'll have a better view from there and the fresh air will help me stay awake." He slams the door as he exits.

I try to close my eyes, but all I see is baby Abigail and the rest of my family back home. Maybe suffering or in agony and pain.

* * *

Sunday morning has come and gone and no one has found us. Logan was right about this spot being deserted. It's my turn to watch the surroundings from the flatbed. None of us have watches on since Whitney lost hers, so I don't know what time it is.

I do know I've been up here for a few hours. The sun was bright when I first got up here and now dusk is setting in, so I know Sunday night is upon us. I haven't heard or seen anything, but the air smells musty.

One by one during the night, we went off into the woods to dig a hole in the ground and relieve ourselves. I'm glad there is a shovel among the supplies in the flatbed. I used my water bottle to wash my hands afterward—not sure if everyone else did the same.

My stomach is growling again. I ate my granola bar earlier, but I'm hungry again. I wish we would have grabbed more rations to bring with us.

I sit up and dangle my legs over the side. I hop down into the grassy area.

"Does someone want to take watch now?" I look into the front window of the truck at Eric. His window is down and he turns to look at me.

Everyone but Whitney has had a turn. She wanted to lookout, but Julian said there was no need for her to. Maybe he's worried she's not up for the challenge because her thoughts would be distracted over baby Adam.

"I can go." Eric swishes open his door.

"No need." Logan stomps toward the truck.

The wind from his body gusting toward us brings a breeze to my face. My guess is he was out at his makeshift bathroom.

"We can get ready to leave now. It's dark enough now. A lot of the watchmen and the leader should have already left for Territory U."

My mind instantly goes to Rich. I hope he found his way to the leaders' meeting along with the others.

Logan slaps the hood of the truck as he storms by it. He swings open the driver's side door. "Let's do this," he says, slamming the door closed.

I open the back door and jump inside. I look over and see Julian stroking the top of Whitney's hand. Whitney remains quiet as the engine roars, and we take off down the uneven road.

* * *

I'm not really sure but it feels to me like we've been traveling for about fifteen minutes. We're still using the backroads. My body sways from side to side and moves along with every bump we hit along the dark path.

"I think we should be able to get on the main road now. It's just ahead…and it will take us to the Hill," Logan says, turning the wheel to the left.

The truck sways and my body shifts with it. We pass several

more large trees. I see the main road up ahead. There are street-lights that align it. The tall, large, oval-shaped streetlamps shine so brightly that it helps bring light to our area.

I need some fresh air, so I hit the button beside me. The window squeaks going down. The air still smells musty, like it did when I was on the bed of the truck—even so, I try to lay my head back on the seat and rest. I hear a loud noise and my shoulders jump. It sounds like crying and tires squealing.

"What was that?" Whitney shouts in my ear.

"There's a large black van up ahead on the main road." Logan sits up, straighter. I see his eyes shift from side to side through the rearview mirror.

"It just plowed right by," Eric says.

Alexa sits up from her slouch.

"Maybe we should stay on the backroads," I say.

"We have to get on the main road, eventually, to make it to the Hill. We will just let the van gain a little distance and then we'll continue on, to get on the main road." Logan strokes his fingers on the wheel. The truck slows down. He stops the truck and turns off the motor.

"Where do you think the van is rushing to? And why did it sound like someone was crying?" I ask. "What else is around here?" I glance around, still seeing the woods surrounding us and several trees. Some trees look dead with no leaves, while others have an abundance of leaves and appear vibrant.

"There's not much." Logan shrugs. "Once we get back on the main road, we will be at the Hill in ten minutes," Logan says, then pauses.

The moon is out now and there are a few stars in the sky.

"But if we stay in the wooded area and keep driving, there's a large gated area. Only the watchmen and patrolmen are allowed in there," Logan continues.

"Logan, you never said what your job involved here." My jaw twitches. "I assumed you used to be a watchman."

"No, I was on the cleaning staff. I cleaned some areas in the mansion and also in the executive buildings. I wasn't allowed in all areas of the mansion…some areas are restricted. I quit because I was sick of picking up after other people. I never had access to certain areas, especially the gated area beyond the woods."

"What's on the other side of the gate?" Eric asks.

"Some kind of camp." Logan shrugs, again. "I've heard some of the watchmen talking about it."

I've only told Eric and Julian about the newbie camps. I wonder if Logan knows about them, too. Now my jaw stops twitching and tightens.

"What do they do there?" I ask.

He turns around to look at me. His face scrunches up, as if he's confused. "I don't know."

"We have to get in there to see what's going on." The lever pops as I open my door. I jump down in a huff and dust wafts up my way. "How far is it?" I look back at everyone else still sitting in the truck. "It must be close. I can still hear crying from here."

"A little under a half a mile from here…down to the right." Logan edges his head to the right.

"Wait a minute." Eric's door rustles open. He jumps down and turns toward me. "We don't know what's going on in there." His face is hard. He places his hand on my chest to hold me back. "We don't even know if that's where the newbie camp is."

"Newbie camp," Whitney shouts. "What are you talking about?"

"What's going on?" Alexa asks. "What's a newbie camp?"

"I thought you wanted to speak to someone about getting rid of the walls. You wanted to look around and find out if you could find any weakness to use against the leader." Logan's eyes widen. "You never said anything about finding a newbie camp."

"Julian, did you know about this?" Whitney asks.

"What is the newbie camp?" Alexa asks, as if we didn't hear her the first time.

"We're wasting time," I shout. I push Eric's hand from my chest. I stomp pass him, but he grabs my elbow and pulls me back.

Logan and Julian plunge down from their sides of the truck. Alexa stamps down as well from the door that Eric left open. Whitney slides over and jumps out, too.

"Would everyone stop squabbling?" Julian says. He holds his hands up. "We're not going to get anywhere like this." He's trying to be the voice of reason. "We're all in this together now, so we might as well tell everyone what's going on."

"I agree." Eric nods. "We heard of the newbie camp while we were back in Territory L." His eyebrows slant together. He looks at me and then back to the others. "Emma, found some papers, and she thinks that's where they take the newborns to kill them."

"Yes," I say, chiming in. "If you must know, I think that's where they took my niece, Abigail. It's been a few weeks since they took her. I need to find her before they do something to her."

"So we're all supposed to just run down to some camp we've never even heard of and expose ourselves to the watchmen and risk being killed." Alexa rolls her eyes. "I think we should just get back on the main road."

I shake my head. "No one's asking you to go." A lump is in my throat. I'm surprised at her harsh attitude. "Besides, it's best if only a few of us go and look around. Eric and I will go with Julian. Logan, you stay here with Alexa and Whitney until we get back."

"This is crazy." Alexa folds her arms. "You're going off on a wild goose chase, and you're going to get us all killed. Why would they slay the children in the woods at some stupid camp? From what I've heard, when they find a baby in Territory L they shoot them on the spot and take their remains somewhere else. Why would they drag them all the way here? It makes no sense."

"I kind of agree with her," Whitney says. "I mean maybe the

babies they take from here," she pauses, and blinks. I know she's probably thinking of Adam. "They would bring to this camp you're talking about, but why bring ones from L, way across the territory?"

"Because they don't bury them in Territory L," I say, shaking my head. "So maybe the midpoint burial I saw on the map next to the newbie camp is where they bury them. Maybe they figure they can bury them next to where they kill them, so it's convenient."

Alexa rolls her eyes again. "That's a lot of maybes and no facts."

"This is all so morbid," Whitney says. "I'm sick of talking about it."

"Whit," Julian says. His eyes focus in on hers. "It's going to be okay. Adam's going to be fine."

Somehow, with my own problems going on, I keep forgetting Adam is Julian's son, too. He must be as torn up as she is over leaving Adam behind. He just masks the pain better than she does.

"If we're going to do this, we need to go now while it's dark." Eric touches the side of his hip. He lays the palm of his hand over his gun.

I nod my head, in agreement.

Whitney and Alexa, disgruntled, get back in the truck while Logan stands watch.

"Take this." Julian hands Logan his Taser but keeps his gun. "That's in case you need to defend yourself." His face saddens as he glances back at Whitney.

"Let's go," Eric says.

"Wait, I'm coming with you." Whitney hops back down.

"I don't think that's a good idea," Julian says. "We don't know what's out there."

"I need to see this newbie camp Emma is talking about."

"Why?"

"If Adam will be taken there because of my wrongdoing, I

need to see where it is." Her breaths sound as if they're getting caught in her throat.

"No, I can't let you do that." Julian shakes his head. "Besides, we don't even know if that will happen."

"I have to."

I stomp my foot. "We're wasting time. Just let her come already."

"Emma's right. We need to go before someone sees us," Eric says.

"Fine." Even in the darkness, I see the tension in Julian's eyes.

I lean down. I follow Eric down the wooded path. Julian and Whitney are close behind me. My stomach is in knots as we stay low behind trees. I feel crackly grass and hard rocks beneath my shoes. We keep running in the direction we heard the noise coming from.

"Watch the holes," Eric says. "My foot just stumbled over one."

Now that we're farther away from the main road it's darker and hard to see. I stumble over a soft spot in the grass. It feels like the soil has been dug up by a small animal. The one I stumbled over wasn't deep but who knows how many are out here and how deep some are.

"Eric, hand me your flashlight," I say.

"What for?"

"Just give it to me."

He hands it over to me. I click the light on. I look down at the hole. This one is the size of a large apple. I snap off the light, and place the small flashlight in my pants pocket. "Keep moving but be careful." I look back at Whitney and Julian.

I touch the necklace that is under my t-shirt. I've rarely acknowledged its presence around my neck since we've been here, but right now I need to know it's still with me. Maybe for comfort because my mother gave it to me or maybe for some stupid superstition that it brings peace and hope and it will make everything okay. Whatever the reason, I just need to know it is still there.

My breaths feel heavy as we continue down the dark path. I'm trying not to step in any of the holes. The crying and shouting I heard earlier has stopped, so I don't know if we're going in the right direction or not. I hear a blast that shakes the ground. My body shudders. It's coming from the area we are approaching. I now know we are still going the right way.

"Over here." Eric nods his head to the right. "There's a fence. Stay low." He grunts as he bends down to his knees.

He crawls through the grass and Julian, Whitney, and I follow. I don't feel any shallow holes beneath the soles of my shoes in this area. Maybe they never figured someone would be foolish enough to get this close, so no holes to make you change your mind and go back are needed.

I swat an insect that lands on my cheek. I wave away another one that is near my arm. I see a large gate about fifty feet ahead, but I don't see anyone surrounding it. No guards, no patrolmen, and no watchmen. There's only a chain-link fence that looks to be about twelve feet in height. It surrounds the entire area.

My face tenses. Why aren't patrolmen guarding the area? Is this some sort of trap we are walking in to? But how would they know we were coming? No one knew I found out about the camp or the burial grounds, so they would have assumed I was coming to the Hill to speak with someone.

I'm back in reality now, and I notice the ground smells like wet grass and the air is thick. We are right up at the fence. I bend on my knees and lace my fingers along the diamond shapes of the fence. My heart jumps because I hear loud voices. To the far right, I see a large square green garbage dump.

"Let's hide behind there." I point. "So no one will see us." I lean down. I crawl on my hands and knees again.

I feel the wetness of the grass seep through my pants. Eric, Whitney, and Julian are beside me as we reach the dump. I lean my hand against it and it feels cold against my fingertips.

"Why are you just standing back here? I know you heard the van pull up," a deep male voice says.

"Why do the guards from L always have to drop off the babies at night?" I hear a squeaky voice say. I wonder if they are watchmen.

"You act like you're brand new," the other male with a deeper voice says, sounding annoyed. "You know it's so we stay under the radar, and no one will see the babies being processed through the territories."

"I know. I'm just sick of getting stuck with this job."

"You only have to stay at it for six more months, then you'll have the chance to move up."

"It won't be soon enough for me."

"I don't mind it. It pays well. The babies are well fed, so they are relaxed and mostly out of it when they get here."

"How many are they bringing over this time?" the one with the higher voice asks.

"The list says five babies, three males and two females, and one six-year-old female."

My shoulders stiffen. Some poor family got away with hiding a child for six years. Now they're going to kill her. How is this even possible?

"That must have been the six-year-old we heard squealing as the van arrived," the deeper voice continues. "We don't get many kids that age. Sometimes, they don't give them the right dosage of chloroform to keep them relaxed for the entire ride over." He chuckles like the horrid conversation is funny. "They should know by now to keep the windows rolled up until they get here. We should get up to the front. They're probably unloading already."

"This is madness," I whisper to Eric. He says *unloading* like they're moving supplies instead of drugged out children.

"We need to get closer, so we can see what's going on," I say, pointing to an area a few feet away on the right. There are four large blue metal outhouses up against the far right side of the fence.

Once the men are out of view, we sprint over to the outhouses. We hide behind them. I sit up on my knees again and lean against one of the outhouses. The smell leaves nothing to be desired. The air shifts and the stench of urine pierces my nose. I peek between the space in between two of the outhouses, and Eric peers behind the other one. Julian follows by looking behind another one. Whitney is right beside him.

We're close enough now that we see them unloading the van. I see the two men we heard speaking a minute ago. Even though a towering light that reminds me of a streetlight shines down. It's still too dark to make out any of their features, but I see that one is tall and the other one is medium height.

Two more men appear, and I know who they are right off. It's Jason and Mike. I saw them on the information box with President Esther when I was at the market. Now they are here, disposing of babies.

"The babies that President Esther decided to keep have already been transported to their final destinations. We have the ones that aren't worthy of being kept," Mike says. He's standing at the back of the van. The rear doors are already sprawled open.

My chest tightens. I only pray Abigail is what they call *worthy of being kept.*

I see babies in tiny car seats, lined up in the back. We never had one for Abigail because we don't have cars. Besides that, we never took her out, since she was always hidden. I've seen pictures of car seats in old magazines that my mother had.

I also see one larger figure—that must be the six-year-old. Both guards hand the car seats to the two watchmen until there are five that lay on the ground.

"This one woke up when we were almost here," Mike says.

"It made no sense to chloroform her again." Jason grabs the

little girl. He holds her by her waist. Her legs are kicking back and forth. "Since we would be giving her the ultimate drug once we got here." He hands her over to Mike. "But once we opened the rear doors, her screams echoed so loudly we grabbed some tape from the glove compartment and used it to cover her mouth. We needed to keep her quiet before letting her out of the van."

Mike takes her and plops her on the ground like she's a rag doll.

The little girl has two pigtails. I see her shoulders bouncing up and down. Her mouth is taped shut, but it doesn't stop the whimpering; it makes the acid in my belly rise.

I hear Whitney's breaths behind me. No doubt, she's probably thinking of Adam.

"Remember back when we would just shoot them and throw the remains in a shallow grave," Jason says, with laughter in his voice.

"Yeah, there's no fun anymore since President Esther decided she wants everything done in a neat, quiet, tidy manner."

"Can we get this over with," the watchman with the deep voice says, like he's irritated with their laughter—even though he was the one doing the chuckling earlier. "I have the briefcase here."

I see a square black case. He pops open the latch. Even though it's dark, the light shines down and I make out a large white syringe.

"Let's start with the oldest child, since she's not in a drowsy state," the watchman with the higher voice says. "That way, she won't have to see what happens to the others."

I see the other watchman take the cap off the syringe. I'm not close enough to see everything. I can only imagine how large the needle attached to it is.

"Bring her closer," the deep voice watchman says.

I hear her shoes scrape against the ground as the guards shove her closer. I hear her whimper, like a small puppy, as they each take one of her arms and hold her down.

I can't let this happen. What if Abigail is in one of those five car seats? That's if she isn't already dead. I blink. Tears want to run down my cheeks like a faucet, but I can't let them. I reach for my gun. I rub my hand across the cold metal. I go to stand, but I feel a warm hand grab mine and yank me down to the ground.

"Whisper, you can't," Eric mouths.

"We can't just let them kill her—or the others," I say, whispering.

"He's right," Julian says, in my ear. "You can't go running over there or you will be captured. There are four of them—"

I cut him off. "And four of us."

"Look, you know Whitney doesn't have a gun, and she hasn't been trained to fight like you have. So, the odds are against us. Besides, we're running out of ammo. I never had a chance to pick up more. If we start a shoot-out with them, we will lose when we run out of bullets. We need to save our bullets for when we really need them."

"We have to at least try. What if Abigail is over there and I don't at least try? What about the other babies over there? What if Adam was over there?"

"Don't bring Adam into this." His expression hardens.

I hear Whitney's soft breaths on the side of me.

"Of course, I would want to save him, along with all the others," he continues. "But we have to be sensible. The gate to get inside the fence is clear on the other side. They will see us before we even get over there and—"

"If we try to climb the fence from this side," Eric finishes Julian's sentence, "they will see us before we climb halfway over it. We have to just sit tight and look out for the bigger picture. We have to let a few die, so we can save many. We have to just hope Abigail is not over there." He touches my face. "What good does it do anyone, if you're captured right now?"

I feel like I'm going to vomit. They would probably kill Julian and Whitney, along with Eric, and chain me up and take me back to President Esther. My throat tenses. I know I can't let this happen. If Abigail or any other child is killed because I am afraid of being captured, I would never be able to live with myself.

Eric and Julian are staring over at the men behind the fence, while Whitney is looking down at the ground as if she's trying to hold back tears. I go to stand again. I've decided to shoot my gun in the air. The loud noise will make them look over at me; and when they see who I am, I'm sure they will come after me. I know Eric and Julian will be mad. But once I've done it, there will be nothing they can do about it. And maybe they can run and save the children from being injected.

Before I stand, I hear a loud banging like thunder in the sky. It's coming from over where the garbage can is.

"Brett, did you hear that?" the watchman with the high voice says.

"It's coming from over there." Even though the noise is to the left of us, Brett points in our direction. I squat down and so do Eric and Julian. "Hey, who's there?" he shouts.

"Let's get out of here," Julian says.

We jump up. We run toward the garbage can. My heart feels like it's beating out of my chest. It beats even faster because we're running in the direction the noise was coming from—we have to go that way to get to the truck. I hear Eric's footsteps trudging next to me. Julian and Whitney are behind me. Their breaths are low like mine are. My gut jerks because I see Alexa running from the area where the garbage dump is.

"W-what are you d-doing out here?" Eric says, through jagged breaths. "You were supposed to s-stay at the truck."

"I was coming to find you guys," Alexa says. "Something's happened."

"What's going on?" I ask. My voice fades in and out. Much

like hers does. She's talking fast and her face looks intense; yet we also need to be worried about the men behind us.

"We could see headlights far off in the distance. We need to get out of here—now."

"Where's Logan?" I ask. I glance behind me. I don't see the men following us yet. They were standing in the fenced-in area. It's probably taking them a while to get down to the gate to come after us.

"He sent me here to get you. He said we have to hurry," I hear her say, interrupting my thoughts.

We start striding faster now. "Try not to stumble over the holes!" I shout, just now remembering them myself.

I don't see the truck up ahead, yet. We still have a ways to go. We're on the dark path in the woodsy area. We're trying to weave around trees and not step in holes. Eric and I are in front. Alexa is close to us. Julian is behind us, trying to make sure Whitney keeps up.

I hear a *thud* behind us.

"Whit, get up," I hear Julian say.

I hear Whitney's strained voice. "I can't. Something's holding my ankle."

I stop running and so does Eric. "What happened?"

I see Whitney and Julian standing near one of the trees.

"Her foot stumbled into one of the holes," Julian says.

"Well, help her get out of it," I say.

"She didn't just stumble over it. Her foot pressed down in the hole and now she's stuck." Julian says in a rough tone.

I snatch my flashlight from my pants pocket. I shine it downward, in the direction of Whitney's foot.

She's trying to yank it up. It won't budge. Julian pulls on it as well. He can't get it out of the hole. I lean down. I grab some of the dirt surrounding it with one hand, and try to shove it out of the way. The dirt and grass feels grimy under my fingernails. My breaths are all over the place. I know the men will catch up to us soon.

I flash the light into the hole with my other hand. I see a silver trap enclosed around Whitney's right ankle. The trap looks like the kind they used to set back home for critters like skunks or squirrels that hung around the farms trying to steal food. The large metal teeth grip her ankle. I see blood staining the area.

Tears fill her eyes. "It hurts," she says.

"We have to get it off, now!" Julian screams. "Maybe we can shoot it off."

"That won't work. You'll only hit her ankle in the process," I say.

"We have to do something!" Julian yells.

"Help me pull on it," I say, bending down.

I put the flashlight in my mouth and hold it steady with my teeth, while I grip my fingers around part of the trap. Julian and Eric do the same. But there's no smooth place to put my hands. All sides are surrounded by metal-looking teeth. I can't get a good grasp on it.

"This isn't working," Whitney cries.

"We have to think of something else." Alexa is still standing. I see her head bobbing, to search for where the men are.

I remove the flashlight from my mouth. "We need something hard and sturdy to bang on it with," I say. "Maybe we can knock the teeth loose."

"There is a shovel and some other stuff back on the truck," Alexa says.

"There's no time to run and get it." Eric smashes his hand across his forehead. "The men will be here before one of us gets there and back."

Sweat is pouring from Julian's face. "We have to think of something else."

"There is nothing else." Whitney plops down on the grass. Her face looks defeated. "You have to leave me," she says softly. Her right knee is bent up to her chin. The metal still surrounds her right ankle.

"That's crazy talk." I point the flashlight her way.

Julian winces. "We're not doing that."

"You have to. It's the only way," Whitney mumbles through tears.

"They will be here soon." Alexa is still keeping watch. "I make out figures, coming this way. It's inhumane to leave her. Emma, maybe you should stay. You're the one they really want anyway."

"You have to leave," Whitney says, ignoring Alexa's comment.

"I'm not leaving you," Julian says.

"They won't harm me." Tears stain Whitney's face. "They'll only put me in the jails for helping you. I'll be alright. L-look at it t-this way. If they are distracted with me, you can get away and w-when you find the leader maybe you can talk them in to letting me go."

"She's right," I say through gritted teeth, because I don't want her to be. "If Rich finds us and takes us back to L, we'll never get to speak to anyone; but if we speak to someone before he does, maybe we can talk them into letting her go—letting us go."

"Are you insane?" Julian barks. "I'm not leaving her. You three go. I'll stay with her."

"Julian, no." Whitney's face is suddenly strong. "You'll be taken in for bigger crimes; maybe even killed because you were a guard that escaped L. All I did was hide you, so I'll only be jailed—hopefully, only until you get me out. It won't be that bad."

"You can't know that," Julian says.

"Whatever you decide, we need to do it now." Eric looks around the side of the tree.

"We can shoot at them," Julian says, grasping at straws.

"You just said we don't have much ammo. They would win any shoot-out we start." Eric is still swiveling his head back and forth.

I hear pounding behind me. I glance over and see male figures running in our direction. It's dark. I can't tell if it's Mike and Jason or the two watchmen. They are still several feet back.

"Please, Julian go—just go, now. If you stay here and you're killed, Adam won't have a father and I will never forgive you."

"But Whit—"

"Just go…please."

He leans down and kisses her forehead. "I'll get you out." He stands.

"I k-know you w-will."

"We'll make sure we talk to someone about getting you out," I say, repeating Julian's words. I snap off the flashlight. I shove it into my pants pocket.

"I know. I trust you." She nods, glancing over at me.

My stomach is in knots. I turn and sprint off. "We need to move faster!" I shout.

I hear loud blasts. They are shooting at us now. I hear another shot, blaring in my ear. It makes me look to the side. Julian has stopped and is shooting his gun.

"Julian, w-what are you doing?" I say, slowing down my pace.

Eric's voice is strained from our run. "You know w-we don't have much ammo."

"None of that matters now…you go ahead. I have to try." Julian voice is behind me now.

I keep forging ahead. I leave him standing there. I hear three more bangs until he's all out.

My breaths are unsteady. I sprint as fast as I can to the truck. Eric and Alexa are behind me.

We keep racing until we reach the truck. Logan is already inside with the motor running. He sees us up ahead and brings the truck the rest of the way to us. I take it he heard the loud blasts as well.

I whip open the passenger's door. I jump inside. Eric opens the right rear door. Alexa hops in. She slides over while Eric glides in next to her. He slams his door closed.

"They c-caught Whitney in a trap," I say. "We couldn't free her and Julian…well, I don't know—"

"Is Julian coming or not?" Logan asks, cutting me off.

We all sit in silence because we don't know. I still have my door open in case he comes; I will slide over and let him in.

"I can't sit here forever or we'll all be taken in." Logan presses on the gas. The truck moves a few paces forward than stops as he releases his foot. My door jerks. "Sorry if you don't agree, but we need to move." The motor blares as he steps on the gas again. I slam my door closed this time.

Before any of us respond, Julian stampedes to our left.

"Stop the truck!" Eric shouts.

The brakes screech as Logan slams down on them.

Julian rustles open the rear back door on the left side. Once he is in, Logan takes off. Julian slams his door closed. The blasts continue until we are out of their line of sight.

"We can slow down now," I say. The roaring of the motor lessens as Logan takes his foot off the gas a little. "They couldn't catch us on foot. They are gone now."

"Do you think they will get their vehicles and come after us?" Alexa says, with a shrill to her voice.

"I d-don't think so." I turn around to look at her; my breaths are bursting in and out. "They have other more important matters to attend to."

"Yeah, you mean like hurting Whitney." Julian blinks a couple of times.

"No, I mean like tending to the babies they were in the process of killing back there." I shift my weight. "I think Whitney will be okay. Like she said, they will just put her in jail for breaking the laws and we will get her out when we talk to—"

"What if we never get to talk to anyone?" Julian's eyes are hard.

"We will."

"You can't know that. Even if we do, the leader of Territory M may not let her go or lighten her sentence. You don't know what's going to happen."

"No, we don't, man." Eric takes over the conversation. "But we will try."

Logan doesn't add his voice to the conversation. I turn back from looking at Julian to look at him, and I can tell he's concentrating on his driving. He grips the steering wheel and the tires squeal as he takes a sharp right along the road. We're no longer along the wooded path; we are back on the smooth street.

I see through the rearview mirror that Julian opens his mouth but then closes it. Instead, he turns toward his window and taps his chin with his fingers.

"At least I tried," I hear Julian say, after a few seconds. "I shot at them until I was out of ammo. I stayed with her as long as I could...but they were almost right up on me."

"You know why we didn't shoot," I say, turning around to look at him. "It wouldn't have done any good. We would have used what ammo we have left and maybe even gotten ourselves shot in the process and still wouldn't have been able to free Whitney. They'll just jail her and we will try and get her out, later. She won't be harmed."

"You keep saying that like you're so sure, but you don't know anything."

"You're right. I don't know for sure, but I pray it's true."

"Great Emma's prayers are going to get us out of everything." He waves his hands up mocking me.

"We're almost there," Logan announces, interrupting our awkward conversation.

I shift to look at him. "Where are we going?"

"We'll be there soon," he says, adding nothing else.

CHAPTER TWELVE

I'M GUESSING FIVE minutes or so have gone by and we're still on the dark road. No headlights are behind us. Alexa and Logan said they thought they saw some; but once I reached the truck and we took off, I saw nothing behind us.

My chest stiffens, wondering what they are doing to Whitney. I know Julian feels the same. I see him through the rearview mirror, pulling on his earlobe.

I see, off in the distance, a series of buildings in a row. They look to be around eight-stories high, with several windows occupying the front. They are white and remind me of a cement statue.

"These are the executive buildings," Logan says. He guides the wheel with one hand and points to the buildings with the other one. "They connect to each other, and also to the mansion, through the underground tunnels," he continues. "And to the left, up on that hill, is the mansion where the leader lives. As you can see, this is why they call this area the Hill."

It reminds me of the mansion where President Esther lives and the weird underground tunnel that leads from the jails to the prison. Only this mansion is not white like the president's. It's dark brick and the fence that surrounds it is black. There is a dark gate that the watchmen stand in front of to let people in and out.

There are several large trees within the gates, but the leaves are not blooming anymore because it's the wrong time of year for that. We are moving into September—the weather is so unpredictable here. The leaves on the trees could turn brown and begin to fall... and next week they could thicken and bloom again. The weather in September could feel like December...and July's weather could feel like October. The more we drive, the more I see why they call this the Hill. There are a lot of hills. It would probably be beautiful to look at, if it wasn't so dark out.

Everyone keeps saying the one in charge or the leader but it's so strange how no one knows who that is. Logan worked there and even he doesn't know.

"We can lie low in one of the executive buildings. It's easier to gain access to them. The mansion has the fence surrounding it, with the watchmen...but the executive buildings don't have either. We will stay there in case the men who saw you back there come after us or the ones we saw with the headlights coming our way try and look for us. Once we're safely inside, we will devise some sort of a plan. No one should be there this time of night." Logan grips the wheel harder and turns onto the street that houses the executive buildings.

"Where are the jails and prisons located here?" I ask. I'm wondering if that's where they have taken Whitney.

"There are no prisons, only jails," Alexa says. "If someone commits a crime they go to the jails until their time is up. If their sentence is longer for a more serious crime, they are transported to Territory L, where they spend their life in the underground prisons."

She clears her throat. "The jail is that building way over there." She points to the right. "If you look beyond the two executive buildings, you'll see it. It's over in that stretch of land that's about two miles long."

I see the area she is talking about. The grass is dried up, and I see a small brown brick building next to it.

"That building is where the jails are." She continues. "I'm sure that's where my brother is being held…and maybe Whitney." She clears her throat again.

Julian grunts, in annoyance, at her words.

So the one and only prison in Craigluy is in my territory. Why am I not surprised? I let out a small groan. Of course the only prison is where the lower class lives. I guess the president feels we are the only territory worthy of housing it.

"The buildings are labeled. The first one is building A, and the second one is building B. Building B is empty now; they used it for conferences, until they started having all of their conferences in Territory U. Now it's closed. Since it's empty, we'll go there," Logan says.

"Won't we need a key to get in?" I ask.

"No, since I used to work there, I know the code to the front door."

"What if the code is different now?" I ask.

"Then there's a shovel and a wrench and some other stuff on the bed of the truck. I will use one of those and break a window."

"The building doesn't have an alarm system?"

"It didn't when I worked there. People might break into homes and stores, but no one would be stupid enough to break into the executive buildings. Most people are scared to come up near the Hill, unless they work here. This area is like sacred ground for the president and the higher ups, along with her men."

The motor roars as we pull up into the driveway of the second building. There are three tall silver parking lot lights that tower over the area and give off light. Instead of stopping in one of the paved spots, Logan pulls way up on the side of the grass along the back of the building. There's a wooded area about a half mile behind the building.

The truck wobbles as he pulls onto the woodsy area. He stops once we're in a hidden spot and turns off the motor. We sit there for a moment. I take it he feels it's better to block the truck from anyone's view. The lamps that tower over the parking area also bring a dim amount of light this way, so hopefully no one will notice us.

"What happens now?" Alexa asks.

"We go in," Logan says. "We should check around the building to make sure it's truly empty before we settle in for the night. I know it should be, but I also didn't think the lights would be on out here if no one was here…so we can't be sure of anything."

We hop down from the truck.

"Be careful of the poison ivy," Logan says. "This wooded area has a lot of it. That's how I know they won't find the truck; no one comes back here. If you fall into some and you're allergic, itching and hives will be the least of your problems; it could be deadly."

We didn't have poison ivy back home—not that I know of—so how will I know if I am allergic?

"All the leaves look the same to me. How can you tell the difference?" I ask.

"They're the ones with the red and green leaves. They come in clusters of three and grow from left to right, not side to side. You won't find any thorns on them, either. There's poison oak growing and some of the shrubs have it, too."

I look up and see several large leaves. The light that shines this way is just enough so I make out the orange, the red, and the green leaves.

We walk through the wooded area, making sure we don't step near the poison ivy. There's a lot of down branches and the leaves crackle as I step on them. I'm surprised an area so close to the executive buildings is not kept up better. We keep treading lightly until we reach the back of the building, where the lights shine brighter.

Then we trudge around the side of the eight-story building until we reach the front. My chest feels hollow as we walk up to the rectangular double doors, because I don't know what's about to happen.

"The panel's over here." Logan edges over to a silver panel

that's attached to the white exterior of the building. The panel has a keypad with numbers. They ding as he punches in a code. The doors remain in their closed position.

"There were several different codes at different times. Let me try another one."

He goes through this process of pushing in a series of different codes.

"We don't have all day," Eric snarls. "Let me get the shovel from the truck."

"No, there's one more code we used to use. I'm sure that one will work." He wipes his face with the back of his hand.

"Yeah, let him try that one, before we smash glass everywhere," I say. "That will certainly lead them to where we are, so that should be done only as a last resort."

"Pipe down. I need to concentrate." Logan leans into the panel and punches in another series of numbers. They beep as his fingers touch the keypad.

Logan's right because the next code works. The large glass doors swoosh and slide apart. I've never seen doors like this before. If I were in another situation, I would think they were beautiful; but since I don't know what's going to happen next, they could be doors leading to my death.

The lights are motion activated. I would have thought, since the building is supposed to be abandoned, they would have cut off all power—but they haven't because the lights click on as soon as we enter the room.

The first thing I see when I walk in is a reception area. There are four rows of seven blue and white cloth chairs. There is a large oval receptionist desk in the middle of the room that looks as if it's made of marble.

The air smells stale, like the building has been empty for quite some time. There is an enormous chandelier hanging from the ceiling. It glows in colors of gold and black.

There is no one around. We follow Logan down a long hallway. The walls are bright white, and I see fancy pictures hanging
on the walls. Logan and Julian take the lead, while Eric and I stay
in the middle, and Alexa lags behind.

We walk pass a set of silver elevators that look like the ones in
the president's mansion. I hear our footsteps echo across the floor
as we leave the hallway and reach what I would call the center of
the building.

There is one single elevator; it's glass and glistens like the moon
at night. There is a circular white sofa that is a few feet away from
the elevator. A set of white granite stairs lead up to the second
floor. It's all so beautiful that it makes it hard to believe a building
like this is not being used anymore.

"It doesn't seem like anyone is here," Eric says.

"It is awfully quiet." My stomach twinges. "Maybe we should
check the entire building. I don't want to end up with any surprise
visitors…like back at the old college."

"Maybe we should split up and check," Alexa says. "Emma
and I can go together." Her voice has a weirdness to it.

"I don't think we should." Eric shakes his head. "If someone is
in here, it's easier for them to get to us if we're divided."

"He's right," Logan whispers. "We're better off if we
stay together."

"Even if someone is in here, they won't care about us. We
all know they really want Emma," Alexa says. The weirdness in
her voice has turned to anger. "She's the one they've been searching for."

Eric turns and glares at her.

"I'm just saying what we already know," she quickly adds. "We
saw it all over the box."

"All this discussing is getting us nowhere." Julian's voice
sounds raspier than usual. I think he wants to hurry and get this

over with, so we can talk about Whitney. "We need to start searching the second floor."

"He's right," I say, trying to add my thoughts to the broken conversation.

I see Eric's eyes squint together with worry. "I wish we could find the power supply so we can cut the motion lights off. If anyone is watching the building, the lights clicking on and off is a dead giveaway."

"There's nothing we can do about that now," I say. "We have to just be careful and watch our surroundings."

"Let's get started then," Eric says.

* * *

We search the entire building and find nothing but plenty of beautiful conference rooms. There are some with glass tables and some with marble tables with large expensive vases on them. There are some with chandeliers and some with lights that have dimmer switches—which is very helpful so we can dim the room to our liking once they click on.

We see a kitchen with a stainless steel refrigerator and other stainless appliances. Even the bathroom floor is white and tan block marble, with its own smaller gold chandelier.

A building with this many elegant rooms should not be sitting unused. Funny how the less fortunate don't have food to eat, but Territory M discards a building like this.

The underground tunnel in the basement is blocked off by a large fence.

"No one's here." Julian plops down in the middle of the reception area. He sits in one of the blue and white chairs. He thumbs his finger across his cheek.

Logan and Eric sit down as well. I lean on the oval receptionist desk in the middle of the room, while Alexa scrunches up next to the wall.

"Now that we know the place is empty, we will stay here for tonight; but in the morning, we need to go and get Whitney." Julian leans forward and nervously taps his foot against the floor. "I'm hoping she's not dead." He stops tapping his foot and pulls on his earlobe. For some reason, he glares at me when he says that. "If she's not, then she should be in the jails, just down the road. We will go there in the morning and see about getting her released." He sits back and folds his arms.

"Julian, I'm sorry, but you realize that we can't just waltz in there to get her released. We'll all be taken in." My throat is scratchy. "We have to be logical about this. I mean—"

"How do you know what's logical?" Alexa cuts me off. She stands from her slouched position. "Since you're the one they really want, maybe we could trade you for her. Maybe, since you're the bigger prize, they will let her go." The earlier anger in her voice is still there.

"No, I don't think that would work." I swallow hard. "And I'm not just saying that to get out of it because I would trade myself for Whitney." I glance over at Julian. "But I think they would take us all in."

"Then, we'll stay here and you go alone," Julian says.

"Why is everybody trying to throw Emma under the bus?" Logan asks, sucking his teeth. "We all need to stick together." He shrugs. "I'm just saying."

"Logan's right," Eric speaks up. "I feel like everyone's turning on Emma now. She's not turning herself in. I assure you that's not going to happen." His jaw tightens.

The conversation makes the muscles jump under my skin.

"All you care about is saving your little girlfriend." Julian stands. "They've got Whitney. If Emma won't trade herself, then

I'll find another way; but I'm going over to the jails. In fact, maybe I'll go right now." Julian forges ahead.

"Wait a minute, man." Eric stands. "That's crazy talk, and it won't get Whitney released."

Julian only makes it a few steps before he stops walking. He leans on one of the chairs and turns toward Eric. "Do what you want, but I'm going." Julian's face is hard. His fists are tightly gripped around the frame of the chair.

"Think about this for a minute." Logan stands. "We have to be smart."

"All I know is we can't leave Whitney there—not after everything she risked for us. We have to at least try. I could never live with myself if I didn't try and get her out of there." His eyes sadden.

"But you won't get her out." I shake my head. "You'll just make it worse because you'll be captured along with her. You're not thinking clearly."

"I won't give you up, if that's what you're worried about." Julian's skin bunches under his eyes. "I'll trade my life for hers. They'll release her from custody and take me in." He paces three steps to the left, then three steps to the right.

"You're being foolish. They'll take you both in," I say. "You're thinking with your heart, not your head. Please stay here tonight and get some rest. We will have clearer heads in the morning. Then we will talk about this again. Do we all agree?"

I search the faces in the room.

"Agreed," everyone replies.

Julian closes his eyes and takes in a breath. "Fine. Agreed." He walks to the other side of the room.

But for some reason, I don't think he really does agree.

* * *

We're in the reception area, lying on the cloth chairs. Everyone takes turns keeping watch while the others get some shut eye. Eric took first watch, then Logan. Alexa is next, then me. I know this is my time to shut my eyes, but I'm having trouble sleeping. Everything that has happened so far replays in my mind.

I notice Alexa lying back down again. I've seen her get up several times. I assume she has been going to the bathroom. I remember her telling me she has menorrhagia. Now, I watch as she scrunches up in a ball and puts her knees up to her chin. She only occupies one chair. Logan sleeps on his back, and Eric is on his side with his legs stretched out. The two of them take up two chairs apiece.

I only need one chair as well. I shift to lay on my right side and see Julian pacing back and forth. It's his turn to keep watch; but I can tell by his demeanor, he is seething inside. I don't know what to do or say to ease his pain. When morning comes, it won't be any better. I close my eyes again and try to sleep.

Only a few minutes have gone by when I hear a swishing sound. I roll over and see Julian putting something in his pocket. He's headed for the front door. He hunches over and scratches his right leg as he makes a quick exit.

I wonder if that's the leg the rat scratched him on.

I jump to my feet. "Julian, what are you doing?" I rush behind him.

He keeps moving along, ignoring me.

"Julian, where are you going?"

"Be quiet before you wake the others," he says, turning to me with a soft but harsh tone.

He turns and steps away from me. The door swishes as he goes through, and I follow.

"Julian, I asked you where you were going." He doesn't answer me, so I continue. "Did you steal the key fob for the truck from Logan?"

"Good thing he's such a sound sleeper. He didn't even notice me swipe them from his pants." He walks faster.

I rush up to him. "You can't do this, Julian."

He growls. "Leave it alone, Emma."

I step in front of him and put my hand on his chest. "I'm not going to let you."

He knocks my hand away. "You're not going to stop me."

"What's going on out here?" I hear Eric's voice.

I turn and see Logan and Alexa are with him.

"Julian's being foolish. He stole the key fob and now he's trying to make a run for it over to the jails."

"Are you crazy, man?" Eric asks.

"Why would you do that?" Logan pats his pants pockets down, looking for the key fob. "I can't believe you stole them while I was asleep. I thought we could trust each other. We're in this together."

"I have to do this."

"Give me the keys." Logan rushes up to Julian. "Or I'll make you give them to me." He shoves Julian in his shoulder.

"Logan, stop it," I say. "We need to talk about this calmly. There's no need for that."

"She's right." Eric is on the other side of me.

"He's not going to listen," Logan says through gritted teeth.

"Do you hear that?" Alexa asks.

All I hear is the low breaths coming from my mouth; but she's right, now I hear a loud pounding noise far off in the distance.

"Yes, I hear it." I feel beads of sweat forming on my forehead.

"What is that?" she asks.

"Let's just get to the truck." I take off. "We need to get out of this area."

The pavement's firm as we make our way to where we left the truck. We pass by the three tall light poles. I notice one thin layer of brightness comes from another light pole along the back of the driveway.

The truck is parked in the wooded area in back of the building, so we have a ways to run. The pounding is getting louder. At the time we parked, it didn't seem that far; but now as our feet bang against the ground trying to reach it, it seems miles away.

The pounding stops. I now hear snorting and a high-pitched yelp. The one yelp turns into another and another. I realize that a pack of dogs is behind us. The soles of my shoes are ripping apart—at least that's what it feels like. The yelping turns into loud barking, and it's coming closer.

I feel the gun on my hip, bouncing into my side. I don't want to have to use it, so I pray I make it to the truck in time. I pass everyone while huffing and puffing—even Eric—as we make our way. They must have watchdogs, looking over the empty buildings for any trespassers. But why weren't they around when we first got here?

My mind is racing and my reasoning doesn't make sense. I wonder if Rich and the watchmen have been watching for us, and they let the dogs loose when we exited the building.

"Keep moving!" Julian screams, interrupting my thoughts.

I hear a beeping noise.

"I unlocked the d-doors with the f-fob." Julian's voice is shaky and so is the key fob in his hand. "I'll go the opposite w-way and distract them. You g-go toward the truck. I'll m-meet you there," Julian continues ranting.

"Julian, no!" I yell back. "Let's all stay together."

"No, I n-need to do this." He's talking fast. "Then I can g-go and get Whitney released."

"Julian!" I scream again.

"If he wants to do it, t-then just let him go," Alexa says. Her breaths are going in and out. "It's the o-only way."

"It's *not* the only way!" I shout. My chest feels like its caving in. "He's *not* thinking straight because he's so worried about Whitney."

Julian shouts as loud as he can, so the animals go toward him. We're a few feet away from the truck, while his feet sprint in the opposite direction.

"It's too l-late to convince him; he's g-gone," I hear Alexa shout out in between faded breaths.

She's right. He's gone now, and there's no way we can stop him. He still has the key with him…at least he unlocked the doors for us. Logan and Alexa dash toward the truck. I slow down a little to look back. I see Julian weaving in and out between several trees. The dogs are still nearing him.

He's running so fast and looking back at the dogs that he stumbles and slams into a tree. He slides down it. He lies on the bottom of the tree…the stump. It's one wrapped in poison ivy. I don't know if he's allergic, but that won't matter now because the dogs are right on him. They nip onto the back of his pants and pull him down to the ground.

I stop dead in my tracks in a huff. I shakily reach for my gun. Eric is right beside me. He knows what I'm about to do and does the same. I raise my gun in the air and pull the trigger. A loud *pop* is heard. Eric does the same thing. Between the two of us, we let out four *pops* in a row. The dogs stop. They look toward us. We turn and head for the truck.

I notice Logan is already at the truck. He's in the cargo area. I see him reaching over the side. I'm not sure what he is looking for. I only remember a shovel and wrench back there and some other junk bunched up in a pile. I see Logan rush back toward the front of the truck with something in his hand.

My shoes are still thumping underneath me. My breaths quickly go in and out. The dogs are still behind us. I sprint faster. I'm trying to escape the doom behind us, while wondering what Logan is doing ahead of us. I see Logan searching the ground. He leans down and picks up something. Then he hops in the front seat of the truck.

Alexa is in the back with the door swung open, waiting for us. Alexa scoots over. I stumble in first and sit next to her. My breaths are uneven. Eric slides in next to me.

The dogs are barking out of control. They are skinny black labs. They jump around like their feet are on hot coals. Most black labs are even tempered and gentle, but these labs have been trained to be vicious.

We slam the door closed to keep them outside. I feel cold and my body won't stop shaking. The gun is trembling in my hand. I will have to shoot the dogs, if they take off toward Julian. For now, they are too distracted with us. They keep pawing and scratching the truck. They are trying to get in.

I look through the window toward Julian. I had hope by now he would have shaken off his fall and made his way to the opposite side of the truck, where the dogs aren't. This is his time to come, while the animals are distracted; but he doesn't come. He is still lying there on his stomach with his face turned to the side. When we were in the ducts he said the rat only scratched him. I think that scratch has helped weaken his system.

"Julian, get up man. Come on. Shake it off!" Logan yells.

Julian can't hear him through closed windows. We can't let the windows down without the key. Even if we could I doubt if it would matter. Julian doesn't move; he just lies there. Maybe hitting the tree hurt him more than we know. Maybe he's unconscious.

I hear loud buzzing, and I see a flicker of light. Lightning ants are jetting around in the darkness.

"Oh, no." Eric shakes his head. "There are lightning ants living in that tree. When Julian ran into it, he woke them up."

Lightning bugs are harmless. The most they do is venture out and glow their light to search for a mate. But fire ants are different; they used to only attack small animals to kill them. They would bite first to get a grip and then sting.

My mother told me back in her day that the lightning bugs mated with the fire ants and the babies they made are powerful. Now, the lightning ants not only attack small animals, they attack people when they feel threatened.

I see more flickers of yellow and green—even some red—and the buzzing sounds like someone drilling a hole. Julian's body shakes uncontrollably. The lightning ants cover his head and part of his face. My throat tightens as I hear him scream out in pain.

"We have to do something," I say. "Eric, crack your door open a little bit and shoot your gun."

"I can't without letting the dogs get near us…besides the noise won't distract the lightning ants, only the dogs."

"This is inhuman. We can't just sit here."

"It's too late. He's gone already," Alexa says.

"You can't know that."

"A thousand ants just bit and stung him in his face. Do you think anyone could survive that?" Her face hardens, like I'm wrong to care—like I'm wrong to hope that he's still alive.

But Alexa is right. It only takes a few angry ones to kill and now Julian has been bitten and stung by hundreds.

Logan reaches over into the passenger's seat. He yanks open the glove compartment. It bangs upon opening. He reaches for something. I now see a book of matches in his hand.

"While you two were distracting the dogs I was trying to figure out a way to get rid of them, if needed," Logan says. "I was able to get an old rag from the cargo area and I found a dry tree branch on the ground."

I wondered what he was doing at the back of the truck and searching for on the ground. Now I know. I watch him in the front seat as he wraps the cloth around the end of the branch. He uses the match to set it on fire.

The dogs are still yapping at us from the driver's side of the vehicle. Logan opens the driver's side door. He waves the lit stick in their faces. The fire singes one of the dog's faces. The dog screeches. It runs away whimpering. The other dogs turn and follow the dog that was burned.

My chest lightens a little, but it doesn't last because we jump out to go help Julian. The lightning ants have flown away now, so it seems okay to go near him as long as we stay clear of the poison ivy behind him. The closer we get, the more I see his still body.

Once we reach him, Eric rolls him over on his back. His chest is not rising. His face is swollen and purple. I call out his name, but he doesn't respond.

Logan leans down and puts his two fingers to Julian's throat to check his pulse. He closes Julian's eyes and shakes his head as he lowers it. We all know what that means. My lips quiver and I blink several times, trying to contain my tears.

"We have to get out of here." Alexa pulls on my elbow. "The watchmen will be coming after us. I'm sure they're behind this."

"We can't just leave him here," I say, with a growl to my voice.

"You guys take the truck. I'll bury him and catch up to you later." Logan wipes the sweat from his brow. "I will use the shovel in the back of the truck."

I blink, noticing the key fob is still tightly in Julian's fist.

"You can't just throw him somewhere, like he was nothing." Eric looks down and back up. "He was one of my best friends. We've been through a lot together."

"I won't do that." Logan glowers. "I will make a temporary grave in the woods and once this is over, we will bury him properly."

My chest aches from the conversation. "I don't think that's a good idea. There may be more lightning ants around the area…we don't want to risk disturbing them again, or getting near more poison ivy."

"And what about the dogs?" Eric asks. "He was my friend." His voice is low. "I can't risk the dogs digging up his body before we return. We need to just carry him to the bed of the truck, and we can bury him once we find a safer place."

"Do you hear that?" Alexa says, pulling on my arm again like she's a five-year-old. "We don't have time for all this back and forth."

I do hear something in the sky. It sounds like fluttering from the rotor of a helicopter. I hear a loud bang, like the ground is opening up. The ground is shaking. I feel another explosion after another. I think they are shooting at us but with what I don't know. The bangs sound like they are coming from a cannon instead of a gun.

Alexa takes off to the left. I follow her. Logan and Eric are close behind. We are rushing behind the buildings now. Alexa runs to the back of the building we just came from. A loud bang stops us in our tracks because it takes out one of the back windows of the building. The banging continues. More windows are shot out. We can't make it to that building without being shot.

There is no fence between the buildings. We dash by building B and keep sprinting ahead toward the next building. The shots sound like they are behind us now. Alexa is ahead of us so we follow her up to building A.

This building has a keypad next to the back doors. Alexa stops next to the panel fixed to the brick. "Logan, what's the c-code for this building?"

He's not as close to her as I am. He doesn't hear her.

"Hurry and g-give me the code!" Her voice goes in and out as she shouts.

"1-6-5-9!" He shouts out. "Or 2-6-5-8."

I hear a series of beeps. I look over and Alexa is slowly punching in a bunch of numbers.

"What are you doing?" I ask. "Those aren't the right numbers."

"I thought that's what he said."

"Move." I nudge her out of the way by pushing her shoulder.

I punch in 1-6-5-9 and it doesn't work. I try 2-6-5-8 and I breathe better as the doors slide open.

"Sorry, I couldn't hear him." Alexa pouts.

"It's fine," I say, rushing into the building.

I thought the building would look identical to building B inside; it doesn't. The lights are motion lights just like in building B—besides that, nothing else is the same. I see it's not elaborate. There are no chandeliers or marble floors. I don't see any furniture anywhere. It looks like a big warehouse.

"Let's go in here," Logan shouts.

We head for a small room off to the right. It looks like an office. There's a metal desk over in the corner but no chair accompanies it. I see several shelves on the walls that are empty.

Eric slams the solid door. The lights automatically pop on. I click the light switch on the wall all the way down so the room is almost dark. Logan goes to the corner. He slides down on the hard floors. Alexa goes near the two-pane window—she leans down as well. The blinds are slightly open. She peers out just enough to see what's going on.

I take that as my cue to sit down behind the door. My lungs feel heavy. I can't control my breathing. Eric sits down beside me.

"I-I can't believe we left J-Julian lying there like that. What are we going to tell Whitney w-when we find her?" My eyes are tearing up like a faucet.

I know I didn't trust Julian, at first; but as time went on, I could see he was a good guy who was only trying to help us. He didn't deserve to die like that—he had a child and a family—it's all so horrible. My entire body is trembling.

"We'll go back and bury him properly, later. You know we couldn't stay there while they were firing at us." Eric's hand is warm as he touches my face. "It's going to be okay." He pulls me close. "It's going to work out."

I want to believe him, but I can't. So far, nothing has gone as planned. I'm no closer to finding baby Abigail or helping out my family or any of the people in Territory L.

Now, I will be taken into custody before I even get to speak my peace. Nothing will ever change back home, once I'm imprisoned for life. Maybe coming here was a waste of time. President Esther will always win in the end.

CHAPTER THIRTEEN

"Do you see anything?" Logan asks. We are still hiding out in the small office in executive building A.

"No, just darkness," Alexa says, peeking through the blinds.

"Do you hear anything?" Logan asks, glaring in my direction.

"No," I say.

I'm leaning against the door and the coldness of the floor is seeping through my body. I'm still shivering over what happened to poor Julian. I can't get the image of Julian's still body and swollen purple face out of my mind.

Eric sits next to me. The room is dim, yet I see his face tells me he feels the same.

"I don't hear anyone in the hallway." Eric bends his knees up to his chest. "They know we came in this building. I don't know why they aren't coming for us."

"Who knows why they do what they do." I shrug. "But I'm sure they've informed the president and she will be on her way here. Maybe they are just waiting for her to arrive before they tear into here."

I wipe my forehead. A strand of hair has fallen into my eye.

"I can't see her coming all the way here just for the likes of us. You know her better than I do." Logan scrunches his eyes. "I've only seen her from afar on the information box. If you say you're so important that she will come here, then maybe she will."

"I agree. I don't think they would wait for her to arrive before they come in and arrest us. They'll surely find us in here, so we can't hide in here all night. Maybe we should try to get out of here, while we still have a chance." There's a faint sound as Alexa shifts her weight on the floor.

"And where would we go?" Eric's voice is rough, like he doesn't agree with Alexa.

"Anything's better than sitting in this tiny room like sitting ducks. I've already tried the windows and they won't unlock. They're shut tight."

"Maybe she's right." Logan nods his head. "If they come in here, we have nowhere to run."

"Maybe we should leave, while we have a chance," I say, agreeing with them. I look at Eric. "I know a lot has happened." I glance around the room. "Losing Julian and Whitney…hopefully, we'll get her back; but I still want to get to the mansion to talk to the leader about Abigail and the walls before Rich hauls us in to jail with her. After we accomplish that we can talk about getting Whitney released."

"We can try to still make that happen…but it will be difficult now that they know where we are. The higher ups should be in Territory U, but the ones left in charge who are chasing us are still capable men…we have to plan out our next move carefully." Logan pinches his throat with his fingers, like this stressful situation will never end.

"If that's the case, then I think we should get down to the tunnels and make our way to the mansion." I stand. "I think our odds are better pleading with the watchmen that were left in charge than pleading with Rich once—and if—he arrives. Sitting here is just wasting time. Once President Esther or Rich are here, I won't get to speak with anyone but them."

"I think we should search the building first, before trying to go down to the tunnels," Alexa says.

"That makes no sense," I say. "We should go down to the tunnels now."

"We can't hide in here forever, so I agree to go." Logan wobbles to his feet. "I just hope the tunnel is not blocked off like in building B."

"Let's do it then." Eric lets out a loud grunt as he stands.

Alexa swipes her hand across her head. It takes her a little longer, but she finally stands as well. "What if it is blocked off? There's no point in going down there. Let's just find another way out."

"There is no other way," I say. "So, let's just go."

The hallway lights click on but we find the dimmer switch and darken the hallway. No beautiful portraits are draped along the walls like in building B. I hear my heart beating in my ears. I have my gun in hand, and Eric has his.

I didn't realize it at the time, but when the helicopters were roaring overhead, Logan grabbed Julian's duty belt with his holsters—he already had his Taser and now he has his gun as well. He has no more ammo; but maybe if we find more, later, he can put it to good use.

The more we hurry through the building, the more I feel my breathing getting heavier. I feel like there's something unknown lurking behind every corner. The air smells like mold. It's noiseless as we make our way down a stairwell to the basement level.

"Over here is where the tunnels should be," Logan says, as he turns left. He's walking a few steps in front of us.

The air smells more like mildew now than it did when we were upstairs. The walls look dank. The tunnel is so narrow that only two of us can walk together at a time without touching the sides. Close spaces have never bothered me before, but this is making me claustrophobic; my belly tenses.

"It's not closed off," Logan says. I hear, from the high pitch of his voice, that he is relieved.

There is no gate or fence blocking our path like in building B. I see the two tunnels switch off. The tunnel in building A was more of a black color and there were no signs of light. The new tunnel we have crossed over into is brownish and floodlights inhabit the ceiling.

"Are there any cameras down here?" I ask. I don't see any sticking out anywhere, but they could be hidden.

Logan shakes his head. "I'm not sure."

"Even if there are, it's too late to turn around now." Eric slants his eyebrows.

My shoulders jerk because the lights begin to flicker. There is a loud roaring. An alarm blares. It reminds me of the alarm we heard in Territory L when the president's speech was starting. The noise is so loud, it feels like the walls are shaking. A cement wall swooshes down out of the ceiling, behind us. It thumps into the ground.

No one says anything. We all begin to plod forward. We are trying to get into the mansion before another wall blocks the tunnel. My ankle stumbles on a rock as we stomp through the tunnel.

Logan is still in front, since he knows his way into the mansion. Eric is beside me, to my left. Alexa is a little behind me, on the right.

"Wait," Alexa cries out. Her breaths are jagged. "I can't run anymore."

My neck snaps around to see what's wrong with her. Before I get a good look at her, something grabs my ankle. I fall down. My head hits the sooty ground. A mist wafts in my face. I shakily raise my head. I see Eric still running. He didn't notice my fall.

Another cement wall bangs down in front of me. Alexa and I are trapped in between the two walls.

"Eric!" I scream, like my lungs are on fire.

"Whisper, what happened?"

"I fell and the wall came down, trapping me and Alexa."

I hear his fists hammering on the wall.

"We've got to get them to go back up," Eric says.

"We can't control it," I hear Logan say. "There's nothing we can do."

My stomach cringes. I try to stand on my feet but I'm wobbly. Using the wall for support, I raise myself up. Once I'm standing, I lean my hand on the wall. I try to balance myself. My eyesight is a little blurry. I turn to look for Alexa. She is a little ways back. She has a weird look on her face as she stares at me.

"Alexa, do you know what happened? Something grabbed my leg and I tripped."

"It wasn't something, it was someone." She cocks her head to the side. "I grabbed your leg, so you would fall." Her voice is rough.

"W-why?" I ask, shakily.

She doesn't answer, but she lunges toward me. She pushes me into the wall. Before I can protect myself, she holds her fist up. I see something white, like a large rock. I feel pressure against my skull. I feel my body go limp. I feel myself fall to the ground.

Everything in front of me goes dark.

CHAPTER FOURTEEN

I BLINK A few times as I open my eyes. I'm lying on something hard and cold. I sway as I try to sit up on the cement floor. I see long metal bars in front of me. It's a jail cell, just like the one in President Esther's mansion where I was sentenced to be incarcerated for thirty days.

I see another cell across from me and one to the right of me. They're both unoccupied. To the left of me is a brick wall. Looking down at my hands, I cringe. There are silver handcuffs surrounding my wrists, making them sting as they engulf my skin. This can't be happening again. Not another jail cell. I don't know if I can take it again.

The last thing I remember, I was in the tunnel of executive building A with Eric, Logan, and Alexa. My jaw tenses because I now remember Alexa tripping me and hitting me in the head with a rock. Why would she do that?

The handcuffs jingle as I stretch my wrists to try and reach for my gun, but I only feel my own hip. My duty belt that holds my holsters is gone, along with my Taser and gun. Even the small flashlight I had in my pocket has been taken.

I hear the stomping of footsteps. "You have a visitor," a tall, skinny patrolman says. His brown eyes match his carefully nested head of brown wavy hair. He has no buttons plastered on his black uniform; so I know he's a patrolman, not a guard. Keys dangle in his hand as he unbolts the lock. I hear screeching as he opens the cell, and my eyes widen. Alexa walks in.

"Don't bother trying to get out of the handcuffs or out of this jail cell, for that matter." She glances around. Her chest rises and falls as she chuckles. The cell door slams behind her.

"What's happening?" My arms feel tight. "Why did you hit me? Why am I here?" I stand to face her.

"You're in jail, right where you belong." Her tone is snarky. Her face scrunches as she continues her rant. "You wanted to talk to the leader of M. You wanted to find the newbie camp. Well, those things aren't going to happen. Remember me pointing out the jail down the street from the executive buildings—well, that's where you are."

"How did I get here?" My brain feels cloudy.

"You were knocked out, apprehended…taken into custody… and brought here."

"Do you work for the president? Have you been working for President Esther all this time?"

I had reservations trusting Julian, at first, and even Logan; but I always thought Alexa and I had the same issues with the president. I never thought she would betray me. I did notice her demeanor has been flighty, ever since we left Whitney's house to come to the Hill. She's had more of an off-putting attitude, but I never would have imagined her doing this.

"Everything you wrote in that book—was that not true?"

She glances down and back up at me. "It was true, and it still is." She clenches her teeth. "I hate President Esther. I don't agree with any of her laws."

My fists are tight. "Then why are you doing this?"

"I liked you, Emma. I really did." She shakes her head. "I liked everything you stood for. When I first met you, I thought we could be friends. But once they took my brother, everything changed. I had to find a way for them to release him."

Her tone softens now. "And I'm sorry, but the only way I could do that was to betray you. I had to keep telling myself that you were selfish and that you were putting us all in danger for your own self-centered reasons. I had to keep those thoughts in my head to be able to go through with this."

"Go through with what? What's going to happen?"

"When you and Whitney returned from the store and you told us how the guards almost saw you, I realized how valuable you are, and I decided to make a trade—you for my brother. I couldn't let my brother continue to suffer. I figured if I told the patrolmen where you were and they informed the Territory L guards, maybe they would take you in exchange for my brother's freedom. So when we were in the panic room, I left to make a phone call."

I didn't notice a phone anywhere within her reach. We don't have them in Territory L, except for in the hospital; so they can call surgeons over from other territories during emergencies. Maybe that's why I glanced right by it. We always communicate by mail or by walking to the person's house, if we need to talk to them.

If the president needs us, our information boxes would just turn on, saying we have a message, or the government would send out a letter. I'm sure the president has a phone, but I didn't see any during my stay there.

"You were in the corner, whispering with Eric. Whitney and Julian were upstairs. So, I told Logan I was going to the bathroom; but instead, I went upstairs to the first floor. There was a black phone plugged into the wall in the den. I noticed it the day she was showing us around," she continues, answering my thoughts on where the phone was. "That's why the patrolmen and the one you call Rich showed up at the house the second time. I called them."

She bites down on her lip. "When the lights went out and I said I was coming back from the bathroom, I was really coming back from the den. Julian and Whitney had gone upstairs to the bedroom. I lifted up the receiver and heard her making arrangements for Mrs. Hutchings to keep Adam. There must have been another extension somewhere in the upstairs bedroom that I didn't know about. After she called the babysitter, I used the phone in the den to make my call."

"I still don't understand. If they knew we were in the panic room, then why didn't they bang down the door and get us? Why the whole charade with them letting us sneak out the back way?" I jerk my hands and the metal around my wrists jangles.

"They were supposed to come in and take you all, but you guys decided to sneak out of the back before they got a chance to." She shifts her weight to her other foot. "When I spoke to the patrolmen on the phone and they found out what I wanted, they immediately put me in touch with Rich. From where Rich was, he was able to call someone to get the power cut off at Whitney's house. It only took a matter of minutes. Guess that's what happens when you're in a position of power like that. You get things done immediately."

She smiles, like all of a sudden she's in love with the power the guards have. "I told him where you were and your plans to make it up to the Hill to talk to someone in charge. He muttered something about how he should have known there was a room behind the bookcase, then he told me to do everything I could to see to it that your little group didn't get to the Hill, especially the mansion. That's where the leader stays, and he didn't want any of you—especially you—talking to them." She shoves her finger at me.

"I told him that wouldn't be a problem because you and the others would probably stay in the panic room—since he hadn't found us when they searched the basement the first time…the group felt it was safe there and no one could get to them. He was pleased and said now that he knew a panic room existed he had ways to break into it. So you guys sneaking out put a wrench in my plans." She grits her teeth. "If you would have just stayed in the panic room," she mumbles. "Everything would have worked out fine. But you decided to sneak out, messing everything up."

"How many times are you going to say that?"

"Whatever." She taps her foot, like my words are making her angry. "I don't know what was taking them so long to come into the house," she continues on her rant. "Maybe they were waiting on special equipment to knock in the doors."

"I guess since you were working with them to keep us in the house, they figured they could take their sweet time coming in to get us."

She rolls her eyes and shakes her head. "Anyway, once I knew you were determined to leave, I had to switch gears, in case you did get out before they came in and caught you. I needed you to think I was with you all the way. I knew after I offered myself up, you wouldn't let me go; but you would think I was such a loyal friend that I would do anything for you."

She pauses, then continues on. "You would never suspect I was working with them. That way, I could spend my time trying to distract you, so they could find us and you would be caught."

"And I suppose that was you who banged on the garbage can while we were at the newbie camp?"

"Yes, me again," she says. Her posture is straight and her chest is puffed out. "Logan wanted to warn you that we saw headlights in the distance. I said I would go do it, instead of him. I saw that as another opportunity to get you taken into custody. I wanted the men at the newbie camp to find you. Rich would know that I was the one who led the watchmen to you, and I would be rewarded by having my brother released. But we escaped that, too. I so wished that was you in that trap, instead of Whitney."

She swipes her hands together. "But it wasn't, so once we made it up to the executive buildings, I had to figure out something else to ensure you wouldn't make it to the mansion."

Her fists are pumped. "I tried getting you alone when we were in building B, so I could knock you out and drag you outside and they could find you; but your boyfriend Eric made sure that wasn't possible. Instead—"

Cutting her off, I ask, "Is that why you pretended to fumble while putting the numbers in the control panel back at building A?"

"Yeah, I heard Logan rattle off the numbers perfectly and I put in the wrong numbers on purpose. I wanted you caught, instead of entering the building to hide. But that didn't work, either."

"Why did you run to building A in the first place then?"

"I was only trying to get us out of the line of fire…or myself, I should say." Her face scrunches. "I have to admit them shooting at us was unexpected…and it rattled me. I just wanted to be near the building and out of the way. When you guys followed me, I had to pretend I wanted in to the building to save us, so I fumbled with the panel to waste time."

"And that's why you were so hesitant to go down to the tunnels to make it into the mansion…because your assignment was to keep me away from there."

"Right again, Emma. I figured if you made it into the tunnels you would get in to see the one in charge, and I would never gain access to my brother. I wanted us to stay somewhere in the building where they could easily find us. I wanted us out of that tiny room and somewhere more accessible. But it all worked out in the end." She shrugs.

"I had no idea there were cameras in the tunnels. I suppose, when the watchmen saw us, they tried to trap us in so we—or rather, you—could be taken into custody. That was my plan all along…so actually going down into the tunnels was a good thing."

She smiles. "I saw the walls coming down as my opportunity to get you alone and knock you out. I was going to drag you back out of the tunnels and out of the building myself. But like I said, since there were cameras it all worked in my favor and they came and got you."

"And what about the others?"

"They were collateral damage. You were my main concern... the ticket to get my brother out. I didn't care what happened to them. I don't think Rich and the others did, either."

I place my hand over my mouth. The cuffs jiggle. I feel like my breaths are caught.

"Don't look at me like that." She rolls her eyes. "Like you're so pure and innocent and wouldn't sacrifice someone else for *your* family. You would do the same thing for your brother or one of your relatives. And you know it."

Her tone is loud, and she shoves her pointy finger in my face. "Besides, they're not going to harm you—you said it yourself. They want you brought in unharmed."

"That was before the latest broadcast."

"So they changed it to harm; it's still not dead." She cocks her head to the side. "At least you won't be killed."

"I don't know." I shrug. "The way they chased us with those dogs and the gunshots raining down from the sky, any one of us could have been a goner."

"Well, Julian got it in the end, not you," she says, with no hint of remorse.

What happened to the spunky girl I met who wrote beautiful words in a sketchbook—the girl that I wholeheartedly agreed with.

"Why are you standing here talking to me, instead of seeing about your brother?"

"They said I had to do a few more things for them before they took me to him. But I wanted to stop here first and talk to you. I need you to know something."

"What else could you possibly have to say to me?" I take in a deep breath and lower my eyes.

"I wish things could have been different." She turns away.

My body tenses at her words because I wish everything was different, too.

* * *

I can't believe it, but I think I fell asleep in here. I hoped I would never sleep in a jail cell again; but I guess after everything that has happened, I'm exhausted. I'm lying on the floor because this boxed-shaped cell doesn't have a cot. My back is stiff and my stomach growls from hunger. I haven't eaten anything since we were hiding in the woods and I had that granola bar.

I stand and glance around. There is still no one across from me or in the cell next to me, either. I jerk on my handcuffs to try and pull them apart, but of course they don't budge. I lean up against the wall and slide down to the floor. I take a few deep breaths because my chest feels like it's caving in.

Where's Eric? I hope he's alright. I'm not sure, but it's probably morning now—so that would make this Monday.

It's eerily quiet. My body shakes, because it's damp and cold here. I bend my knees up to my chin and bury my face in my hands. The cell door screeches open, but my head feels like lead and I can't raise it to have another argument with Alexa. I'm sure it's her and she's gearing up for round two because there was something she forgot to say to me—but I can't stomach it.

I hear loud footsteps coming near me, but I still can't look up.

"So, the chosen one needs a nap."

I know that voice. It's crude and unmistakably cocky. My chest constricts. I feel the pressure rising in my chest as I look up at him. His green eyes pierce right through me, just like always. My words get caught in my throat and I can't speak. I had hoped to never see him again—but I knew, deep in my gut, that wasn't possible.

"Why so quiet? Were you not expecting to see me?"

I remain silent.

"You've never had a problem speaking up before. What's the problem now?" There's a *thud* as he kicks my shoe with his boot.

My shoes squeak as I slide them closer to me—and out of his path of vengeance.

"Where's Whitney?" I finally ask, trying to add strength to my voice, even though I feel my knees tremble.

"So, she finally speaks," he says, leaning down next to me. "She does have a voice." He mocks me. "But Whitney is not the one I'd thought you'd ask for. I thought you'd be whining for your little boyfriend, Eric." His nostrils flair.

"I know Eric can take care of himself." I slide even closer to the wall. "I'm not worried about him."

"Well maybe you should be." He stands.

I can't help but stare at his leg. I thought I shot him in the right leg. Or was it the left? Everything's blurring together and I'm feeling dizzy. I know I shot him. Why is he standing there like nothing happened?

"You're wondering why I'm still standing, walking." His eyebrow rises. "You're not so tough after all. All that training you did..." his voice trails off. "And you couldn't even shoot a gun properly." He leans his head to the side and there's a popping sound as he cracks his neck. "You just grazed me." He sneers. "I was out of commission for a day or so; but after they cleaned it at the hospital and applied a few bandages, I was good as new."

My heart races at his cockiness. "I saw blood."

"Not enough blood." One of his eyes narrows. "To keep me down for long."

"Long enough so you couldn't call it in."

His eyes glare. "I did call it in."

"But my shot must have kept you down long enough so you couldn't call it in until we were already beyond the gates of Territory M."

"It doesn't matter now, does it?" His jaw flexes. "We eventually caught you."

He takes out a set of keys from his pocket. They clank together as he leans down again and dangles them in front of me.

"W-what are you doing?" I don't want my voice to shake but it does.

"Just wait and see." He raises his other hand to my cheek. His finger feels sweaty as he slides it down the side of my face. I flinch to get away from him and his hand falls. He laughs a wicked laugh and turns his attention back to the handcuffs around my wrists.

He turns the key and the handcuffs release. They clank as they hit the cement floor. He yanks me up, like I'm a limp rag doll.

"Why are you taking off the handcuffs?"

"You think you're so tough. I want to see you try and get away from me. The handcuffs will only get in your way. We wouldn't want that, now would we?" He clicks his tongue.

Here he goes, playing his games again. He wants me to make a move, so he can pound me into the ground.

"Let's go," he says.

I turn away from him. He shoves me in my back. I fall forward before balancing my weight.

"Go where?"

"You ask too many questions." He grabs my elbow. "Just wait and see."

His words are mysterious. His grip makes me tremble, but I try not to show it. I can't let him know that his presence still unnerves me.

"Rich, you beat me to her. Did you get the same orders I did?"

I glance around and see a tall guard with a bald head, a silver goatee, and scary gray eyes standing at the door of my open cell. He has on a brown uniform, so I know he is a watchman.

"I'm here to take the prisoner back to L, so she can be jailed there for escaping."

"Those aren't the orders I have." He brushes his fingers over his goatee. "She's to be taken to the mansion. *He* wants to see her." His skin is as pale as the white floor underneath me.

I now know the leader in M is a man.

"That doesn't make sense. She defied the laws, and she and her friends need to be taken back to L. That's what President Esther would want. Those were the last orders she doled out before she left for the leaders meeting. The watchmen captured her and brought her here. I heard it over the radio. Now why would they bring her here if she was to be brought to the mansion?"

"Well, he's in charge of this territory and he doesn't want that. He left explicit instructions before he left for the meeting…and I'm just following his orders." His face his hard, like stone. "The watchmen who apprehended her made a mistake. You need to release her into my custody. I'm sure he has already talked to the president and she knows what will happen once the young lady is caught." He walks closer to me. His eyes bore into me. I'm almost as frightened of him as I am of Rich.

He has his own set of handcuffs for me. He clicks the cold metal around my wrists and I shiver.

"Let's go," he barks and yanks on the cuffs.

"Mitchell, this isn't cool. You know she's my prisoner," Rich growls.

"If you have a problem with this, then follow me over to the mansion…you can use the phone there. Call over to U and see what's going on for yourself. I assure you, if he's doing this, I'm sure the president already knows."

Rich rolls his eyes and mumbles something under his breath. I see his face harden as he stands there. I already know he doesn't think the leader here knows what he's doing, and I'm sure he hates taking orders from him.

* * *

The watchman wrestles open the back door of a large silver box truck. He throws me in and tells me to sit down. We're outside of the jails in the parking lot. It's the same building Alexa pointed out to me when we were driving to the executive buildings. The building is brown brick and about four-stories high. The grass is dried up and looks unmanaged.

The door rolls down and bangs closed. I collapse. There are no windows in back, so I can't see outside to look at anything else. Everything looks hazy and the brightness of the white truck walls makes me squint. The coldness I feel underneath me is the truck's floor.

My head feels like fire because my thoughts are jumbled, and I don't know what will happen next. The white wall that sits in front of me blocks my view, so I can't see the driver's area or the passenger's seat. The air is thin and smells like floor cleaner.

The ride is somewhat bumpy. My body sways from side to side and my handcuffs jingle. I can't help but wonder where my friends are. I didn't see any of them over at the jails. Are they at the mansion? Or were they caught at the mansion and are now being driven back to Territory L by Rich's hands?

The ride seems like it was all of ten minutes; before I know it, the door swishes open and Mitchell, the watchman with the silver goatee, stands before me.

"Let's go," he says. He motions for me to hop down.

We are in a large garage of some kind, and I see several large white and black vehicles—some jeeps, some trucks, and some vans. He grabs ahold of my arm and leads me through the garage. The garage is big enough to be considered a warehouse. It feels damp and smells like oil.

He leads me to a set of elevators that are black metal. He pushes the up button and the doors screech open. We enter the elevator, and he jams his finger onto the button for the third floor. The elevator jerks and rises upward. We bypass the basement, the first, and the second floors. We reach the third floor, the elevator dings, and the doors swoosh open again.

"This set of elevators only goes as far as the third floor. We will have to get on another one to reach our final destination on the fourth floor," he says to me, as if I should care. He grips my elbow this time and forces me ahead.

There is a long hallway in front of us. The white walls in the hallway match the white walls in the truck I just came from. I'm not used to such brightness. I see a black metal door to the left of us and another one to the right of us. Every few feet we walk, I see another door.

My hand tightens, wondering what—or who—could be in each room we pass. My insides quiver as we continue down the hall. Mitchell lessens his grip on my elbow. I could make a run for it, but this place seems more like a maze than President Esther's mansion was. I would never find my way out.

I hear taps on the floor. I see a man in brown pants and jacket, with black buttons on his left side—a watchmen—fastening his suit, coming toward us. He's a little taller than me, and he has dark hair and broad shoulders. But the tapping I hear isn't coming from his black boots—they kind of skate along the concrete floors.

The tapping is coming from the female who is behind him. She is light-skin and has blonde hair that reaches her shoulders. Her face is thin with high cheekbones, and she is severely underweight. I'm too far away to see her eye color, but I recognize her. Her name is Molly Travers. I remember her being in one of my classes in school. Back then, her eye color was brown—I'm sure it hasn't changed.

Why am I distracting myself with eye color? Maybe it's because she has a strange look on her face, like a deer caught in headlights. Maybe the look on her face worries me. Another watchman is behind her—he's short stocky and has bushy eyebrows that match his hair. I notice she doesn't have on handcuffs, but he has his hand perched on her shoulder. Like a bird, he guides her where he needs her to go.

Mitchell barks orders at me. "Keep your eyes ahead."

I don't listen to him; I keep watching them. They don't quite make their way to where I am; they turn into one of the rooms on the left before I reach them.

"I said eyes ahead," he sneers, as he grips my elbow tighter.

I roll my eyes. "I heard you the first time."

We reach another set of elevators. Mitchell pushes the up button. It only takes a few seconds for the doors to open. He shoves me inside. He jabs his finger onto the button for the fourth floor. The doors ding and close. The elevator roars upward and my stomach flip-flops with it. There are several more floors, but we only go up to the next floor—the fourth. The doors swing back open. Mitchell grips my arm and snatches me off.

"Go to the right," he says.

I turn right, and there is a large brown door in front of me— larger than all the others. It's like a large garage door, but it has a handle.

"Turn the knob," he says to me.

I open it and take my time walking in. The room smells like fresh linen.

"The rooms have names. This is the fight room." There is a snicker behind his words. "If you master this room, you will go to the war room next."

"Master," I mumble to myself.

"Never mind." He shakes his head. "You will never go to the war room."

This room is double the size of the jail cell I was just in. The four walls are a light Granny Smith apple green. A large rectangular mirror is built into the wall to the left.

"She'll meet you here, in a minute," he says, with a smile that shows all of his teeth. "I'm not allowed to stay and watch." He takes the keys from his pocket and undoes my handcuffs. They click as they unfasten.

"Make the most of your time," he says. His boots click as he walks away.

The door slams and my shoulders jump. I have to get my thoughts in line before the *she* he mentioned arrives. I move toward the mirror and stare at myself. Most of my hair is still in one long braid—only a few strands are unruly.

"It's only going to get messed up again."

It's Alexa's voice. I turn around to face her. "Why? What's about to happen?"

She moves closer to me. "I want you to know, I don't want to do this." Her voice is soft. "But it's the only way. They're watching." Her eyes squint toward the mirror.

It must be a two-way mirror.

"I'm sorry," she continues. "For this."

Before I have a chance to breathe, she pops me in my face with her fist. The pain shoots through the right side of my jaw, like someone has stomped on it with a boot. I double back and bang into the mirror. The mirror shakes and clinks. Before I regain my composure, she wallops me again on the right side of my sore jaw.

"I d-don't want to fight y-you," I say, through jagged breaths. "This won't s-solve anything."

"It will help my brother get out."

She swings at me, but I duck. I grab her around the waist. I ram my head into her stomach. I back her into the wall with a bump. She wobbles and stares at me.

"I thought a-all you had to do is trade h-him for me."

"I t-told you t-there w-was a few m-more things they needed me to do. They j-just informed m-me that this is one of t-them."

"So h-how can you trust them n-now? They c-could change the deal a-again."

"S-stop stalling, Emma, so w-we can get this over with."

She twists her waist. Her right leg goes up. She swings her right foot behind me. She kicks me in the back of my left knee. My feet slip from underneath me. I fall to the ground, hard. My spine hits the floor with a *whack*.

"E-even if you win, that s-still doesn't mean they will let your b-brother go."

She moves toward me. I wobble from side to side. I manage to sit up, a little. I'm on my butt now. My elbows still connect to the floor. I kick her in her right thigh. She only sways back a little. Her face is stiff.

She's silent now, but she keeps gunning for me. She bangs down on top of me and grunts. Her knees are digging into my thighs. She quickly smashes her right fist into my neck. I fall back down all the way. My spine meets the floor with a wallop, for a second time. She's little, but her weight is enough to make a sharp pain go through my side.

I think she aggravated the old injury I encountered while training with Eric—now, both sides hurt. She tries to wrap her tiny fingers around my neck. I have to act fast before she gets a good grip. I shove the palm of my hand into her nose. I smash her face away from me.

She falls to the left of me with a *thump*. I jump up with a huff, to get on my feet before she hits me again. My heart pounds in my chest. I run to the mirror and bang on it with my knuckles.

I yell, "Can we stop now?"

In the reflection, I see Alexa stampeding for me. I turn to face her. Her right fist is moving toward my jaw again. This time, I use my elbows to protect my face. My left elbow blocks her right punch. My right elbow blocks her left punch.

She swings again. Before she makes contact, I lunge down to the ground and bend on my knees. Alexa's fist hits the mirror with a *bang*.

"Ouch," she says, screaming out in pain.

She turns to me with her left hand wrapped around her right wrist. I think she hit the mirror so hard her wrist may be broken. She's holding onto her right wrist and rubbing it with her left hand. The mirror now has a squiggly crack down the middle of it.

"I h-have to save my b-brother," her voice shakes.

Tears gather in her eyes. I think the pain in her wrist matches the pain she feels trying to save her brother.

"This isn't the way."

"Then tell me, what should I do to get him back?" The shakiness in her voice calms down, but the intense look on her face remains.

Before I speak, she continues.

"My brother has been there for me through some awful times. You remember back at the old college? You said you saw blood in the pool."

"Of course I do." I nod. "There was a pink blanket and underneath the blanket was a tiny white dress. It was bloodied, shredded, and the right sleeve was sliced apart."

"That dress was for the baby I had that didn't survive. The blood in the pool was mine."

Her words make me wince.

"My father used to hurt me. He always thought girls were useless, so he doted on my brother. He said I would never amount to anything. He never cared for me. My brother saw that and took up for me." She's still holding on to her wrist and rubbing it.

"My mom died in a car accident," she says, continuing, "when I was ten years old and things only got worse. Over the years, my father drank. When he was inebriated, he would hate me even more. He would come home from work and if I didn't have dinner started or have the house cleaned, he would hit me. He would say that was women's work and now that my mom was gone, it was my responsibility."

Her eyes are filled with tears. My eyes water along with hers.

"That's how I got these bruises around my wrist that you noticed back at the old college." She glances down. Her arms shake. "He would hold on to my wrists and shake them violently. Time and time again, my brother would step in and tell him to leave me alone."

I swipe sweat from my forehead.

She takes in a much-needed breath. "I met someone in college. He was kind and nice to me. I stupidly let myself get pregnant. I knew the rules. I knew if I didn't apply myself and do well in college, the baby would be taken and I may be sent to Territory L."

She uses the index finger on her left hand to rub both of her eyes. "The thought scared me because all I heard about Territory L was horror stories. I knew I didn't want to go there, and I didn't want to be here, either. I felt like I didn't belong anywhere. My father was irate and would hit me, even while I was pregnant." She looks around the room. "The final straw was one day when he shoved me into a wall. My brother said enough was enough. That's how we became runaways."

"There was no family—no one you could go and stay with?" I scratch my chin.

"We have no other family here." She shakes her head. "My father was an only child and so was my mother." A tear falls down her cheek. "Our grandparents, on both sides, died years ago. Like I told you earlier any other relatives we had moved to California or Arizona."

"I'm sorry." I don't know what else to say. My insides ache for her. I know I should hate her for betraying me; but looking at her now, I feel sad.

"Resume fighting," a loud booming voice echoes across the room.

"The blood you saw in the pool was because I had a miscarriage." Alexa continues with her story, ignoring the intercom. "I had slowly started putting things aside for the baby. The night we ran away, I only had enough time to snatch a few things. The pink blanket and the white dress were some of the things I grabbed." She glances down and back up.

"It was a girl?" I ask, crossing my arms.

"I didn't know for sure, but I hoped." She bites her lip. "If I was going to have a baby, I wanted a little girl. I enjoyed sitting at the pool. There was no water in it but, for some reason, it comforted me. One day, I was sitting there gathering my thoughts. I was staring at the dress and blanket, wondering what she would look like. My stomach started to cramp. I'll spare you all the gory details, because I don't like to relive it." She shakes her head. "Long story short, I was only two months pregnant at the time and I miscarried right there—right at the pool."

That's why she had menorrhagia. I watch her shake her head again, like she's in disbelief.

"Resume fighting at once," the loud voice says, again. This time, there's a tap behind the mirror that goes along with it.

I know they're getting angry, but Alexa continues talking like she doesn't care and I want to hear the rest of her story.

"I was so upset that I wiped up some of the blood with the dress. I ripped the sleeve because I was angry about what happened to me. I know it's for the best; my boyfriend didn't want anything to do with me after I got pregnant." She takes in a breath.

"I'm sure I would have been a terrible mother. What kind of life would my child have had, anyway, when I can't even take care of myself?" she asks, rhetorically. "We had just come back from burying the remains when you spotted us sneaking back into the old college. So, we weren't just out getting supplies like we said."

I don't have time to let the weight of her words wash over me because I hear a rattling noise along the mirror this time.

I didn't notice, at first, but there is a square black box in the corner of the ceiling. A loud voice comes from the speaker, again.

"Alexa, you haven't done what we asked, to the best of your ability. You will be dealt with accordingly."

Now that we aren't fighting each other to the death and are engaged in civil conversation, they're done with us—well, especially Alexa. I guess I should be grateful they let us converse for as long as they did.

"Alexa, you can go now." The voice is muffled. I can't make out who it is.

Alexa wipes her face and edges toward the door.

"Once again, I'm sorry." She turns back to me. "I know I said this earlier, but I need you to understand. I would never do this if I knew they would kill you; but they won't, and you do for family."

The door echoes behind her.

She's right; you do for family. I think I am doing what is right for my family as well, but maybe I am wrong. I left them all behind, so who knows what has happened to them now.

The loud overbearing voice from the speaker continues. "Now you know how it feels when a friend betrays you."

What does that even mean? I haven't betrayed anyone. Why are they trying to teach me a lesson?

"Alexa was your friend and she turned on you," the voice says. "Now you see what happens when you trust people."

"Who's speaking?" I wipe the beads of perspiration from my forehead. I feel sweat pouring down every inch of my body. My t-shirt is damp, and now smells like a gym.

The door slides open and a tall dark-skin man walks in. He looks to be in his fifties. He has brown eyes. His hair is short, dark, with waves in it. There is a patch of gray right in the front. The closer he gets to me, the more I realize he's the man I saw in the wedding photo with President Esther. It's her husband, Henry—the one who disappeared and no one knew where he went. He is dressed neatly in a gray suit and a spotted gray tie. His dress shoes are shiny and black.

"Sorry for the accommodations," he says.

His face looks sincere. His voice is soft and his eyes are somber—not loud and blaring like it was over the speaker. He says accommodations like I will be staying here—I thought this was the fight room.

"We don't normally treat guests like this, but the circumstances are different in this case." He continues talking gibberish that I don't understand.

"What do you want with me?"

"I know you've wanted to speak to the leader. Well now's your chance—that would be me—I'm the one in charge."

"You're over Territory M!" My eyebrow rises.

"You seem surprised. Do I not look like I could be the one in charge?" His left eye squints.

"I didn't say that."

"But your tone implied it."

"It's just that you're Henry, President Esther's husband. I saw you in her wedding photo. You two looked happy and in love."

"Yes, we used to be; but that was a long time ago."

Mitchell said the leader had gone to the meeting. But he's not at the meeting now—he's standing right in front of me. Maybe he got back earlier than expected.

He's a small pip squeak of a man. President Esther is thin as well, but her body language and voice commands such a presence—his voice is trivial and he seems weak. I can't imagine him being married to President Esther or even being the president himself, for that matter. He looks like he couldn't give an order to a mouse, let alone a whole nation.

"I wanted to speak to you about getting rid of the walls and making us one whole nation again. There shouldn't be any division between the classes. We all should be able to go to college and strive for better jobs. No children should be killed. Babies should be born, no matter how much money you make."

I don't know why I'm talking so fast. My heart is racing. "I would also like to know where my friends are. Where are Eric and Whitney and Logan?"

"Slow down, child," he says. His eyes widen. "Pancakes," he says. A small chuckle follows his words.

"What?" I don't understand what he means.

I'm not a child, but that doesn't bother me as much as the word *pancakes* does. "I'm not joking." My jaw stiffens. "I came all the way here to speak to you."

"I realize that." He puts his hand in his pockets and takes them back out. The way he moves his hands makes me wonder if he's nervous about something. "I have been waiting for you."

His words make me cringe. I think about what Logan said. They knew I would come here one day, and I shouldn't be harmed.

"We have a lot to discuss, but we can't do that on an empty stomach. I'm sure you're hungry. I'm in the mood for pancakes. I will have my staff make us a stack or two."

"What time is it, anyway?" I ask. My face scrunches up. The conversation is weirding me out.

"It doesn't matter; you can have pancakes any time of the day."

"With all due respect, sir—I didn't come here to eat. I need to talk about the walls."

"We will eat first, then we will talk. Come with me. First, we will stop off at the infirmary. It's across the hall and down the way. It takes up most of that side."

"Why? I'm not sick." I let out a large sigh.

"Your upper lip doesn't imply that."

I put my finger to my mouth and I feel wetness above my lip. I thought it was just sweat from my fight with Alexa; but now I grasp, I'm bleeding. There is red on my finger. I guess the fight took more out of me than I realized. The pop she gave me made my nose bleed.

"Let's go," he says. His voice is more commanding than before. Maybe he's not as weak as my first impression led me to believe.

CHAPTER FIFTEEN

THE WALLS IN the infirmary are bleached white, and there are two rows of eight cots each. The room feels cold, which makes me shiver.

"This side—the west side of the infirmary—is for my staff." His chest puffs up like he's proud. "The east side is for me and—"

"President Esther," I say, cutting him off. "I'm surprised she doesn't have her own infirmary in her mansion." I shift my weight on the cot. "But she chooses to use the main hospital or the hospital in Territory U where her high-class friends are—or she makes my father work for her."

I should take that back. I now know my father begged her for the job. I remember hearing Jason and Rob, two of President Esther's guards, say that when we were hiding behind the hospital, trying to escape Territory L. I suppose it's because he wanted to be able to watch over me.

"You are feisty, aren't you?" He glares at me, but it isn't the kind of glower that Rich gives me.

Rich looks at me as if he wants to kill me. Henry's stare is more of an inquisitive one, like he's trying to figure me out. No matter what kind of glare it is, it still makes my jaw pang.

"And you're right," he says, continuing. "The president does use my side of the infirmary when she is here. I don't like to go out much, so I like to have all the things I need close-by."

"Sorry it took me so long to get here, sir," says a woman with long red hair and green eyes. She looks to be no more than thirty years old. She wears a white uniform that matches the walls. It's weird to see. Back home, the nurses at the hospital could never wear white.

"I was on my lunch break. Hillary is off today, and I'm the only nurse in the infirmary. Doctor Bush is busy handling an incident in the war room on the fifth…" her voice trails off, like she knows she has said too much in front of me.

Mitchell mentioned the war room. I wonder what they do there. If it's anything like the fight room, I never want to go there.

"It's fine, Claire."

Henry seems so kind to his staff—nothing like President Esther.

I lay my head back on the pillow on the cot. I'm amazed at how fluffy and soft the pillow is. If the infirmary pillows are this wonderful, what must the rooms the guest stay in be like.

I watch Claire as she takes blue latex gloves out of a box and snaps them on. She grabs a square white cloth and wipes the moisture from my lip.

"Let me take a look," she says, with a nice wide smile. "Look up," Claire says.

My eyes go wide.

"Glance to the right," she says, belting out orders. "Now left," she says.

"I thought I am here for a nose bleed," I say.

"Claire knows what she's doing," Henry says. "Let her do her job."

I know he's right, but my jaw flinches at his words anyway. Even though his tone is soft, his words still command.

"It's not bleeding anymore," she says.

"I didn't think so," I say. "I do know what to do for a nose bleed. Tilt your head back, pinch your nostrils closed, and apply an ice pack, if needed. I don't understand why I needed to come here."

"That's all well and good, but I do want to make sure the bleeding doesn't start back." Claire pushes my forehead back.

"And that's why we came here." Henry's eyes scrunch. "You'll find, young lady, that there is always a reason for what I do. Always," he repeats, as if I didn't hear him the first time.

He talks to me like I'm five years old. Maybe he does that to everyone. I glance around, looking for Alexa. I don't see her anywhere. I know her wrist is hurt, so I wonder where she is. Henry brought me to his staff's side, so I would think she would be here. I know he wouldn't take her to the side that is for him and President Esther. I can't see the other side. There is a wall that separates us.

"Keep your head back for a little while longer. Place this ice pack on the bridge of your nose, just in case." She turns from me to Henry. "Sir, can I speak to you for a moment?"

"Yes," he answers.

They walk a few steps away from me, but they're close enough that I still hear what they are saying.

"Alexa's waiting outside. I will examine her more fully, once she's brought in. I'm sure her wrist is only sprained," Claire says.

"I'll be taking Emma with me. Then you can escort Alexa in." Henry glances at me. "Emma, if you feel up to it, we will leave now."

"I'm fine." I stand. The ice pack smacks the floor. I pick it up. It's cold to the touch and stings my hand, so I throw it on the cot.

"Follow me then." His steps are quiet against the cement floors. "And bring the ice pack with you."

* * *

"Where are we?" My breaths are caught in my throat. Once again, I'm in an unfamiliar room.

The elevator took us upward and dropped us at the tenth floor. We are in a large room with purple walls. There are several windows that give the room light. It smells like musk. There is a white sofa in the middle of the room with a square glass table in front of it.

I take in a breath and continue searching my new surroundings.

In the corner of the room is the kitchen area. I see stainless steel appliances, like in Whitney's kitchen. There's no bar area, like in the president's quarters—maybe he doesn't drink. I also see a staircase to the right of us that must lead up to the second floor of his quarters. My guess would be his bedroom is up there.

"These are my quarters." I have already figured out where we are by the time he opens his mouth to answer me.

"Sit." He grinds his teeth. He belts out another command, but in a nice way, as he throws his hand toward the sofa. "My maid, Nancy, will bring us something to eat. You must be famished. She will have my chef, Thomas, make us anything your heart desires."

"Why are you being so nice to me?" I swallow hard. "I've invaded your territory, looking for you to beg you to get rid of the walls. According to President Esther, I've caused disruption and chaos in Territory L and I want to do the same here. She claims I want to start a war. Why am I no longer handcuffed? Why have you brought me here? Why have you taken my friends away?"

He seems annoyed at all of my inquiries. "Everything will be answered, in due time. Right now, I want you to sit and eat."

He talks in circles, just like the president, all the while never answering my questions. He walks over to the left side of the room. There is a small brown box on the wall. He presses the button on the intercom.

"Nancy, please bring my lunch. Emma will have the same."

"I'm not really hungry," I lie.

I could eat—my stomach growls. But I would feel bad, enjoying a meal while my friends are probably having nothing.

"You still haven't sat down yet." He turns to me with a hard look on his face.

"Sorry." I plop down and air wafts up in my direction. I don't need the ice pack any more, so I place it on the sofa next to me.

"Thank you." He smiles and sits at the opposite end of the sofa. "I understand you have questions, but I never delve into important things until after I've had an enjoyable meal."

From the way he waits for his meal and talks about food, you would think he would weigh more. Yet, he's very thin. His shape reminds me of a pencil.

It doesn't take long before the door shrieks open and a woman walks in. She's younger than I imagined. She has ebony skin and is tall with a medium build.

"Here is your usual, sir." She smiles at me. She has beautifully high cheekbones that stand out when she smiles. "He has the same thing for lunch every day." Her brown eyes are wide. "It's his favorite."

The plates on the silver tray she carries in the palm of her hand clink as she tries to hold it steady. "Would you prefer to eat in here or in the dining room, sir?" Her hair is brown, shoulder length and it swings as she moves her head.

"I would prefer the dining room," Henry says.

He stands and I take that as my cue to stand as well. I follow him and we go left, pass by the kitchen, through a set of double doors. It leads to the dining room, where the walls are orange. The table is glass and oblong-shaped. There are a set of six white chairs—two on each side and one at each end. Henry sits at one end and I choose to sit at the other end. I don't want to sit too close. This is all strange, and I need to keep some boundaries.

Nancy carefully sets down the tray in the middle of the table, but it clanks against the glass anyway. She glides toward me and puts a plate in front of me. She is so bubbly that it seems as if she's walking on air as she glides back down to where Henry is. His plate clinks as she places it in front of him. She returns to the tray and picks up the glass pitcher.

"Here's your water with lemon, sir." The water plops into his glass. Her white high heels click along the floors as she walks it to him and smacks the glass in front of him. She doesn't wear a stiff maid's uniform—instead, she has on a lovely flowered red dress that sways as she moves.

"Water, Emma?" she asks, knowing my name already. Her eyebrow rises. "Henry only likes water with lemon at lunchtime. I could get you something else, if you like."

"No, water's fine," I say.

I don't want her going to any more trouble than she already has. My hand vibrates because now I feel bad for not sitting closer to Henry. If I had known all the walking she would have to do because of the long table, I would have sat near the middle.

"I try to get him to eat in the living room, sometimes, so he can be more comfortable. That sofa looks so cushiony." She grins at me as she pops my glass with water down. "But he won't hear of it. He follows a strict routine and he prefers to eat in here." She winks at me. "Maybe you will get him to change."

"That will be all, Nancy," Henry says, with a chuckle.

My shoulders tense. What makes her think I could change his mind about where he eats? She talks to me like I have some pull here. It seems like she already knows me and we're old friends. And the way she jokes with Henry, it's like they are more than servant and boss. This is quite different than the way President Esther would order her maid, Helen, around.

I'm so distracted with Nancy that I haven't looked at my plate yet. I smell cheese. I look down to see a grilled cheese sandwich. The only grilled cheese I've had is with the yellow cheese the government hands out, but this looks like so much more. It looks delicious and, I have to say, my mouth is watering. The cheese is white and thick. There is a thin layer of bacon on it along with a tomato slice. The bread is grilled to perfection and has to be the thickest bread I've ever seen.

"I hope you enjoy it, Emma," Henry says. "Eat up. I decided to save the pancakes for the morning."

"What kind of cheese is this?" I know it's not important, but I'm curious.

"It's called provolone. Do you like it?"

"Yes." I nod. "I do."

I don't mean to, but it's so wonderful, I smack as I eat. I wipe my mouth with the cloth napkin that is next to me. I sip the water that I was given and that too taste better than normal. I guess the lemon gives it a citrusy taste.

It's funny how they don't serve bottled water here. Their tap water isn't contaminated like ours, so they aren't stuck drinking water that's supplied by the government.

Henry crunches loudly and I can tell he's enjoying it as well—after all, Nancy said this was his favorite lunchtime meal. To think of people getting their favorite meals every day boggles my mind. I was just happy to have food to eat, let alone get my favorite—or even three meals a day, for that matter.

A set of four windows is to the right of us. The sunlight hits the glass table and makes it shine.

"Now that we're almost done eating, can we get down to business?" I ask.

"I agree." Henry clears his throat. "Now that our bellies are full, we will talk more sensibly."

I could talk sensibly on an empty stomach before but apparently he couldn't.

"I believe every person should be treated equally and have a fair shot at a nice life." I shift in my chair. "I'm not saying people with less money deserve a handout, but I believe we should have a chance to go to college to better ourselves—that way we can make it here or to Territory U if we want. If you're a doctor, like my father, I believe you should receive the appropriate wages for your job description. It's unfair that just because you live in Territory L and you're a doctor, you don't get paid equally."

"I thought you wanted the walls torn down. If that were the case, there wouldn't be any doctors in L; we would all live in the same territory. So which is it Emma? Should all doctors live in the same territory or should the doctors in Territory L just get paid higher wages?" His tone is demeaning.

He's twisting my words around. "I just want everything to be fair. I don't want babies being killed anymore." I swallow, hard, thinking of Abigail. "I want all children to have a chance at a good—"

"I thought you wanted to know what happened to your friends," Henry says, cutting me off.

"What?"

"Your friends," he says, standing. "Earlier, you asked why you weren't cuffed and why your friends were taken away. I thought you wanted to know what happened to them."

"Well, I did—I do, but I need to know about the walls and—"

He cuts me off again from my rambling.

"I can't answer everything at once."

He's not answering anything I ask; he just keeps interrupting me. My shoulders sink. I can't believe I made it all the way here. I made it all the way to the Hill for this—a game of twenty questions with no answers.

"Why don't we start with where your friends are, and how they are doing?" He links his fingers together. "Come with me," he says, unlinking them.

My chest aches because this conversation is getting me nowhere. I feel like I'm talking to a brick wall. I'm starting to think talking to President Esther was more engaging than this. She talked to me in a snotty uppity way, but at least she answered most of my questions. Even when she had no intention of answering me, she would plainly tell me that, instead of giving me the run-around like Henry.

My feet feel like lead as I stand. I feel this is another trick and I won't really get any answers.

"Hurry, Emma, time is money," he says, squinting his eyes.

We walk up the staircase to the second floor of his quarters. The walls here are silver, and the air smells like jasmine. There is an open door on the left. I see a king-size bed with a gold bedspread. I'm guessing that's his master bedroom.

We keep going pass that door and his shiny shoes slide up to another door on the left, only this door is closed, like its private—secret. He pushes in a series of numbers in the keypad next to the door. The buttons beep, then the door pops and unlocks. The door whizzes open on its own.

He grins. "Some things are off-limits."

We step inside a small hallway no bigger than a tiny closet. Another door stands before us. This door has a different pad—unlike the keypad we encountered earlier.

"Sometimes, you need extra security," he says, with another grin.

He turns from me and put his eye up to the square-shaped pad. I hear a beep and the second door pops and snaps open.

"It's eye recognition software," he explains to the confused look on my face.

As I step ahead, my body shudders. The room is white, much like the room I was held in earlier. There is a beige sofa to the right of me. To the left is a large rectangular gray table with eight chairs surrounding it. It reminds me of a table you would use if you were in a business meeting.

He moves pass the table, toward the wall. The wall has large cherry framed shutters with artwork on it. He pushes a button. I hear a motor start up that sounds like a whirling noise, as the shutters slide to the right. Once the shutters are removed, I see several small boxes. They look like small information boxes, just like the ones Whitney had in her panic room. But there are more of them, probably twenty boxes—four rows, five screens on each row.

"Sit," he says, tilting his head toward the business-like table.

I plunk down in one of the gray chairs. It's soft and feels like what I would imagine velvet to be.

"This is my monitoring system." He is still standing. His chest puffs out, like he's proud. "There are a lot of rooms here, and a lot of comings and goings. I need to know what's happening in the mansion, at all times."

"You said my friends—"

"Yes," he says, cutting me off. "I told you I would show you how your friends are doing. They were in the jails, like you were, but I had them brought over to the mansion."

There is a panel next to the screens. The long panel has silver switches and buttons and they are numbered. He switches on all of the screens in the fourth row. The other screens remain dark. My body goes numb, because one of the screens shows Eric. He is sitting on the floor in a white room, staring up at the ceiling, like he's trying to figure out his escape plan. His right wrist is handcuffed to a post. There is a tray of uneaten food next to him. He looks tired and despondent. I wish I could help him.

My throat constricts. I sat down with Henry and ate a full meal, while Eric took a stance and wouldn't eat at all. I figured if I ate like Henry wanted me to, he would answer my questions; but so far, he has answered none. I guess that's a half-truth. I was hungry and I wanted to eat, so I did. The mucus in my throat thickens. I stand. I walk up to the monitors. I touch the screen, tracing Eric's face with my fingers.

"Don't waste all your time on that one," Henry says. "There are a few more screens you need to see."

Two more screens pop on. There's Logan on the floor. He is lying on his stomach, like he's dead to the world. It's like there is no life left in him to fight. His ankles are tied and his wrists are, too. My heart sinks for him. He helped us a lot, and he didn't betray us. Now he is caught, like we are, just for being near us.

"He fought more than Eric did, so we couldn't just handcuff him to a post. We tied his ankles and wrists with wire so he would stop fighting." He takes in a breath. "He eventually calmed down."

I stay silent and look at the next screen he turned on. It's Alexa, in the infirmary. She's lying on a cot, with her right wrist bandaged. She is on the cot near the one I was on. She's taken my place, only she has tears in her eyes, like she is sorry for all she's done.

This is no better than being in the jails. Why would Henry bring them here, only to torture them again?

"Can I visit Eric? Will you release him? Could you take the handcuffs off him? Where's Whitney? What did you do with her?"

"So many questions, so little time." There he goes with his riddles again. I don't get him or his motives. "There's another screen you should see before you beg for Eric to be released, or to see Whitney. You may want to use your energies on someone else."

My heart beats unsteadily at his words. The next screen snaps on, and I blink a few times. I can't believe what I'm seeing. It's my sister, Taylor. She is also in a white room; but she lies on a cot, not on the floor like the others. Her hands and feet are tied, like Logan, but she is also gagged—he wasn't.

"We had to cover her mouth. She wouldn't stop screaming." He pauses. "Something about what have we done with her baby."

My eyes are glued to the screen. She has big crocodile tears rolling down her cheeks and her once-brown eyes are bloodshot. She has on a blue uniform, just like they made me wear when I was housed in the jail in Territory L. What is she even doing here? My chest lightens to see her again, but seeing what she's going through makes it instantly heavy again. Her long sandy hair is tossed all over her head.

"You can't do this." My nostrils flair. "She's already been through enough. You have to let her go. She's a good person; she's doesn't deserve this."

"She hid her baby, which you and I know is against the laws."

"The laws are stupid. Just let her go. I'll take her place." The vein in my neck pulsates. "Please let her go." My voice is getting louder. "Let her out of her cage!"

"Emma, calm down." He glares at me. "There's another screen I need to show you."

"I don't care about your stupid screens. I won't calm down, until you let her go."

"I'm warning you." He steps forward. "I said to quiet down."

"Stop telling me what to do."

"Mitchell, get in here, now," he says.

I hear the door swing open. My body jolts, seeing Mitchell standing there. How is he all of a sudden here? Where did he come from? Before I speak, I feel a warm, strong hand around my mouth. I swallow hard. I jerk my elbow back to hit him in the gut, but my elbow never reaches its target. I feel something sharp and cold pierce my neck. I know it's a needle.

"Sorry, I had to do that," Henry says. "But this was getting out of hand. If you're going to keep having outburst like that, this arrangement is never going to work."

He says arrangement like I've made a deal with him, when clearly I have not. His voice fades in and out and my eyesight blurs. Mitchell's hand is still over my mouth. The room is getting dark. I feel my body go limp. My breaths get weaker and weaker.

CHAPTER SIXTEEN

I FEEL DROWSY and nauseated. I don't know what they stuck me with, but my head feels like a heavy weight is sitting on it. My eyes burn as I glance around the room. My face drops. Across from me sits Taylor, on her cot. The room smells like brown sugar. I see a bowl of oatmeal on the cement floor. I don't know how they expect her to eat it with her mouth gagged. I wobbly stand and move toward her.

"Taylor," I bellow. I rip the tape from her mouth. "Are you okay?"

She remains silent. Her blue uniform is rumpled and her white sole shoes look dingy.

"It's me. Emma."

Her voice trembles, like she's scared. "I-I know who you a-are."

"Taylor, what's wrong?" I ask, removing the wire from her wrists and ankles.

"I-I just can't b-believe it's you. I-I thought I w-would never see you a-again." Tears flow from her eyes, matching the ones that flow from mine.

I lean in, hug her, and I feel her body trembling. She's thinner now; I feel the bones sticking out on her back. It's so good to see her. I don't want to let her go. After a few minutes, I lean back and stare at her.

"Did they hurt you?" I remove a few strands of hair from her eye.

She shakes her head. "No."

"What happened? How did you get here?" I ask.

I step back. I stop once I feel the wall against my back. I need to lean on it for support to digest her story.

"You first," she says, as her voice settles a little.

I understand her not wanting to talk about what she's been through, yet.

"I only wanted to do the right thing." I take in a breath. "But maybe everything I do is wrong." I sniff. "I'm sorry I couldn't save you and get you out of jail." I slide down to the floor.

"It's okay, Emma."

"No, it's not." I swipe my hand down my face. "I came here with Eric and Julian. I met Eric while I was jailed in Territory L. Julian was a friend of his. I wanted to talk to the leader here. I stupidly thought he—who I now know is, President Esther's husband, Henry—could help me go against President Esther."

Her eyes go wide.

"Eric was by my side the entire time. Eric never let me down—not even once."

I'm talking fast. I want to get my story over with.

"We hid out, at first, in an abandoned college. We had to keep a low profile so no one could locate us until we devised a plan. I met a few people here in M who wanted to come along with Eric, Julian, and I to help. Some I now call friend; others betrayed us, so I cannot."

I swallow hard. "Long story short, I was eventually caught because someone betrayed me. I was jailed, but only for a little while. For some reason, Henry had me released and brought here, to the mansion."

Her eyes widen again as I mention Henry's name a second time.

"I'm still unclear why he would bring me here; but since I am here, I tried talking to him and pleading my case."

"How did that go?"

"Not so good." I shake my head. "So far, I've been getting the runaround. Henry has barely answered any of my questions. For some reason, he tolerated me—that is, until I saw you chained on his monitoring system and I screamed at him for how he was treating you. Then he drugged me and had his watchman, Mitchell, throw me in here."

"He stomped in, with a sour look on his face, carrying you. He kind of shoved you over in the corner, then looked at me and said, 'don't get too comfortable, she won't be staying long.'"

Now that I know I won't be here long, I need her to tell me what happened to her before I'm taken away.

"I want to know what—"

"Who is this Eric person?" she asks, cutting me off.

"That's not important," I say. "We might not have much time and there are more pressing things to talk about."

"Tell me about Eric."

I don't believe her. We're in crisis and she wants to talk about someone she doesn't even know.

"He's just a b-boy—a man—a m-male friend. What does it matter?" I shrug.

"It matters because you smile a little every time you mention his name; and you've mentioned it several times since we started talking. Also, you're stuttering, so I know you must like him."

I grin because I've missed her—I've missed this. I miss her bugging me over nonsense like when we were little. I miss her teasing me because I forgot to bring home the milk mother asked for from the market. I miss her getting on me because I didn't do so well on a test I had in school. I miss having a big sister to talk to. After she met Nathan and especially after she got pregnant, there was no time for joking or mischief. Everything turned serious and it was like I was the older sister, instead of her.

"Do you like him? Or, maybe it's love?"

"I don't even know what love is." I bite my lip. I feel my shoulders tense. "I've never been in love—never had a boyfriend, for that matter—but you already know that. But I guess I do like him. He has these dreamy amber eyes that I could just get lost in. He's strong and independent, but he's also moody and mysterious, at times. He has this wall that's sometimes hard to break through. It's just," I hesitate. "I enjoyed spending time with him back in the jail. I was getting to know him and, I have to say, seeing him was the highlight of my day."

I shift on the cold concrete floor. I know I'm blushing.

"But now that we've been on the run, everything's been different. We've barely had time to talk about anything but this journey we're on, and I kind of feel like we're losing the closeness we were starting to share. I know it sounds stupid. I don't have time for a love life, not with everything that's going on around us; but we kissed on the lips—only once." I hold up my finger to emphasize my point.

"It was nice, and I sometimes wish I could be a regular girl and go on a first date and fall in love like a normal person." I rub my hand through the front of my hair. "But that's never going to happen for me, because I've started all this and I don't know how any of it's going to end."

"You don't know that." She tries to sound reassuring. "You don't know what's going to happen in the future. Maybe all of this will turn out fine and you will be able to date Eric, like a normal couple. I have to say, it is nice falling in love. When I first met Nathan, he was all I could think about."

"I know," I say, with a chuckle in my voice. "You talked about him so much I was sick of hearing his name."

"Anyway," she says, rolling her eyes. "It was so nice, at

first—that is, until I got pregnant and he didn't want any part of it and he ran off with his parents." She blinks. "I want that for you—I really do. I want you to experience a first love. Everyone should."

Her face drops, and she stares down at her hands. I know the conversation has turned, making her sad again.

"Tell me how you got here. What happened?"

I'm trying to change the subject, since the banter has shifted and I know I may not have much time left. I bend my knees up to my chin.

"About a week after you escaped, President Esther sent down word that she was fed up with the ingrates of Territory L and she was having every single home searched. They only had time to do a few houses a day; but they would all eventually be investigated, whether occupied or abandoned. Once they started searching houses, they found so many babies and children being hidden that the jails became overrun with mothers—my age, some older, and some younger. For some reason, they grabbed me and said they had to move me here…to Territory M, because there wasn't enough room."

She drums her fingers along her right thigh, like she's in deep thought.

"I tend not to believe them though…" her voice drifts off.

"Why is that?" I slide my legs back down to the floor.

"Because they moved Theodore, too, for the same reason, saying the male jails were also overrun because so many fathers were jailed. But, as far as I know, Theodore and I were the only ones brought here. We were the only ones in the van, unless another van was following behind us; but I really don't think so."

"T's here?"

"Yes, probably in a room like this one."

That must be the other screen Henry was trying to show me, but I didn't give him the chance.

"There has to be a reason Theodore and I were the only ones shipped here." Her eyes widen.

"You think it's because of me?"

"Yes," she says, nodding. "Now that I know you're here, I believe that's the reason."

My leg twitches. Why would they bring my family here? Unless they are going to use them as leverage over me.

"Maybe they'll take you to see T next." A small smile seeps onto her lips. "That would be nice."

"Yes, I would love that." My chest pounds. "You mentioned earlier that the van they brought you and T in was empty."

"It was."

"And you're sure no other van followed behind you."

"I told you I didn't think so. Why?"

"It's nothing." I squirm.

"I think it is something or you wouldn't have asked."

"There's a guard named Samuel that I'm kind of worried about." My knee shakes while talking about him. "He was so nice to me, like a big brother." I add.

"You already have a brother."

"I know that. I'm just saying he was so kind to me and I'm sure he was jailed or even imprisoned as a lifer for helping me out. I just wondered if you knew of him."

"I never met anyone named Samuel. I'm sorry. I can't tell you what happened to him because I don't know."

"That's okay." I glance around the room. "I was just curious."

"Does Eric have competition?"

"Stop being stupid," I say. My face feels hot. "I told you he was like a big brother to me. He was there for me when I needed someone—the way I should have been there for…" I lean my head into my palm. My temples are throbbing. "I'm sorry, Taylor." I look back up and blink. "I'm sorry for everything. I wish—"

"Don't," she says, cutting me off. "I can't talk about her." The small smile fades, and her eyes leak like a faucet.

We have talked about so much, all the while avoiding this subject. I know it's because it's too much for both of us to handle, but I need to get this out.

"I wanted to save her. I really did." I wipe my face.

"Please, Emma. I can't." Her shoulders shake. "Abigail is gone now. I'll never see her cute little pudgy face again, or the birthmark on her cheek that reminds me of—"

"The one on your left cheek." I'm trying to get her to laugh. I just want to make the situation lighter, but I know there's no way to.

"Very funny." Her face winces. "I was going to say I'll never hear her coo or laugh or gurgle. I'll never hear her cry again." Her whole body trembles. "It was just me and her in that tiny room alone...every day. You got to come and go, but it was like she was attached to me...a third arm, and now she's gone...just like that, gone. It hurts too much to think about it, so I try not to."

She wraps her arms around herself and rocks back and forth on her cot.

I stand and slide over near her. I clutch her palm in mine as I sit down on the cot next to her. I feel the warmth of her hand as I gently squeeze it. I so want to tell her that I think Abigail may still be alive. But what good would it do, if it turns out she's not.

I haven't had time to question Henry about it. I'm sure he won't give me a direct answer anyway, only the runaround. It wouldn't be fair to get her hopes up. I can't do that to her—I won't. So I'll keep it to myself until I get more information.

"What's wrong?" Taylor asks.

"Nothing," I reply, releasing my hand.

"You're all quiet."

"I was just thinking of Mother and Father." I shrug.

It's not a lie, entirely. They were in the back of my mind, and I did wonder why she hadn't mentioned them. As soon as I told her about Abigail I was going to ask about them. Since I decided not to tell her about Abigail, now is the time.

"Why haven't you mentioned them? You're here, and Theodore is here. Where are they?"

She gulps and looks down at the floor. She wipes tears from her face. "They are fine." Her tone is so soft, I barely hear her.

"Where are they?"

"They're still living at home. Father's still working at the hospital…" her voice trails off. She pauses for a moment, like she's thinking of what to say next. "Mother visited me every chance she got while I was jailed. So did Father. They both visited T as well. They're sad over what happened to Abigail, although they tried not to show it when they visited me. I know they are trying to keep my spirits up. And they miss you terribly, but they know what you're doing is important."

"Do they really know that?" My mouth goes dry. "They're not disappointed in me for running off and leaving you all behind?"

She bites down on her lip. "No, they understand."

"Are you sure they are okay? If something was wrong you would tell me, wouldn't you?" The dryness in my mouth has moved down into my throat.

"Don't worry, Emma; like I said, they know why you have to be here. They are fine, Emma, really they are." She pats my hand, trying to reassure me.

Her face freezes. I don't believe she's telling me the truth. A cold chill rushes up my spine. I feel something has happened that she doesn't want me to know about.

Before I bombard her with more questions, the door rustles open. Mitchell is back with his bald head and silver goatee. I take in a deep breath. I know my time is up.

"It's time to go." He towers above me. "I will be taking you to your next destination." He says destination like I'm going on a wonderful trip, instead of whatever torture they have planned for me.

I guess I'm not standing fast enough for him. He sighs, grabs me by my elbow, and yanks me up.

"Hey, don't touch her," Taylor says. Her brown eyes go cold.

"It's alright," I say. "I'll be okay. You just take care of yourself." I blink. "Try to eat something. I'm sure the food here is better than what we had at home." I smile. "I love you."

She smiles back. "I love you, too."

"Hopefully, I'll be back to visit soon."

"Hopefully." Her smile fades. She probably doesn't believe that's true.

"You shouldn't speak of things you're not sure of," Mitchell says, grunting.

His face is like stone and his voice has a growl to it, reminding me of Rich's attitude.

CHAPTER SEVENTEEN

"IT's so GOOD to see you," I say to my brother, Theodore.

I release the hug. We never show affection; but the way he hugs me, I can tell he missed me as much as I missed him. He looks more muscular and his sandy head of hair has almost been shaved down to nothing. He has on a blue uniform like Taylor, but his rubber-soled shoes are still bright white. His cage smells like lemons, like he's been scrubbing the floors.

"I wasn't sure if I would ever see you again," he says. "How did you get in here?"

"One of the watchmen brought me. His name is Mitchell. I'm not sure, but I think he may be Henry's right-hand man, like Rich is to President Esther."

"Where is he now?"

"He's waiting outside the door. He said I could have a few minutes with you. Taylor said you were here, but she didn't tell me about this."

I touch his right cheek. It's bruised. His left eye is surrounded by a black and purple circle.

"She probably didn't want to worry you."

"Well, I am worried. Does your face hurt?" I remove my hand.

"No." He shakes his head. "I'm fine."

"What happened?"

"A guard put his hands on Taylor. When they were dragging us to the van, he was way too rough with her. I didn't like it, so I punched him—needless to say, he punched me right back. I'm not going to let anyone hurt you or Taylor."

"You've turned into someone I can respect, you know that."

"And you couldn't respect me before?" He gives a small smile.

"You know what I mean. Instead of just looking out for yourself, you've really stepped up and looked out for our family."

"I know you didn't like me being a guard." He stops and takes in a breath. "But it wasn't all bad. It taught me how to defend myself. It taught me how to be a man. I grew up."

"That's funny because it did some of that for me, too." My chest rises and falls. The words are hard to say. "Why did they bring you and Taylor here?"

"I'm not sure." He paces the tiny room. "I know it has something to do with you. Maybe if you saw that we were here, imprisoned, it would get to you."

"But I already knew you were imprisoned back in Territory L."

"Maybe seeing it up close and personal would bother you even more. They could use it as a power play, so you would stop doing what you're doing."

"You mean talking to someone about the walls coming down. Or starting a war, as the president says." I roll my eyes.

"Yes, both things." He nods. "How's that going?"

"Not so good." I shrug.

I open my mouth to say more, but the door opens and Mitchell is standing there.

"Time to go," he barks.

"I thought I would have more time."

I didn't even have time to ask him about Mother and Father. Maybe he would have shared more information about them than Taylor was willing to. I was given way more time with Taylor. We were able to talk about so many things. I wanted the same time with Theodore, but I guess I should be grateful for what I was given.

"You have one last stop." He squints both eyes. "I said let's go."

T grips my hand and squeezes. "I love you, sis."

"I love you, too," I say, releasing my grasp.

* * *

We reach another black metal door. Mitchell opens it and shoves me inside.

"Last stop," he says, yelling. The door closes and I feel a waft of air wash over me. The room smells stale.

I look over in the corner and see this is Eric's room. He hasn't noticed me. He is no longer chained; he's lying on the floor, doing push-ups. He grunts as his muscular frame moves up and down. I watch as he does ten more push-ups.

Once he is done, he lays his stomach against the floor to rest, like he's taking everything in. He lets out a breath, rolls over, and notices me. He has an awkward look on his face as he jumps to his feet.

"Whisper," he says, brushing off his black pants. "I didn't know you, or anyone, was in here."

"That's okay," I say, softly. I can't help it; I'm staring at him. His chest ripples and glistens with sweat. I realize this isn't the time nor place for this, but I can't stop my whole body from trembling.

"What's wrong? Why are you looking at me like that?" He uses his gray t-shirt to wipe off the moisture around his neck.

"I guess," I pause, hesitating, not able to gather the right words. "This is only the s-second time I've seen you without your shirt on. I guess you look—well," I pause and look around the room. I'm stumbling over my words. "You look even more chiseled than the last time I saw you. I-I'm used to seeing your arms when we worked out. When I see you like this. Sorry." My face feels hot and I know I'm blushing. I feel a warm tingle go up my spine. Seeing him like this unnerves me.

"Sorry," he says. "I'll cover up." He throws down the t-shirt with one hand and uses the other hand to grab his black hoodie that lays on the floor and puts it over his strong frame. The zipper whizzes as he hurries and fastens it. "I can't put the shirt back on until it dries."

"It's fine." I glance down and back up.

"I didn't expect to see you here." He marches toward me.

"I didn't expect to be here."

"How are you? Where have you been? Did they hurt you?" He rambles. He clutches my chin in his palm and strokes my face with his finger. "The last thing I remember was the wall coming down in the tunnel, separating us. You were shouting, but I couldn't get to you. A watchman appeared out of nowhere and used a Taser on Logan and me, before we could draw our weapons."

"No, I'm not hurt," I say, remembering his last question. I shake my head, causing his hand to fall. "Just confused," I say, followed by a gasp. I notice a cut and dried blood on his upper lip. "What happened?" I touch his lip with my finger. It's warm and soft to the touch. "Are you alright?"

"I'm fine. You know I can handle myself."

"I do know that. What happened?" I ask again. "Henry has cameras monitoring the entire mansion. I saw you on the monitoring system a few hours ago. You were handcuffed. How did you get out of them?"

"If he's watching us, maybe we shouldn't talk here." He glances around the room.

"I don't think it's wired for sound. When I was watching with him, we could only see rooms, not hear people speaking. I could be wrong though; maybe he just didn't have the sound turned on. I don't care if he hears." I frown. "I just want to know what happened."

"After we were Tasered, I woke up in the jails; but I didn't stay there long. They tossed me in a van and brought me to the mansion. Then they threw me in this room and I've been here ever since."

He shrugs like it's no big deal. "My gun and Taser were both gone. I never saw Logan in the jails. He wasn't in my cell, so I don't know what happened to him. I just figured he's still in jail or he ended up in a room just like this one." He scratches his cheek.

"I refused to eat for a while. But I knew if there was any way I would make it out of here, I would need my strength; so I changed my mind and decided to eat the cold meatloaf and mash potatoes that were given to me."

He picks up the t-shirt again and wipes more sweat from his forehead. "When a watchman came in to take my tray, I asked if my handcuffs could be removed, if I promised not to try and escape. He decided that was okay and undid the handcuffs but kept a gun on me the entire time, until he exited the room. I wanted to move around freely, so I could work out and keep fit for what's to come next."

"That was smart of you."

"Now, what happened to you? There is a small cut underneath your nose. I suppose we're both banged up."

Taylor didn't notice, nor did Theodore; but Eric's so observant. He seems to study every inch of my face, so I should have known he would.

"It's nothing." I shake it off. "It doesn't even hurt."

"I don't agree—it's something. Who did this to you?" He touches the cut. I flinch. I didn't realize it was still painful. I guess it would be, since it only happened a few hours ago.

"Alexa betrayed me…actually us. She tripped me back in the tunnels and I fell. While I was trying to stand back up, she hit me in the head with a rock or something and knocked me out. I ended up in the jails, where Rich showed up to take me back to Territory L."

I take in a breath, glancing around. "That is until Mitchell, one of the watchmen, stopped him. Then they brought me here to the mansion."

I see fire in Eric's eyes. His jaw clenches. "Did Rich do this to your face?"

"No," I say, shaking my head. "I know he wished he had. He still hates me. But I now know Henry, the president's husband, is the one in charge. He had other plans for me. He brought me to a room they call the fight room. They had me fight Alexa. She punched me in the nose. That's how this happened."

I flinch again, rubbing my finger over the cut. "Long story short, they were watching us fight from another room. At the time, I wasn't sure who," I say, knowing that was his next question. "Henry was watching. I don't know how many others. During the fight, I ducked and she hit the mirror, instead of my head. Since she was hurt, we started talking, then the fight was over. It was a two-way mirror. Henry came in and got me. I've been with him this entire time, trying to get information but basically getting the runaround."

I step back and try to breathe. "If it's any consolation, I do think Alexa is sorry for betraying us. She just wants to save her brother...get him out of jail. We can't fault her for that."

The hard look in his eyes tells me he doesn't really agree.

"She's been through a lot of stuff no one should ever have to endure."

He ignores my last statement; maybe because he's been through a lot of things no person should have to endure, either, but he's never betrayed anyone because of it.

"Can we go back to something you said earlier? You said you were confused. About what?"

"They've been parading me around to various rooms." I'm

surprised after everything I just said he wants to go back to that, but I continue anyway. "It's like I'm on some kind of good-bye tour."

"What do you mean?"

"It's like they want me to say good-bye to my loved ones as if this is the last time I will see them. They brought Theodore and Taylor here, and I've already been to see them; now I'm here to visit you. Mitchell said you were my last stop, so I take it I won't be seeing Logan, and I still don't know where Whitney is. I fear after this, they are going to do something bad to me; maybe even kill me."

"Remember what Logan told you and what the president said on the box. They don't want you killed."

"But so much has happened." I shrug. "Maybe all of that has changed now. I don't know."

There's a sinking feeling inside of me.

"Everything's going to turn out okay."

I blink. "You don't know that."

"Is there something else you're not telling me?" His glare is strong.

"I just," I say, hesitating. "I feel horrible for the thoughts I'm thinking. But I feel like after I leave this room, there's no turning back and…"

There's an unmovable weight standing on my chest. "If I'm right and I somehow devise a way to escape, first I need to save Taylor. I don't think she can save herself. I also need to save Theodore. He talks a good game, but he may still need help and—"

"If you have a chance to run and save your family at the same time, you do that." His finger feels warm as he wipes a tear from my face.

"I just don't want you to think I don't care about you or that I'm being selfish. Because I do care for you…"

My words drift off because I can't say the words *in love with you*. I feel things for him—maybe I do love him, but I don't know if I'm in love with him, yet. I've only known him a short time, so it can't be that. I'm being naïve to even think so. Besides, I don't know what being in love is supposed to feel like. I lean against the wall for support.

"I won't think that." His words break my thoughts. "I would never think less of you. I need you to know that. It's okay if you don't come back for me or leave me behind. I can take care of myself. I'll be okay."

His eyes are glued to mine. He rushes toward me and pulls my face to his, kissing me hard on my mouth. I feel a surge go up my spine. My back is up against the cold wall. That icy feeling changes to warmth as I feel a wave of heat pouring from his body onto mine.

Our first kiss was nice and tender; this is something different. This is passionate. My toes curl. I didn't want it to end. But it does end, because the door opens. We finish the embrace as Mitchell stampedes in.

"Ms. Whisperer, we have to go now."

He uses my last name. It sounds strange, because no one else has done that. I know it's because he means business. It's really time to leave.

CHAPTER EIGHTEEN

I'm SITTING BACK on the sofa in Henry's quarters. Mitchell dropped me here and told me to make a list of twenty questions I want answered. The room smells citrusy, now. Maybe Henry sprayed some cologne. Maybe he had Nancy spray something. I don't know why I'm dwelling on the way the room smells; maybe it's because I can't focus on the pen and paper in my hand.

My hand trembles as I move it toward the paper. I suppose I'm unsure if I can write down twenty questions for Henry. What will it matter, if he will only give me the runaround? I finally start to write and write. The pen squeals as the questions flow.

I feel like over an hour has gone by when the door swings open and Henry steps in. I hand him the paper. It ruffles in his hand as he glances over it.

"Interesting," he mumbles. He scratches the gray patch in the front of his head. "I'll be back in a minute. Stay here."

He glides up the stairs to the second floor of his quarters. I know I shouldn't, but I'm curious. I follow. How much more trouble could I get in when I'm already drowning like I'm in water. I use small strides so Henry won't hear me. I didn't notice the first time; the steps are tan and cushiony and soft.

As I round the corner, I hear talking. It's coming from the first door on the left, his bedroom. I lean against the wall, to hear what he is saying. He's on some sort of speaker or intercom system.

"You were supposed to keep her busy until I had a chance to get there." A chill goes up my spine; it's President Esther's voice and she doesn't sound happy. "The leaders meeting is taking longer than I originally hoped." Her voice is squeaky, like always.

Leaders meeting—she's the only leader, so why do they call it that.

"If I hadn't been commanded to leave the meeting early, come back here, and babysit, I could have helped you discuss the kill-all project."

"No," she says, roughly. "Your presence isn't needed. You never add anything of value anyway. No one misses you." She talks down to him. "You're only around to be my eyes when I can't be around. I told you before, since she was seen in the area, she may be caught soon and you were more valuable there—to detain her."

The way they converse with each other makes it hard to believe they are husband and wife. My throat tightens. Why must I be babysat? What is going on? The kill-all project must be about killing the babies.

"I realize that." He seems angry. "I've been stalling her." He takes in a deep breath. "But it's time we answered some of her questions. You already know we can't kill her. And harming her doesn't work either." I hear him smack his lips. "We already tried that with Alexa and she won the fight. Emma's tougher than we thought. I don't know if that's a good or bad thing." He lets out a small chuckle.

His laugh makes my side ache.

"We need her on our side," he continues, "so she will stop the rebellion in Territory L. Maybe if she understands some of what we do here—maybe she will agree to help. We need to get the people in L back on our side."

"They may not even listen to her," President Esther says.

"We won't know unless we get her to try."

"We could try harsher ways to get her to comply. Since harming her isn't working, we could harm the ones she cares about. After all, that is why we have them in custody."

I gasp quietly. I knew that was the reason my brother and sister were brought here, to persuade me to do what they want. They know it as well. Hearing it makes it all the more real.

"I'd rather not go that route, if we can help it," Henry says, trying to be the voice of reason. "Let's just see how answering some of her questions works out." He sounds somewhat stronger.

I sense the conversation is about to end, so I turn. I creep back downstairs. I pray he doesn't hear me.

I make it back to the sofa in one piece and plop down on it.

"Ready to begin," he says, almost standing right in front of me.

My heart jumps. I don't know how he made it back downstairs so fast. Good thing I left the hallway when I did.

"I don't like to talk business in here. Follow me to the den." He tilts his head to the side.

* * *

We walk by the kitchen and dining area and go to a room with a white wooden door. The door is partially open and it swooshes as Henry opens it all the way. We step onto a large room with light gray walls. This room is double the size of my bedroom at home. I suppose this is the den he was speaking about. The floor is light wood and creaks slightly as I walk across it.

There are several windows—two large ones on the right and left sides of the room—that give off light into the room.

Henry slinks down in a large cushiony tan chair. The chair has over a dozen button-type circles embedded in it. The chair looks like leather to me—the type a belt would be made of, only much softer. In front of him sits a large tan desk. He says the desk is

Victorian. I'm not sure what that means, but the shiny gloss that the desk gives off is lovely. It occupies the middle of the room. Tan must be one of his favorite colors. He seems to use the color around his quarters quite often—reminding me of Esther's quarters.

I trickle down across from him in a smaller chair that also feels like leather. I'm close enough to look him in the eye while he answers my questions. I need to see if he's lying or not.

He clears his throat, like he's going to say something, but he doesn't. He picks up some of the papers on his desk and shuffles them around. There are a few pens scattered around also and they screech as he pushes them to the side.

His hand wobbles as he reaches for a pitcher of clear liquid that is on the desk in front of him. Maybe he's nervous about answering my questions.

The liquid sloshes and glistens as he takes ahold of the pitcher's handle. I'm assuming its water. He takes his glass that's beside him and pours some for himself. He glances down at an empty glass that's near me, then up at me. I shake my head to signal I don't want any. He understands my silence and the pitcher clanks as he sits it back on the table. Maybe Nancy supplied this room with fresh water since she knew we would be occupying it.

"Well, Emma," he says. "Shall we begin?" He crinkles the papers in front of him as he peers at my questions. "You want to know why I hide and no one knows who is in charge of Territory M. You also want to know why I don't have better control over the territory and if I'm just a mouthpiece for the president. I think those questions go hand in hand," he says, placing the papers down. He clasps his hands together.

He clears his throat like he's uncomfortable. His hands are still clasped and his elbows bang against the Victorian desk.

"As you probably already know, I spent several years as president over the territories. I was happy when my term was over. I didn't want to do it anymore—"

"My mother said the people didn't want to elect you for another term."

"That wasn't the only reason." His eyes harden. He unclasps his hands. "I also felt it was time to give someone else a chance. It's not always easy reigning over thousands of lives. Making sure people are kept safe—"

"So instead, you rather have your crazy wife divide the nation so poor people have nothing," I say, cutting him off.

"First of all." He holds up his hand to stop me from talking. "I was proud and happy when my wife took over as president. The ideas she had, at first, were going to do great things for our world. Her first term was wonderful; she never wavered on all the promises she made."

He turns his chair away from me. His hands shake again, like he's nervous as he hits a button on the wall. There are two windows behind the desk. The top window is oval-shaped and the bottom window is larger and rectangular. Tan and orange curtains drape across the top window.

The already bright room becomes brighter as the mid-size tan and orange curtains are pulled apart and opened wide. Maybe this little distraction is giving him a break from answering my question.

"When she was elected for a second term…well, that's when things changed," he says turning toward me, again. "I never agreed with her that she should remain in office until the day she died or until she decided to remove herself from office. I believe others should be given a chance to lead, but she wouldn't listen to me. And the people were so happy with her that they agreed, so there was nothing I could do. I had no idea her plans would change so drastically once her second term sta—"

"And once you found out, I'm sure you did nothing about it—did you?" I sit up straighter in my chair.

"You need to stop cutting me off and let me finish, young lady." His words echo the hard look on his face.

I sit back. "Sorry."

"The position was making her hungry for power. The people didn't know this. I saw the change in her before anyone else did. Behind closed doors, she would tell me things. Things like she liked people praising her and hanging on her every word. She liked having control over everyone. It was like she was becoming a different person."

The table clanks as he bangs his fist on it. "A person I could no longer identify with. She wasn't the same woman I married, not anymore. That's when I decided to leave her. The person I loved so deeply had evaporated before my eyes. I came to live here on the Hill. The place was empty and I made it my own. I thought maybe the separation would do us some good, and she would come to her senses…be the woman I married again; but she changed even more—for the worse, not for the better."

"My mother told me you all were friends and once the president changed, she stopped inviting her and my father up to the mansion."

"Your mother is correct. That did happen." He clears his throat again, like the conversation still makes him uneasy. "The woman I married was gone. I didn't know who the person standing before me was, so I stayed here and decided to never go back." He blinks. "I was living here when I found out about the division of the territories. I didn't agree with her. I even tried to talk her out of it, but she wouldn't listen. So the area I lived in became Territory M."

He shifts in his chair. His hand shakes as he raises his glass to his lips. He gulps down a sip of water.

"If that's the case…" My voice drifts off. I'm deep in thought. "And you wanted to get away from her, why would you follow her orders now? Why do you let her tell you what to do now, when you know the things she's doing is wrong?"

"I guess it's because I like watching over Territory M. I like having something to do with my days."

"But you're just a mouthpiece for the president. You don't really implant any of your ideas into anyone. You just do what she says and watch over everyone to make sure they stay in line. What kind of life is that?"

"If you must know," he says, leaning back. "Although we will probably never be together again, I still love my wife. My hope is…maybe, if I play along with what she wants, she will come to me and want to reconcile. That's why we're not divorced. I believe, deep down, she still loves me, too; and maybe, if she stops this nonsense…one day…" His voice quivers.

"To answer another question from your list," he continues, not finishing his previous thought. "That's why I stay hidden. I don't want people to know I'm the one watching over them. They would think I believe in the things my wife is doing. I don't."

His fingers are clenched around the glass as he takes another sip of water. Maybe the conversation is stressing him out. "That is why I have Mitchell go before the people with information. My actions embarrass me and I'd rather not be seen. The only time I leave the Hill is to go to the leaders meetings, once a month, in Territory U."

"But all of the watchmen and the people that work in the mansion know that you're in charge here, or that you're taking orders from President Esther, so how long do you think it will be before everyone finds out?"

He takes a moment and glances around his desk. There are two small gold lamps, with black shades and dangling gold chains used to cut them on and off, sitting on both ends of the table. He nervously plays with the chain dangling from the lamp to the right of him. The clinking continues until he finally decides to speak again.

"I've been hiding up here for years, Emma, and no one knows. If anyone does, they don't discuss it. They know it's the president's doing and they wouldn't challenge her nor tell a secret she doesn't want told."

"Yeah," I say, rolling my eyes. "Who would want to go against her when they know they would be thrown in prison or worse?"

"So now you see why I'm here and taking orders from her," he says, sounding relieved that this part of my inquisition is over. "Can we move on to the next question?"

I shrug. "I guess."

My throat burns because I don't believe everything he's telling me. There has to be another reason he would be at the president's beck and call. Could it be that he's still in love with her and hopes she will change some day? Could I be wrong? I just don't see that as being all of it.

"In order to answer your third and fourth questions, we will need to take a little walk." He stands. He leans over to grab his glass and gulps down more water.

He slams the glass down and some of the water sloshes out onto the desk. He was the one who agreed to this, so I don't know why he's so fidgety. I do know, from overhearing his earlier conversation with the president, that he thinks pacifying me by answering a few questions will make me cooperate with what they need me to do.

CHAPTER NINETEEN

I FOLLOW HIM down a long hallway with more bright white walls. We are back on the fourth floor. I'm getting much-needed answers to some of my questions, but my throat still feels scratchy. I see the door to the fight room I was in. I didn't notice it before but above the painted black doors are bronze signs that remind me of a street sign, only smaller. The sign on the room I was in says: FIGHT ROOM 1. I glance down the hall and see a sign that says: FIGHT ROOM 2.

"You'll notice that the rooms are labeled," Henry says, reading my mind. "When you were down on the third floor—"

"You mean visiting my friends and family, one by one," I blurt out.

His eyes shoot daggers at me since, once again, I'm cutting him off.

"As I was saying," he continues. "The rooms are labeled there as well. Eric is in holding room 5. Taylor is in holding room 3. My point is, most of the rooms have names. I like things to be neat and organized, and I feel this is the best way to accomplish that."

I remain silent and continue following behind him. We turn a corner and the silence disappears. I now hear shouting and crying.

"I know I can do better. Please give me another chance."

I try not to stare, but I can't help it. I see Molly, again. The last time I saw her, she was in the hallway on the third floor. That was several hours ago. Why is she now up here on the fourth floor?

"Too late little girl…you had your chance," the short stocky watchman with the bushy eyebrows says.

"There are no second chances here. You wouldn't do any better anyway, so why cry over it." The other watchman, with the dark hair and broad shoulders, has a firm grip on her arm.

"But my parents need this." Her shoulders slouch. "They were counting on me." Her blonde hair swings in her face.

I don't know what has just happened, but my body cringes for the pain she is in.

"Is everything okay here, Paul?" Henry asks. "The young lady seems quite upset."

"She's fine, sir," the dark haired one says. His hair sticks up, like spikes coming from his head.

"I wasn't talking to you, Tony." Henry's voice is strong. "I was talking to Paul."

"She wants us to give her a second chance in the fight room," Paul says. "But we were explaining to her that there are no second chances. One is all you get." He glares back at her.

Tony still grips her arm tightly.

"My family needs this."

I now see her eyes are red from all the crying she is doing.

"They want to move up so badly…this was our only chance. I'm sorry. I will do better next time, now that I know what's expected of me."

"I'm sorry, young lady." Henry steps to her. "But they're right. One chance is all you get. If we made an exception for you, we would have to do it for all the others, and we can't do that. No bending the rules." He steps back from her.

"There are a few more fights on the docket for today. Once they're done we will take whoever's left to the van to be transported back to Territory L." One of Paul's eyes narrows.

"You'll be comfortable in your holding room until then," Tony adds.

"Let's continue, Emma." Henry shoes tap as he, again, forges ahead of me.

***

There's a keypad next to the door. Henry pushes in a series of numbers and the door beeps and unlocks. This door doesn't have eye recognition software attached—maybe because more people than just Henry have to use it. He slams the door behind us. We have walked into a room that has a silver door, instead of a black one. The signage above the door reads: STAFF ONLY.

The lights come on and dimly illuminate the area. My eyes widen as I look at where we are. The room is oval-shaped and quite large. There are several mirrors that surround the room. I take it they are two-way mirrors. Henry goes to a panel and clicks on a switch. The lights pop on and I see a light green room on the other side of the mirror. It's much like the one I was in with Alexa.

"That's fight room 1." Another light pops on. "Fight room 2."

Lights keep flashing on, until there are seven rooms surrounding us, behind seven two-way mirrors. I gasp.

"Have a seat." Henry barks another order at me. "You can see all of the fight rooms from this discussion room. Sometimes, we have several fights going at once. But most of the time, it's only one or two, since we don't always have that many eyes to keep watch. Some days, my men are out on other assignments."

In the middle of the room is a square black table with four black chairs surrounding it.

I drop down, like he asked me to. He slides down next to me.

"You wanted to know how people are accepted into Territory M. Well, this is only part of it." He scratches the gray patch at the top of his head. "Part of the journey. There are three major components." He holds up his fingers to emphasize three. "It starts on the third floor.

Half of the third floor contains the holding rooms where your friends and family are being held."

He nods his head toward me. "The other side of the third floor contains holding rooms where there are table and chairs. That's where we question young people we pick, to see if they're worthy to move here."

"Worthy." I mouth.

"Yes, worthy," he repeats.

I guess I am louder than I thought. My eyebrow rises. "What makes someone worthy?"

"The president and her men—"

"Henchmen," I add. "Sorry, it won't happen again," I say, knowing I cut him off again.

"They decide who should have a chance to move here. It starts with the family as a whole. They spend hours going over all of the families that live in L. They've watched, over the years, to see the way families carry themselves. Even if you're poor, you can still carry yourself in a dignified way. What I mean by that is, take two families. Both have run out of rations for the week. Both don't have money to buy more food until the next week. The free block of cheese and bottled water that the government hands out has also run out. The family that toughs it out and maybe tries to find work down on the farms for the day is the family we would have to try out."

I know what he is speaking of. People work down on the farms in Territory L as their regular permanent jobs; but sometimes, when the farms are unusually busy, they offer day work to anyone who needs it. But you are only allowed to work one day a week for extra rations. The next day, they let someone else in need work for rations. If no one else shows up, then you can stay and work the next day; but they try to make the whole process fair.

"Some families don't want to work anymore than they already have to on their regular jobs, so they won't go down after they've finished their nine-to-five and try to get work on the farm. Some families just go home and pout or have their children go to the market and beg for scraps. Some even go so far as to have their children beg in the streets for food. Families like those are ones we don't want here. Even poor people can show some sort of class."

He seems to dote on the words *class* and *dignified*. I guess he feels he carries both. He crosses his leg, putting his left leg on top of his right knee.

"So that's how the process starts. Once they decide who shows worthiness, we then look exclusively at the young people that live in the home. If the offspring have moved out and no longer live with the parents, their process is almost the same. We look at how well they did while in school and at their character, now. As far as the young people that still reside at home, we go through their school records to see what kind of students they were when they were in school. The ones with the higher grades, usually over a three-point-five, are allowed to try and move here."

He pulls down on his spotted gray tie. He looks uncomfortable. "Once they receive a letter in the mail that they are worthy to try out, they take the bus down to the president's mansion. When they arrive there, a van awaits to bring them here, to my mansion."

"How often do these letters go out in the mail?"

"Only a few a year. Sometimes more, or less, depending on what we decide in our monthly leaders meetings. It just so happens that we are having trials a few days this week…that doesn't happen all the time. It's a good day for you to see things. Make sure you pay attention."

I let out a slow grunt and continue listening.

"After they arrive here, they stay in one of the holding and questionnaire rooms on the third floor. The rooms are quite large. There is a cot on one side of the room and, like I said earlier, there is a table and chairs on the other side. They are also fitted with a bathroom; whereas, the rooms your family and friends are staying in have no bathrooms." He shifts his weight.

"If one is needed, a watchman comes and walks you to the necessary accommodations. There are several bathrooms along the hallways on each floor. There is a silver panel near the doors with a button above it in those rooms. If the bathroom is needed, that's how they communicate with someone to get their attention."

"What if they're chained to a post and can't reach the panel?" I ask, thinking of Eric.

He thumbs his fingers along his chin. "I suppose they're just out of luck then."

"What does that mean?" I know what it means, but his words make my throat burn with anger. He doesn't care, so I want to drill him some more.

A knock at the door makes my shoulders jump.

"I'll be right back," he says. He stands, never answering my question.

He comes back, after a few minutes, and sits back down with a pad and pen in hand. "We only have a limited amount of time." He checks the watch on his wrist. "Now, on to the questions we ask the young people in L." He rattles off several questions. "We ask them what a better life would mean for them. What kind of job do they dream of having? What would they study in college? How would those moving here enrich the life of the others that already live here? If they made it to Territory M, what kinds of choices would they make to ensure they were never sent back to Territory L? If they had children and didn't do their best to move on to Territory U, how would they feel if their child was taken away and they were sent back to L— would they put up a fight, although they already knew what the government's laws entailed?"

"What kind of answers are you looking for?"

"Smart, positive answers that show how intelligent they are, or could be, one day. Answers that show how hard they plan to work for their futures. Not someone who hesitates or takes too long to come up with an answer. Someone who's quick–witted and can think fast on their feet...like you."

He glances at his watch again. "What we don't want to hear are answers that are meant to just pacify us...what I mean by that..." He shifts in his seat. "We don't like those who just say things because they think it's what we want to hear. There are those that think they can fool the system. We can tell when someone's not speaking from the heart."

"What do you mean?"

"We hook them up to a lie sensor. It's a machine to detect if someone is lying," he says like I don't know what a lie sensor is.

"As soon as we know someone is lying, they are exiled back to Territory L. Some people speak their truths; but it's just not the answer we were looking for, so they are also banished back to L." He thumbs his fingers along his cheek this time.

"We should move on to the next step, or we won't have time to get everything in." His suit jacket ruffles as he shifts in his seat. "Once, and if, they pass the questionnaire portion, they are then allowed to move to the fight rooms."

He stands and clears his throat. He walks around the room and looks through each two-way mirror.

"As you can see, these are the fight rooms." He sounds almost proud. "You were in one yourself," he adds, as if I could forget Alexa and me going at it, like a pack of wild dogs. "We like to see courage and strength in our young ones. We want to see that they can take care of themselves. We need to know that they can think fast on their feet."

"Is that why Molly was crying? Did she not do well in the fight room?"

"No, she did not." He's standing near me now. He taps his fingers on the table. "She will never tryout in the war room, because she never made it past the fight room."

I've heard the war room mentioned a few times. I wonder what that means.

"You need to show strength and no weakness."

"What does that mean?"

"It means she didn't even try." He sounds annoyed. "She just stood there and cried. She never even fought back. That's weakness and neither she nor her family can ever move here."

"I didn't realize you were so big on weakness." I stand.

"What are you getting at?" He pulls on his tie.

"Why do you let President Esther control you? I know you said it's because you still love her and you hope by doing what she wants you may get back together; but I believe it's something else."

I know I shouldn't, but I have to speak my mind. I clear my throat. "I would say that makes you weak."

"I don't agree. We don't like weakness; strength is the only thing that has value in our world."

He says *we* like he and the president are still a team. I would call what he's doing weakness, even if he won't.

"I'm starting to think you like all of this fight room, war room garbage. Maybe you use still being in love with the president as an excuse."

"I do still love her, but I don't agree with the division of the classes. But if it has to be this way, then I don't believe there's any harm in making sure the people who are qualified make it here and the ones who aren't stay where they are."

"But that's just it…it doesn't have to be this way, if you would just stand up to her. But you won't, because you want her back."

"This conversation is getting us nowhere. We should get back to your list of questions. I think you need to sit."

"Fine." I bang down in the chair.

"As I was saying, Molly stood there and cried. If she had at least swung at her opponent or ducked…but she didn't. She cried and screamed. Her opponent wanted it more than she did, and that's why her opposition moved up to the next level."

"Who was her challenger?"

He falls silent.

"Maybe her competition was too big for her to handle."

"That's not possible. We make sure we size everyone up to ensure they would be good rivals with each other. We never have two people sparing whose attributes don't match. We would never have a small person with a bigger person or a tall person with a short person. That wouldn't be fair; we want a fair fight. We put the tall with the tall, the thin with the thin."

Everyone in Territory L is thin, I think.

"The frail with the frail," he continues. "Males fight males. Females fight females. Mitchell and some of my trusted men help me decide. Esther has her guards send them here and then we weed the weak out for her."

"Why didn't my family ever receive a letter?" I blurt out. I know it's selfish to think of myself at a time like this, but I need to know. "Why wasn't I allowed to move up?"

"President Esther didn't feel your family was fit enough to move."

"I don't believe you. I think it's because she fell out with my mother and father."

"You think whatever you want, but that is the reason."

"Then why did you have me fight Alexa? What did that prove?"

"Esther wanted you to feel pain, to feel what it's like when you don't do as she asks. And I wanted you to see what the fight room was like, before you help me decide."

"Help you decide?" My throat tenses.

"Yes, we have a few more fights today. This will be interesting." He chuckles. For someone who claims he doesn't like doing what the president wants, he seems to enjoy it. "We knew Alexa was your equal. You were a guard and she was homeless…living in the streets. You're both strong…that makes a good match."

My stomach becomes skittish. If I hadn't been trained by Eric, I wouldn't have been up for that fight. Now, I may never see Eric again, and I'm stuck in some room, getting ready to witness a ridiculous battle that's not my own.

"I've cleared the room. Mitchell and the other men won't be in here. There will only be you and me."

I swallow, hard.

"We're going to train our eyes on fight room 1," Henry continues.

I turn to the two-way mirror on the right. Two males walk into the room. I stand. I slide up closer to see better.

"The male on the left with the blond hair and pointed chin, that's Davis Redford…and the round-faced male on the right with the curly brown hair is Kevin Wise." Henry swipes his hand through his hair. "They're both the same height, same weight, and both are nineteen years of age. Do you know them?"

"No," I say, while turning around to Henry. "I don't remember them from school, or the hallways I should say."

Since females and males didn't have any classes together, why would I recognize them?

"My brother might know them." I turn back around to face the mirror.

Henry walks over to a bronze box on the wall. He flips a couple of the silver switches. That must turn on an intercom, since Henry talks into it.

"You can start now." Henry puts his hands in his pockets, then takes them back out. He does that a lot; it seems to be some nervous gesture. He walks back to the table and slouches down in the chair.

I continue to stand and watch. I slide my finger down the mirror and it feels cold to the touch.

Davis lunges for Kevin. There is a *thud* as Kevin's back slams into the wall. Kevin groans but quickly recovers. He punches Davis in the mouth with an openhanded fist. Davis's eyes are wide as he wobbles back, trying to keep his balance. He steadies himself.

Before he fully holds his stance, Kevin comes for him. Kevin kicks him in the stomach. Davis falls. His back whacks the floor with a *thump*. His head hits the floor, moments later, with a *bump*. He yells out in pain. Sweat glistens along his face and body.

Davis tries to stagger to his feet. Kevin jumps on top of him and pins him down with his elbow on his throat. Davis frowns. Wrinkles appear along his forehead.

"Can you believe these two are friends?" Henry stands. "If he can use that much aggression on a friend, can you imagine what would happen if he were Kevin's enemy?"

Henry lets out a slow sigh. I can't tell if this whole routine makes him happy or saddens him.

"You're the one making them do this. You're the one making him turn on his friend."

"Like I said before, we have to separate the weak from the strong. This is a process that needs to be followed."

I roll my eyes. "So you say."

"Gentlemen," Henry says. He's back at the intercom. "You can stop now. We've seen enough."

Tony, the watchman I saw earlier with Molly, steps in and escorts both males out.

"Now, we decide." Henry sits back down. He motions with his finger, so I will sit down as well. "They both did extremely well, but we both know one did better."

"Kevin did," I say, while sitting down. "I suppose that means Kevin gets to the next level and Davis doesn't."

"You would be right. But that's not always the case…" His voice drifts off.

He writes something down on the pad he has on the table. "Sometimes, it's an equal fight and they both move on to the war room. You never know what's going to happen."

He's right about that. I never would have thought this was how you were accepted into the upper territories.

"There will be another fight starting in room 3 in an hour, but Mitchell and some of the others will judge it and bring their findings back to me. When I'm not around Mitchell handles the trials for me. You and I are needed elsewhere."

CHAPTER TWENTY

W<small>E ARRIVE ON</small> the fifth floor, where the war room is. We walk inside and the room reminds me of the one we just came from, except the walls are light blue and there is an oblong black and white marble table with six chairs in the center. There is only one large two-way mirror, instead of many—like the fight rooms have. There is a small black box on the table with several silver buttons attached.

This time I sit down without being asked, because my leg jolts at what's to come. As I look inside the two-way mirror into the small box-shaped room they call the war room, I see a light flash on. I see a bronze table with one metal chair. There is a headset on the table and something else that I can't make out. Maybe some sort of eyewear.

Another watchman I haven't encountered yet storms in. He has on a brown uniform like the others. He's tall with fair skin and an oval-shaped face. From here, I make out he has blue eyes. His brown hair is wavy along with his matching brown goatee.

"That's Wyatt," Henry says. "It's his turn to control the war room. We call it the war room because in a war, you need to know how to make the right decisions to survive. Here, you do the same, only in the form of questions."

Wyatt rummages around in the room. I have no idea what he

is doing. The door screeches as he leaves. He quickly returns with a female in tow. He slams her down in the chair. Her green eyes are wide as she glowers around the room, like she doesn't know what to expect. She has red curly shoulder-length hair and wide dimples.

"Wear this headset and place the goggles over your eyes," Wyatt says.

Her hands shake as she places the bulky headset over her ears. The goggles have a rubber piece that Wyatt stretches over the back of her ears. It lands firmly around the back of her head.

"As we go along, you will hear questions. Speak your answers out clearly, so everyone hears."

He says *everyone* like there's a crowd of people watching, but there's only me and Henry—and Wyatt, of course.

"This is Lindsey Bowers. She went head-to-head with Molly in the fight room, hours earlier. Of course she won…that's why she is here now. Do you know her?" His eyebrow rises.

"I can't say that I do."

"I think you do."

I think he is mistaken; I don't remember her. But he is right about one thing; she is about the same weight and height as Molly, so I suppose it was a fair fight.

"She's twenty years old and was in one of your sister's classes," he continues, like I should already know this. "She had a four-point-zero and she worked down on the farms ever since she graduated from school. She still resides at home. So, if she gets to move here, her entire family will have the pleasure of coming with her." He gives a thin smile.

"Since she has exceptionally good grades, we wanted to test her when she first graduated…when she was eighteen; but sadly, she became sick from pneumonia that year and wasn't able to make the trip." He clears his throat.

"We thought of testing one of her older siblings," he continues. "We decided she was the best candidate for her family to move up, so we waited. Once she was better, we already had a list of others to try out, so she had to wait a few years until her turn came around again. Now her older siblings have moved out and are married, so they can't move on her good merit. And they're not good enough to move on their own—they haven't shown the drive that we want. But her parents can move and her one brother, who's nineteen and still lives at home, will be able to as well."

"What if there are three offspring, only one has done exceptionally well, the others have done nothing with their lives as you would say, and they all still live at home; do the parents still have the right to come?" I ask. "Earlier, you said you test the offspring first, since you want to see how they are raised and that gives you the best inclination on how the parents are, so they can move up. So, if some of the offspring aren't doing well, what gives them the right?"

He smiles and all his teeth show. "Fair question." Apparently, he thinks it's a smart question and he likes it.

"Sometimes, we have to be impartial. If a parent has one child that does exceptionally well, we figure they should have a chance. Some offspring are just bad seeds and it's not the parents' fault, so we make exceptions. If all three in the brood are horrific, then we know it's the parents' fault and we wouldn't want them here. If one apple is rotten in a field of good apples, then the parents have the right to come; but they have to leave the bad apple behind. They're of the age where they could move out and get a job anyway, while the parents move ahead."

"What if the parents don't want to kick a child out and move up?"

"Then they stay in Territory L. There are plenty of parents that move and do leave the offspring behind. Their hope is their descendants will marry, or at least get their lives together, and be able to come here one day on their own merit."

"Can you tryout a second time?"

"No," he says, tapping his fingers on the table. "One chance is all you get. If you blow that chance, you will *not* get another," he emphasizes.

He shifts in his chair and changes the subject. "We'll see what they see through the goggles, on the screen here."

He presses a button on the box and there is a flat panel on the table that opens, revealing a screen. The screen reminds me of a small information box. It's just big enough so that anyone huddled around the table is able to see. There is also a silver microphone planted firmly on the desk.

"Now, let's watch."

The screen shows what, to me, looks to be a forest. There are beautiful green trees and vibrant green grass. The sky is a ray of blue and off-white. A black and tan dog—maybe a German Shephard—appears. It barks loudly, and then lies down in the grass. The screen closes in on the dog's leg; it appears to be red and swollen. It seems to be infected.

A loud voice booms in the war room and the room I'm in. "As you can see, the dog is sick and only has months—maybe to a year—to live. What would you do, if this was your pet?" It's coming from the speaker. Henry controls it, flipping switches on the panel.

"You can answer now," Wyatt says to the girl in the room.

"I-I d-don't know," Lindsey says. Her voice trembles. "I guess I-I would take the dog home and love it for as long as I can."

Henry's pen squeaks as he writes something down on his pad. He turns to look at me. "What would you have done?"

"I'm not on trial here."

"I know that. I just want to see how you would handle the situation."

"I would probably put the dog down, so it doesn't have to live its last few months in misery."

"Excellent. That's the answer we were looking for." He smiles. "That's exactly what we would want one to say."

"What will happen to her, now that she's given what you think is the wrong answer?"

"There are more questions to ask, but that one is the first strike against her." He shifts in his seat. "Wyatt, please continue." He speaks into the microphone that is fixed next to the panel.

Wyatt does something on his end and the next moving picture appears on the screen. There is a run-down street, reminding me of the street I live on back in Territory L. There's a gravel and dirt road. There's a neglected boarded-up house with a woodsy area behind it. We hear the faint sound of a baby crying.

Henry flips the switch on the panel and the loud voice speaks again. "If you heard this child crying in Territory L, where no children should be, what would you do?"

Lindsey rocks back and forth in the chair. "I would call the patrolmen, since no babies are allowed in Territory L."

Henry glares at me. I guess he knows I would answer differently—after all, I did hide my sister and her baby. If I had to do it again, I would still do the same thing. He scribbles on his pad and then turns to the microphone.

Is this all a tactic, so they could get Abigail further and further away from here? Henry's been keeping me occupied. Yes, I've found out useful information, and some of my questions have been answered; but I still haven't been able to get any answers about Abigail or the newbie camp.

We keep going like this through several more questions. Some questions, Lindsey answers like I would; others, she answers differently.

"Let's move on, Wyatt," Henry says.

"Two pictures appear on screen, simultaneously. It should take you only five seconds to pick which one is closest to the career you would like."

I see a patrolman and a guard. What kind of games are they playing?

"You expected to see a nurse, or a teacher, or even a doctor… did you not?" Henry looks at me. "Well, this is a test we like to use." He turns back toward the screen. "For specific reasons…what do you think it entails?"

I shrug. "Not sure."

"I would choose the patrolman," Lindsey says. "The patrolmen live at home…so that way, I would get to spend more time with my family."

Henry's eyebrow rises. He scribbles again on his pad. I'm all ready for him to turn, look at me, and ask me what I would do; but he doesn't.

I think Lindsey's answer was a good one…a fair one…but I know that's not what he's looking for. He probably wanted her to say she would be a guard, since some of them live at the mansion and they make the most money.

His voice interrupts my thoughts. "All I will say is you should pick the job that will make you the most money."

He said what I was thinking.

"Are we almost done?" I ask. I've seen what I need to. Now, I would like to talk about Abigail.

"Are you bored?"

"No, I just want to move on to a different topic."

"Wyatt, next slide please."

I squirm in my seat.

The next image I see is a rainy and dark sky. It seems to be a video and not just a slide. The wind is roaring strong and the leaves on the trees sway back and forth. The rain gets heavier and the drops become massive.

"If the government informed you a storm was nearing, and they asked you to pack a few things and go to a shelter of their choosing, what would you do?" The loud voice booms over the room, again. "Would you stay and try to protect your belongings and your home or leave with the clothes on your back, like we asked?"

"I-I w-would leave like you a-asked." Lindsey's voice is still shaky.

"What if your parents decide to disobey us and stay in the home; would you stay with them or defy them and leave?"

"I-I would do as the government asks and leave my parents behind." Her green eyes are wide and her face looks even more sunken than before. She searches the room, like maybe that was the wrong answer.

Henry scribbles on his pad again. "Next." He speaks into the microphone, while looking through the mirror at Wyatt.

A new video appears. I see a howling gray wolf. Drool runs down his chin and all of its teeth show. It looks vicious, like it would kill, without hesitation. The screen shoots to a silver gun, laying on the grass.

The voice blares around the room again. "Would you try to make a run for it or pick up the gun and shoot it?"

"I don't know how to use a-a g-gun, so I guess...I-I would try to r-run." Beads of sweat surface. Lindsey wipes her forehead.

My chest tightens. I feel she would never make it, if she ran. Even if I didn't know how to use a gun, my first instinct would be to pick up the gun and try to use it. I feel that's my only chance of escape. But no one's asking my opinion.

"Last one," Henry says.

The screen shows a man begging in the streets for food. People are walking pass, like they don't see him.

"If you saw this man, begging in the streets, would you go home and bring back food or just step over him and forget he ever existed?" the voice over the intercom howls.

"I r-really shouldn't t-talk to strangers, so I would go home;

but it would be h-hard to forget about the man. It's so s-sad that he has no food while I do, at least, have a little."

I'm surprised. Her voice got stronger at the end. I'm proud that it did, although that's not the answer I would have given. I would have brought back what little I could and helped the stranger out.

"That will be all, Wyatt. Take her away." He writes on his pad, again.

"Now," he says, turning to me. "We've been doing this process for years. Since we mostly base it on how the children are raised, we decided that there should be a process for those who have never had children. If you are a grown male or female and have no children, you skip pass step one and go directly to the war room. You see a different set of slides and videos than the ones you have seen here today…with a set of different questions. To get to that point…like I said before, you have to be the type of person who looks for extra work if you ran out of weekly rations. Someone who would not go begging in the streets. Those are the ones who would do well here."

"Is there a cut-off age, for those who are childless? Those that have never had a child at all."

"If you haven't tried to better yourself by age sixty, there's really no reason for us to test you to move here. We feel there are not many years left to their lives anyway, so why bring them here only to die. They might as well live out their days where they have resided all of their lives. Besides, it shouldn't take a person sixty-something years for them to become the person we need them to be."

"What about those children who have recently moved out?"

"I believe I answered that, earlier, when I said we look at their schooling and character to see if they deserve a chance."

"I know…but I'm asking about the parents. What if the parents have no more children at home…will the parents get to come on the good merit of the child that has moved out?"

"No, once the child has left home, all ties are cut…but there are exceptions. Sometimes, if a child has recently moved out, is still in their twenties, and is accepted to come here—we could test the parents in the war room, just like we test the parents who are childless. Sometimes, we get busy with other things and moving people up in the system becomes a lower priority. If that's the case, and the child should have been tested while still living at home, the parent shouldn't be denied for that…so then, we'll test the parents as well. It's all done on a case-by-case basis."

He stands and clears his throat.

"The point of all of this is that we really need to make sure the male or female will be a welcome addition to our society. We don't need someone moving here, if they are just going to bring our society down." He glowers at me. "What's that sour look for?"

I didn't realize I have a certain look on my face, but I guess I do.

"I don't understand why all of this is necessary just to move up into the next territory."

"You don't realize the money that is spent and the time that is taken to ship someone over here, let alone an entire family. We have to find suitable housing for them. We need to make sure they can handle college here. We have to decide what career they will have. We need to make sure the job is something they can handle. We have to make sure we locate them on the right side of the territory… a part of the territory where they will fit in and can evolve nicely."

He puts his hands in his pockets and takes them right back out. "It takes time, so we don't make a decision lightly. Do you realize the expense of bringing someone here only to have to ship them right back to Territory L, if they're not a good fit here?"

He seems annoyed that my expression hasn't changed.

"It's one thing, if they've done something wrong and are going back to be imprisoned; but shipping someone back, because they don't fit in, is different. We have to find new housing for them back in L. Nine times out of ten, the house they lived in before the move has been torn down already."

He motions for me to stand with him.

"Are we going back to your quarters, so you can answer the rest of my questions?"

"No, we're done here."

"But I want to know why I was spoken about here, in M, over a year ago? And, why the president would want me here."

"You already know the answer to that, Emma." There's a growl to his voice. "Your parents were friends with the president."

"But that doesn't make sense. My brother and sister weren't spoken about—only me."

"You are the last eighteen-year-old in L—*they are not.*" He emphasizes. "Let's go." He nods his head toward the door.

"But you haven't answered my questions about Abigail. I wrote that on the list as well." I hear my voice crack, and I don't like it.

We walk into the hallway and the door shuts behind us. Mitchell is standing there, waiting.

"Mitchell, take her to one of the empty rooms on the third floor." Henry walks away. "There's something I need to take care of."

He must be taking me to one of the rooms like my friends are being held in, with the cold floor and white walls.

"Yes, sir." Mitchell glares at me. "Ms. Whisperer, you need to come with me."

I follow, even though I don't want to.

CHAPTER TWENTY-ONE

I DRAG BEHIND Mitchell. We're already on the third floor, where the holding areas are. I don't want to go there. I want the rest of my questions answered. I guess I should be happy I received any answers at all. I know I only received them because they want me to do something for them.

Mitchell walks over to one of the holding room's black doors. Next to the door is a clear plastic hanging file, mounted to the wall, with a thick white pack of papers sticking out. There are around six sheets of paper. He mumbles while searching through them.

"Almost every holding room is occupied. We may have to find you...no, I see one that's available. I'll take you—"

My thoughts are interrupted, and his voice cuts off, when I hear a loud siren. It almost reminds me of the sound I heard when it was time for the president's Monday night speech.

"Don't move. I'll be right back." He nods his head toward me, and I see the wrinkles in his forehead move slightly forward.

He takes off down the hallway before I even respond.

I rush over to the file and grab the thick bundle of papers. They rustle in my hands. I want to see what holding room Logan is in and if Whitney was brought here. My fingers tremble. I know I need to hurry before he comes back. My eyes blur, reading over the tiny black words.

I see Logan's name; he is in room 6. I move my head up and down, searching for Whitney's name. Before I spot her name, my heart pounds because I see the name Samuel on the list. It says he is in room 1. So he was brought here.

I wonder how he is doing and if he is still okay. I have to find holding room 1. My knees tremble as I forge down the hallway. I pass room 2 and keep trudging until I reach room 1.

I know the door will probably be locked, but I need to try anyway. I reach my hand near the knob. Before I jiggle the door handle, I hear loud quick footsteps, returning.

"This is not where I left you. What are you doing way down here?" He smacks his lips. "I have to hurry and get you to your room." Mitchell's voice sounds panicked.

"Why? What's happening?" He seems more worried about what the sirens mean than why I'm not in the spot he left me.

"That's none of your concern," he says with stern eyes. "Let's go down here." He yanks my arm.

I thump down to the floor and cry out in pain.

"What's wrong with you?"

"When you jerked me like that I think I turned my ankle the wrong way. It hurts." I rub my right ankle to emphasize my point.

"Get up, now. I need to be somewhere else." He grabs my arm to pull me up, but I make my body go limp. I remain on the floor.

The sirens grow louder now.

"I don't think I can make it to another room."

He rolls his eyes, like he doesn't believe me. "I don't have time for this nonsense. Just get in here. It's already occupied—but whatever."

He rolls his eyes. His breath is hot in my face. I notice there is no keypad on the wall like there is to get into the fight and war rooms. His keys clank as he unlocks the door to holding room 1 and pushes me in. "Don't get to comfortable. I won't be gone long."

My stomach drops. What does that siren mean? The door

slams behind me, and I stand there trembling. I can't believe I got away with that. I wanted to get in here to see Samuel, and it actually happened.

The room is dark and smells like medicine. I hear deep breathing, so I know he's in here. I see a dark figure. The lights aren't motion lights, so I feel along the wall until I come upon a switch. I flip the light on. The room is bright now and it's just like the one the others are being held in.

Over in the corner, on the floor, I see Samuel with his knees bent. His head is hunched over and he looks almost dead. He has on black pants but no shirt, and there are purple bruises all over his physique. Seeing the bruises makes my body shiver.

"Who's there?" he asks. His voice is muffled; he's talking into his knees.

"Samuel," I cry out.

He lifts his face to mine.

"Samuel, what have they done to you?" I run over to him.

"Emma…Emma," he says a few times, like he can't believe it's me. His voice is soft. He blinks his red eyes.

I lean down next to him.

"Are you alright?" he asks.

"It doesn't matter how I am. What happened to you?" I rub my palm against his cheek. His face is warm and kind, like always.

"After I let you escape from L, the guards took me to the jails. President Esther was furious that I helped you—"

"You didn't help me escape," I say, cutting him off.

"But I didn't try and stop you, either." He shrugs. "And I did use the Taser on Mike, so I did help you."

"I'm sorry."

"Don't be. I wanted to help you." He blinks. "Anyway, after I was jailed, two guards held me down in my cell while Rich beat me. He used his fists and punched me everywhere he could, except my face."

"Why not your face?" I am grateful they didn't bruise his face, but I wonder why.

"He didn't have the authority to beat me like he did…and he knew if the president found out, she wouldn't be so pleased with him; so by not injuring my face, she would never know. I'm not a snitch. I won't tell, and he knew that about me."

Good ole Samuel, I think, rubbing his face again.

"But why did they bring you here? Not that I'm not happy to see you."

"While I was jailed, I received word that my father passed away in the home I had him in. I hadn't been able to keep up on the payments, since I was no longer working. I knew he would probably be kicked out soon. Before that happened, he had a stroke and died. They wouldn't give me a lot of the details, but they did say he didn't die instantly; it took a few days. I feel in my heart that they didn't even admit him into the hospital or try to save him, since I wasn't sending regular payments anymore. Why would they?" He shrugs.

"I asked if I could please leave and make proper burial arrangements…after all, I was the only family he had left. My sister and my mother are gone." He sniffs.

I know this is hard for him. I remember the story he told me about how his sister died and then his mother.

"I told them that two guards could come with me. And after the arrangements were made, I would come right back and serve my time; but they said no and moved me to the prison. I was labeled a lifer. I sort of loss control after that and got in a fight with one of the guards bringing my tray of food one day. He beat me on my back with a baton, so badly that I had welts. I needed to go to the hospital; but they couldn't take me there, so they shipped me here to the infirmary. When I was doing better, they brought me down to this holding room. I'm not sure what's going to happen next." His shoulders are still slouched. He looks defeated.

My voice quivers. "Why—w-why couldn't they take you to the h-hospital in L?" I'm nervous at what his answer will be.

"Emma, you don't know what's going on back there?" He shakes his head. "It's terrible."

He takes in a breath, like the words are hard to say. "Ever since you left, it's been nothing but complete chaos. There are so many people hurt that the hospital in L is overrun with the sick and injured. There was no room for me there. Since my injuries weren't life threatening and I'm a guard…or I *was* a guard…they figured this was the best place to bring me. I've been here and to Territory U a few times, for meetings and other things—but never like this…" His voice drifts off. He looks down and then back up, slowly. "Never as a prisoner." He looks like he's ashamed.

"Can I ask you a question?"

"You know you can ask me anything."

"Did you know Henry was in charge here? I mean, since you've been here a few times."

He rubs his chin, like he's in deep thought, before speaking. "I never saw him when I was here…but I kind of had an idea. Some of the watchmen would hint at things. But I never spoke of it, since I couldn't be sure…and I don't like to speak about things unless I know it's true."

"I understand…that's what makes you so good and kind. Those are some of the things I like about you."

"Emma." He looks at me with soft eyes. "I need you to know something. No matter what has happened, I'm glad I helped you. I would do it again—it's just…I don't like this feeling."

"What feeling?"

"Feeling helpless…being locked up with no way out and hurt where I can't defend myself."

"Why couldn't they take you to the hospital here in M, so you could get the care you need?"

"You know as well as I do that's impossible. The hospital here is only for the people of Territory M."

"Well, why aren't you still in the infirmary?" I stretch my knees out and sit down, all the way, onto the floor.

"Dr. Bush and Nurse Claire said I was doing better, so I could come here. The pain has lessened, although the bruises still show."

"I'm so…so sorry, Samuel. Your father died and you couldn't even be there for him. This is all my fault."

"I knew you would feel that way. I don't want you to. None of this is your fault." He cups my chin with his hand and raises my face to his.

His gaze is on me. I shudder. I get that same feeling I had before—the feeling that he sees me as more than just a little sister.

"I missed you." His voice is soft.

"I missed you, too," I say, as my voice cracks. "I feel terrible. I feel like everyone is hurt because of me and my choices—"

He cuts me off. "No, Emma."

"No, let me finish." Tears run down my face. "Julian died because of me. Whitney's missing because of me. Eric and my brother and sister are locked up because of me. All the rioting in L is because of me. I don't know how to live with all of that. Y-you didn't s-see the h-horrible way that J-Julian died. It was terrible." My shoulders hunch and I lean into him for support. "I h-had to shoot Rich b-back in L and now here…I had to s-shoot a patrolman."

"I'm sure it was only because you had to…to save your own life."

My whole body shakes. I haven't let the weight of everything wash over me, until this moment. I had to be strong in front of my brother and sister; they needed me to be there for them—not the other way around. And Eric was my trainer. He trained me to be strong and independent. Sometimes, I feel like I can't break down in front of him. I can't show any weakness—only strength. Samuel is someone I can let my guard down with and show all of my emotions to.

"Don't be so hard on yourself," he says.

He leans into me even more and, before I realize what he's doing, he kisses me on my lips. The kiss is soft and much different than the time he kissed me on my cheek. The kiss lingers for a moment. I know I should pull away. I'm with Eric. No, we never said we were exclusive; but this isn't right. Eric is the one I want to be with.

My thoughts are interrupted, when the door swishes open. We break away as I hear footsteps. Mitchell stomps in.

"Time to go." He pulls me up by my elbow. "I should have never left you here; but there was an emergency, and I couldn't have you roaming the halls. This was the closest room I could find, since you hurt your ankle."

He's still trying to explain, like he's afraid he may be in trouble for just dropping me off anywhere. "But your ankle looks fine now, doesn't it?" He glares at me.

I barely get a chance to wave good-bye to Samuel before Mitchell rushes me out of the room into the hallway.

CHAPTER TWENTY-TWO

I'm in a holding room now. They place me in holding room 8. My chest relaxes because they did not handcuff me; but I'm sure my friends don't share the same fate. I see someone has left a change of clothing on the floor. There's a pair of black jeans and a brown t-shirt laying there. I wonder if anyone else is given a change of clothing—or am I the only one.

I sigh. I can't even think of changing clothes, right now. My thoughts are glued to the bruises on Samuel's body. He sacrificed his job and the money he needed to send home to his father because of me. I don't know how I could ever repay him for that.

I'm trying to divert my thoughts from the kiss he gave me. It wasn't passionate, like the last kiss I shared with Eric, but it was nice and gentle—and, if I'm being honest with myself, I must admit I did enjoy it.

I'm trying to distract myself from the fact that I still haven't gotten any answers about Abigail. And I don't know how my parents are doing back in L. Taylor was so vague about them, and Theodore didn't mention them at all. Now that I know things are so bad there, I wonder if they are still alive. The thought leaves a sour taste in my mouth.

My body tenses because my door swings open. Maybe it's someone bringing me food, or asking me if I need to use the bathroom, or taking me down for a shower. My eyes widen. It's Wyatt. He was the one running the controls in the war room, earlier.

"I'm going to need you to come with me," he says.

"Why?" I stand. "What's going on? Does this have anything to do with the sirens I heard earlier in the day?"

"The sirens were because runaways were trying to break into the mansion."

My eyes widen. "I don't understand."

"Most runaways don't like living here, in M. They don't like the rules here, but they also don't want to be sent to Territory L because the rules there are even harsher. They basically feel they don't fit in anywhere, so they run away and hide out to live on their own terms."

I can't help but think of Alexa and her brother.

"Some runaways are tired of hiding though. They decide to let us know of their disdain against the way things are run here by trying to sneak into the mansion and destroy things. They know they will be caught, but they feel at least they did something to support their cause before being brought in."

Now they remind me of myself.

"My feeling is some of them want to be brought in. That way, they finally have a hot meal in the prisons, instead of living on the streets and having none," he continues.

I understand that. During my time in jail, I had three meals a day. The food came regularly. That didn't happen all the time when I was at home.

"Some even go so far as to try and sneak pass the gates of Territory U. Their hope is to sneak in and make trouble for the territory. They don't care if they are killed in the process; they just hate the people of U for being rich, and they want to terrorize them for as long as they can. The gate for U opens for medical personnel to go to Territory L and M, for other government officials to go in, and sometimes for different supplies to be shipped over between the territories. Those are the times when they try to sneak through."

"But there are watchmen, everywhere. How do they even get close enough to get in? I'm speaking of here, in the mansion."

"They find ways." He shrugs. "After all, you got close, didn't you?"

I nod and say nothing. He's right. I might have actually made it, if it hadn't been for Alexa.

My silence only lasts for a moment. I've wondered where Henry's men stay and since he's in the mood for telling, I think this is a good time to ask. "Where do you reside?"

"The watchmen stay on the eighth and ninth floors of the mansion." He chews on his bottom lip. "There's no time for any more questions. We need to hurry."

I follow him down the hallway. We round the corner and end up in front of Samuel's room. Wyatt dangles keys from his pocket, then he puts the key in the lock and I hear a click. Air wafts against my face as Wyatt swings the door open.

"Let's go," Wyatt says. "We don't have much time."

Samuel walks out of the door. His face looks pained.

"I have no idea where we're going, but maybe you should stay," I say.

"No, I'm coming." Samuel's breaths are cagey.

"We don't have time for bickering. Everyone's asleep now, so it's the best time to go. Coming or going?" Wyatt's eyebrow rises.

"Coming," Samuel replies. He grabs my hand in his.

I jerk my hand from his. "I can't leave my brother, or sister, or…" I hesitate.

"We're not leaving for good…just getting some information for you," Samuel says. "You'll be pleased, once you find out where we're going."

My lungs twinge, but I keep following them. The hallways are dark at night, and I barely see in front of me. It's a good thing the lights aren't motion activated or the henchmen would know we were walking around.

Wyatt knows his way around. We take a set of stairs—they're a little ways beyond the elevator. We go down to the first floor. Our steps are light as we make our way to a side door. Wyatt pushes in a series of numbers in the keypad on the wall. The numbers beep and the door pops open.

"We'll use my truck," he says. "Hop in."

The truck is a dark gray pickup, with a bed on the back. Wyatt's, along with a few other cars and trucks, is parked right near the door. It reminds me of the truck Julian borrowed for us— except this one looks fancier. The tires are larger and the exterior emblems are gold. Three people can sit in the front seat, just like in the other truck we had.

I jump in with ease, and slide over to the middle. It takes Samuel a little longer. I hear a soft groan come from his mouth. I'm sure this kind of movement can't be good on his sore muscles and bruised torso.

"I'll take the backstreets. The watchmen at the front gate won't spot us." The steering wheel squeals as Wyatt turns it.

The street stays smooth until we turn onto a road a little ways down. The road turns bumpy and my stomach does uneven spins. The look on Samuel's face tells me he's not enjoying the unevenness, either.

"We're here." Wyatt glances over at me. "I managed to turn off the cameras monitoring both of your holding rooms, and the one for the door we exited out of. So no one should notice you're gone, for a while. There are no cameras out here. They don't want a record kept of what's going on here, so that's one less thing we have to worry about."

I'm sure they saw me on the cameras earlier, when I was in Samuel's room. I wonder if Mitchell will get in trouble for leaving me there.

The motor slows down to a soft purr. Wyatt clicks off the ignition. He swings his door open. I swallow hard. I recognize this place. There's a long fence in front of me that surrounds the area, along with a locked gate in the middle.

This is the place I saw earlier. It's the place where I saw watchmen injecting small children. My legs feel numb. It's the place that I assumed was the newbie camp. I'm grateful, but why would he bring me here? How would he even know I wanted to come here?

I bounce down behind Wyatt and the dirty ground wafts around. Samuel is a little slower getting out on his side. Instead of leaping down, he puts one foot on the ground and then the other. The air is still thick and smells like smoke.

I make my way over to Samuel's side. "You okay?"

"I'm good." He gives a half-smile, but I'm not convinced.

"He'll be fine. He's been through worse scrapes than this," Wyatt says.

"When we were little kids, before the division of the territories that is," Samuel says.

"Wish we had more time to reminisce…maybe later." Wyatt heads toward the gate. "We should go this way." He points.

I guess they're old friends; but he's right, I can't dwell on their connection right now.

We walk pass the green garbage dump. It hasn't been moved since the last time I was here. I follow Wyatt to the gate. I hear Samuel's slow breaths behind me. There's a loud bang, like a door slamming shut.

"Over here." Wyatt points to the right, where the outhouses are. It's the exact same spot I hid in the last time I was here.

We crouch behind the outhouses. We're close enough to see what's going on. I see Jason and Mike, leaning on a black van. It's the same van that was here before. We are all hiding against the outhouses, but it looks like Samuel is leaning on it more for support.

Samuel looks at Wyatt. "Why are they here?"

"Not sure." Wyatt's eyes widen. "They're usually not out this late. Normally, they bring the babies over between ten and midnight. It's going on two. They should be done by now."

"Those are the last two," Jason says.

"We're out of here." Mike jumps in the front seat of the van and slams the door.

Jason hops in the driver's seat. The motor roars. Brett races over to the gate and opens it. The truck peels out of the lot. Brett shuts it back.

"Avery," Brett shouts to the male with the stocky build.

I didn't catch his name the last time I was here.

"Can we get out of here now?" Avery gripes. "That stupid Emma opened her mouth and now they bring kids over all times of the night. I never get any sleep anymore. It's insane. We don't get paid enough for this."

"At least there were only two, this time, and now we can go home."

"My wife's getting upset over all the long hours I've been keeping."

They slide away to the other side of the area and get into a jeep. The jeep bounces and tears out of the fenced-in area. The jeep skids and halts. Avery jumps out of the passenger's side, closes the gate, and locks it with a key. He jumps back in. The jeep's motor races and they take off.

I flinch at the thought of two more babies being injected.

"I will use my key to get in," Wyatt says. His breaths go in and out, like he's nervous. "They shouldn't be back tonight."

I'm surprised there's no keypad.

"Why are you doing this?" I ask. I don't want him getting into trouble.

"Samuel asked me to, and I can't turn down an old friend."

I turn to Samuel, and his eyes find mine.

"I know about your sister's baby—"

"B-but I didn't have time to explain any of that to you. That day—"

He cuts me off this time. "That day, after I knocked the guard out and you got on the elevator, you were trying to tell me something. You said you saw something, but I wouldn't let you finish because the other guards were coming. I needed to know what you were talking about, so I went into Esther's quarters. I saw a drawer was left open and—"

"I was in a hurry, but I know for sure I slammed that drawer closed before Mike found me."

"Sometimes, when you use force to slam a drawer, it pops back open." He gives a small smile. "Anyway, good for you it did. I looked through that drawer, saw the files, and I knew what you wanted to tell me."

"Why would you waste time like that when you knew the guards were coming?"

"It didn't matter." He shakes his head. "I couldn't run from them. They saw what I did to Mike on the hall monitor. I had to take my punishment, to deal with it."

"Can you two lovebirds reminisce later? The gate is open. We should hurry," Wyatt says.

The phrase *lovebirds* makes my body tingle. I look over. Wyatt has the gate unlocked, and he is already inside.

"This fenced-in area goes back for miles. The graves for the children are this way." He runs and we follow. "I brought a couple of flashlights." He stops moving.

He has a duffle bag over his left arm. He brought supplies with him. The bag shrieks as Wyatt unzips it.

"We could have come without you." Wyatt stops talking and tosses me a flashlight. "But Samuel knew you needed to do this… to look for the baby's grave yourself. We didn't think you would take our word for it."

I cringe every time he says the word grave.

"I knew you would want to do this yourself," Samuel says. His eyes catch mine. "Not hear a report when we got back."

He's right. I have to do this myself.

"I also have these." Wyatt shuffles in the duffle bag and hands me a stun gun. "They had your duty belt, with your guns and Tasers in them, locked in the weapons room…and I wasn't able to get to them, but I was able to grab these stun guns. They also keep these in the weapons rooms, but they're not in locked drawers… probably because they're not as powerful as the other weaponry. I know they're not much, but at least it's something. Here's a holster and another duty belt. It's small, so it should fit your waist."

"Thank you," I say. "For everything." My chest relaxes. I don't know how I will ever repay him or Samuel.

Samuel wraps a duty belt around his waist and thumps the stun gun in place in the holster. I do the same.

"We should go this way." Wyatt races across the hard ground.

The front area where the men injected the babies is just dirt, gravel, and dead grass. There are floodlights hovering over the area; but as we go deeper in, the lights disappear and it's pitch-black. It smells like death. My skin crawls. We keep running pass an old shed. My breaths catch in my throat, as I wonder what could be in there.

"That's where the watchmen hang out when they're waiting for more children to be brought over. There are a few cots in there and a fridge…"

Wyatt's voice drifts off as he runs ahead. He just answered my question though.

We keep racing, until we're deep into a wooded area. My eyes blur when I see lots of gray headstones. I assume this is the mid-point burial grounds.

"They're not marked by name," Wyatt announces. "They don't want proof laying around that could be used against them. But they do have a way of keeping track."

"Why do they care about keeping track?" I ask.

"They always need a system in place, in case they need to exhume a body, for some reason. They want to make sure they exhume the right grave. They go by the first and second letters of the first name and the first and second letters of the last name."

"That doesn't seem too hard," I say.

"I'm not finished yet. There's more. The letters match up with numbers. The letter *A* goes with the number 1 and letter *B* goes with the number 2. Do you understand?"

"It's a little confusing." I wrinkle my nose. "But I think I can figure it out. So *AB* for the first two initials in Abigail would be the numbers 1 and 2 and the last name Whisperer would be…" I shut my eyes and take in a breath. I'm trying to figure it out in my head. "*W* would be 23 and—"

Samuel completes my system. "And *H* would be the number 8."

"So the grave would be marked with the first number, a space, then the second number, a space, then 23, a space, and 8," I say. "1 2 23 8."

I keep saying the numbers over and over in my head, so I won't forget.

"Yes, that's it," Wyatt says. "The graves are scattered all about, so you will have to go around and just look for those numbers. I suggest looking for the number 1 first and ignore the rest that way you can just check all the number 1 graves and find if the other numbers follow."

I nod. "Sounds like a plan to me."

"Let's get started," Samuel says.

I shine my flashlight. I see a few headstones that start with the number 1 in the first row, but the other numbers don't match. We stomp into the next row, where I don't see any headstones with the number 1 as the first digit.

We keep searching, until I see more headstones beginning

with the number 1. I see 1 2 23 but then the last digit is 9. The letter *I* equals 9. My chest stops pounding in my ears. I don't see any digits that match Abigail Whisperer's name.

"She's not here," I shout. "Those digits aren't here," I say, again. I'm trying to make myself believe it, but my hands still twitch.

"We need to keep looking. Now that so many babies are being brought over, they ran out of space in this area. They've started to put them farther back, deeper into the woods. They even had to extend the fence so they would all fit," Wyatt says. "They just kind of stick them where they can, now."

The pounding in my ears starts up again, as we trudge deeper into the woods.

"I'll look here." Wyatt stops in front of more headstones. "You take the middle and Samuel will take the last rows."

We separate.

I smell decay. It makes me want to hurl. I snap my flashlight on a row of brown headstones this time. One by one, I search. I see so many digits that my eyes burn, but I still don't see the digits matching her initials. I finally finish my section. I can't search anymore. I'm cold and my feet feel heavy. I go back to where Samuel is, and he gives me a despondent look.

"She's not here," Samuel says.

"I didn't find her, either." Wyatt says. "We should start walking back now."

We're back near the front now, where the headstones are more neatly arranged—not strewn about and thrown anywhere. Although we have accomplished something, my throat tightens and I feel like we've accomplished nothing.

"Why does everyone look so glum?" Wyatt asks. "I thought this would be a good thing. I don't know the entire process." He shakes his head. "I don't know why some babies are chosen to stay alive and others aren't; but I do know if she's not here, then that means somebody adopted her."

"I realize that." I shrug. "Now the search begins for where she is. What if I never find who took her? Should I just be happy and pray she's gone to a good home where no one will hurt her? I mean, it's not even a legal adoption. I don't understand how…"

My voice drifts off. I hear a loud slam, like a van door shutting.

"They're back," Samuel mouths. "Get down."

I snap off my flashlight. We all squat where we are and hide behind a few of the headstones. My stomach is roiling. I feel like I can't control my breathing. It's still dark where we are, but a few feet ahead, there are spotlights helping us to see what they are doing.

I see the black van, near the now open gate. I hear the roaring of a motor. The jeep tears in and stops next to the van. I thought they had all left for the night, but they are back. My stomach feels like it's dropped to my knees. Why are they back?

CHAPTER TWENTY-THREE

BRETT AND AVERY are the first to jump out. They close the jeep doors behind them.

"I can't believe they radioed me to come back as soon as I got home," Brett says. He smooths his brown watchmen's uniform, like it was wrinkled from the ride.

"*You.*" Avery, the other watchman mocks. "At least *you* don't have a wife breathing down your neck. She wasn't too happy that I had to leave as soon as I walked in the door."

"The first two babies went down easily, but I don't know about this next batch," Brett says.

He says *batch* like they're a group of apples, instead of human beings.

"No one's happy about this." Mike, the guard from Territory L, walks in front of the van. "But this is our new reality."

"Sorry to interrupt your dinner," Jason, the other guard, says roughly. "But they caught three more, so this couldn't wait until morning."

"It's always waited before," Avery says. "What's so different now? Why couldn't you just hold them at the hospital until morning, like you used to?"

Avery pounds his right fist into his left palm.

"Rich said it had to be done now. The hospitals are overrun," Jason says.

He bangs his boot into the van's tire. He seems annoyed by the watchmen's attitudes. "Do you think I want to be here right now—?"

Mike cuts him off. "None of us do. But this is an unusual case."

"Besides, we don't have much room left," Avery says. "I thought they discussed getting rid of the headstones. We don't have room for everything to be nice and neat anymore. We need to start burning them or throwing them on top of each other."

The conversation makes my flesh tingle.

"We're in talks to secure another area for the graves, near here…so it may not come to that," Mike answers.

Mike's blond hair swings from side to side as he moves his head. It's longer than it was when he cornered me in President Esther's quarters. Even Mike's newfound look can't distract me from the nausea in my stomach.

"Now, can I continue what I was saying?" He rolls his eyes. "This is an unusual case because we have a twelve-year-old."

The queasiness in my stomach gets worse.

"Are you serious, man?" Avery chuckles.

Mike folds his arms. "Do I look like I'm joking?"

"How did they let this one slip through the cracks?" Brett shakes his head.

"Twelve years—sheesh." Avery hawks and spits on the ground. "How could someone hide a kid that long without getting noticed?"

"Back when I was a patrolman, if something like this happened, heads would roll." Brett wipes his mouth.

"None of that matters. She's here now." Mike puts a cigarette to his lips and lights it. I had no idea he smoked. "We need to get rid of her first, and then we can inject the two males. The babies are six and seven months old."

"Why her first?" Avery asks. He doesn't seem to take direction easily.

"We chloroformed her just like we did the six-year-old the other day, but apparently it wasn't enough." Jason clenches his right fist, like the situation angers him. "She woke up on the ride over and started screaming her lungs out."

"She wouldn't shut up, so we had to pull over and tape her mouth shut." Mike throws the cigarette on the dusty ground and stomps on it. It's like he's angry that the little girl wouldn't follow his horrid directions. "She won't go down easy, so we need to get rid of her first."

Jason nods his head at Brett and Avery. "You two get the injection ready, and we'll get her out of the van." He turns and heads for the back of the van.

I need to stand and do something, but Samuel squeezes my hand. He's trying to calm me; he knows what I'm thinking. I glance over at Wyatt, to the left of me, but his head is down, like he's disgusted.

I look over at the men again and see Avery and Brett, coming out of the shed with the same briefcase they used the last time. I know now that's where they keep the injection supplies to kill the babies.

The van door slams shut, and I see Jason holding the twelve-year-old girl. She's thin and has brown curly hair that seeps to her shoulders. He's struggling with her. She's twisting her body from side to side, putting up a fight.

My chest constricts. I'm happy she's not making things easy for them, but I know it won't matter. In the end, they will win.

"Put her down, here." Mike points to a spot on the ground.

Jason drops her and she plops down. Her mouth is taped and her hands are tied but her feet flop around, like fins on a fish.

Jason looks at Brett and Avery. "We weren't expecting another trip tonight, so we didn't have much rope left in the van…we were only able to bind her hands. We figured, better to have her hands tied than her feet."

"Yeah, hands are made for slapping, so better to have those tied," Avery says, with a chuckle in his voice again, as his whole chest rises.

It's like they think this whole thing is a big joke.

"You don't have to explain things to them," Mike says. "They tend to their job, and we tend to ours."

He seems way more aggressive than I remember. He's starting to remind me of Rich.

Wyatt is next to me. His breathing is heavy, like helping us was more than he bargained for.

Samuel has a tight grip on my hand, like he's holding on for dear life.

A loud noise, like the gate opening, makes my knee jerk. Who else is coming? The men must also wonder, because their heads whip around to look. I'm too far back to see if anyone is entering. While they're distracted, the twelve-year-old girl jumps to her feet and makes a run for it. She dashes our way.

"We've got a runner!" Avery shouts. The other men turn back around.

Her hands are still tied. Her feet bounce up and down on the pavement as fast as they can. Her shoes bang against the dusty ground as she runs.

"Shoot her!" Brett shouts.

Jason yanks his gun out of his holster, but he's too slow. Mike has already cocked his gun. He has it trained in the little girl's direction.

"We can't let this happen," I mouth to Samuel.

"Just let it be." His face saddens. "There's nothing you can do," he mouths.

"I have to at least try." I stand.

Samuel tries to pull me back down. I snatch my arm from him.

I know it's insane, but I can't just stand by and watch this without trying something. I run until I'm near the girl. She stops running when she sees me. I rip the tape from her mouth, so she can breathe better.

"P-please h-help me," she says.

Her breaths are uneven. Her face scrunches up. Tears stain her cheeks. Her jeans are dirty and ripped. Her shirt has holes in it. She's as thin as a rail. Where on earth have they been hiding her?

She's weak from the chloroform they've given her on the ride over. She looks as if she will fall down at any minute. Now that she's closer, I see her eyes are hazel like mine.

"Please stop." I stand in front of her, facing the watchmen and the guards. "I'm begging you."

They stare at me with blank faces, like they don't know what to do with me.

I hear an eerie voice. "Still heroic, Emma, I see."

It's coming from behind the men. I know it is Rich. My body shivers and my knees feel weak.

"Always trying to save the world." He steps out in front of them.

That must have been him coming in when I heard the gate screeching.

"Jason had such an attitude when I told him this had to be done tonight that I thought I should check up on him to make sure he was doing his job right. And now I see that he isn't. None of you are." He growls. "But I made it here just in time to enjoy the show." He moves closer toward me.

I add strength to my voice. "What show?"

I haven't seen Rich since that day I woke up in the jails. I assumed he was mad that I was taken to the mansion and angrily went back to Territory L. Now he's back and right in front of me. I fear the worst is about to happen. I only have a stun gun, and I know from training that I'm not close enough to Rich to do any damage to him.

"This show," he says, then clicks his tongue.

He raises his gun. Before I know what's happening, he takes a shot. The loud bang makes me flinch as it passes by my left shoulder. I turn to find the little girl lying on the ground. I see blood around her head and neck.

"No!" I scream. My voice echoes. "What have you done?"

I fall to my knees and feel dirt underneath me. My shoulders hunch and I shake uncontrollably.

"What have I done?" He laughs like something is funny. "What have you done, Emma? Everything that just happened here is your fault. That little girl could have died a nice quiet death—a death of dignity. Because of you, she was shot in the head."

"Dignity!" I shout, trying to find my voice. "Injecting someone full of poison is not dignified."

"That little girl died this way because of you." His face is hard and his eyes are cold. He stomps closer to me. He bangs his gun into his holster. "And you're still running at the mouth. Come here."

He grabs my arm and wrenches me up. He practically pulls me on top of her. "Look at her!" he shouts.

Her small oval face is frozen in death. A bullet hole graces her temple. Blood surrounds every part of her skull. Her body is scrunched into a small frame. I can't look anymore, so I turn away.

"I said look at her!" Rich still has ahold of my arm, and he shakes me until I turn to the little girl again.

"Why'd you have to do that to her...why?" My eyes well up.

"I told you before, it's your fault." His hot breath is in my ear. "Look at her."

He grabs my chin and pulls me down to her level. "Look what you did."

"What was her n-name?" I manage to ask, even though his grip is tight around my mouth.

"Isn't that sweet." He turns to the other males. "Emma wants to know her name." He's in my ear again. "Why does it matter?"

"I j-just need to know."

"Melissa," he says. He lets go of my chin, but the nails on his other hand are digging into the skin on my arm.

"I'm so s-sorry, Melissa." I say, my voice still shaky.

"If you're so sorry, maybe you should get down there with her." He shoves me down right next to her. I fall to the ground with a *thud*. Dirt flies. "Maybe you should take a well-deserved bullet to show how sorry you really are."

My leg won't stop trembling.

"Don't," I hear Samuel say. "She's been through enough."

I turn on my side. Out of the corner of my eye, I see Samuel has moved from behind the headstones and is now standing. So is Wyatt.

"Look at this, boys. Samuel here is going to save his little girlfriend. Now sweet little Emma has two men vying for her heart. The other one is over in the holding room."

He lets out a wicked laugh as his chest bounces up and down. "Well, I suggest you kneel back down before I beat you senseless again, like I did back in Territory L—except this time, it will be to the death."

Samuel still comes forward.

"So, I don't scare you," Rich says.

I quiver. "Please l-leave him alone."

"And your little girlfriend thinks she can help you from the position she's in." I feel the heels of his boot squishing onto my side.

"Rich, this will stop now," I hear a voice call out. It sounds like Henry's. "This is not the way we run things—not in Territory M."

He walks toward us in the same suit he had on earlier—apparently, he never went to bed. Mitchell stands next to him in his brown watchmen's uniform.

I try to sit up on my knees. I can't help staring at the dead life-less little girl next to me. Some of her blood seeps over onto my t-shirt. I cringe. I even have some of it on my hands.

"That little girl should have never been taken down that way," Henry continues, with force. "Gunshots are a thing of the past and only used when absolutely necessary. You know we use needles now."

"She was a runner, sir. I didn't see any other way to take her down. But I am sorry her life ended so horribly," Rich says.

I know, and everyone within the sound of his voice knows, he's lying. His chest is still puffed up with pride at the way he took the girl's life.

"I will make sure she has a proper burial with a handsome headstone." He cocks his head to the side. "Unmarked, of course."

He says *proper* like anything about her assassination was proper. She should have a suitable burial and a headstone with her name on it. Somewhere, her parents can appropriately mourn her death—now that would be proper.

"Will you need anything else from me tonight, sir?" Rich's voice is almost weak, like the words are hard to say.

I know Rich has no respect for Henry. I remember hiding in Esther's mansion in Territory L and overhearing him tell her that he could do a better job running Territory M.

"No, that will be all." Henry's glower moves from Rich to me. "Emma, you will come with me. Brett and Avery, finish the burial process for these children."

He glances down at poor dead Melissa and then back at the van where the sleeping babies lie. "Mike and Jason, put Wyatt in a holding room—until I have a chance to deal with his disloyalty. Then take Samuel back to his holding room."

I wobbly stand. "Please, don't hurt them." I use my pants as a towel and wipe the sweat and some of Melissa's blood from the palm of my hands.

"You need to worry about yourself," Rich growls.

"I said that will be all, Rich." Henry's voice is robust. Once again, I think maybe Henry isn't as weak as I first thought.

Rich rolls his eyes and lets out a slow grunt. He kicks some dirt up from the grimy ground with his boot as he stomps away.

I give Samuel and Wyatt one last glance, before I make my way over to Henry. I follow Mitchell and he places me in the back-seat of a long black car. It reminds me of the one that picked me and my family up for the party at President Esther's mansion. The seat is leather and cool to the touch.

Henry is in the passenger's seat and his eyes find mine through the rearview mirror. He squints them. I know he's not happy with me, so I stay silent. Mitchell starts the motor and drives away.

CHAPTER TWENTY-FOUR

I DON'T KNOW why, but they brought me to Henry's quarters. Mitchell snatched my stun gun away from me, along with the duty belt and holster I had surrounding my hips. I'm sitting in the dining room where Nancy had served us that extravagant meal. It's also where we played twenty questions—well, that's what I like to call it.

The room is dark, now. The shades are drawn and the glass table no longer reflects the light from the window. I'm not sure of the time, but it has to be at least three in the morning.

The room fills with a lavender scent.

"So, this is how you choose to repay us." It's President Esther's voice.

I swallow hard and recoil. I hear the heels of her shoes clicking along the floor as she comes near me.

"My husband was kind enough to answer your questions... answers, from my understanding, you've wanted to know for a long time. Instead of being grateful, you chose to repay our kindness with idiocy. You chose to go behind our backs into the newbie camp and search through graves...graves that are none of your business."

My eyes widen. She is now standing in front of me. She has on a light blue pantsuit with gold heels.

"What do you have to say for yourself?"

I remain silent.

"Speak up, child. I can't hear you."

"The graves are my business, if you have my niece buried there. That was on my list of questions that was never answered."

"You only know about the newbie camp because you stumbled upon it by accident. You were in my quarters going through private documents. So don't you dare get indignant with me."

"How did you even know we were in the newbie camp?"

"Did you ever think that some things don't concern you—that some things should remain private," she continues, without letting me speak, without answering my prior question. "Some things are only for the leaders of the community to know. Some things you don't understand but are for the good of the territories."

"Breaking into the president's quarters is cause for death," she continues. "Do you realize that, Emma? At the very least, for what you've done, you should be imprisoned and labeled a lifer."

"Then why am I not? Why did you play this little game with me, having Henry answer some of my questions?" My heart hardens. "Why did you show me the war room and the fight room? Why didn't you take me back to Territory L and lock me up as soon as I was captured? Why?"

Her eyes glaze over, like she doesn't care for my tone, so I continue. "You weren't being kind by answering some questions; you wanted something in return...you always do."

"Sweet, smart, unshakable, Emma." Her blood red fingernails tap on the glass table. "You pretend you're not scared of anything, isn't that right?" Her eyebrow rises. "You think you can solve all of the nation's problems and, for some reason, the people in L think the same thing. For some reason," her voice grows louder. "The lower class are running rampant and there's destruction in the streets. They seem to only listen to the ramblings of a teenage misfit, a misguided fool."

Her words are harsh, but I can take it. "I don't think I can solve all of the nation's problems. I just know what's right and what's fair. We should all be in one unified territory and not be defined by how much money we make. We should all have an opportunity to go to college and make better lives for ourselves. Even if some don't want to do that, they should be able to be friends with the wealthy. Poor or rich, we should all be treated equally."

"The territories, not here. They are the ones who like to hear your disputes. I've heard this speech already. I care not to hear it a second time." There's a snarl to her voice.

"Then, why am I here?"

"I need Territory L back to normal. I need the looting and fires to stop. You should want that as well." Her eyes glower at me. "After all, your family does live there and so do you."

"You think I want this? I don't."

"Then you should have no problem going on the box and making a speech. I want you to tell them the looting and anger needs to stop, and they should be happy and satisfied with the lives they have now. I want them to see me as their president again—a president that's only trying to help, not hinder them. I only want what's best for them. Surely you see that, with the answers Henry gave you during your question and answer session."

"I saw nothing of the sort."

"You saw that I do allow people to better themselves and come here. It's a fair process. I pick those who are doing well in school and are obedient to their parents. I pick families that show pride in their communities and don't whine and cry about where they live. You now know that I only want what's best for everyone."

"I now believe that *you* believe you are doing the right thing— maybe because of the way you were raised. I know, from what you told me, part of your family was rich while the other side was poor—"

"So, I've seen both halves." She locks her fingers together.

"Or maybe you're just pure evil," I say, finishing my thought. "I don't know, and it no longer matters to me. It's not my job to understand you. I feel it is my job to help the people, so I will make a speech on the box; but I'm not going to tell them that they should be satisfied the way their lives are now. I will not tell them that every word you say is gospel. I *will* say the fighting needs to end, since it's only hurting them in the end."

She glares at me and unlocks her fingers. Then she looks over at Henry with disgust. He's been hovering in the corner this entire time, leaning on the windowsill. He was so quiet, I almost forgot he was even here.

"What if I tell you where your niece, Abigail, is?"

"What did you say?" My heart thuds, unevenly.

Her mouth curls up. "You heard me the first time."

I don't know how to respond, so I say nothing.

"I could torture your sister or your brother or even that boy, Eric, you seem to like; but I think out of all of them, you would prefer finding your niece. When the guards caught up with Samuel, he was looking at the papers regarding the newbie camps. Since he found the maps, I knew you had, too; so I knew that's what you were after. Since you left your family behind to find her, she's the one you most care about."

"That isn't the only reason I left." I find my voice and sit up straighter in my chair. "I also want the walls torn down."

I feel a twinge in my heart at her harsh word. I care about my entire family—it's just Abigail is the one I know couldn't take care of herself. I pray the others somehow could.

"Clearly, you now know that's not going to happen, since my husband Henry is in charge. You must know he follows my orders." Her eyes slip over Henry's way again. "I know everything that goes on around here. I see everything, and I control every-thing." She clears her throat.

"When they first went looking for you, I told them not to

harm you," she continues. After they couldn't find you, I became furious that you were doing such a good job of staying hidden, so I changed the alert to harm but not kill you. I need you alive, so you will make this speech."

"Well, your men came awfully close to killing me when they shot at us back at the executive buildings." I stand, trying to get my point across.

"That was only to scare you. I control you," she says, her voice growing louder. "And I control Henry."

Henry looks away, like he's embarrassed.

"What will it be? Will you make a speech in order to find out where Abigail is? It's your choice."

"Fine." My mouth goes dry. I'm not sure if I'm doing the right thing. "But I want to know why she was chosen? Why she was adopted—or whatever you want to call it?"

"We decided, years ago, that instead of killing all newborns... some would be killed and others would have a chance at life."

She sits down like the conversation is making her weak, so I sit down as well. "Some of the women in Territory U were having trouble conceiving children. There was talk that some of these women would pay handsomely, if there was a way they could care for some unwanted child that wasn't theirs...like some sort of adoption so—"

"But those children are wanted. They have families that love them."

"Don't cut me off again, Emma." Her eyebrows slope together, and her mouth curls up. Now she sounds like her husband, Henry.

"I decided if some lonely rich woman in U wanted a child because her husband worked all day and she needed someone to love—or for whatever reason—why shouldn't I give her what her heart desires. I had the supply, and she had the money."

I roll my eyes; babies aren't supplies.

"The money could be put back into the upper communities

to make more homes, libraries, and jobs. And the babies have a chance at a decent, good life. It's a win-win."

Her chest puffs up; she almost seems proud of her misdoings. "I decided that the babies with the most chance of being adopted…"

Illegally adopted, I think. I shake off my thoughts and continue listening.

"…are the ones who are prettier, chubbier, well-kept. Granted, I will say some babies aren't that fat due to lack of food in L, but some are better off than others when we find them."

"Light-skin?" I ask.

"Light-skin or dark-skin has nothing to do with it."

I bite down on my lip.

"So, the better babies go to U and the others are killed," says President Esther.

"What if a baby goes to U and doesn't get picked by one of the rich women?" I ask.

"They come back to the newbie camps and are killed. I almost decided to stop the process. The requests for babies weren't coming in like they used to. So you should be happy Abigail got in when she did."

She smiles and her lips purse together like I should be grateful.

"Lately, more babies have been killed than saved. We have reason to believe the demand for them in U will pick up again; but until that time, killing them will be the case. I know you won't mention anything about the babies during your speech—or derail and say the people should go against me, like you did during your speech at your party—or you will never find out where your precious niece is."

She clasps her fingers together again. "It's nearly six in the morning. We all better get some rest, so you can make your speech this afternoon. We wouldn't want your eyes to appear puffy on camera, now would we?"

CHAPTER TWENTY-FIVE

I SPEND THE next few hours lying on a nice soft large bed in Henry's quarters. Why should I get a nice bed while my friends and family are still sleeping on the cold hard floors? That is, except for Taylor—at least she had a cot. I hope that's still the case. Henry takes the master bedroom, of course, and Esther takes one of the other masters. They led me to a bedroom down the hall from theirs, and said I needed to rest.

The walls are beige, the bed is queen-size, and the spread is golden. I have a small circular window, but I am instructed not to touch the blinds.

Now that morning has arrived, the sunlight shines through, hits the room, and makes it glimmer.

I couldn't close my eyes at all. Every time I tried, I thought about that little girl being shot in the head. Now, all I think about is the task ahead of me.

Once again, I am forced into making a speech that I don't believe in. During the speech at my party back in L, I spoke my mind; and look how well that turned out—I was jailed. The last time the president wanted me to make a speech, I was able to run away and get out of it; but this time, I don't see any way out.

Since we've been here, all of the days have run together; but I know this is Tuesday. If I have to give the speech tonight that means this will be a special report, since it will not be given during the regular Monday night broadcast.

A knock at my door interrupts my thoughts.

"I brought your breakfast, Emma," Nancy says, entering my room.

She has on a bright yellow dress with matching yellow heels. "President Esther wants you well fed for your speech. She had Chef Thomas make you an omelet with toast and turkey bacon. I also brought you some orange juice." The bottom of her dress sways as she moves.

"Later, Penelope is coming over from Territory U to have you fitted for another guard's uniform." Her lilac perfume fills the air.

I should have known I would need to look like a guard again—one of her own—to make my speech. I scooch around and sit up straight on the bed. The covers bunch beneath me.

"I'll leave your breakfast here, Miss." Nancy plops the tray down on a marble table that's in the middle of the room. "Make sure you eat all of it." She smiles.

"I'll try." I give a half-smile back. "Thank you."

I hate to lie to her, but my stomach is queasy and I know I won't be able to get any of it down.

After wrestling with it for a moment, I decide I should eat. I'm not sure what will happen later, and I might need some added strength. I gulp down some juice. The fork screeches against the plate as I cut a small portion from the omelet. It's quite good, but I don't want anymore. Just like I thought, the food doesn't make my stomach any less queasy. I shove the plate away.

I need to think about my next steps right now. I'll try finishing the food later.

* * *

Earlier, in the bathroom mirror when I was washing up, I noticed that I have pinkish—almost red—eyes and wrinkles under them. Now, it's seven in the evening and I'm being primped and pampered to look appropriate.

Penelope hasn't changed much since the last time I encountered her. She fitted me for my guard's uniform back in L, and made sure my hair and makeup were appropriate for the speech President Esther wanted me to make.

She has on a pink pantsuit that offsets her gray eyes nicely. Her perfume is strong like Nancy's was; only it smells like roses, not lilacs.

"Hold your chin up, dear, and widen your eyes," Penelope says. Her blonde hair is attractively pinned in a bun at the back of her head.

She takes out a small bottle with clear liquid. I blink rapidly as the substance splashes in my eyes.

"This should take care of the redness. Now, on to some makeup to cover up the bags under your eyes."

She pats my face with a cloth and brown bits of makeup drift around.

I hold my nose because I want to sneeze.

"Now, we will have to do something about your hair," she squeals. "I realize that wearing one long braid is your hairstyle of choice, but that won't do for tonight."

I haven't dwelled on my hair in weeks. This morning was the first time I really acknowledged it as I was looking in the mirror.

She unbraids it and combs it out, making the thick strands feel heavy against my shoulders. I don't like wearing my hair down; it feels like it's strangling me and I can't breathe.

"There's not much more we can do with it on such short notice," she says. "Let's try some hairspray to keep it in place."

She sprays, making a thick chemical mist fill the air. I cough and wag my tongue, trying to get the taste out of my mouth.

"I will leave you be now, dear," she says. "Your uniform is on the bed, there. I will be waiting in the hallway, until you're ready to leave. Don't dawdle."

She glances down at her gold wristwatch. "We should be downstairs in fifteen minutes to get ready for the eight o'clock broadcast." She whacks the door closed behind her.

I stand, frozen. I can't believe this is happening again. My hands shake as I pick up the black guard's uniform. It's brand new and has one shiny silver button plastered on the left side. After all the upheaval I've caused, I'm surprised she is still willing to give me that one. I guess, if it was gone, I wouldn't look like a guard anymore—and that's what she needs me to be when speaking to the people.

Now that I have managed to slip on my uniform, again, it feels foreign against my skin. The thick black boots still weigh me down, like lead upon my feet.

My mother's necklace has always been with me, underneath whatever t-shirt or turtleneck I wear. It's still there now—the small silver dove tingles against my neck. I try to remember my mother's meaning for it...peace, love and hope. I take in a much-needed breath. I don't know what's going to happen after this.

CHAPTER TWENTY-SIX

I REMAIN SILENT all the way down in the elevator. All I hear are the gears flowing and the *thump* as we halt on the second floor. I follow Penelope off the elevator. Her heels click in front of me. We walk down a long lighted hallway, until we reach a room near the end. There are camera crews everywhere and the hustle and bustle of people, shuffling around the room, getting ready for tonight's broadcast.

I shudder. It reminds me of the party at the president's mansion. Except, there weren't camera crews everywhere, like now. I stand off to the side, out of the way. Penelope stands beside me.

I see President Esther walk in dressed in a gold suit with golden heels to match. Once again, her hair flows to her shoulders. She nods her head and Penelope scurries over in her direction. I remain where I am, until Mitchell walks toward me.

"Henry wants to see you, before the broadcast."

All the lighting in the room makes his bald head glow. "Come with me."

He leads. I follow. We walk down the hallway, pass the elevators, to a room on the right. It reminds me of a small kitchen. There is a mini stainless steel refrigerator, along with a round white table and four chairs.

"Sit beside me, Emma." Henry pats the cushion next to him.

"The broadcast doesn't start for another ten minutes. I think there are some things we should discuss." He sits on a turquoise sofa that is off to the side of the room.

I really didn't want to spend the next ten minutes talking to him. There are things I need to go over in my head before my speech; but there's no way of getting around this, so I drop down beside him.

"Before you start, may I ask a question?"

"Yes, Emma." His eyebrows furl. "Go ahead."

"How did you know we were in the newbie camp? Why were you up that time of night?"

There are six square windows that have shades drawn; a small bit of light flows underneath. Henry stares over at the windows before answering.

"If you must know, Esther had just arrived and we were going over some business. Brett called it in to Mitchell, and he came and told me. He said there was an unusual case down at the camp. They had a twelve-year-old. Since they never had a child that old before, I came down to make sure the burial process was being done properly."

The words *burial process* makes my skin crawl.

"I still can't understand why you take orders from her. I know you said it's because you want her back, because you still love her. You do things you don't believe in to gain her love again—that's not the kind of love I would want." I shift on the sofa.

"What would a girl your age know about love?" He seems annoyed at my comment. "When you're older and really know what love is, then you can come and talk to me."

His jaw flexes. "We've already dealt with this subject, and I do not want to discuss it further. There are a few things I want to say to you, before you speak tonight. As you have probably already noticed, there are several reporters here from Territory U."

"Yes, I did notice," I say. "Why is this broadcast such a big deal?"

"At your last-eighteen-year-old party, there was only one camera to broadcast the event to all three territories over the box, like usual—so the camera went unnoticed. This time is different." He places his hand to his mouth and clears his throat. "This time, the higher ups in Territory U want to run a story about it in their local newspaper. You probably don't know this, but Territories U and M have newspapers. Well," he pauses and clears his throat, again.

"Newspapers are for the older folks that like the paper feel—others like to read the news on their tablets. That's an electronic device that can be used for things such as reading, looking at the local broadcasts, streaming shows and other things. I take it you don't know what a tablet is, since you don't have those things in L."

"I don't." I shift on the sofa. I feel warm. But I imagine it's like the e-reader my mom told me about.

"Anyway, the reason there are several cameras here is because they don't want only information from the box; they want several records of what is being said, so they can write about it in print later. They see your failure as a big deal—"

"My failure?" I wipe beads of sweat from my forehead.

"When you upstaged your own party and gave that heart-felt speech, Territory L landed in an uproar and agreed with your words. What you didn't know was that some of the people from Territory U and M agreed with you as well."

My heart jumps in my chest at his words.

"Once you escaped, they were eager to see what you would do…how you would set out to accomplish your goal of making everyone equal and getting the walls torn down."

"Why have I never heard this before?"

"Esther didn't want you to know. She would have my head, if she knew I was telling you now." He glances over at a silver information box that sits near the wall, like he's nervous.

"Why are you?" My eyebrow rises.

"My wife is embarrassed that some of her high-society friends actually agreed with you and would like to hear more of what you have to say. They wanted to see what you could accomplish, after you ran away to Territory M. But all they've seen is the rioting and destruction of Territory L by that territory's own hands. They want to write a series of reports on you about why no one else should step up and try to go against the president again—it doesn't work and only brings down the societies. Not only will you be making a speech for the people in L to stop the revolt, you will be answering questions for the local newspaper from U on your failings."

He scratches the back of his neck. His expression shows he needs to explain further.

"Reporters want to do a story on the last eighteen-year-old who stood up to the president and also to corner you with questions on how you feel since all your ramblings were for nothing. My wife told you that you would only be making a speech, not about the questions to be asked. She wants you caught off guard, so you will fail even further in front of everyone."

"And you—do you want me to fail, too?" I ask.

"No, I don't. That's why I am telling you this. You're a strong, determined young lady. I don't want you getting up there looking like a fool. I'm telling you this, so you will get your thoughts together. Yes, I suggest you stick to the talking points the president already went over with you for your speech. Don't deviate off topic, like you have in the past. I know you tend to go your own way and do what you want, but please don't make the mistake of doing that tonight."

He clears his throat again. "I'm warning you, if you do...you won't like what follows. But when asked a specific question by a reporter, say what you need to—that will be the time to speak your own mind. Now you should run along. I'm sure my wife is waiting for you."

I roll my eyes and stand. "I'm sure she is."

"Emma," he calls.

I turn back around.

"I don't always follow all of her orders." He winks.

I'm more confused now than when I sat down beside him. I'm not sure if I will comply with his wishes during my speech, but it was nice of him to warn me about the questions coming my way. If I don't say what the president wants, she won't give me the answers about Abigail. But what if it's all a lie and she doesn't give me answers about Abigail anyway?

My heart thumps in my chest. No chance of making a run for it; Mitchell is waiting outside the door to walk me back to my destination.

Now that I'm back in the broadcasting area, I see Rich has slithered in and is standing next to President Esther. He has on a black guard's uniform that now mimics my own. They are over at the podium I guess I will be speaking from. He scowls at me for a moment, before turning away to look at something else in the room.

CHAPTER TWENTY-SEVEN

"TONIGHT, WE HAVE a special broadcast going out to the people of Territories L, M, and U." President Esther's eyes lurk across the room, until she finds mine. She taps her long fingernails on the podium, like she's scared of how I'll react once I get up there.

The room is quite large and is a soothing deep blue, like water. I stare at the walls, trying to calm myself. The room holds no windows for light; but that doesn't matter, because the ten or so reporters that surround me have flashing cameras and the light trickles around every time they take a picture of Esther.

The males have on pinstripe suits with pointed toes on shiny shoes. The females have on sharp-colored suits that land at their knees and heels with spiky tips. Their recorders hiss and hang on to the president's every word. I wonder if they will do the same when I get up there.

Rich stands next to President Esther, and Rob stands on the other side of her. My guard uniform feels heavy against my skin. I want to rip it off and run away; but I can't, not this time…too much is at stake.

I don't see Henry or his watchman, Mitchell. I assume he's still back in the room I left him in, since he stays away from cameras.

I haven't heard a word President Esther has said; but I know she wants me to move closer, because she motions her hand and waves me up.

"Please listen to what Emma has to say. I'm sure you will find it enlightening." She steps off to the side as I approach.

My leg feels numb as I step up to the podium. Flashes of light from the cameras pop in my face, making me blink and feel even more uncomfortable. To the right of me, I see Rich and President Esther. To the left of me is Rob. I guess if I say the wrong thing, they will be close enough to pounce on me at any second.

"H-hello people of Territories L, M, and U. My name is Emma Whisperer."

I glance down at my boots. The people already know who I am. I didn't have to introduce myself.

I look back up and try to compose myself. "I stand before you today to send a message to Territory L. Since I've been away, there's been rioting, rebellion, and strife. I know I told everyone that they should stand up for what they believe in and not to listen to President Esther because she does not want what's best for us—"

A short pale-faced man, with red hair and mustache, shouts out from the audience. "Are you changing your tune now?"

He looks to be in his mid-forties. Another flash of light pops in my face, so I blink and turn away from the camera, making my eyes line up with President Esther's. She smiles with delight and the knots in my chest tighten. I didn't think it was time for questions and answers…maybe I am wrong.

"Are you changing your tune now?" he asks again, as if I didn't hear him the first time.

"No," I say. "I'm not. I believe that the president believes she is doing what's best for us—"

"That just sounds like twisted gibberish you're spewing up there." A woman, who looks to be in her thirties with long blonde hair, stares at me. "Could you speak in terms someone from Territory L will understand?"

That comment makes my blood boil. Is she saying the people in L are too stupid to understand what I am saying? Is she saying that the lower class...I can't finish my thought, because my head starts to pound. I rub my forehead roughly and sigh.

"What I'm trying to say is...we should not destroy our territory to get our point across. Making the area we live in into a disaster zone is no good for anyone. We should not destroy our homes, our markets, our workplaces—especially when we do not have the money to rebuild. I beg you to stop, now." I glance around the room.

"Please, think of your loved ones and what will happen when we have no place to buy food, no homes to live in, and nowhere to work to earn money. This is not the way we show President Esther she is wrong. We are only making things worse for ourselves. Please...please, stop this now."

I close my eyes and take in a breath. That wasn't hard to say, because I believe in that. What I don't believe in is my next sentence—the sentence that the president wills me to say—that we should be happy and satisfied living in squalor with menial, low-paying jobs and no continued education. We shouldn't strive for anything better. My hand tightens into a fist.

"Is that all you needed to say?" the man with the red hair shouts.

"What's your name?" I ask.

"What was that?" He pretends not to hear me.

"I asked you what your name is."

"Why is that important?"

"You seem to have a lot of questions, and I want to address you appropriately."

"It's Tim...Tim Chesney."

"Mr. Chesney, what position do you hold?"

"If you mean my job, my career? We can all see I'm a field reporter."

"Did you always want to be a field reporter?"

"Yes."

"Do you want to move up one day or is field reporter the only job you ever want to hold?"

He has on a tan suit and he shifts his pink tie like he's uncomfortable. "I would like to move up to producer one day."

"What if you couldn't? What if your boss said you weren't good enough and field reporter is all you will ever be? How would you feel?"

"I suppose that wouldn't be fair. If I want to move up, I should have that chance."

He grunts out his answer like he's annoyed by my question. Maybe he feels everyone should know this because it's just common sense. I know that's how I feel.

"Miss," I say, calling out to the tall woman with the blonde hair and blue eyes. Her white dress is so bright it almost blinds me. "What is your name?"

"I don't see how that's relevant to anything, but it's Jessica Jennings."

"Thank you, Ms. Jennings. Do you have children?"

She bites down on her lip. "I have two."

"Are your children in a good school?"

"One of the best in our territory."

"How would you feel if your children weren't allowed to obtain higher education just because of where they lived and a label that was placed on them?"

"I know where you're going with this. You're a smart young lady." Her smile is thin as she winks at me. "It's funny how the tables have turned and you're asking the questions instead of us." She shifts her weight to her opposite hip. "But to answer you, no one should be placed in a box. No matter what race, gender, or religion, you should be able to get a higher education, if you would like to."

The cameraman turns the lens to President Esther and Rich. Out of the corner of my eye, I see Rich's fists are clenched and President Esther's face is like stone. I don't know if this is going to work, but I'm not reading a speech and telling the territories that President Esther is wrong. I'm asking questions and letting their answers tell them what they should already know.

I'm sure this strategy won't work. President Esther will still see this as a betrayal against her. If that's the case, it will ruin all chances I have of her telling me where Abigail is.

My jaw twitches. I need something more. I need to get Territory U on my side. Then the president can't turn on me or go against me. I believe she wants the people of U to like her, since some of them are her closest friends and allies. Henry already said some of the people in U agreed with my speech; now that I know that, I will use it to my advantage.

I clear my throat and continue. "I was wrong for escaping Territory L; but when I was made a guard, I have to admit, it scared me a bit."

I'm lying but trying to gain sympathy from the masses. "I felt my only plan of recourse was to run. I wanted to come to Territory M and see about the walls coming down. So far, so many other things have happened that, sorry to say, I haven't had time to do that."

That's a lie, also. I talked to Henry about it and just got the runaround.

I take in a deep breath and continue. "I believe if my friends and I have a chance to walk freely into Territory U and are able to talk to some of the citizens, maybe they would sign a petition or something to show that the majority feel we should all live as one or at least live where we would like to."

I glance over at President Esther; she is gritting her teeth. I know she's mad, but I haven't crossed any lines. She never said

I couldn't speak directly to the citizens of U. She only expressed interest that I put the citizens of L in their place.

"That's an interesting idea," Tim says, as he snaps another photo of me.

"I agree," Jessica says. Her pen swivels as she writes on her pad. "President Esther, I realize we elected you president and all decisions are yours to make; but would it be so bad if Emma and her friends start a petition? I'm curious to see how many will sign it."

I hear heels clicking as the president walks toward me. Her stride is slow and her posture is rigid, like she wants to pull every strand of hair from my head. She stands in front of the podium. I scoot over a little to give her room.

"Ms. Jennings, I am curious to see how many of the people in Territory U would sign it, too. It was my understanding that Territories U and M were happy with the way things are now. I thought the reason I was elected a second time was because the people are happy with every decision I make. Only Territory L seems to have a problem. I would have no problem letting Emma and her little friends go to Territory U and roam the area, looking for ones who are skeptical."

The eerie politeness of her voice sounds weird; I know she's not being truthful. She doesn't want to look bad to the upper class and her rich friends.

"And what happens if a majority signs her petition to have the walls come down?" Jessica asks.

"I guess I would have to seriously consider the needs of the people and have the walls torn down. But we will cross that bridge if, or when, we come to it."

"So when can we expect to see Emma and her friends in Territory U?" Jessica asks.

Funny, the first time Jessica opened her mouth she annoyed me; now, I believe she could turn out to be my greatest ally.

"Not sure about that, Ms. Jennings. Possibly next week or, at the earliest, maybe in a few days. Once it happens, you'll be one of the first to know."

"I appreciate that." Jessica scribbles in her pad, again.

"Thank you," Tim says, with a grin. "This is an interesting story for the paper."

"I'm happy to help." Esther turns to me, then looks back to the crowd of ten. "I'm pleased you're all so excited."

I feel President Esther's temperature rising. The heat from her anger radiates on to me.

"That's enough for tonight. I think the young lady is tired. Enough questions have been answered."

"I didn't get to anything on my list," another man shouts out from the back of the room. He's tall and robust with a pointy chin, and he has a recorder in his hand. He stands in between the others who have been calm and quiet.

"Sorry, Steven." She lets out a small cough. "They'll be other broadcasts, other times for questions—just not now."

He looks at her and nods. She called him by his first name. I wonder if they're old friends.

CHAPTER TWENTY-EIGHT

I'M BACK IN my holding room now, sitting on the cold floor. As soon as President Esther stepped down from the podium, Rich ushered me out of there, like I was a criminal who had committed murder. He threw me in here and hasn't come back since. I take it they didn't want the reporters asking me any more questions.

I can only imagine what my punishment will be for my insubordination. I'm sure nightfall has come and gone. I am unable to sleep. I know my eyes have turned red again. I occupy my time by putting my hair back the way I like it—braided in one long ponytail down my back.

A gust of wind blows through as the door opens. I hear loud footsteps and I look up to find Rich standing over me. He grips my elbow and forces me up.

"I hope you got a good night's sleep. President Esther wants to see you," he says, with a snarl. "For the life of me, I can't understand why you're still alive."

He shakes his head, like I'm a puzzle he's trying to solve. "You keep pulling these stunts and you keep getting away with it. I don't get what she sees in you." His breath scorches my cheek. "You'll go to the bathroom and get showered and changed first."

"Why do you hate me?" I turn to him. "I know your sibling died. It must have been your brother—"

"Don't start that again," he grunts.

"The last time you said *he*. So I know it must have been your brother. But that wasn't my fault—even so, I apologized; but I feel like there's something more. Is it my skin color?"

"I don't care if your black, brown, white, or green. That has nothing to do with it."

I was, sometimes, looked at differently growing up, since I had parents of mixed races—so that seems to be my fallback point whenever I find out someone doesn't like me.

If that's not Rich's problem, then what is? I want to know how I've wrong him. I don't know why this bothers me so much. I guess I should let it go, for now, and dwell on what President Esther has in store for me.

He yanks me by my braid and twirls me around until I'm facing the door. "Let's go." He pushes my back.

He drops me off at the bathroom down the hallway, where I shower. A change of clothing is left for me on the back of the door. After I'm done brushing my teeth, I open the door and he's waiting for me.

I figure we are going to Henry's quarters and the president will be there; but I am wrong, because we're on the first floor by the main entrance. Rich holds onto my elbow. I see President Esther coming near me. She no longer has on her gold pantsuit; this one is black. The crease in her forehead deepens.

"Very clever, Emma. Once again, you managed to sway the room in your favor." Her eyes glow with anger. "Yes, you did succeed in telling Territory L to stop the fighting for their own sakes, making you look like you really care for their well-being. But I also told you to tell the lower class that they should be happy and satisfied with the lives they have now—"

"And I did that." I pipe up.

"No, I don't think you did." She twists her skinny finger in my face.

"Well, I wanted to, but you ended the broadcast before I could."

"Really, Emma? Is that the card you want to play?"

She keeps using my name in a creepy way. She's standing right in front of my face now and her teeth shine.

She continues to talk. "That would be a bald-faced lie. I will tell you what you did. You managed to twist everything around so you wouldn't say that. You cleverly positioned yourself to ask questions so the answers would help the lower class see they shouldn't be satisfied and should strive for more."

She keeps talking, without taking in a breath. "You asked questions and received answers that made you look good and afforded you the opportunity to get your point across, without being the one to make me look evil. Instead, the reporters made me look that way. Well played, Emma, well played."

She swipes her hands together. "Wouldn't you say so, Rich?" Her mouth curls up at the corners.

"Yes, Madam President. I would."

"I take it this means you're not going to tell me where Abigail is?" I ask.

She nods at Rich. "Outside, now."

Mitchell is there and he opens the front door. Rich heaves me outside. I shudder as I am shoved, once again, into the side door of a long black car. The backseat has two long rows that face each other. President Esther sits, with her legs crossed, next to Mitchell. I sit on the other side, next to Rich. Rob is the driver.

The car sways and bumps along the path. I hear the tires rumbling underneath us.

The car stops and I am forced out. I stand in a field of freshly cut grass. The air smells like daffodils.

"Where are we?" I ask, but no one answers.

We stand there, for a few minutes, before a white van rustles up beside us. I know it's not the van that brings the babies, that van is black. My gut feels like bugs are roaming around in it.

"President Esther, I didn't mention anything about the babies or the newbie camp during the broadcast," I say.

"Did you hear that, gentlemen?" She looks at Mitchell, then Rich. "I think Emma is trying to plead with me. I think she may actually be afraid of what's to come."

Before I respond, the van door whips open. Jason and Mike get out. They are armed with guns. I now see the driver is Paul—Tony sits in the passenger's seat—watchmen. I remember them from the mansion. They were the ones escorting Molly from the fight room.

"Everybody out," Jason says. "Line up."

I see my friends and family members jump out of the van, one by one. They line them up in a neat little order and hold guns to their backs. Standing before me is Logan, Eric, Theodore, Taylor, Samuel, Whitney, and even Alexa. Next to Alexa is Wyatt, who I now call a friend for helping me the other night.

Logan looks exhausted and so does Whitney. Taylor's eyes are so red, they are the color of plasma—I can't tell if it's from crying or tiredness. Samuel looks weak and is hunched over in pain. Theodore and Eric seem to be the healthiest of the bunch. They both stand tall and proud. Eric's gaze is glued to me. I can't look at Alexa, not after everything she's done to me—but I know she had her reasons.

They all looked like they've showered and changed to fresh clothing, just like I have—except, I wear a guard's uniform, while they all wear black or blue pants with matching knit shirts. Some have on matching cotton hoodies, while others don't. They all have on the same style black boots.

"What's going on?" I ask.

"You announced to the world that I should let you and your

friends stroll in to Territory U and see how many people you can turn against me."

"That's not exactly what I said."

"Close enough," she snaps back. "Since I had to agree with you in front of the reporters and the nation, you're going to get your wish. Otherwise, I look like a fool and am made out to be a liar. I will let you and your friends go freely into the next territory. But there are rules." She repeats herself. "There always have to be rules. Rich, read the guidelines."

She slants her eyes his way.

I can't believe this is happening. We finally get a chance to try and get the walls torn down. Maybe that's why she let everyone shower and change. I suppose the president wants us to look presentable in Territory U.

If we get some of Territory U—some of her high society friends—to agree with us, that will be a start and maybe she will tear down the walls just to please them. And even if she won't tell me Abigail's location, maybe by being able to walk freely through Territory U, we will somehow find her. And if the walls are gone, she can come back home. I know there are rules, but they can't possibly be that bad.

I pull my head out of the clouds as I feel Rich loosen the grip on my arm. He starts to read from a piece of paper that was stuffed in his pocket.

"Emma and the others have one shot to make it over to Territory U. They will have to run from here to the gates of Territory U. It's about a half mile stretch from where we are standing. Whoever makes it will get the chance to freely walk through the territory and start their little petition. Whoever doesn't will be remanded back to the holding rooms, where we will decide what to do with them, later. You only have five minutes to make it there, before the gates start to roll down."

I look over the grassy area to the walls of Territory U. The walls cover the entire territory just like they do in M and L. Barbwire emerges from the top. The gate is black. Instead of it having two side by side double doors that open and close, it rolls down from a pole above it. It reminds me of a garage door that goes up and down.

"No one's allowed down near the walls unless they're leaving or entering the territories. No arrivals or departures are scheduled for today, so we're safe to punish you accordingly without any prying eyes around. The men at the gate will leave it up. On our orders, they will push a button and it will start to go down." Rich pats the radio communicator on his hip.

"But you said all my friends would get a chance in Territory U."

"That's not what I said, at all. I said I will allow Emma and her friends to roam the territory. I didn't say how many friends."

"This isn't fair." My voice cracks. "That's about an eight minute run. What if no one makes it in five minutes? This is insane. We had a deal."

"Deals are broken every day," she says. Her lips curl. "But don't worry. I'm sure some of your friends can run the stretch. Some of them have to now, don't they dear, or the reporters will say that I lied when you and your friends don't show up. We wouldn't want that now, would we? I know you couldn't care less about me and my needs, but you should try your best to make it so you get your message heard and your petitions signed in Territory U."

I feel acid rising up from my belly. I lunge at her. I know I'm being stupid. Rich tugs me back before I can even get close to her.

"Those who do make it into Territory U will have—"

"You will be given ten days," President Esther says, cutting Rich off as if he's reading too slowly. "Or should I say given *free reign* for ten days—starting today. My men will stand down. You will roam freely and talk to whomever your heart desires. Once the ten days have expired, I will expect you to be waiting at the gate to cross back over. Alexa is going with you. I need to test her loyalty further, since she didn't finish the fight against Emma as I asked, before our deal is completed. She will spend her time in Territory U helping you—you should make her feel welcome."

I glance at Alexa. She is staring at the ground. I guess she doesn't want to make eye contact with anyone.

"How do we know you won't eliminate us after all this is done?" Theodore asks.

"You don't," she says. "I would like to know, does everyone standing here want to go?"

No one answers, but I see a lot of nodding heads.

"Whitney, you don't have to," I say. "I know you have Adam to get back to."

"Funny little Emma," President Esther cackles. "You actually believe if Whitney doesn't want to go, I will let her run back home and be with her son? She hid you and your friends. She went against the laws. If she stays, she will be put back in the holding area to await further instructions. And her son—well, that's something to be discussed at another time. We have more pressing things to go over."

"It's okay, Emma. I want to go. I have to believe in my heart Adam's safe, for now." Her eyes divert the president's way. "I need to do this in Julian's name. I know he died because he believed in this cause." Her face saddens.

Someone must have told her what happened to Julian, on the van ride over.

"You all must know, depending on my mood, when all this is over, I could have you labeled as lifers and remanded to the prisons. Every one of you standing before me has broken a law, maybe two."

"Then why not just remand us now, instead of playing these little games?" Eric asks, with heart in his voice.

"Like I explained earlier, if I don't let you do this, the people in U may lose trust in me...and the ones in the other territories, who have already loss faith and whose trust I'm trying to regain, will remain lost. I'm also curious to see what will happen. How many of my followers will you get to turn against me?"

She says *followers* like she's a rock star and they are her groupies.

"Before the fun begins, we have another matter to tend to. The punishment for Emma disobeying me on the podium and doing what she wanted."

My throat constricts. I thought my punishment was having me and my friends run to a gate that could close down on us at any second and, if we don't make it, being banished to a holding room forever or labeled a lifer or worse. What more could there be?

"One or more of her friends will suffer."

My leg jerks.

"One or more of you won't be going on this little journey. You won't get your chance to run. You will stay here in the holding room. You may be beaten every day that I hold you here. I may starve you to death, or I may walk you across hot coals and burn your feet. It is Emma's decision. Who will stay, while the others get a chance to run and make it into U?"

My voice shakes. "I c-can't m-make a decision l-like that."

"Look at your comrades." Rich places his gun under my chin and raises my face so my eyes meet my friends.

My insides twists. I feel like I'm suffocating. How can I pick one person to stay when I know they may be tortured over and over again? This isn't a choice anyone should have to make.

"I'll stay," I say, turning to President Esther.

"You're not in this equation. You know it has to be one of them. You are the main one the people of Territory U want to see."

"I'm giving you sixty seconds on the countdown clock," Rich says, with glee in his voice.

All kinds of thoughts are rambling through my head. My esophagus feels like its closing. I can't make Taylor or Theodore stay. I can't make Samuel or Eric or even Wyatt stay. Logan's strong, but he doesn't deserve this either. Alexa betrayed me, but I know why…she was only trying to save her brother. After everything she went through with her father, does she really deserve this now?

"Pick one." Rich is in my ear. "Hurry, Emma. Who will it be?" He clicks his tongue.

"Give her time, Rich," President Esther says, like she's settling a small child. "This isn't an easy decision." A small chuckle comes behind her words.

My body trembles. I feel like I'm going to faint.

"If the president will allow me to, I would like to make this easier for you." Rich glances her way.

She nods back that it's fine.

"You can't pick Alexa or Logan. Those two will definitely be running for the gates to try and make it into Territory U. Neither of them will be allowed to stay here. You have to pick someone else to stay here in the holding cells and be tortured."

How is this any easier now than it was ten seconds ago? I know his reasoning. I haven't known Logan that long and Alexa betrayed me. He figures my first choice would be to go for one of them to stay here and be tormented. But now that they've been taken out of the equation and they have to run, I still don't know who to pick.

"Too slow!" Rich shouts. He raises his gun and points it. I hear a loud blast. My eyes widen when I see Alexa fall to the ground. Blood trickles from her neck and her lips gurgle. Everyone around me gasps.

"Why did you do that?" I scream.

"I aimed for her carotid artery. I knew that way she would fizzle out fast. I didn't want her to suffer. What good is she… she couldn't even complete a simple task like finishing the fight with you."

My mouth drops and I don't have any more words. Her body

shakes, uncontrollably. We all watch as Alexa struggles and takes her last breaths.

"You didn't care about her anyway," Rich continues. "She betrayed you."

"That doesn't mean I wanted her to die," I say, with a groan. My insides ache.

Rich motions to Mike and Jason with his weapon to pick her up and move her to the van.

"No one wants to see that." He scrunches up his nose. "Not while Emma has a decision to make."

I don't know why, but I glance at President Esther. I know it may be stupid, but I need her support. Surely she didn't know that Rich was going to shoot someone—that couldn't have been planned. I look at her, thinking maybe she will stop this; but she doesn't.

"Time's running out, Emma." Rich shoves me in my back with the gun. "Pick someone…pick someone!"

I look at the area where Alexa stood a few seconds ago. The grass has turned red because her blood has been absorbed there. I gaze back at my friends.

"Do it now, Emma." He shoves me in the back again, like this is a game. "I can shoot someone every thirty seconds if you like."

He aims the gun again. He's talking so much I can't even think straight.

Eric's strong. I know he'll take whatever they throw at him. Wyatt seems to be strong as well. I know I've only just met Wyatt, but he helped me earlier. He threw away the only life he's ever known to get me to the newbie camp. Taylor's not strong enough. And Theodore…well, Theodore is my brother.

I bite down on my lip. This is an inhumane decision to make, let alone in sixty seconds.

Whitney has a child. And she did everything she could to help us. Then there's Samuel—

"Time's up!" Rich shouts, breaking into my thoughts. "Choose now or else."

I hear the *click* of the gun cocking and my body spasms.

"Eric," I say, quietly.

"What was that? We can't hear you?" Rich glares at me. He knocks me in my shoulder with his.

"Speak up, child," President Esther says. "So everyone hears."

"I choose Eric," I shout out. "Eric stays behind." My chest tightens as soon as the words leave my lips.

"Good girl," Rich says.

Eric's eyes sadden, and he looks away from me. He didn't even see me mouth I'm sorry. Tears well up, but I can't cry. I won't.

"That was fun and all, and I really wish we could hold Eric here to be crucified, but he's not the one," Rich says. "Taylor should be the one to stay."

"No, that's not fair. You said I get to choose."

All I see is red in front of me. I ball up my fists and hit Rich in his shoulder. I go to punch him again; before I can, he pushes me back as hard as he can and I bang to the ground.

"Boys, put Taylor in the van."

Theodore lunges toward Jason and Mike, but they turn their guns on him.

"I wouldn't try that if I were you," Rich says.

I stay on the ground watching as they pull Taylor, kicking and screaming, to the van. They throw her in back, right next to Alexa's dead body.

My mind is still racing. I don't know how to help her. Rich shouts at me to stand up.

"Now that…that's over, we can focus on the gate." President Esther looks toward Territory U.

I haven't even had time to wrap my head around the events that just happened, when she says, "Your five minutes start now."

I hear the *boom* of Rich's gun. Everyone takes off, running. I stand there like my body is numb. I can't put one foot in front of the other.

"Emma! Emma, run." Off in the distance, I hear Samuel's voice. And Theodore's.

What if I don't run? What if I don't try to make it? The people of Territory U are expecting to see me there. No matter if I make it or not, she will have to let me inside the walls. But by now I know, President Esther always has a trick up her sleeve. What if, for some reason, she decides it's not worth it and if I don't make it she leaves me behind?

I feel like I'm moving in slow motion as my heavy boots pound underneath me. I sprint as fast as I can. It reminds me of my days running through the woods to take supplies to Taylor and Abigail.

I see Eric and Whitney far ahead of me. I have already caught up to Samuel. I realize his strength isn't what it once was. He moves at a slower pace. I hear his shallow breaths as I pass by him.

"Y-you can do this, Samuel," I say, lagging behind to make sure he's okay. "Just stop for a minute and catch your breath."

To the right of me, I see Logan. Up ahead of me, on the left, is Theodore. I don't see Wyatt anywhere. Once Samuel seems to get his second wind and surges ahead, I look for Wyatt. I see him coming up from the rear. He's even slower than Samuel.

Before I shout out to him, I hear hooting and hollering coming from every direction. I look around to see males, in dark baggy clothing, running as well. Before I fathom what's going on, I feel something—or someone—grab my ankle. I bang down on my knees with a smack. I hit my chin on the ground and lay in a stretch of grass.

Wyatt is beside me now. "Are you alright?" He's kneeling down.

"W-what was that?" I ask.

"It's t-the runaways," Wyatt says, between jagged breaths. "S-sometimes they h-hang around, waiting for an o-opportunity to get into Territory U. R-remember, I told you about them."

"Y-yes, I d-do remember." I pull myself up to my knees. "B-but they aren't sneaking in…everyone sees them." My breaths finally even out.

"M-maybe they figure they will make it in while the w-watch-men are distracted with u-us."

I look over to see a runaway grab Whitney. The runaway shoves her down. Eric comes to her rescue. Eric punches him. He crashes down. Eric helps Whitney up. They continue racing toward the gate.

I know she's not used to any of this. I'm glad he's looking out for her. A runaway jumps on Samuel's back. They fall backwards to the ground. Samuel tries to turn on his side. The runaway is still on his back. Logan and Theodore come to his aid. They knock the runaway off. I see them belting out punches before helping Samuel up. They head for the gate.

"Why are the runaways fighting us, if we're heading for the same goal—to enter the gates?"

"I have no idea. Either way, w-we have to get up now. We're losing time."

I know he's right. Time must be running out; I hear grinding metal. The gate starts to roll down.

I jump to my feet. "Let's go," I shout, and then I take off.

There are probably twenty or more runaways in dark clothing, darting over the area. Wind splashes in my face. For a moment, I can't see where anyone else is. Finally, I see the gate is halfway down.

Eric makes it through first, with Whitney. Theodore is next, and then Logan and Samuel.

I sprint as fast as I can. I hear Wyatt's boots thumping right behind me. He is doing better now at keeping the pace. The gate is almost all the way down.

My breaths are getting caught in my throat. I pick up speed. I thrust down on my left hip. I use my hands to push my weight all the way under. Dust and dirt wafts all over. My hands feel like fire. Wyatt is a few seconds behind me. His body slams down on his butt. He tries to use his elbows and hands to scooch himself under.

The motor roars as the gate rolls down faster. His body looks like dead weight. He's not sliding fast enough. I wobble on to my knees. If I can get to him I will help pull his legs. Help pull him under.

Before I—or anyone else—reach him, the gate crashes down. It lands on Wyatt's chest. He shouts, in pain. The gate continues until it hits the ground with a *boom*, crushing him underneath it.

Instantly, I see blood coming out of Wyatt's mouth. His chest isn't rising up and down. I turn away. I know he isn't with us anymore.

My heart rumbles in my chest. I'm sweating. I wipe my nose with my hand. I crawl away from Wyatt's lifeless body and move toward the wall. I need to lean against it for support. My back is against the wall now. My knees are up to my chin. I glance around. Everyone's breaths are as short as mine are. No one looks at Wyatt. We all know he's dead.

Eric and Whitney are both lying on the ground, breathing heavily. Samuel wipes the perspiration from his face. So does Logan. Theodore looks at me and gives a thin smile.

Three of the runaways have made it in, as well. They are across from me. They are all males. They are also lying on the ground, trying to catch their breaths.

I look at the runaways. "W-why w-were you trying to s-stop us from getting through t-the gates?"

"We w-were instructed by that g-guard, R-rich, to make it hard for y-you," one of them says, between jagged breaths. "W-we will b-be rewarded and be able to s-stay in U, for life."

The other two look down at the ground. I suppose these runaways are different from the ones Wyatt told me want to terrorize the people of U—they must actually want to live among them.

I turn away from them and look over to the right. I see a small building with a few windows. I also see a tower. I suppose Esther's men reside in there to watch over the territory and to open the gates for those allowed in and out.

All of a sudden, two watchmen emerge from the tower. I know they are watchmen; they have on brown uniforms, instead of black ones. They have their guns drawn. They fire on the three runaways. My body jerks at the loud report of gunfire.

They manage not to hit any of us. The runaways lie there, deceased, in bloody clothes.

My stomach turns. I want to hurl. I was just speaking with one and now he's dead. I don't know how many more dead bodies I can take seeing.

They put away their guns. Apparently, we weren't their targets, the runaways were.

My breaths slow down. I glance around at the others. I can't believe Wyatt's gone, and now the runaways are shot right in front of us.

Everyone remains silent, until I finally notice Whitney opening her mouth.

"W-what happens now?" she asks. She wipes the sweat from her face.

"We need to find a proper place to bury Wyatt's body. After all he did for us, we can't just leave him here." I stand and brush off my uniform. "After that we can find a place to stay and figure out how and where we will start getting our petitions signed. Today marks the first day…so we need to hurry."

"I agree." T stands as well.

Eric and Samuel nod and stand but remain silent. So does Logan.

I hear a deep voice say, "We'll bury the runaways."

It's one of the watchmen from the tower, who was just shooting at us—or should I say at the runaways—a minute ago. His brown eyes glow as his boots stomp, rushing toward us.

"Why did you shoot the runaways? Why couldn't you just let them go to the jails or prisons?" I ask.

"They know when they try to enter that they are taking their lives into their own hands. They know upon entering the gates they will be shot at. This is the risk they take."

I feel bad for them; apparently, Rich lied and told them they would get to stay here if they did what he asked.

"We'll bury him along with the runaways." The watchman points at Wyatt like he's unimportant. "You need to get going." His eyes narrow.

"He's our friend," I say. "We should do that."

"And I don't take orders from you." He grits his teeth. "You take them from us." He glances back at the other watchmen still on the tower. "Move." He tilts his head to the right. "Get out of here—away from the gate. Now!"

"Emma, he means it. We should go." Samuel's eyes find mine.

"I agree." T swipes his brow. "There's nothing more we can do here. We need to start our journey and pray it does some good."

"I know the area," Samuels says, rubbing his chin as he looks around. "I've been here a few times to pick up supplies. I just wish Wyatt was still with us. He knew the area better than I do."

He sniffs. "That's not the real reason I wish he was with us. He was a good person...a good friend." His eyes soften, talking about Wyatt. "Anyway," he says, shaking his head. "I came here a few times, before I was permanently stationed at the mansion." He blinks. "After that I came back a few times on special assignments. I may know an area where we can lie low, until we figure out what to do next."

Eric finally speaks. "Let's go then."

Whitney finally wobbles to her feet. She walks alongside

Logan, behind Eric and Samuel. Theodore comes to where I am, so we can walk together.

"It's going to be alright." He rubs my shoulder. "Even with all the deaths we've just encountered."

"I know." I nod. "We know Abigail's alive and that's a big accomplishment. Now we just have to find her, get enough signatures to have the walls taken down, and get Taylor back—hopefully unharmed. Shouldn't be too hard, right?" I give a half-smile.

T smiles back. "No, it shouldn't."

Dear reader,

Please continue the journey with Emma Whisperer and her friends by reading Book Three in the Extinction series, *Journey to Territory U.*

Will Emma get her petition signed? Will President Esther honor her pledge? Will the walls finally come down? Will Baby Abigail ever be found? What is President Esther hiding underground?
Grab your copy, today!
Sincerely,

L.J. Epps

P.S. Here's a sample.

JOURNEY TO TERRITORY U

CHAPTER ONE

WE ARE NOT far from the gates of Territory U. I can't believe I'm here after everything that has happened. My breaths are caught in my throat as I look over at Theodore, Eric, Samuel, Logan, and Whitney. President Esther, who is over our little nation of Craigluy, has divided the people into three territories. Territory L stands for the lower class. That's where I live; we are considered poor. Territory M is the middle class, where people have better homes and more money. I was able to sneak into M with Eric while riding in the back of a work truck. Julian was the driver who helped us sneak in. The guards at the gate knew Julian and never suspected we were hiding in the back.

I was only in M for a few weeks, and the time just flew by. I made a few new friends while I was there, as well as some enemies. Hard to believe it's September now. I blink a few times and take in a deep breath.

Now my friends and I stand inside the walls of U, where the wealthy live and have anything their little hearts' desire. They are richer than those who reside in M, and I'm sure their houses are bigger and better.

President Esther made us run to the gates of U before they

came down. That was her way of deciding who would have the chance to walk around the territory freely, trying to get petitions signed…and to make us suffer, if we didn't make it into U. She likes to play games. The petitions will decide if she will let the walls come down, so we can all be one whole unit, again—one entire nation of Craigluy. My hope is if the walls come down, the killings will stop.

President Esther decided long ago that the poor couldn't take care of their own. She provided contraception, so people would stop having babies. Any children illegally born were taken away and killed. I recently found out that some babies are adopted by the upper class, while other babies are killed.

When I left my home in Territory L for Territory M, my main goal was to find out about my sister Taylor's baby—my niece, Abigail. I now know she is alive and probably adopted by one of the rich families. Now that we've made it into Territory U safely, I can find her. My second goal was to have the walls taken down… the petitions being signed will mean I may have my chance at doing that.

We didn't all make it safely inside the gates. Wyatt was crushed by the rolling gates. It was a horrific death. No one should die that way. I hadn't known Wyatt that long. In fact, it'd only been a day or so; but he was kind to me. He went out of his way to help me find the newbie camp where I looked to see if Abigail had been taken and buried.

My sister Taylor also didn't make it into the gates of Territory U. Evil President Esther made her stay behind in Territory M. She has Taylor in the holding cells in her husband Henry's mansion. President Esther says Taylor may be tortured. My hands tingle, thinking of my sister going through such pain.

Now I pull my head back into reality and search my surroundings. The grass seems greener here and the air smells fresher, like clean linen. I know it's probably my imagination. From where we stand, all I see is a field. We're still near the walls and too far back to be able to see any houses or streets, but everything seems livelier in Territory U.

I'm still wandering around in amazement, trying to catch my breath, when I hear the motor rolling the gate up, again. I look back at the gate and see Rich walking in. His green eyes are glued on me. I know he has hated me ever since he had me cornered in my jail cell back in Territory L. When I was locked up for thirty days, doing my time, he had no problem displaying his displeasure for me. Jason and Mike, two of the guards from L, are with him. Why are they here?

Order your copy today! Click the link below.
www.ljeppsauthor.com

Dear reader,

Have you read Book One in the Extinction series, *Extinction of All Children*? If you liked the second book in the series, check out the first book. See how Emma Whisperer's journey began in Territory L.

Sincerely,

L.J. Epps

P.S. Here's a sample:

EXTINCTION OF ALL CHILDREN

CHAPTER ONE

TODAY THE WIND is colder—sharper—and it whips right through my bones. Even so, I continue to run as fast as I can through the wooded area. It smells damp like rain, and mud sticks to my shoes. The air feels thick like sand is choking me. At times, it is hard to breathe; but, I continue on. I have to make it back home before dark. If I'm found on the streets after dark, it means I'm not following orders. And my family might not receive our daily supplies; supplies we need to make it in this land.

Even though I make this trip through the woods at least three times a week, today I feel weaker, more sluggish, as if it is my first time. But, it isn't the first time, and it will not be the last, since I'm the one my family counts on.

No, I'm not the boy of the family. Boys are considered stronger, but my brother Theodore—we call him T, for short—is nineteen and not a fast runner; so, he couldn't make the trip that I have to. That isn't the real reason. The real reason is that they say they need his talents for other things, and he can't get hurt.

I have to pace myself. The trees seem thicker and wider, which is odd, since they should be thinning out. This time of year, the leaves should be falling towards the ground, but they aren't.

This land is different, and the seasons aren't exactly on point. Sometimes, it is hard to even tell what time of year it is. Ever since our world was taken over and broken into territories, everything seems to blend together.

I know I'm tiring because my thoughts jumble. Why didn't I wear my hair in a ponytail? It is long and thick and reaches beyond my shoulders. I usually know to put it up, out of the way, on days like this. The wind slaps me in my face, obstructing my view. Maybe I should put my hood up; but, it won't stay on, and there is no time to fight with it.

The pack on my back that I used to carry to school starts to feel heavy, as if lead weighs me down. But, I can't soften. I'm almost there, and, not only am I bringing what my mother asked for, but I've also made the most important part of the trip. The part of the trip my mother will ask me about first. She always does; it is always the same.

I need to hurry. It will be dark soon. Normally, I make the trip early, before dusk arrives. But today, I spent more time at the market, looking for what mother asked for. I groan. I don't know how many more times I can make this trip; especially, once winter is upon us.

Not to get food but the other thing, the thing we aren't supposed to talk about, the thing we aren't supposed to mention until we are within the four walls of our small home.

I've been thinking about it for a while now, but how can I tell my parents when they depend on me so? How can I tell them that the last winter was unbearable, and I don't think I can make it through another one? I turned eighteen two weeks ago. Why wasn't I happier about that? Maybe it is because I'm the last child to turn eighteen in our territory, and there will never be another.

A full list of outlets that carry the Extinction series can be found here: www.ljeppsauthor.com

Dear reader,

Thank you so much for purchasing and reading my novel. I hope you enjoyed reading about Emma as much as I enjoyed writing about her. In case you're wondering if Emma's quest will continue, the answer is yes; it will continue in Book Three, *Journey to Territory U.*

I would be grateful if you left an honest review. Let me know if you loved, or hated, Emma's adventure. I always appreciate receiving feedback.

If you have any questions, please contact me through my website: *www.ljeppsauthor.com*

I would love to hear from you.

Sincerely,

L.J. Epps

ACKNOWLEDGMENTS

I have to thank my sister and my brother-in-law, for believing I could write the sequel to the Extinction series and for being excited about it.

Thank you to my beta readers and to my editor, proofreader, and beta reader, Helen Burroughs of HKelleyB's Editorial Services.

BOOKS BY L. J. EPPS

Romance

I Wish I Could Remember You

Young Adult

Extinction Series:

Extinction of All Children

Journey to Territory M

Journey to Territory U

www.ingramcontent.com/pod-product-compliance
Lightning Source LLC
Chambersburg PA
CBHW020240200626
46816CB00001BA/56